PRAISE FOR *LONDON YIDDISHTOWN*

"Vivi Lachs's new book is a novel and successful experiment in re-creating the experience of everyday London Jews in the middle decades of the twentieth century. Lachs draws on the work of three neglected Yiddish writers to explore the needs and hopes of Jews who too frequently escape the attention of historians. We learn much about gender roles, courting and marriage, tensions between parents and children, religious observance, and social mobility among Jewish Londoners."

—Todd M. Endelman, professor emeritus of history and Judaic studies,
University of Michigan

"Vivi Lachs's *London Yiddishtown* is a triumph. It unearths for an English-speaking audience the authentic voice of the Jewish East End during the years of its dissolution and eventual dispersal. It gives us, in all its sympathetic richness and ironic humor, the internal contradictions of a community that fractured as much from within as from without. Here, in the work of these hitherto-unknown Yiddish writers, is the gold that Arnold Wesker would mine for the theater just a few years later."

—Jerry White, emeritus professor of modern London history,
Birkbeck, University of London

"Vivi Lachs is a leading authority on the understudied subject of Yiddish in England. In *London Yiddishtown* she has added to the history of its development and use in the 1930s and 1940s, including biographies and translations of three important prose writers."

—Anita Norich, Tikva Frymer-Kensky Professor Emerita of English and
Jewish studies, University of Michigan

"A fascinating window into a previously closed world for those no longer able to access the rich past of their Yiddish-speaking forebearers."

—Rachel Lichtenstein, author of *Rodinsky's Room* and *On Brick Lane*

"Yiddish London comes alive in this wonderful selection of stories from the East End of the 1930s. A joy to read, these vibrant episodes of Jewish immigrant life, sometimes humorous, sometimes moving, are expertly translated and historically contextualized by Vivi Lachs, providing the reader with a unique look at the Yiddish subculture that bubbles just below the surface of contemporary English Jewry. Offering a window into a Jewish life that has disappeared, the stories in *London Yiddishtown* reveal immigrant hopes, fears, dreams, and aspirations, and do so while painting a vivid picture of a community walking between two worlds."

—Eddy Portnoy, author of *Bad Rabbi and Other Strange but True Stories from the Yiddish Press*

"What a treat. A book that brings to life exactly where and how my parents lived. For anyone, though, following the people who came out of Eastern Europe and created Yiddishtowns in London, Manchester, New York, and elsewhere, this is a wonderfully detailed, scholarly, and human read."

—Michael Rosen, author of *Many Different Kinds of Love*

London
Yiddishtown

London Yiddishtown

East End Jewish Life in Yiddish Sketch and Story, 1930–1950

Selected Works of Katie Brown, A. M. Kaizer, and I. A. Lisky

Translated with Introductions and Commentary by Vivi Lachs

A YIDDISH BOOK CENTER TRANSLATION

WAYNE STATE UNIVERSITY PRESS
DETROIT

ISBN 978-0-8143-4847-5 (paperback)
ISBN 978-0-8143-4848-2 (hardback)
ISBN 978-0-8143-4849-9 (ebook)

Library of Congress Control Number: 2021934628

"Brick Lane Restaurant," lithograph by Pearl Binder, 1931. © Estate of Pearl Binder. Cover design by Tracy Cox.

I have made significant attempts to contact the family of A. M. Kaizer, who has no surviving children. Despite finding his brother Solomon Kaiser, who passed away in 1986, I have been unable to trace any other siblings. If there are relatives of the Arnold and Bertha Kaizer family of Golders Green, please contact the publisher.

Wayne State University Press rests on Waawiyaataanong, also referred to as Detroit, the ancestral and contemporary homeland of the Three Fires Confederacy. These sovereign lands were granted by the Ojibwe, Odawa, Potawatomi, and Wyandot Nations, in 1807, through the Treaty of Detroit. Wayne State University Press affirms Indigenous sovereignty and honors all tribes with a connection to Detroit. With our Native neighbors, the press works to advance educational equity and promote a better future for the earth and all people.

ייִדיש
Yiddish
Book
Center
Regenerating Jewish Culture

A Yiddish Book Center Translation

Wayne State University Press
Leonard N. Simons Building
4809 Woodward Avenue
Detroit, Michigan 48201-1309

Visit us online at wsupress.wayne.edu

This book is dedicated to two close friends: the late Chaim Neslen, who continued to run the Friends of Yiddish single-handedly for years after the East End community had disappeared, and the late Barry Davis, born and bred in London, who kept contact with the last generation of Yiddish actors and writers.

It is also dedicated to the families of Katie Brown, Summer Lisky, and Arnold Kaizer, and to other descendants of Yiddish writers who do not know enough Yiddish to read the work of their parents and grandparents in the original.

CONTENTS

YEHUDA ITAMAR LISKY

ARYE MYER KAIZER

KATIE BROWN

ILLUSTRATIONS

ACKNOWLEDGMENTS

One never writes a book on one's own, and I am indebted to many people who inspired me to begin this project and gave me ideas and advice regarding Yiddish and London history.

This project is supported by a Yiddish Book Center Translation Fellowship (2019). I was touring North America with my previous book, *Whitechapel Noise*, and during a conversation with Mindl Cohen at the Yiddish Book Center, I realized that the idea I had had on the back burner for some years could become a reality. The fellowship was inspiring and illuminating. I would like to give huge thanks to Mindl, Margaret Frothingham, Lisa Newman, Abigail Weaver, and my workshop leaders, Liz, Danny, and Jim, my dear friend Ellen Cassedy, and my wonderful co-fellows: Caraid, Julia, Julian, Maia, Matthew, Miranda, Miriam, William, and Zeke. I value the generous New York hospitality of Denis Paz, Ellen and Jeff Blum, Marilyn Neimark, and Alisa Solomon.

I am particularly grateful to my mentor and friend Heather Valencia, who is meticulous, delightful, methodical, and knowledgeable. Her comments and thoughts went beyond the call of duty as we spent hours poring over texts in her lovely home in Scotland. We even managed to fit in the odd walk.

I was, as always, given marvelous advice and photos by my dear pal David Mazower. His broad knowledge of Yiddish culture, his fabulous London photo collection, and his ebullient generosity enriched this work.

I have felt well supported by my editor, Annie Martin, whose comments and suggestions, delivered with warmth and a light touch, have been incisive and helpful. I would also like to thank Emily Nowak, Kristin Harpster, Carrie Teefey, Jamie Jones, and Kristina Stonehill at Wayne State University Press, whose teamwork made the whole process run so smoothly. I am particularly grateful to the anonymous peer reviewers of the book, whose detailed comments and criticism were supremely helpful, and I am indebted to Mindy Brown for her detailed, careful, and knowledgeable copy-editing.

A number of my friends and family were wonderful readers. I'm grateful for the hours put in by Sarha Moore, Simo Muir, Nadia Valman, Nicky Lachs, Steve Ogin, Ruti Lachs, William Pimlott, Alex Graffen, Tamara Gleason, Ester Whine, and Marion Brady. I also had many conversations and advice on the East End, Yiddish writers, and the Yiddish language—in person, on the phone, via email, Facebook, and Zoom—for which I'd like to thank Dovid Katz, Sima Beeri, Bob Chait, Todd Endelman, Shane Baker, Elinor Robinson, Haya Vardy, Itzik Gottesman, the late Mike Valencia, Leyzer Burko, Dawn Cesarani, Rokhl Kafrissen, Andreas Schmitges, Brurye Wiegand, Davina Cooper, Emma Uprichard, Barry Smerin, David Feldman, Tony Kushner, Edith, Jude, Erin and Liam Lachs, and Liz Iyamu.

I would like to thank the organizers and participants of the Yiddish Open Mic Café—which continues the tradition of the Friends of Yiddish and has given me a space to try out some of the ideas in this book.

I could not have done the background research needed without the collection of London Yiddish newspapers and journals in the British Library and the YIVO library and archives. I would like to thank the librarians, and my teachers at the YIVO Yiddish course: Dovid Braun, Miriam Trinh, Sheva Zucker, Anita Norich, Barbara Harshav, Chava Lapin, and London's Helen Beer.

I have been delighted by the contact I have had with the families of Summer Lisky and Katie Brown, and would like to thank Francis Fuchs, Abi Fuchs, Bella Fox, Geoffrey Shisler, Abi Shisler, Carol Shapiro, and Betty Capper. In my attempts to find Kaizer's family, I knocked on the doors of his old neighbors in Golders Green on a rainy day, and I would like to thank Trevor and Ingar Fenner and Naomi Klein for their memories of the family and for sending my search forward to Esther Held and Nitza Spiro.

For assistance in photo research, in addition to those I have already mentioned, I would like to thank Goldie Morgentaler, Ruth Kessentini, Kathi Diamant, Hazel Karr, Rabbi Pini Dunner, Maya Pasternak at the Montreal Jewish Public Library, Sarah Tuckman, and the librarians at the Tower Hamlets archive for their warmth, generosity, and attentive email contact. I appreciate the technical help with images from Annie Challis, Jude Munden, Rony Cohen, Jeremy Grant, and Melanie Rozencwajg.

A NOTE ON THE YIDDISH

Yiddish transliteration of words, names, and titles generally follows the YIVO system. I've made exceptions to this for clarity and context. When the Yiddish is clearly nonstandard in titles, I use the nonstandard version; for example, the word *Idisher* is not corrected to *Yidisher*. When there are known English spellings for Yiddish (or Hebrew) words, they are used; for example, the word *Torah*. However the word *haftoyre* remains in Yiddish transliteration. Names of writers are generally presented as they spelled their own names in English and as listed in Prager's *Yiddish Culture in London*. Yiddish place names are complicated by towns that had multiple names and changing borders. When places in Eastern Europe are referred to, the Yiddish name and location is given first, followed in parentheses by the name of the place today and, where necessary, the present-day country.

The Yiddish that was spoken on the streets of the East End was sometimes called "Cockney-Yiddish," "anglicized Yiddish," or what the scholar Khone Shmeruk termed "local London color."[1] These descriptions refer to the way English words became incorporated into daily conversational Yiddish and, indeed, became commonplace in the London Yiddish press. Katie Brown, A. M. Kaizer, and I. A. Lisky all used English words in their stories and sketches, often in direct speech, but not always. In the original Yiddish text, the English words were spelled out phonetically, using Yiddish/Hebrew letters. Brown uses the word *bedrum* (bedroom) in the first line of the story "Breadwinners"; Lisky uses the word *doks* (docks) in the story "A Guinea a Day"; and Kaizer uses the word *tiket* (ticket) in "When You Go to a Yiddish Theatre." (When Kaizer published his story collection *Bay undz in vaytshepl* in 1944, he was aware that the English words might not be understood by some of his readership, and so added a six-page glossary of his English words translated into Yiddish.) The use of anglicized Yiddish adds character to the Yiddish stories, but it has no similar effect in English translation, and my including such phrases would break the narrative flow. I therefore decided not to highlight the use of anglicized Yiddish except on one or two specific occasions where the English word itself is the focus, such as *finndish* as the incorrectly used word "finish" in Kaizer's story "*Roni Akore* and the Dressmaker."

INTRODUCTION

In around 2000, I was perusing the bookshop at London's Jewish Book Week in a hall in Central London. It was filled with stalls of new books, but on one second-hand stall was a row of old Yiddish books. I had just begun to learn Yiddish and was intrigued by one of the titles: *Bay undz in vaytshepl* (This Whitechapel of Ours) by A. M. Kaizer. It made me laugh, having never seen the East End area of Whitechapel written in Yiddish letters before—*vaytshepl*. I bought that and another book of stories, published in London with the title *Produktivizatsye* (Productivization), by I. A. Lisky. I had read many East End stories and memoirs in English and was curious to find out what the Yiddish writers, whom I had never heard of, would have to say. However, the two books sat on my bookshelves waiting for my Yiddish to improve enough to read them.

At around the same time, I began going regularly to the Friends of Yiddish meetings that took place in Toynbee Hall in Whitechapel on Saturday afternoons. A small group of very elderly Yiddish speakers, augmented by a couple of Yiddish learners like me, read poems and stories, sang songs, and told jokes in Yiddish. I couldn't understand most of it, but I particularly loved Phyllis, who with a broad London accent would read a different sketch by Katie Brown each week. I managed to understand whole sentences here and there in the story, but never seemed to be able to catch the punchlines at the end, at which everyone laughed.

A few years later, when my Yiddish had improved enough to think about taking the dusty books from the bookshelf, I ended up on a rainy summer holiday in a small village in the Italian mountains with the two books of Kaizer's and Lisky's Yiddish stories and a large Yiddish-English dictionary. As the images of the East End community began to emerge, I found that they spoke to me personally about the world of my grandparents, aunts, and uncles, and they excited me as a historian. Some time later, when I acquired copies of Katie Brown's two books and devoured them with ease, I realized that, through these three writers, I had stumbled onto a new peephole into East End Jewish life.

Further surprises were inevitable when I started researching. While working on the translations for this book, taken from my now four storybooks of London Yiddishtown, I was scouring the Yiddish press at the British Library to find out who these writers were, and in what cultural and literary environments they had been writing.[1] Lisky's book had come out in 1937, Kaizer's in 1944, and Brown's in 1947 and 1951, yet I discovered that almost all of the stories or a version of them were first published in the early to mid-1930s in the Yiddish daily news-papers, and that Brown and Kaizer were particularly prolific. The stories I had translated from the books were sometimes identical to the earlier versions, but some were substantially altered to reflect the changes over time; and reading the two versions together added subtle nuance to their storylines. I also found scores of articles and reviews about London Yiddish literary culture, and obituaries of the writers and editors. I slowly began to build up a vibrant picture of the Jewish East End as it changed through the thirties and forties, different from anything I had read before.

London Yiddishtown offers two perspectives on the Jewish East End of the thir-ties and forties, both of them of interest to Londoners, Yiddishists, historians, and story-lovers. One perspective is the emerging landscape of the Yiddish-speaking Jewish community in the selection of stories by Katie Brown, A. M. Kaizer, and I. A. Lisky, translated into English for the first time. The stories are all set in Jewish London, mainly in London's East End, and, although they are fiction and satire, they give a sense of the political atmosphere, the community debates, and personal feelings of the time. Where necessary, individual stories are preceded by a short background note so that the reader today will have some of the information that the reader of the time would have known. A second perspective is a new history of the London Yiddish literary community gleaned almost entirely from articles, reviews, and reports in the local Yiddish press. Brown, Kaizer, and Lisky were part of a family of poets, fiction writers, satirists and playwrights, critics, journalists, commentators, and reporters, and even actors and artists. They were a close-knit community whose members supported, critiqued, and challenged each other. Sometimes the atmosphere was one of intense and loving encouragement. At other times there was a feeling of backbiting, bitter disagreement, and competition. This vibrant but small community is described in the final essay in this book, "The Liter-ary Landscape of London's Yiddishtown and the Fight for the Survival of Yiddish,

1930–50," and in the biographies that appear before the stories of Brown, Kaizer, and Lisky. Thus *London Yiddishtown* creates a picture of the past that is viewed through both the stories of its storywriters and the articles of its journalists. This combination offers us an intriguingly intimate view from community insiders.

JEWISH LONDON IN THE THIRTIES

From the mid-1880s, Whitechapel in the East End of London was Britain's Yiddish-speaking metropolis. Immigrants brought their Jewish Eastern European culture into their new homes, workplaces, and leisure activities, and the area bustled with Jewish daily life and cultural activities taking place mostly in Yiddish. London was one of the centers of an emerging transatlantic radical Yiddish press, and revolutionary anarchists and union activists argued politics in Yiddish in the workers' clubs and cafés. There was a developing Yiddish theatre, and arts and literary institutions were established. The streets were plastered with Yiddish signs, posters, and ads, and Yiddish talk and discussion emanated from the plethora of shops, market stalls, workshops, and synagogues. At the turn of the twentieth century, many Yiddish writers and journalists lived in the East End, writing about London and publishing in London, such as the poet and socialist activist Morris Winchevsky and the writer Yosef Haim Brenner.[2] Both Brown and Kaizer grew up in this Yiddish-rich environment, absorbing the East End community's daily routines, intimacies, and eccentricities.

By the 1920s, however, the Jewish East End was in decline. Winchevsky and many Yiddish writers, activists, and actors had left England for America, and Brenner had gone to Palestine. Upwardly mobile Jewish immigrants, such as Kaizer, had moved or were moving away from the East End to the suburbs of London, expanding the Jewish communities in East London's Ilford and Gants Hill, North London's Stoke Newington and Stamford Hill, and North West London's Cricklewood and Golders Green. Those remaining in the East End, like Brown, were mostly an older generation of working-class immigrant tailors, cabinetmakers, and market-stall holders who still spoke Yiddish. Many of these Yiddish speakers did not want to pass the language on to their children, worried that it would hold them back or cause them to suffer anti-Semitism. The children, who were in or had been through Anglo-Jewish and local-authority schooling, were, in any case, firmly anglicized. The tension between the old Yiddish culture and modern English living is the subject of Brown's humor and Kaizer's satire. In one of

Brown's stories, Rachel is embarrassed by and rejects the Yiddish language of her parents, complaining to her mother that they now live in England and "it's time to forget Yiddish."[3]

But for the older generation, Yiddish was unforgettable. It was a Jewish language: a combination of old German, classical, biblical Hebrew, and Slavic and other influences from the countries where Jews had lived and to which they had migrated. It had a hold on immigrant Yiddish speakers, not only for its familiarity as a mother tongue, but also for how it could speak to and describe a cultural experience in a particularly Jewish way. The richness of the spoken language and extensive literature contained the history of the settlement and movement of Jewish people. As other languages, such as English, became incorporated into daily Yiddish speech, the changing language mirrored the experience of becoming an English immigrant community. The next generation, growing up in London and speaking English, may have had some understanding of domestic Yiddish but had no way to access the nuance of fluent Yiddish speech or the Yiddish written word.

As the worldwide depression overtook the UK in the 1930s, unemployment surged, and although the north of the country was hardest hit, the textile industry was affected, which impacted East End Jews working in the tailoring trade. Jewish families tried to feed their own households while also supporting extended family living in Eastern Europe, as news reports described starvation conditions and growing anti-Semitism there.[4] At the same time, there was increasing anxiety about the rise of fascism in the East End, where, bolstered by Hitler's victory in 1933, Oswald Mosley's British Union of Fascists, clad in black shirts, were vocal and aggressive on the streets. Lisky arrived in London in 1930 and witnessed the growing tensions in the East End, which became the themes of his stories.

The Jewish community was full of conflicting views about how to respond to key issues of the day, which led to clashes. There were Zionists campaigning for the British authorities to allow more immigration to Palestine, non-Zionists afraid that Jews would be seen as a nation and thus less welcome in Britain, and anti-Zionists completely opposing the Zionist project.[5] There were antifascist activists who wanted to respond to Mosley's fascists with confrontation, and those who wanted to keep a low profile.[6] There were those who wanted proactive public Jewish marches and demonstrations against Germany's violence toward its Jews, and those who wanted to wait and only be a part of a British-led response.[7] Reports on these taut political struggles filled the weekly Yiddish press *Di post* (The Post) and *Di tsayt* (The Times) and the weekly English-language *Jewish Chronicle*.

During the 1930s, the Anglo-Jewish establishment was in the middle of significant organizational and communal change, with a move away from the Jewish upper middle class and aristocracy's exclusive hold on leadership positions. During the nineteenth century, Anglo-Jewish authority had wielded communal power through the United Synagogue, the Board of Deputies of British Jews, and charitable bodies, such as the Jewish Board of Guardians. They had been led by established wealthy families of British Jews who had fought for recognition and Jewish emancipation. After World War I, however, the balance of leadership in the Anglo-Jewish community began to change, and these same institutions became dominated by Jews who had immigrated in the 1880s and their descendants.[8] People like Morris Myer, the editor of *Di tsayt*, art critic Leo Koenig, and Kaizer took positions in Anglo-Jewish institutions. One result was the ideological change in these organizations from non- or anti-Zionist to firmly Zionist leadership.[9]

Immigrants who had become financially secure and could support their fellow immigrants became known as *Alrightniks*.[10] For example, the writer Judah Beach, who cofounded the Ben Uri Art and Literature Society in 1909, offered his home as its gallery throughout the twenties. The poet and writer Moshe Oved, who had a jewelry shop in Central London, provided financial assistance to help Yiddish writers like Brown publish their books.[11] *Alrightniks* had feet firmly in both camps. On one hand they were Yiddish speakers with strong links to Eastern Europe, and passionate about maintaining and developing a Yiddish literature. On the other hand they fully engaged with Anglo-Jewish institutions, becoming part of their inflexible bureaucracy. Upward mobility, however, also created a growing distance between the middle-class immigrants who had left the East End and the workers who remained. So, despite greater participation of Jews with immigrant backgrounds, the Anglo-Jewish institutions still did not speak for the whole working-class East End Jewish community. The readership of the London Yiddish press was declining as the number of Yiddish speakers decreased, yet it was there that Brown, Kaizer, and Lisky, as journalists in fiction, gave voice to the East End Jewish community.

FICTION IN THE LONDON YIDDISH PRESS

From the mid-nineteenth century, the modern Yiddish press, from Eastern Europe to America, not only provided news and opinion to its readers but also published the creative and literary work of Yiddish storytellers. It gave publishing opportunities and a way of making a somewhat meager living to writers from the most famous, such as Sholem Aleichem, to the local writers of the region. The papers published short stories, serialized novels, humorous and satirical sketches, and poetry and feuilletons in almost every edition. Some stories published in the press were literary works written in genres that were popular at the time. Other serialized cliffhangers were soap operas designed to keep their readers hooked. There were also those who wrote local stories that referred to the specific details of the daily life and politics of their region's Jewish community. The English Yiddish newspapers were no exception.

After immigration accelerated in the early 1880s, the first regularly published Yiddish papers were the radical *Der poylisher yidl* (The Polish Jew) and *Der arbayter fraynd* (The Worker's Friend). In 1897 the Leeds weekly *Idisher ekspres* (Jewish Express) became a London-based daily paper; it was incorporated into *Di post* in 1926. The competing daily paper, *Di tsayt*, was established in 1913; after *Di post* folded in 1935, *Di tsayt* became the main London Yiddish paper until it ceased publication in 1950. After 1950 *Di idishe shtime* (The Jewish Voice) was the main Yiddish weekly. There were many shorter-lived papers, including one of importance here: Baruch Weinberg's weekly *Der Familyen fraynd* (The Family Friend), which ran from 1922 to 1926. The editors of the newspapers paid internationally known writers, including Zalman Shneur and Sholem Asch, for their serialized novels, and also employed local writers for a regular supply of stories and sketches.[12] Readers were able to read fiction about Eastern Europe, America, and England. During the thirties and forties, Brown, Kaizer, and Leyb Sholem Creditor (*Der eygener*) were called "our three Whitechapel humorists."[13] They wrote short sketches that satirized behaviors and incidents in the London community. They were published in regular columns, and they produced scores of satirical and comic sketches over the decades. Lisky and the writer Esther Kreitman wrote short stories that included local material but often in a more literary vein. They saw their work as connected to fiction writers across the Yiddish-speaking world rather than to local satirists. These five writers were not the only writers producing fiction on local themes. Abish Meisels, for example, wrote a novel partly set in England that was serialized in *Di tsayt*.

I chose to translate the short stories of Brown, Kaizer, and Lisky because they published books that made their material accessible across time. Kreitman would have been included—because she also published in book form—but her short-story collection, which includes nine stories set in London during the Blitz, has already been translated.[14] Kreitman, Creditor, Meisels, and many other London Jewish writers, poets, and playwrights will appear in this book as part of the wider story of the London Yiddish literary milieu.

INTRODUCING BROWN, KAIZER, AND LISKY

Katie Brown, Arye Myer Kaizer, and Yehuda Itamar Lisky were storywriters and journalists who wrote for the Yiddish press. Yiddish was their mother tongue. It was the language of Jewish communities across Eastern Europe, including the small Eastern European towns where Brown, Kaizer, and Lisky were born. Brown and Kaizer arrived in London as children, and Lisky as a young man; yet although they learned English and were familiar with the English-speaking Anglo-Jewish society and the wider English society, they chose to write in Yiddish for a small Yiddish-speaking audience. The subject of most of their stories was London's Jewish East End, and they knew its streets and buildings, its people and communal institutions, and the local and national politics. Their journalism included topical articles, theatre and arts reviews, and travel reports, and their journalistic eye for detail was incorporated into the Whitechapel of their stories.

I will introduce the writers here according to the chronological order of their writing careers in London (Brown, Kaizer, and Lisky). The stories reproduced in the chapters that follow, however, appear in the chronological order of their books' publication (Lisky, Kaizer, and Brown).

Katie Brown was born Gitl Bakon in Ulanov, Western Galicia (today, Ulanów, Poland), in 1889. At the age of twelve, she and her parents moved to London's East End. After getting married at sixteen, she lived in Chicksand Street off Brick Lane,

Portraits of Brown, Kaizer, and Lisky: Katie Brown, 1930 (courtesy of the Mazower private collection); A. M. Kaizer from *Loshn un lebn* (May–July 1966); I. A. Lisky, c. 1940 (courtesy of the Menke Katz Collection, Vilnius, Lithuania).

and stayed there for the rest of her life. She became involved in the Yiddish theatre as an actress, playwright, and songwriter, before, in the 1920s, writing regularly for the Yiddish press. From 1923, she wrote a women's advice column for the weekly paper *Der familyen fraynd* (The Family Friend), and in 1930 she edited the women's pages for *Di post*, writing much of it herself. During the thirties Brown wrote more than 130 humorous sketches of East End life that appeared in *Di post*. During the mid-1940s, Brown had a new contract with *Di tsayt*, for which she edited around sixty of her earlier stories. Some of her revisions are substantial, illuminating the huge changes wrought by the war years on the East End community. Selected stories taken mostly from the later *Di tsayt* versions were published in two book collections: *Lakht oyb ir vilt* (Laugh If You Want To), published in 1947, and *Alts in eynem!* (Everything Together!), in 1951. Together they comprise eighty-six stories and sketches, two poems, and a one-act play. Further stories were published in the literary journal *Loshn un lebn* (Language and Life). A novel, *Unter zelbn dakh* (Under the Same Roof), was serialized in *Di idishe shtime* (The Jewish Voice) in 1953.[15] Brown was active in the Workers' Circle (*Arbeter ring*), a left-wing mutual-aid society, and between 1935 and 1941, she contributed to and coedited their journal, *Arbeter ring*.[16] A selection of her short stories, translated into English by her nephew Sydney Bacon, was published in 1987.[17]

Brown's sketches address small episodes of daily life, to which she gives a comic twist. They may be incidents in the home or encounters on the street, the theatre, or other places she frequented. I have translated eleven of her sketches here, chosen because they highlight generational misunderstandings and point out how the different attachments to Jewish identity of parents and children created unresolvable fractures. Throughout these largely domestic dramas, we see how political tensions from both within and outside the Jewish East End affect marriages and parenting. The story "Breadwinners" shows the generational flip that happens as children financially support their parents and reject their parenting. "*Krismes Prezents*" explores the difficulties of juggling English and Jewish holidays in a nonobservant secular family. "My Prince, the Socialist" examines the terror the older generation feels as their children take their radical politics into the English gentile world. "When a Woman Becomes a Person" offers tongue-in-cheek advice to women on gender issues and how to deal with their husbands' complaints.

Arye Myer (Arnold) Kaizer was born in Yordanov (Jordanowo), Poland, in 1892, the son of a Hasidic kabbalist *rebbe*.[18] In 1895 the family moved to London, where Kaizer had a religious upbringing in the East End: first in Sidney Square, Whitechapel, and later in Tredegar Square in Bow. He spent World War I in the Jewish Legion in Palestine, returning to London in 1920 and becoming a journalist for *Di tsayt*. He was general secretary of the Federation of Jewish Relief Organizations of Britain, regularly traveling to Eastern Europe to report on the situation of the Jewish communities there. On his return from the Ukraine in 1930, the federation published his report as a pamphlet, *Mir zenen hungerik* (We Are Hungry), and reports from other trips were published in *Di tsayt*.[19] Between 1930 and 1950 Kaizer moved first to Stoke Newington and then to North West London. He was involved in setting up the Association of Jewish Journalists and Authors in England (later renamed the Association of Jewish Journalists and Authors of Great Britain), and he arranged and chaired many events, some in his own home.[20] During the thirties and early forties, more than 150 of his sketches and humorous stories about Jewish life in Whitechapel appeared in *Di tsayt*. A selection of thirty-seven of them was published in the book *Bay undz in vaytshepl* (This Whitechapel of Ours) in 1944.[21] Later stories appeared in *Loshn un lebn*.

All but one of Kaizer's witty and satirical tales translated here were first published in *Di tsayt* in the thirties. Kaizer's tales are of community foibles within communal institutions and the foolish or self-centered behavior of Jewish East End folk. I chose to translate ten of Kaizer's stories that explore secularization and religious decline, class hypocrisy, and local politics. In the story "Where It Bubbles," set at the opening of a new community kitchen, pompous benefactors describe their favorite meals. In "Choosing Cantors" the assorted desires of a synagogue congregation and the real motivations of those who work there are brought into relief. In "The Whitechapel Express" upward mobility can be seen in the clothes worn by the community wives and in the fish they buy for the Sabbath. "When You Go to a Yiddish Theatre" is a romp about who goes to see a Yiddish play and how they behave. "*Roni Akore* and the Dressmaker" pinpoints minutiae of the decline of religious practice and attendant cultural loss.

Yehuda Itamar Lisky (Summer Fuchs) was born in Yezerna, Eastern Galicia (today Ozerna, Ukraine), in 1899. A younger brother of the writer A. M. Fuchs, he came to London in 1930.[22] He was politically active on the left in communist-leaning organizations, including the Workers' Circle. Lisky wrote articles and short stories for *Di tsayt* and coedited *Di tsayt*'s evening edition, *Di ovent nayes* (The Evening News). A collection of his short stories, titled *Produktivizatsye* (Productivization), was published in book form in 1937, with a version of some parts of the stories published earlier in *Di tsayt*. Lisky wrote two novellas: *For, du kleyner kozak!* (On Your Way, Little Cossack!), came out in 1941, and is set during World War I in a small village in Eastern Europe. *Melokhe bezuye* (A Humiliating Profession), published in 1947, concerns the London Yiddish literary circles and depicts well-known personalities thinly disguised with pseudonyms.[23] Along with his wife, Sonia Husid (the critic and essayist known as N. M. Seedo), and the Whitechapel poet Avrom Nokhem Stencl, Lisky was on the editorial committee of the literary journal *Yidish london*, and he was published in *Loshn un lebn*. Two of Lisky's Eastern European stories appeared in an English translation by Hannah Berman.[24]

Produktivizatsye contains twelve stories. The six that revolve around London's Yiddishtown are all translated in this volume. The stories concern the East End's clashing ideologies of communism, Zionism, fascism, and Jewish class difference. The title story, "Productivization," tells the story of a metalworker whose son has been given a scholarship to become a doctor. Through scenes in a bathhouse and Gradel's Restaurant in Aldgate, we hear the debate among Sam Stricker, Mrs. Stricker, and the communist Vogman over whether a professional can be productive. "Fascist Recruits" looks at how gentile East End workers find an identity and community in the fascist party. "On the March with the Hungry" describes how the desperation of unemployment affects members of an East End family in different ways, and how they choose to respond. "Ideological Speculation" follows a father and son-in-law who rent out property in the East End and speculate about buying land in Palestine. In "A Guinea a Day," "authentic"-looking Jewish East End extras are needed for a film about the first Frankfurt ghetto of 1462.

COMMON THEMES, DIFFERENT PERSPECTIVES

Brown, Kaizer, and Lisky knew each other well and often attended the same events. Kaizer and Lisky served on the same committees, chaired meetings, and spoke at events for the Association of Jewish Journalists and Authors, the Ben Uri, and the London branch of the Yiddish Scientific Institute (YIVO). Brown and Lisky were both involved in Workers' Circle committees and were weekly participants at the Friends of Yiddish Sabbath Afternoons. Brown and Lisky wrote for *Di post*, and all three writers wrote for *Di tsayt* and later *Loshn un lebn*. Yet as much as they had in common, they inhabited different political and religious spheres. These differences are apparent in the ways they approached the same themes. Viewed together, their writing reflects the spectrum of views and experiences of the immigrant generation. The examples here will address their portrayals of Zionism, gentiles and anti-Semitism, and the relationships between women and men.

Portrayals of Zionism

Lisky was not a Zionist at this stage in his life. In his story "Ideological Speculation," he depicts the cynicism of some Jews who identify as Zionists only to further their capitalist venture to buy land in Palestine. He portrays two characters: One is a cold-blooded property speculator who has no interest in Palestine other than for the money to be made from buying and renting property there; the other is an East End worker who is emotionally attached to the Land of Israel yet also drawn to the prestige he gains by associating with the wealthy West End Zionists of the Zionist Organization of Great Britain. The story depicts Zionism as an ideology adopted by people with nonideological motives.[25]

Kaizer, on the other hand, was a Zionist. He had lived in Palestine, and he attended and reported from the annual Zionist congresses. His story "Moses in London" depicts the political and ideological differences and in-fighting among Zionist groups in London. Albeit with humor and a light touch, he criticizes how the narrow focus, dogma, and bureaucracy of the different right-wing, left-wing, and religious Zionist organizations obstruct their wider Zionist aims. Clearly frustrated by the Zionist structures in Britain, Kaizer makes fun of all of them, and thus shows them to be morally shallow. Even at the end, when there could be some unity, the organizations cannot pull themselves out of their competitive squabbles and ideological positions.[26]

Lisky's and Kaizer's stories were written in the mid-thirties, but Brown's stories that contend with Zionism were published more than a decade later, after World War II and just after the establishment of the State of Israel. In each of the stories "I Need a Flat" and "My Prince, the Socialist," a mother talks to her children about the prospect of their immigrating to Israel. In "I Need a Flat," the existence of a Jewish state gives the mother new confidence and pride in being a Jew in England, and she tells her daughter that it is the duty of Jews to support Israel. In "My Prince, the Socialist," a mother fears that her son's radical public speech will be dangerous for a child of immigrants. The mother sees Israel as the only safe place for Jews, where they will no longer be a target of anti-Semitism. In both stories, the children's lack of interest reflects their diminishing engagement with their Jewish identity. Israel does not hold their hopes for the future; England does.

The difference in perspectives on Zionism reflects the writers' differing political viewpoints, their positions in the community, and the change in atmosphere from pre– to post–World War II, although there is some irony in Brown's promotion of the State of Israel, which scorned Yiddish in favor of Hebrew. Placing the stories together, we get a sense that, although Zionism was constantly fragmented and debated, and encompassed a wide spectrum of types of Jews, it became enmeshed in an English Jewish cultural identity.[27]

Portrayals of Gentile Characters and Anti-Semitism

Lisky regularly included gentile characters in his London stories. They sometimes appeared as protagonists, and when they do not, they are alluded to in conversation. In the story "Fascist Recruits," Bill Smith and his employees are all gentiles, and the two main characters join the British Union of Fascists (BUF). Although anti-Semitism is not shown as their primary motive, they do participate in demonstrations where BUF members hold placards with anti-Semitic slogans, shout anti-Semitic chants, and hold street meetings in Jewish areas of London. In contrast, the story "Productivization" takes place entirely in Jewish spheres, without a gentile character. Yet BUF fascists are conjured up in the talk in Gradel's Restaurant, and the women in the bathhouse discuss their anxiety about Hitler and fascist policy in Germany. There may be no gentile characters depicted, but their presence is felt, and anti-Semitism is an underlying fear.

Kaizer, on the other hand, rarely brings in the outside English world. The single gentile character in the ten stories translated in this volume is the bus conductor on the "Whitechapel Express" who asks the Jewish workers for a tip on the races. Although this may point to a Jewish stereotype, it is clearly meant as an inside joke about the gambling problems among East End Jews. More poignantly, earlier in the same story, Yerukhem, the philosopher, interjects an anecdote about the loneliness of traveling in a Rolls Royce. In the end he spits out, "It should only happen to anti-Semites." This is a topical reference to Oswald Mosley, the leader of the BUF, who gave rousing speeches at BUF rallies from his Rolls Royce.[28] Yerukhem's comment shows fascists residing in isolated luxury, a world away from the conviviality of the Jewish East End community's cocoon.

Gentile culture also appears only occasionally in Brown's stories. In "Jewish Readers!" she contrasts the polite and demure way English people read newspapers with the utter lack of decorum and rudeness with which Jews read newspapers. Brown uses the English as foils to poke fun at Jewish stereotypes and at the same time take pride in their feistiness and excitability. The story ends with a bus passenger shouting at the woman sitting next to her for not letting her read her newspaper over her shoulder. She yells that this stingy behavior is the reason people are anti-Semitic. Although her depictions are humorous, Brown portrays her characters as afraid of appearances in the gentile world, and not just because of anti-Semitism. In "Davy Becomes a Prize Fighter," the mother instructs her young son that boxing is not a fitting profession for a Jewish boy. This leads Davy to suggest that he would publicly display his Jewish identity by wearing a Star of David in the boxing ring. The mother's anxiety, however, is not that he will get anti-Semitic heckling from the audience but that he will be lured into an English gentile world and marry a gentile woman. The fear of assimilation overrides her fear of anti-Semitism.

Brown's and Kaizer's stories were written for an internal audience to entertain the readership of the Yiddish press and are less focused on the world outside of Yiddishtown. Lisky, on the other hand, wanted to show the relationship between the Jewish community and the wider world, and he aimed to have his stories translated for an English audience. He wanted his politics to have a broad reach.

Portrayals of Women and Men

Brown spent years writing a women's advice column for *Der familyen fraynd* and a women's page for *Di post*, so it's no surprise that a fair number of her stories concern the marital relations between women and men. In the story "Pessimism and Optimism," the female narrator mocks her husband's failings, yet she does so without making him look foolish. In contrast, in the story "When a Woman Becomes a Person," Brown does not hold back from letting the husband character look weak and silly. Brown's tongue-in-cheek style is clever, and in her advice to women, ineffectual men are the butt of a lot of jesting. In "A New Play in Whitechapel," Brown portrays how men need significant bolstering, and the sensible women are depicted as low-key but in control.

Lisky also describes a number of husband-wife relationships. In his stories the husband, as head of the household, makes the final decisions, but it is the wife who has the dominant intellect and speaks the most sense. In "Nationalist Feelings and Class Interests," we learn that, after Mr. Klepman's gentile partner left their business, it was due to Mr. Klepman's wife's "brains that they no longer lived in the small East End street, and now belonged to the 'highbrow' set." In "On the

March with the Hungry," it is Mrs. Barsht who keeps the household together by borrowing money and going to the soup kitchen while her husband is overcome with despair. In "Productivization" Sam Stricker's wife has to edge her view in between her husband's muddled thinking, but her perspective is the one that is validated in the end. The wives are seen only as appendages to their husbands, yet their common sense forms the bedrock of their families.

Relations between men and women do not feature strongly in Kaizer's stories. He tends to describe husbands and wives as existing in their own nonoverlapping spheres. Thus the men are the benefactors of the communal kitchen in "Where It Bubbles," and the women on the Whitechapel Express do the shopping for the Sabbath. The husbands are not absent from the Whitechapel Express, but they are busy reading newspapers and Yiddish books and muttering psalms while their wives are knitting, gossiping, and getting bargains on the fish. The story where we see the interaction between husbands and wives is in "*Roni Akore* and the Dressmaker," where the husbands dance to the tune of their wives, who are taking advice from their dressmakers. In this instance the show will not go on without female approval, and the women are the ones who do the negotiating through telegrams from the seaside.

The depictions of women and men are fictions created from observations and experience, yet they may reflect the writers' own personal lives. Brown was happily married, with a busy family life. She was a woman writing in a man's world, carving out a space within which she could act out some of her frustrations. Kaizer was a dedicated family man, inviting the community into his home for Yiddish cultural events.[29] Lisky had a turbulent marriage to Sonia (N. M. Seedo), a feisty communist intellectual.

Zionism, fascism, and the challenges facing the Jewish family were burning and urgent issues of the day. Aspects of these topics leapt out of newspaper headlines and daily news reports, and they were hotly debated in opinion pieces and features, reports of meetings, and reviews of events. These topics would also appear in fiction in a variety of guises. The views that we are offered through Brown's, Kaizer's, and Lisky's eyes complement each other, sometimes contradict each other, and show us a range of positions in these debates.

Brown, Kaizer, and Lisky penned their works with an energy that displayed a passion for the East End and its Jewish community, a passion for documenting the East End, and a passionate desire to continue a meaningful Yiddish-language culture in London: a culture they already knew was in decline. They wrote in a literary atmosphere that was full of contradictions: anxiety and determination, hopelessness and humor, paralysis and desperate activity. They held onto hope amid the chaos of worldwide depression, and they wrote to counter the despair about the future of Yiddish writing and Yiddish culture. They wrote about their experiences of Whitechapel. They may not have imagined that, years later, when the Yiddish East End had disappeared and was largely remembered with nostalgia and sentimentality, their local stories, written for a local audience, would offer new perspectives on the East End culture of the thirties and forties.

Map of the Writers' Yiddish East End During the 1930s and 1940s
Drawing by Sarha Moore

1. Petticoat Lane Market ("The Lane") on Middlesex Street and surrounding streets
2. Soup Kitchen for the Jewish Poor, 17–19 Butler Street. (The street name was changed to Brune Street in 1937.)
3. Gradel's Restaurant, a popular kosher restaurant at 2–4 Whitechapel High Street
4. The Makhzike Hadas Synagogue, on the corner of Brick Lane and Fournier Street
5. Whitechapel Library and Art Gallery, 77–80 and 80–82 Whitechapel High Street
6. Adler House on Adler Street was a venue for weddings and events that also housed, at various times, the Jewish National Theatre, the Jewish Free Reading Room, the New Yiddish Theatre Company, the Beth Din Rabbinical Court, the United Synagogue's Burial Society, the Jewish Institute's Advisory Centre, and the Folk House.
7. Pavilion Theatre, 191–93 Whitechapel Road
8. Carlos' Café, where Stencl's inner circle met, Fulbourne Street
9. Offices of *Di tsayt*, 325 Whitechapel Road
10. Jewish Communal Restaurant, 214 Whitechapel Road
11. Israel (Yisroel) Narodiczky's home (a focal point for writers and intellectuals), 48 Mile End Road
12. The Narodiczky Press print shop, 129–31 Cavell Street
13. Temple of Art Yiddish Theatre, 226 Commercial Road (which opened and closed in 1912)
14. Hessel Street Market
15. Grand Palais Theatre, 133–39 Commercial Road
16. Circle House, Workers' Circle, 22 Great Alie Street
17. The Jews' Temporary Shelter and reading room, 63 Mansell Street
18. Stern's Hotel and Kosher Restaurant, 3–5 Mansell Street

Yehuda Itamar Lisky

דאָס אידישע פֿאָלק

Published by THE JEWISH PEOPLE.   Editor: I.A. LISKY

Portrait of Lisky (1930s) presented to him by his newspaper,
Dos idisher folk, probably in the 1970s. (Courtesy of Francis
Fuchs, private collection)

Front cover of Lisky's short-story collection *Produktivizatsye* (Productivization), 1937. (Photograph by the author)

BIOGRAPHY

> Lisky's depth does not lie in the lofty problem itself, but in the way he
> interprets and cultivates it . . . and a tragic intensity lies in the simplest
> voice of his protagonists.
>
> Joseph Hillel Lewy, *Di tsayt*, 1943[1]

Yehuda Itamar Lisky was born Yehuda Isomer (Summer) Fuchs in 1899 in
Yezerna, Eastern Galicia (today Ozerna, Ukraine), the youngest of four boys.
His father, Haim Fuchs, was a merchant who traveled to villages and fairs in the
locality to trade with the peasants, and he sometimes took Summer with him.[2]
Summer had a religious education, went to one of the Jewish philanthropist Baron
Hirsch's vocational schools, and had a private tutor. His older brothers, Avrom
Moyshe and Shia, left home when Summer was still young. By the time Summer
was twelve, his brother Avrom was traveling and writing in Europe and America,
on his way to becoming the well-known Yiddish writer A. M. Fuchs.[3]

Summer left Yezerna during World War I, when the Russian army occupied
Galicia; he worked in a tavern in Lemberg (today Lviv, Ukraine) before returning
home at the end of the war. In 1924 he went to study in Vienna, where his brother
Avrom was now living. He became part of the literary circle of the Yiddish poet
Mendl Naygreshl, and he began writing.[4] In order for Summer's writing not to
be confused with that of Avrom, Naygreshl suggested that he change his name
from Fuchs to Lisky, derived from the Polish word for fox.[5] In Latin letters on his
publications, Lisky wrote his name as "I. A. Lisky," approximating the Yiddish
initials of his name. While in Vienna, Lisky met many young Jewish writers. He
became close friends with Mordecai Husid, from Bessarabia, who was studying to
be a Hebrew teacher, and who later also became a published writer.[6]

Lisky (far right), Seedo (Sonia Husid; half in shot, far left), Mordecai Husid (second from left), and two others. Probably in the countryside near Vienna, late 1920s. (Courtesy of the Jewish Public Library Archives, Montreal)

In May 1930, while Lisky was sitting in a café, a group of fascists came in and demanded to know what strange language he was writing. When he told them, they ordered him to get out. Afraid of the political climate, Lisky left Vienna that same day. He traveled to London, moving into his brother Shia's family home on Hanbury Street in the East End.[7]

ARRIVAL IN LONDON

In London Lisky sought out the Yiddish literary circles. He became involved with the English branch of the Yiddish Scientific Institute (YIVO), which had been established in Vilnius five years earlier. YIVO's aim was to promote and preserve Yiddish culture, and Lisky used his contacts from Vienna to bring over the highly respected poet Zalman Reisen as a guest of the London branch. Lisky was applauded for his article about Reisen in *Di tsayt*, which not only helped to raise the profile of YIVO but also brought Lisky to the attention of the London Yiddish literary world.[8] He began to write articles for *Di tsayt* and *Di post*, and several of his stories about London Jewish life were published. He also worked on *Di tsayt*'s evening paper, *Di ovent nayes* (Evening News), and wrote for the Eastern European and American Yiddish presses.[9]

Around the same time, Sonia Husid, the sister of Lisky's friend Mordecai, arrived in London from Vienna, where she had also been studying. Lisky was still living with his brother Shia and family, although now at 135 Bethnal Green Road.[10] With his address on a slip of paper, Sonia turned up on Lisky's doorstep straight off the boat. They became friends, and Lisky found Sonia lodging at 50 Carysfort Road, Stoke Newington, an area in North London where upwardly mobile Jews from the East End had settled and where many Eastern European refugees came to live during the thirties. Lisky began introducing Sonia to the literary groups he was involved with, and Sonia, writing under the pen name N. M. Seedo, attended events at the Association of Jewish Journalists and Authors and became a member of the Workers' Circle. By 1935 Lisky and Seedo were living together on Carysfort Road.[11]

When Lisky was still studying in Vienna, his group of writers wrote in a variety of literary genres. Mordecai Husid wrote short stories in a modernist style; Fuchs was a realist; and Lisky's mixture of realism imbued with moments of fantasy made him a "modern realist who does not fanatically observe the rules of realism, and so makes the subject independent of a fixed outside world."[12] Since

Portrait of Seedo c. 1930 and letters sent to Lisky and Seedo by Mordecai Husid, 1933–35. (Courtesy of Francis Fuchs, private collection)

leaving Vienna, Lisky and Husid had corresponded, and in 1935 Husid suggested that Lisky, Fuchs, and he produce a collection of their short stories.[13] Perhaps due to their contrasting writing styles, the book did not materialize. Fuchs already had a substantial publishing history, and in 1937 both Husid and Lisky had their own short-story collections published.[14]

Lisky's *Produktivizatsye* (Productivization), published by Narodiczky Press, contains twelve short stories: The first six are set in Poland, and the following six, those translated in this volume, are set in the East End of London. Some of the stories were based on his earlier stories in *Di tsayt*.[15] A prepublication review by Morris Myer, the editor of *Di tsayt*, began with his utter delight at the publication of the book. It was like giving Lisky a metaphorical bear hug, with thanks for his keeping Yiddish Whitechapel on the map.

> This book shows that Yiddish is productive: that even here in London, where Yiddish-speaking Jews find themselves like those shipwrecked on a small island in the middle of a wide English-language cultural sea bubbling with life, it can be productive and creative. Here, the Yiddish word will not be drowned in the huge, foaming English sea, as long as there are people with the passion and desire to express themselves in Yiddish: create stories

and scenes of Jewish life in our own language. . . . I. A. Lisky has done
this. He has observed, responded to, and taken on specific characteristics of
Jewish life in London and has described them in his stories.[16]

Myer's sense of exuberance, however, does not stop him from being sharp and
critical of the London stories, which he called one-dimensional. Myer critiqued
what he saw as only a surface examination of characters' emotions and motivations. The characters lacked psychological intensity because they were made to
push ideological positions. This, he argued, limited the internal wrangle of Lisky's
protagonists in their struggle with the big questions in life, such as their place in
the universe, what they should do, and why. Myer also complained that some of
Lisky's sentences were awkwardly constructed, and that his lack of realism, his
journalistic style mixed with episodes of imaginative fantasy, and his "strange-
sounding expressions" were a barrier to understanding the stories. Despite this
stream of criticism, Myer concluded that "these failings in no way cast a shadow on
the significance of Lisky's creation, and they do not lessen the enjoyment that one
gets from reading his stories."[17]

By this time, the local community knew Lisky as an active participant in the
literary and political worlds about which he wrote. They might have seen him at an
antifascist demonstration or at a rally demanding an end to the unpopular means test
for unemployment benefits. Lisky, however, wanted a wider audience than the local
London Jewish community. He wanted the art critic and writer Leo Koenig, who
was then the chair of the Association of Jewish Journalists and Authors and published across the Yiddish-speaking world, to write a review of *Produktivizatsye* for
an international audience. Koenig however, unlike Morris Myer, preferred to review
internationally known writers, and tended to ignore local writers at the beginning
of their careers. Seedo felt that Lisky had been snubbed by Koenig, who had not
even offered him an author's reception, which was the standard sign of respect that
all London Yiddish writers expected on publication of a book.[18]

FAMILY LIFE AND ACTIVISM
AS A MARRIED COUPLE

In the late 1930s, after contending with many logistical and bureaucratic hurdles,
Lisky and Seedo managed to bring Seedo's mother over from Eastern Europe, and
in 1938, Lisky and Seedo got married. They continued their joint activities. They

were active in the establishment of the *Yidisher kultur-gezelshaft, YKUF London*, which was a branch of the international Yiddisher Kultur-Farband, a communist-leaning association promoting Yiddish culture. Lisky was the honorary secretary of YKUF, London and both Lisky and Seedo were editors and contributors to the YKUF journal, *Yidish london*.[19] Seedo was instrumental in setting up a lecture course on the development of Yiddish language and literature at King's College, University of London, and when the lectures proved popular, Lisky pushed for the establishment of a permanent chair in Yiddish at King's, although that failed to materialize due to lack of funds.[20]

As the war loomed, Lisky's brother A. M. Fuchs, now a well-established writer, escaped Europe and arrived in England. After being interned on the Isle of Man for three months, he was warmly received by the Yiddish writers' community. Three days before the war broke out, Seedo and Lisky's first son, Irving, was born. Seedo describes how she was transformed overnight from a literary and cultural activist into a housewife. She felt "pushed out" of the Yiddish, political, and social worlds that had given her spiritual sustenance. Seedo and the baby were evacuated out of London, and she grew to resent Lisky, who remained in London and whose activities not only continued but increased.[21] By 1942 Lisky was the vice chair of the Aid-to-Russia Fund, and was also involved with the 1942 Committee, a pro-Soviet fundraising group set up by the novelist Simon Blumenfeld.[22]

As a result of the damage the Blitz had caused, property prices in London's bombed-out streets significantly dropped. In late 1942, Seedo and Lisky, now with a second child, Francis, managed to purchase property on Carysfort Road, the street where they were already living, with the security of a diamond hat pin that Seedo had been given by her mother. Between Lisky and his brother Shia, the family owned a number of houses on the street. Lisky hoped to bring in an income that writing did not provide by renting rooms to immigrant families, but rents were so low in those areas that, after paying the mortgage, the couple was still left struggling financially.[23] Lisky and Seedo's marriage, rife with both personal and political disagreements, did not survive, and they divorced in the fifties. They did, however, still live in the same street, maintain frequent contact, and later remarried.[24]

FURTHER PUBLICATIONS AND TRANSLATIONS

Lisky published two novellas in the 1940s. *For, du kleyner kozak!* (On Your Way, Little Cossack!), which came out in 1941, is set during World War I, in a small village in Eastern Europe. *Melokhe bezuye* (A Humiliating Profession), published in 1947, is a London novel.[25] In the latter, Lisky provides vignettes of the time using thinly disguised characters based on Lisky and Seedo, Morris Myer, Leo Koenig, and the poet Itzik Manger, among others. The story moves through a variety of local settings: a Yiddish literary event; a meeting at a printer's office in White-chapel; a strategy meeting in the Workers' Circle center, Circle House, during the "Battle of Cable Street"; a house party for London intellectuals in Hampstead; and a meeting with a translator. It shows the feelings of self-doubt and rivalry within the writers' circles. The novel depicts the Yiddish writers' intense conversations about the nature of art, literature, and beauty while also portraying the hardships they experienced over getting published in London. The *Jewish Chronicle* reviewer described how Lisky "threw down a 'challenge' to the Jewish community which . . . by neglecting the writers and artists in its midst, converted their calling to a *Meloche Bezujo* (humiliating profession)."[26]

Lisky's fictional alter ego was his writer-protagonist, Haim Aysnberg. In Seedo's later memoir, *In the Beginning Was Fear*, Lisky appears as Abram Eisberg. Seedo describes how every Yiddish writer dreamed of having their work translated into English to gain a wider audience and greater prestige, yet it rarely came to fruition.[27] Lisky, however, did work with two translators, the writer Hannah Berman and the journalist and communist activist Isaac Panner. Berman's translations were published as *Geese* in 1951 and *The Cockerel in the Basket* in 1955.[28] The collaboration with Panner was less successful, and although a manuscript exists for the story "Ideological Speculation," it was never published.[29]

From 1958 Lisky edited *Di idishe shtime* (The Jewish Voice) with the journalist Leon Creditor. He published his own newspaper, *Dos yidishe folk* (The Jewish People), from 1966 until 1988. Lisky remained a regular at Avrom Nokhem Stencl's literary Sabbath Afternoons, then known as "the Friends of Yiddish Language," where he provided a news briefing of current affairs each week.[30] He also wrote in English for the *Left Review*, *New Life*, and the *Jewish Chronicle*.[31]

In 1988 Lisky was attacked in his Stoke Newington home during a burglary and lost the sight of one eye, making it impossible for him to continue editing *Dos yidishe folk*. He died a year later. The *Jewish Chronicle* obituary called Lisky "one of the country's last significant Yiddish writers . . . whose optimism about the future of Yiddish was an inspiration to young students of the language."[32]

PRODUCTIVIZATION

In London in the mid-thirties, Jewish communists were mostly Eastern European immigrants. They congregated largely in Jewish groups, which gave them more in common with the worldwide Jewish communist movement than with the Communist Party of Great Britain. Many East End Jews were drawn to communism because communists were the ones actively strategizing to oppose fascism in Britain, in contrast to the Anglo-Jewish authorities whose response was slow and tepid. Many were members of the Workers' Circle, which was instrumental in setting up the Jewish Labour Council, which later became the Jewish People's Council Against Fascism and Anti-Semitism. Jewish communists were strongly represented in groups like the Stepney Tenants' Defence League, and formed the ideological base of the Jewish Cultural Club, the Jewish Fund for Soviet Russia, and the London branch of YKUF. Lisky was involved with the latter three groups, and served as secretary of the last two.[1]

In this story characters allude to the communist response to the activities of the British Union of Fascists (BUF) in London. The BUF was formed by Sir Oswald Mosley in 1932, and throughout the thirties members held meetings and rallies across London, dressed in their recognizable black shirts.

The antifascist activism described in this story all refers to events from 1934. That year, the BUF held a series of meetings at the Albert Hall in South Kensington, where Mosley delivered lengthy speeches. In April 1934 one large rally attracted ten thousand fascists. The meeting proved such a successful boost for the BUF that they followed it up a few weeks later with an even larger public event at the Olympia Hall in Hammersmith. It was widely advertised, and tickets were free. Antifascist protesters got hold of tickets and attended the event in order to disrupt the meeting. When the protestors began heckling, the Blackshirts descended, violently kicking them and beating them with brass knuckle-dusters. In September 1934 the BUF planned an open-air rally in Hyde Park. The Jewish communists put out a leaflet in Yiddish encouraging East-enders to attend a counterdemonstration. Despite the *Jewish Chronicle*'s advice that Jews not attend, many joined the massive crowd of 120,000, who completely outnumbered the BUF by more than 20 to 1.[2]

The Anglo-Jewish establishment, which had opposed Jewish antifascist activism, was also concerned about growing anti-Semitism in Britain. They worried that the overrepresentation of Jews in the professions might aggravate or even cause anti-Semitism. In 1937 the Board of Deputies of British Jews funded a survey, to be carried out by the Jewish Health Organisation of Great Britain, to ascertain the situation, produce data to counter anti-Semitic claims, and deter young people from going into professions they saw as already over-represented in parts of the country. The report was never made public.[3]

Although this story is set in London, the title, "Productivization," refers to the debate over programs created in Imperial Russia of the 1880s, which sought to encourage Jewish artisans to work in industry and on the land. By the 1920s this idea was being discussed across the Jewish world. In part this debate was fueled by the anxiety that Jews were seen as unproductive, which made them the targets of anti-Semitism; encouraging Jews to become productive, it was thought, would avert anti-Semitism.[4]

Three other locations are mentioned in the story. Gradel's Restaurant at 2–4 Whitechapel High Street was an established kosher restaurant and popular with the immigrant community. Several bathhouses in the East End were mainly patronized by Jews, including Schevzik's on Brick Lane, and others on Little Alie Street, Goulston Street, and Old Ford Road, Bethnal Green. The World Zionist Organization's central office was located at 77 Great Russell Street, WC1.

It has been a long time since the small, crowded home on the second floor was happy . . .

At night a gas lamp lights up two damp, cramped rooms; each with a single window peering out onto the small, gloomy Whitechapel street like a glass eye. This flat is in one of the leased houses of the area, belonging to speculators who let them out for a weekly rent.

Sam Stricker, a Jewish metalworker, has lived on the second floor for around twenty years, and has never missed a week's rent. He is so reliable that his landlord has said on many an occasion: "Mr. Stricker, you're a decent man." Mr. Stricker's friends and neighbors think he is lucky because his son won a scholarship to study medicine. Yet this situation is precisely why their home is not happy.

Sam Stricker has absorbed the hard coldness and grey hue of his neighborhood into his appearance. All week he looks grey, is covered with dust, and his metalwork produces a rusty residue that deposits its color onto his long face and broad nose. His meager earnings barely provide enough for his wife and children, of whom Abe, the sixteen-year-old, is the eldest.

Sam works for himself and never wastes any time, working late into the night, except on Mondays, the worst day of the week, because that's when he pays rent for both his home and his workshop. He pays the two rents to the same landlord, and because Sam Stricker is a decent man, he doesn't wait for a rent collector to come round and remind him; he just takes the money to his landlord—a squat man, built like a safe: tough, rich, and always locked into his own thoughts.

On Monday nights Sam Stricker trudges over to a small shop belonging to his landlord's son that's stuffed full with gold, silver, and diamonds. He hands over the rent book and the rent, and the landlord signs it with curly, wavy strokes inscribed with an old, shaky hand, and as usual, twitches his watery right eye. When he returns the rent book, the landlord inquires with an affectation that comes from seeing himself as an expert in dealing with good tenants:

"And how's your Abe doing, Mr. Stricker?" He knows that Sam loves people asking him about his Abe, and Sam quickly begins to tell him what a clever boy Abe is and how much they praise him at school.

This Monday evening, however, Sam Stricker came with an eager look in his eyes, clearly wanting to speak with the landlord. He wanted to ask him what to do with Abe. His expression, like a silent question mark, was particularly agitated because of a conversation he had had with Mr. Gradel in his restaurant.

Mr. Gradel was a sort of Jewish politician who was well up on everything happening in the news, especially the economic crisis that was making people so desperate. He knew precisely how many Jews had been driven out of Germany, and why the situation was so worrying for educated people today, particularly for doctors across Europe.

"We mustn't let our children study today," he told Sam. "They slave away and work themselves to death before they've finished studying, and subsequently they are superfluous to society, like in Germany. Jews have to be productive, become artisans or work on the land."

When Sam heard this opinion, it made his head spin. It seemed as if some pressure was pushing through a small opening in his brain. His tense, dark brow furrowed, and it was clearly hard for him to contain the jumble of incomprehensible thoughts. Later, he said to his wife:

"I always thought that the world needed important people, educated people, and I've suffered because I'm just a simple man." And glancing at Abe, he thought: *The world and its wagon are going backward.*

He knew that his neighbors, his good friends, and acquaintances in the street were no longer jealous that Abe was doing well in school, had won a scholarship, and wanted to become a doctor. When he talked to them about their own sons going into their businesses, and heard what good support they were to their fathers, he pictured the old, pinched face of the landlord, and heard his words clearly in his head: *Really it's better for Abe to work with you in the workshop. Times have changed, you see, Mr. Stricker. I've read in the papers that we Jews have too many educated children. Hitler and Mosley weren't completely wrong in the slogans they declaimed. It's us ourselves who are guilty. We push ourselves forward too much in the eyes of the world. Jews must become workers. You must have heard what problems Jewish intellectuals and doctors are facing nowadays.*

Recently, these opinions kept tumbling about in Sam's head. At home he walked to and fro in the cramped little rooms, restless, anxious, and muttering. He kept telling his wife what advice the landlord had given, but because she did not want to listen to his babbling, he became more agitated.

At work, as he stood from early morning until late at night in his dark, poky, smoky workshop, his blackened, overworked hands shaping the sheet metal, copper, and brass, he made a decision. He would bring Abe into the workshop, and Abe would become a worker and not a doctor. Jews must become productive. But the decision was so difficult to make that the sweat poured down in large drops onto his sooty face, so that he resembled a boiling, blackened pot.

The landlord's advice gnawed at his heart, but even though he had decided not to go along with his wife's opinion, he could not bring himself to say: "Abe, stop studying. It isn't practical." His wife's grievances constantly came back into his mind: *And you are a worker Sam. And are you doing well?*

In a small, densely heated basement corridor, good for sweating, people came
into the bathhouse through a heavy brown wooden door. Women came only once
a week on a Tuesday afternoon. The women from the back streets of Whitechapel
all knew each other. They sat on the bathhouse benches, huddled up together in
the hot steam. Their chunky, naked, hunched backs looked like one huge piece
of red, melted, wet flesh, steaming and sweating. Under their hot armpits hung
large, slippery breasts, propped up on their protruding bellies. Between their
burly swollen legs stood buckets of hot water. The women scratched their scald-
ing hot skin and rubbed their flesh with their hard, swollen hands. They all spoke
at once, shouted, coughed, choking on the steam. Louder than all of them was
Sam Stricker's wife. Naked, except for a wet cloth around her head, she walked
around cursing:

"I hope he cracks his head open! He made his sons into gold-dealers and doctors but he advised *my* husband to make my Abe a worker."

The puffy wrinkles on her tense red face showed the bitterness she felt toward
the landlord, whom her husband had consulted. One word tumbled over the next
as her agitation grew stronger. She felt the frustration of someone who knows she
is right but sees people trying to delude her and make a fool of her, even when
she tries to defend herself. She also felt strong resentment toward her husband
for being so stubborn. She strained her ears to hear what the other women were
talking about. They all started to curse Hitler:

"He should die a violent death, and in three months' time everything'll be just
fine. For one pound I'll get ten."

"Have you really bet a pound on Hitler being killed?" Sam Stricker's wife asked.
A new idea came to her, and as it flittered over her face, her expression changed.

"In our street the bookies are giving odds of 50 to 1," a woman cut in. Sam
Stricker's wife suddenly longed to make a bet on Hitler dying a violent death. She
thought she'd ask her husband about this, but just as suddenly she remembered his
words that trapped Abe in a net, and she started to sweat even more.

That night she told her husband what she had heard in the bathhouse and
begged him to make a bet, hoping it would distract him from the idea of making
Abe a worker.

"One mustn't tear a child away from his studies," she said to him. But her
words, just like every other time, fell on deaf ears. Sam was tired from work and
didn't want to listen to what she said to him. She shouted louder, and turned
away so as not to hear the news he had brought from the street and from Gradel's

restaurant. He wanted to tell her that Mr. Vogman, a good friend of his from the restaurant, knew all about what was happening in the world. With an effort he said:

"The women in the bathhouse don't know what they're talking about. For ages I've wanted to take you with me to the restaurant so that you can hear what people are saying."

On *Shabbes* Sam Stricker is a free man. Dressed up in his best clothes, with his waistcoat, watch and chain, and his wife by his side, he went to Mr. Gradel.

The empty, quiet streets and alleys of Whitechapel had the cheerful serenity that Jewish citizens feel on *Shabbes* when they cease their work and business dealings. The young women, who you see all week at the entrance to the shops shouting their wares, were now standing at the street corners, by the damp, blackened walls, listening to the speeches of the missionaries.

In one of the alleys, in front of a wall, there was an old, battered sign engraved with the name "Mr. Gradel's Restaurant." Displayed in the window under a grubby Star of David was a hard lump of cooked meat. Mr. Gradel considered himself to be a great innovator in putting a lump of meat in his window, just as he also considered it noteworthy that he did not have the radio playing on *Shabbes*, even though he was not observant. This chunk of food drew customers in faster than the piece of fried fish or slice of fruit cake the other restaurants put in their windows.

Gradel wandered around his restaurant; his clammy face was ever ready with a good-natured smile in his green eyes. He always sat at a different table and had a lot to say and argue about, not only with Jews working on the docks, tailors, pressers, or cabinetmakers, but also with dim-witted, ignorant, or homeless old bachelors who stay in the hostels in the back streets of Whitechapel.

Just today he told the story of how Vogman, whom the Jewish regulars consider to be a Bolshevik, invaded the "Olympia" with his friends during the first big fascist meeting in London. Smiling at Vogman, who was sitting at a table in the corner, Mr. Gradel proudly described Vogman's daring in asking the fascist leader Mosley such pointed questions that his black-shirted supporters had almost had a heart attack, and, in great agitation, had attacked him like wild animals:

"But it was the Blackshirts that got the real beating. Vogman thrashed them with his fists, and he didn't even feel it when they ripped his trousers off him." Mr. Gradel had a fit of coughing.

"Absolutely right what you did!" shouted Mr. Cohen, a man with a fat neck, a flabby belly, and broad shoulders like an ox.

"You are *not* right," chipped in Mr. Shpiegel, a Zionist who was standing there eating Mrs. Gradel's homemade pickled herring with bay leaves. "Jews mustn't get involved with politics, they must be productive," he yelled, as he looked around the room.

The people in the restaurant were indignant that the Zionist warned them not to get involved in politics. They hated him, because although he was a poor man, he had pushed himself into the circle of the rich Zionists in Great Russell Street who buy noble titles from the king, and who treated Shpiegel with respect. And although the restaurant regulars had recently argued with Shpiegel because he constantly bored them with his Hebrew blathering, they were nevertheless happy that now Mr. Cohen would get a mouthful from him. They couldn't bear Mr. Cohen either, and it irked them that he considered himself a communist. He always clapped Vogman on the back in a friendly way and said with a cajoling smile: "Red Front, comrade!" They knew that Mr. Cohen was a liar and a usurer. Vogman, on the other hand, was one of them, and since he had made a fiery speech about a united front in Hyde Park, the restaurant regulars had begun to regard him with new respect.

As usual, the restaurant was lit by a large electric lamp, and a big nickel-plated kettle was boiling water for tea. Beside the damp walls, blackened with constant tobacco smoke, there were small tables where the clattering of dominoes could be heard. Anarchists, Bundists, and communists wearing shapeless caps sat there playing. Blue with cold, their serious hardworking faces, with red noses and unshaved chins of sharp, prickly stubble, were strong and intense.

Mr. Gradel turned to the door abruptly with a comradely smile:

"Hello, Sam." He immediately noticed that something was not right because Sam had come with his wife.

"Hello," answered Sam with a subdued look. He and his wife sat down at Vogman's table. Sam stretched out his work-worn hand: "How do you do."

Vogman smiled. Sam felt awkward and ashamed of himself. Here was Vogman, also a worker, yet he understood so much. And he, Sam, could not even work out his own problems. Sam's wife looked embarrassed. It was clear that she regretted having come.

Mr. Gradel brought two cups of hot tea and some slices of fruit cake to the table. He breathed heavily, sucking in his cheeks, and, as usual, began to speak:

"Have you heard yet, Sam, what a prank Vogman played on the police? Come on, Vogman, tell him." Sam was pleased that Vogman began to speak because his wife would now hear something that was worth hearing.

Vogman willingly told her about his exploit:

"I was trying to hand out leaflets to workers outside a fascist meeting at the Albert Hall, calling them to unite and fight together against fascism and capitalism. But the police stopped me getting anywhere near them. So I jumped on a bus that passed by the Albert Hall and threw the leaflets out of the window and shouted 'United front, fight fascism and capitalism!'" Vogman's eyes shone as if he was reliving it. But Sam didn't want to hear him talking about the fascists; he had something else in mind.

He wanted Vogman to tell his wife about the situation for Jews in the world today, so that she would see that he, Sam, was right. But he was plagued by doubt and needed convincing himself. Vogman knew what was going on everywhere, especially in Germany, so Sam wanted to hear what he would say about his plan to put Abe in the workshop, and whether allowing his son to study might bring more trouble later. He knew that people said that nowadays you should let your children be productive, but his own wife wouldn't listen. She didn't want to tear the child away from his learning, but what did she know? The foolish woman had no understanding of the times we live in.

In front of Vogman, Sam wanted to hide all the joy he felt when he spoke about Abe. He felt awkward as he spoke. His tongue was rigid in his mouth. At the other tables a discussion began about the rumors concerning the situation for Jews in other countries.

"You're asking me again what's happening now in Germany? Listen Mr. Stricker!" Vogman's tone was cutting, like a diamond on glass. "The terror in Germany today could be in England tomorrow, and also in other countries if we don't fight capitalism, anything could happen."

"Still talking about politics?" Mr. Shpiegel the Zionist butted into the conversation.

"Shut up," Mr. Gradel good-naturedly interjected. "Vogman knows what he's talking about, never mind politics."

"Why have the Germans chased the educated people out of Germany?" Sam's wife suddenly asked.

"I love discussing politics with women," Vogman answered her. "It's because a capitalist state can't aspire to or use all the possibilities that educated people bring to the workforce. As far as they're concerned, they've got enough intellectuals. The capitalists need people who can make gas bombs and other poisons to kill people in war, and make a lot of money out of it. They don't need intellectuals who can't do those things, so they're left to become unemployed."

"That's not what I'm talking about," Sam Stricker barged into the conversation, flinging his wife a resentful look. Clearly he hadn't completely understood what Vogman had said.

"I want to ask you about productivization, Vogman. Should my Abe be a worker, or should he continue studying to become a doctor? You know that he won a scholarship." His eyes lit up as he spoke about Abe.

Vogman became very uneasy. He lifted his hand, kneading a small bit of bread between his fat fingers, gave a coarse laugh, and his face flushed:

"Are you afraid that if your son studies to become a doctor, he won't be able to afford to live in a palace like you live in? I've told you more than once; a doctor and a worker, both can become unemployed. In a society where there's unemployment, both of them can become unproductive. A doctor and a worker are equal if they're both aware of class war. Let your son study. The working class needs to have educated people. He should gain as much knowledge as he can. All workers need to study; your son needs to study to become a doctor and also to grasp the science of the proletariat. We must all learn the laws of economics, so that we understand what constitutes a trade and what kind of state the working class needs. Yes, a doctor and a worker are equal: both are proletarians."

That evening Sam Stricker did not speak to his wife again.

FASCIST RECRUITS

This story has two connected themes: property speculation and fascist activity.

The property speculator Bill Smith's fear of cheap housing being destroyed refers to the 1930 "Greenwood Act." The act, passed by a Labour government, allocated funding for slum clearance and rehousing. The Depression had delayed its implementation until 1933, but even then it was slow to come into effect while the definition of what constituted a slum was debated.[1]

Fascist activity of the British Union of Fascists (BUF) and antifascist and communist counterdemonstrations often took place, as the story indicates, in outdoor locations in central London, including at Hyde Park Corner, Regent Street, and Charing Cross Road. There were also many smaller street-corner meetings across London, and particularly in the East End, as the BUF targeted Jewish areas.[2]

The story "Fascist Recruits" is based on an earlier story, "A shuster in london" (A Cobbler in London), published in *Di tsayt* in 1931. The earlier story concerns only the cobbler and his wife buying property; in that story the name of the cobbler is Simons, an anglicized Jewish name. The earlier story relates to the ongoing tale of Jewish immigrants' upward mobility as they became workshop masters, attempting to get a place on the property ladder and move out of the East End. The readers of 1937 may not have remembered the 1931 story, but the change does reflect Lisky's changing focus.

"Be cleverer than other people, if you can, but don't let them know."

Once again, this thought brought a cheerful look into the eyes of Bill Smith the cobbler—eyes soaked with the faded greyness of the walls in which he lived. He pondered this verse from the Gospels, which he read every week as he walked past the large billboard outside the church, and he thought to himself, *It's a very clever idea, possibly the cleverest quotation they've put up there.* His shaved upper lip was turned down, and with a sort of dull hopefulness he shook his dusty, bald head in the half-dark shadow of the workshop, where he sat on a low bench, at a filthy table.

A number of fifteen- and sixteen-year-old boys worked with him, as well as one older worker. They patched the shoes of the poor, and of the tramps who dragged themselves there from faraway streets for a night's lodging at the cheaper hostels.

The cobbler hired only two types of workers: boys with elongated heads and shifty eyes, and lanky youngsters with large, round heads and green, dreamy eyes. A sense of neglect emanated from them, a trace of the cramped, damp, and dingy dwellings where they grew up. Children from the poorest streets in London ended up in Bill Smith's workshop, straight from state primary schools, and those who hung out in the doorways of large pubs that swarmed incessantly with drunken men and women. These educational establishments barely taught the children how to correctly sign their names, yet they did qualify them to become Bill Smith's workers.

In the cellar flanked by the high walls of blind, smoky buildings, the monotonous knocking of the cobblers' hammers ceased only late in the evening, after the wailing radios in the streets became silent and the big-city advertising lights were switched off.

At the end of the working day, the cobbler would stay on in the workshop with only the older worker, Jim. Apart from Jim he didn't hire anyone for longer than a year; he didn't want the expense of more experienced workers who commanded higher pay. But he could not send Jim away, even though recently the pale youth with his long, gaunt face hadn't wanted to sit in his proper place at the benches, and at the end of normal working hours, he'd refused to work overtime, and the cobbler was often left on his own.

The cobbler's face had turned grey from overwork, and the veins in his neck were swollen, but as a result he had saved penny after penny and put all the money in the bank.

Another person lived under the same roof as Bill Smith. His wife's large face and broad nose was covered with the thick dust exuding from all the old things she bought and sold. Her mouth was constantly open; she loved talking, but not to her husband. They led separate lives, with separate bank books. But when the value of the two bank books reached a particular *quantity*, their relationship as husband and wife reached a new *quality*. The couple united in one thought—to buy a house.

With the help of his wife, and of the Mortgage Society, the cobbler Bill Smith became a houseowner with a quarter-century loan. The house that he bought was in a small, dark, smoky alley, and was rented to poor workers. The cobbler received the rent money from them, and a plan to buy more houses had begun to gather momentum.

The cobbler's eyes, still soaked with the faded grey walls of his home, had taken on a new glow. His eyes were often strained at work, as if bank books and bills were spinning about in his head, and more than once, while working, an idea popped into his mind, inspiring him. In these moments, each time he struck the hammer it hit the tack into the sole of the shoe with precision.

His road to riches was a long one, and on the way he had plenty of time to be unhappy. He often felt irritated with himself, and he resented his wife because they had no children like respectable people had. When people have children, they grow up, go out to work, earn wages, and bring money home. The mother of the house would cook a bit of food, and the father would get richer. *The children would then have to pay him for board and lodging.*

The cobbler had no one to help him get rich or to rely on while he went to look at a bargain of a house that the estate agent suggested he buy. And because he didn't have anyone, he had to leave Jim in charge, that strange dog . . . but he certainly couldn't leave the boys without some supervision.

Jim knew he was indispensable to his boss. This sense of his own importance made him somewhat insolent, an attitude he tried to disguise with submission and humility. But his tongue began to feel looser, and he often tried to give the cobbler advice or tell him about the things he had recently done.

But Bill Smith did not willingly listen to Jim's stories or his advice. It really upset him once when Jim came to work wearing a black shirt and boasted that he'd got the shirt for free from the fascists, and had even had a good ole drink with them in the pub.

There was a roguish twinkle in Jim's eyes. For him, drinking was bound up with feelings of joy, debauchery, and power. These feelings came from his childhood, when he too had hung out at the entrances of pubs, absorbing the warm, strong, smoky air as it carried out into the cold, damp, foggy night each time the pub door opened.

"We shouldn't have any political parties, only we, the fascists, should exist," he yelled, grimacing with childish obstinacy. He felt very proud that people saw *him* in the street every Saturday evening, among the crowd of young people, servant girls, and old women who went to buy Mosley's paper, *Black Shirt*. Jim spat out the words like sharp pins. The cobbler resented it and thought: *I sit here working myself to the bone until late at night, and he just works a few hours and then has time to run off to the pub with the fascists, that bloody black-clad lot who drag people to the pub and make them into loafers.*

But he kept his resentment silent, just like he didn't react with a disapproving frown when Jim told him that, on the street where he lived, the small, older houses were being torn down, and big blocks of council flats for workers and poor people were being built in their place.

One day, just like any other day of the week, the cobbler was bent over his low bench, with his apron tied around his waist, but he couldn't work. Numbers were flying about in his head so much that the tacks broke under his hammer and didn't stick into the soles of the shoes. He calculated: *I have to buy these houses; they are valuable all standing in a row.* The profit was there for the taking. *The estate agent is a decent person; surely he wouldn't cheat me.*

The cobbler, however, didn't remember how many houses there were in the terrace; was it three or four? As he strained his memory, a thought came back to him about what Jim had told him that he'd read in the paper. The Labour Party promised that when they came to power they would tear down all the slums and the City Council would build nicer, bigger new homes . . . But now the cobbler didn't want to think through this idea to its end. Better for him to drop in on his estate agent and have a chat with him—and he looked outside silently.

Wearing a pair of shapeless shoes with twisted toes, the cobbler Bill Smith crossed like a cat, small and fast, from one street to the next, with an anxious glance, trying to avoid the constant torrent of wheels dragging over the stones in a zigzag race. Running amid the melee were all sorts of different people, each with their own particular burden. The cobbler felt that the ideas that had blocked him suddenly freed up like the wheels on the stones, and he ran quickly, totally absorbed in himself. Then from one moment to the next his legs gave way.

Would the City Council really tear down the old houses and build new, nicer, bigger blocks of flats? A despairing expression crossed his face, and the grey in his eyes became paler. All at once it was as if the outside world became distant, and his mind began fiercely imagining—the streets and alleys suddenly veered to the side, only to turn themselves over: *London is tumbling down . . .* He saw the houses being uprooted from the ground like shrunken ruins, smoking and covering whole mountains with dust; taken away in pieces in big lorries, and disappearing among the dense crowds of workers with bare arms.

Bill Smith stopped and stood leaning against a cold, unfamiliar building to catch his breath. The thought that they were going to rebuild London was still swimming around in his head. He bent over, burrowing like a mole, with fear in his heart that his breath might give out in the middle of the street. With all his strength he clung to his will to undermine these proletarian homes: The proletarian future the social democrats had constructed with individual homeowners had been built on sand. It was not protected from those who intended to destroy it.

It was only his resentment against his wife that kept him from collapsing. He grabbed at the opportunity to throw the blame onto someone else, make some other person responsible for the destruction of his life's plan, for his lost battle for existence, for the disappearance of his economic security. He thought bitterly: *Why didn't we have any children, young boys who could have become fascists like Jim. They would have helped put an end to all political parties and local councils.* And so new energy flared up in him, as if he was spurred on by a fresh inner power. His eyes shone with a glittering thought: *They also recruit older members to the fascist party.*

Bill Smith started to display a new sense of confidence among the groups of half-disturbed young people in black uniforms who constantly gave speeches and prided themselves on terrorizing the Jewish neighborhoods. This fresh hopefulness manifested in a particular way when, on Regent Street, in Hyde Park Corner, or along Charing Cross Road, he encountered the resolute looks in the obliquely veiled eyes of frosty women who walked around wearing paper placards and shouting contrived curses against the Jews. These vulgar fascist slogans instantly crept into Bill Smith's head, and his ideas started developing with greater force.

He now had an important and respected job in the fascist party. His role was to be the first at street-corner meetings that the Blackshirts organized, and to walk about with an intense look in his eyes, attracting others to join them. And when a crowd of listeners had gathered, he was allowed to ask a barbed question, one that he had practiced and learned by heart.

His joy, however, was always thwarted by the communists, who held their own meetings at the same time and on the same street. He couldn't bear how a bigger crowd of listeners gathered around them, and he felt bitterly offended by the communist slogans, and especially by their shouts: "Rats, rats, we gotta get rid of the rats!!!"

With an old habit of reading everything he saw, his eyes took in all the captions. But he often mixed up the different slogans, written with the wrath of the oppressed and the energy of justice, on the flaming flags carried by the organized trade unions, the socialist youth, and the workers' organizations. And under the red flag, he saw many of his neighbors standing with the workers, people who were considered to be upright citizens on his street. And he heard the powerful call coming from the dense crowd: "United Front. Fight fascism and capitalism!!!"

And Bill Smith did not know how or why his hatred and fear had suddenly begun, with sickening obstinacy, to turn into shame, and how he suddenly felt totally helpless and lost. So he pulled the collar of his old coat farther around his bare head.

IDEOLOGICAL
SPECULATION

We first encountered the character Mr. Shpiegel in the story "Productivization," which gives background to how he is seen by certain groups within the East End immigrant community where he lives. By the early thirties, interest in Zionism across the British Jewish community had substantially increased and continued to grow, although it was not very active in the East End. East End Jews were more concerned with the fascist threat from the BUF on their doorstep, and were drawn toward left-wing organizations that were proactive in the antifascist struggle. East End Zionists were more likely to be members of the Poale Zion (Labour Zionists), and there were often clashes between Zionists and communists. Shpiegel, however, looks toward the West End Zionists. The majority of London Zionists, who were immigrants and children of immigrants, lived in middle-class suburbs such as Notting Hill, Willesden, and Golders Green. They sent their children to local Zionist youth movements, such as Habonim, further enmeshing Zionism in the fabric of Anglo-Jewish life and encouraging settlement in Palestine.[1] Speculating on land in Palestine was a growing business venture. A notice in Di tsayt of June 1934 announced the arrival in London of an agent from a property firm in Haifa who was selling land on Mount Carmel, claiming that for the sum of 110 pounds one could buy a plot of a thousand square meters.[2]

Mr. Jacob Shpiegel's son-in-law lives in Golders Green. As well as selling fine fox furs with thick tails from his fur shop in Whitechapel to wealthy Jewish women of the area, he also deals in property. He buys old houses and rents out rooms to workers and poor people. Business is going well: He is rich.

The father-in-law walks around the properties with an umbrella and a fat cashbook, in which he writes down the rent he collects. He is a devoted rent collector and looks after his son-in-law's business well. In the evenings he goes to his son-in-law's house, sits down in a comfy chair, takes the cashbook out of his pocket, and hands it to his son-in-law. One evening he said:

"It's not good, Michael!"

The son-in-law gave him an uneasy look, and his narrow eyes gleamed like false diamonds as he listened carefully to how many homes will, in a few days' time, become empty.

"We have to throw out the tenants in houses 26, 28, and 30. They've lost their jobs and won't be able to pay," Mr. Shpiegel continued, as he turned his attention to the hot tea that he started to drink.

The room was warm, and every corner was filled with electric light.

"I won't make allowances for anyone, not even Mr. Riklin, even though he has paid punctually until now," Michael replied with annoyance. He glanced at his father-in-law with a worried look in his eyes.

As usual, Mr. Jacob Shpiegel became sidetracked in the conversation and abruptly changed the subject to Zionism. For a long time he had carried in his heart a deep love for the Holy Land and would constantly say to his son-in-law:

"Oh, Michael, how good it would be if you bought a plot of land in Palestine. We could build a house, plant a garden with fruit, and live a peaceful life."

Mr. Shpiegel frequently attended events at the Zionist Organization and saw himself as an ardent Zionist. He loved the small, shining brass plaque nailed up on the wall beside the entrance door with the Hebrew inscription: *The Zionist Organization of Great Britain*. Every time Mr. Jacob Shpiegel opened the weighty door, he gazed warmly and intimately at the plaque; his fingers were drawn to it, as if it were a *mezuzah*. He would have liked to touch the plaque and kiss his finger.

He went up the stairs slowly, from one floor to the next, cracking jokes with the young women whose dimpled smiles he could see through the office doors and who said:

"Shalom, Mr. Shpiegel."

He opened the door of the large hall with reverence and was delighted to see the large crowd of important Zionists who had come to take part in a memorial for a Zionist leader. At moments like these he felt totally content. They always asked him the same question:

"Mr. Shpiegel, when will you settle on the soil of the Land of Israel?"

"Yes, yes, we must be productive," he answered with a soft, dreamy little smile.

Then one evening his son-in-law greeted him with the words:

"Father-in-law, I want to buy land in the Holy Land."

Michael had just come in from Lyons' Corner House, where he and his wife had enjoyed tea and pastries to the sweet music of the *Hatikvah* playing in the background. The thought of buying land had come to him because he felt envious of speculators he knew who were making fortunes in Palestine. He'd been mulling over the idea for a while, but now it had matured and transformed his emotions into a passionate nationalism. His heart softened, and he sensed that he should follow his father-in-law.

So the son-in-law also became a Zionist. He listened with more interest to the news that his father-in-law brought home from the Zionist Organization, and was delighted when he told him that entire shiploads of Jews were traveling to Palestine, that it was prosperous there, and that land prices were shooting up like flowers after rain.

One evening, the father-in-law said:

"Listen, Michael, the plot in Tel Aviv that you bought for two hundred pounds would now fetch two thousand pounds. Land prices are going up."

Michael was silently drinking his tea.

"Why don't you sell the plot?"

Michael grimaced and answered:

"You're a fool, father-in-law. I won't sell it." Suddenly, he had a new idea. "You know what," he continued. "I'll build houses there and rent them out. There's no difference between Palestine or Whitechapel. In fact, in Palestine the rents are higher. You can go there and be my rent collector."

"That's a wonderful idea, Michael," Mr. Shpiegel answered.

With wrinkled brows, the two Zionists bent their heads and began to make calculations on their new speculation.

"This is good business," the son-in-law said.

"We're building our land and becoming productive," answered the father-in-law.

A GUINEA A DAY

"A Guinea a Day" gives a fictional account of the Jewish East End involvement in the making of the film Jew Süss. Jew Süss is a British historical drama based on a book by Lion Feuchtwanger, which tells the story of the controversial figure Joseph Süss Oppenheimer in the 1730s. In one scene in the film, Oppenheimer visits his mother in the Frankfurt ghetto. The outdoor crowd scenes in the ghetto described by Lisky in this story are in the middle of the film, with the East End actors on set for barely two minutes.[1]

Jew Süss was directed by Lothar Mendes and stars Conrad Veidt. Mendes was a Jew, and Veidt was married to a Jewish woman; both men escaped from Nazi Germany to Britain in the early thirties. The film's producer, Michael Balcon, hoped that, through parallels in the stories, the film would draw attention to the Nazi atrocities of the day.[2] Although the film was well publicized when it came out in October 1934, and received good reviews in the English and Jewish press, no accounts mention the hiring of East End Jews as extras. However, ex-Eastender Cyril Sherer remembers that old Jewish locals were hired as extras on the Jew Süss film set and given instructions on how to act.[3] Lisky gives us an intriguing fictional back story with so much detail that it leaves the reader wondering whether one would be able to find his face among the extras.

A hundred and fifty Jewish men and women should have made some money.

Back Street became aware of the news when it woke up in the morning. Out of the blackened houses, as full of holes as rotten teeth, bits and pieces emerged to be laid out on the windows, doorways, and barrows. Giblets, dead fish with pale gills, overripe fruit, stale beigels, peas, kidney beans, sauerkraut, pickled cucumbers, garlic, *tefillin*, *mezuzahs*, prayer shawls, and *tsitses* were all for sale.*

In the nooks and crannies of the street, people whispered to each other. A man with a pale, pointed face and high, bony shoulders asked his neighbor:

"Are you going, too?"

"Yes."

"Where will we meet? In Aldgate, or over in the square?"

"The square would be best!"

"What time?"

"No later than seven in the morning."

"Have you heard that Shavl has become a big shot with them?"

"How did our Shavl get to be the breadwinner for all of us? Is it already slack time in tailoring? I saw him over at the union, sweating over his dominoes."

"You may be ribbing Shavl, but God knows where he picked up that young man in the green jacket."

"It looks like the bloke in the green jacket has put him in charge!"

"We'll have to persuade Shavl to let us have a few days' work. What do you say, eh? And a guinea for each day!"

Back Street was really buzzing.

Shavl and the young man in the green jacket were standing on the street. On the wall opposite them, torn bits of posters were eerily flapping about, and beneath them sat two wizened old women. The words streamed continuously out of their mouths like smoke from broken chimneys:

"Beigels, beigels, beigels, three a penny."

The young man in the green jacket looked up and down Back Street, and with an expert eye decided that the alley they had constructed in the studio out of paper and planks was nothing like the reality. If they could take a photograph of Back Street just as it really was, it would be worth paying any price. But then he realized that this Jewish lane was not great for filming purposes. In London there are more remarkable neighborhoods: Chinatown, the Italian Quarter, Hoxton, the Docks. Each area was distinctive and worth filming.

"So, Mr. Shavl, have you sorted out all the cast yet?"

---

* The spelling "beigels" mirrors the pronunciation used in the East End: "buy-guls."

"There are more people here than we need," Shavl answered.

"You should bring in more characteristic faces, you know what I mean?"

The young man in the green jacket had a satisfied smile on his face from his success in putting real Jews into the ghetto scene. This scene was really important to the great film that was being made here.

"Mr. Director," said Shavl, "I'll bring you some real, dull-witted, old-fashioned Jews, with twisted faces, hooked noses, shifty eyes, and thick, bushy eyebrows. You won't need to put them in costume, and they'll seem even more authentic than Jews in the ghettos of the past."

The German filmmaker slapped him on the back and said, "Good, Moritz, good." Shavl was delighted and swallowed his distaste at being called Moritz.

"Get me two Torah scrolls as well, Mr. Shavl, because in the film there's an important scene where the main character needs to kiss Torah scrolls."

Shavl was very happy with the job. His eyes shone with confidence, and he answered imperiously:

"In Whitechapel there are more than enough Torah scrolls . . ."

Shavl showed up in the yard where the unemployed hung around looking for work. People there knew Shavl hadn't been hiring workers lately, and that he himself would soon be standing among those who hire themselves out. But when they got wind of the chance to earn good money, they began to look at him a bit warily, not knowing whom he would approach.

Shavl approached various unemployed men in worn-out coats, with caps worn backwards to tuck under their turned-up collars. With an amicable expression, he whispered secretly to them before going back to the union alone.

He hurried up the hill, up dark, worn stairs, arriving sweating into the smoky hall with its bare, dirty walls and damp ceiling. In the corners of the room, workers with sunken cheeks and empty mouths sat on long wooden benches at small, filthy tables pockmarked with cigarette burns. Destitution cried out of their eyes, their pale faces, sallow cheeks, and pinched noses. The cry of their child and the groan of their wife gnawed at their brains. They were talking about jobs: "Look, here's Shavl." The bunch of dark heads turned toward him as one:

"Yes, early tomorrow, be in Aldgate on time." And from there Shavl went off looking for Torah scrolls.

. . .

He bent down to enter the narrow door of a small shop and surveyed the jumble of religious books, secular books, prayer shawls, and phylacteries.

"Is Mr. Berl here? I'd like to speak to him."

A red-haired man emerged from a corner, looking startled. He had a low forehead and a broad hooked nose that overlapped the dark, spiky hair on his upper lip. With suspicion and mistrust in his eyes, he asked:

"Who are you looking for, and what do you want?"

"Listen, Mr. Berl, I need to get hold of two Torah scrolls," Shavl stammered.

Mr. Berl's nose twitched; he looked at Shavl as if he was crazy. What did someone like Shavl the tailor want Torah scrolls for? He knew Shavl got things done, and that he'd been a guv'nor a few times. But why did he suddenly need Torah scrolls?

"Listen, Mr. Berl," words popped out of Shavl's mouth like frogs from a marsh. "Very early tomorrow morning, lots of Jewish men and women are going to be in a film. They're going to be paid a guinea a day." He babbled and sweated until he managed to make it clear to Mr. Berl that the men and women from Back Street and elsewhere would be appearing in a film based on a historical book, in a scene set in the first Frankfurt ghetto.

Mr. Berl blinked, dropping his gaze onto a large, locked cupboard, and after agreeing to a deal with Shavl for such and such an amount, he told him to come early the next day, but informed him:

"Remember, Shavl, shush, no one must know who gave you the Torah scrolls."

Shavl was happy but unsettled, because films made his head spin. He had often sat in the picture palaces, watching for three hours in the darkness, straining his eyes toward the pale light where sounds and voices were moving on the screen. Shadows shimmered, getting entangled with images that intoxicated him with sharp excitement and sweet joy. As if in a dream, stories of crime, intrigue, love, espionage, battles, and emperors all got mixed up in his mind. He'd never wanted the experience to end, wishing the day would go on forever.

At sunrise the men and women of the back alleys trudged over to the underground station at Aldgate. In the empty streets with grey walls that constantly stared out onto the endless monotonous commotion across the big city, the heavy footsteps of the city's workers could be heard; workers who were employed on the railway, on bridges, canals, and the roads. They strode out, some with tools on their shoulders and others emptyhanded. Here and there heavy wagons rolled up, carrying meat to the butcher shops, laden with carcasses of cows and calves with open stomachs, bloodied heads, and long, dangling tongues.

The Jewish workers, looking anxious, wandered to and fro in the cold. Their exhausted, crumpled faces appeared blue in the damp air, yet they were livelier than usual, and their normal deathly yellow-green pallor was not apparent. They were restless because Shavl was late.

"How will we get there? What will we do there? Will we really get a guinea a day?"

The man with the high, bony shoulders, desperate to ingratiate himself with Shavl, gave a shout: "Here he comes," and ran to meet him. Shavl was walking with hurried steps, his long arms encircling the two Torah scrolls wrapped up in grey cloth. The man helped him, making it easier to hold them under one arm.

Shavl explained that his landlord had blocked his way and threatened to throw him out if he didn't pay his rent immediately, and he shouted:

"What a dirty dog."

The young man in the green jacket was standing beside the big gate of the film studio, waiting for the crowd. First of all, he took the two Torah scrolls and passed them on to a tall steward in a stiff top hat. He then passed white slips of paper to the Jews as he led them through long, dark, narrow corridors. Their rough, tired faces expressed a sort of dull surprise, because they had imagined something completely different.

"What do you think Shavl?" asked the man who was hovering around him. "It looks like a barracks here, where soldiers get drilled."

Shavl disappeared inside with the young man in the green jacket.

"We have designated you to act the part of the rabbi. If you do it well, you'll be paid eight times more than the others. Now remember that you are the rabbi of the Frankfurt ghetto."

Shavl's legs started shaking, and he blushed.

"Don't worry." The young man in the green jacket winked at him impudently. "Come on!" He tugged Shavl by the sleeve, leading him into a room full of mirrors.

. . .

In a large courtyard they were preparing to film the crowd scene. They arranged the electric lights to cast so much light that the sun wouldn't be seen. In the small alley made out of paper and wooden boards, two large white horses stood in thick, leather reins, harnessed into an old-fashioned gilded coach with big painted wheels. The eminent Jew who had to sit in this coach was, according to historical description, a frequenter of the royal court. He was very rich, played an important role, occupied a high position, and supplied beautiful women for the kaiser.

They had employed a famous actor to play the part of this Jew. Broad and tall, he swaggered around the courtyard in splendid costume, his eyes made up with thick black mascara, and with a somewhat lewd expression on his face. His chubby cheeks, also heavily made up, had a pinkish sheen. He wore a small monocle pinched into his left eye, and put on airs and graces. The young man in the green jacket hovered around him submissively and whispered quietly that he must kiss the Torah that Shavl, the rabbi, would hand to him.

Instead of the payment slips, the Jews in the dark corridors now held small, twisted bundles of old rags in their hands. The men were decked out in brown overshirts and long, green smocks with a yellow patch on the front. Some of them had matted beards attached to them and disheveled wigs on their heads. The women were dressed up in wide, long dresses, padded so that they had large bellies and full, high bosoms. They wore large, matted wigs with tousled hair.

They all went out into the courtyard. The famous actor was already tired from the effort of wandering around. He sat near the director, a short blond man with cunning eyes that attentively watched the lights being arranged.

Shavl was standing in his designated place and was not allowed to move. He looked truly dignified, in a shiny robe and a tall fur hat, a full beard, and thick side curls reaching to his waist.

"Remember that you are a rabbi, Mr. Shavl," the young man in the green jacket informed him again. "Don't forget to raise your eyes to heaven, then cast down a religious glance, and then you have to look up toward that window over there."

Out of the small window shone two large black eyes belonging to a young girl who was dressed up as an old mother. She wore oversized black silk clothes, had a grey wig with a bonnet perched on her head, and she sweated profusely.

. . .

The Jews were placed onto the set of the ghetto, where they were split into two groups. The young man in the green jacket spoke to them:

"You should know that the scene we are about to film represents the first Frankfurt ghetto—remember that," he yelled in Yiddish. "The great actor who has got into the coach represents the rich and eminent Reb Yosef, who saved a Jew from a blood libel. Reb Yosef came into the ghetto to visit his old mother. As soon as you see the carriage with the white horses appearing, you should all rush up to him and shout—'Long live the great, good, rich Reb Yosef—long should he live—long should he live.'"

The Jews, with their dull-witted faces, looked, in their costumes, like wild prisoners. They scratched themselves under their itchy stuck-on beards. The wigs would not stay on their damp, sweaty heads, and under their caps they slid to one side.

"Shout out the lines I told you to say."

Muffled, hoarse, and high shrieking voices spread across the courtyard . . . once, twice, and up to ten times.

"Ready."

A beam of electric light streamed out. The horses moved from their place. The costumed men and women started following the coach and shouted, clamored, and shoved each other as they accompanied the coach, which stopped a few paces farther on. The famous actor got out. He bowed down before Shavl, kissed the Torah scroll, and waved to his mother, who was looking out through the window. Shavl didn't take his eyes off the old woman either; he felt attracted to her.

The scene had already been filmed a few times on the photographic plates of the camera equipment, but the director said the scene the Jews had acted with their running, shouting, and jostling didn't work. The famous actor, who had earned thousands of pounds for his talent, had disappeared.

Then they really made the Jews work again. The strong electric light stung their eyes and burned their faces. The dust and the sweat tickled and irritated their skin. They worked until they had performed the cries and jostling properly. In the evening they breathed a sigh of relief.

•   •   •

Shavl hung around the yard. He had taken off his fur hat and beard a while ago and was no longer a rabbi. But something made him not want to join the rest of the crowd, and the man with the bony shoulders was pointlessly hanging around him. The Jews were paid the guinea for the day's work, but they weren't happy, because they were told that tomorrow they would not be needed.

Shavl carefully counted the eight guineas he'd received a few times, and thought that if only he could fall in love with the pretty girl with the large black eyes who played the role of the mother, she could surely manage to persuade them not to send him home together with all the other Jews—and maybe he could advance his career a bit.

NATIONALIST FEELINGS AND CLASS INTERESTS

"Can you spare a ha'penny sir?" The repeated chant did not bring any success today. The children of Brick Street had been standing for a long time in front of the high wall, impatiently waiting for the motorcar that came every morning at a set time. They went away noisily. One child carried another in his small, thin arms. Others, with dirty bare bottoms that could be seen through their torn trousers, dragged ropes behind them, tied to stolen or begged-for broken boxes and planks.

Brick Street is poor. Impoverished workers live in the small, dark houses. The one large house at the front belongs to Mr. Klepman. It is his factory where, during the week, girls make dresses, supervised by a manager. Today, the submissive words with which the manager always greeted his boss stuck in his throat, and he decided, once again, to telephone Mr. Klepman at home.

The town had devoured the light half of the day. A dark fog drew in from the distance onto the quiet streets of this more affluent London suburb. A car waited in front of one of the houses; a house identical to the other houses in the terrace, with a small front garden. The chauffeur was impatient, waiting so long for his boss, and kept looking around him resentfully. He worried that today's fog would grow dense and cover the houses and streets with a smog that crept into your eyes and throat.

The hands of his gold watch showed Mr. Klepman that he should have been in Brick Street a while ago, but he was still standing, gloomily looking out at the day. He suffered with his kidneys: an illness that suited him exactly, just like the stiff pressed trousers that he wore with a straight crease, like all rich English businessmen, suited him.

But it was another strange feeling that made him uneasy. He couldn't remember what he thought . . . he couldn't bring it to the front of his mind. It evaporated in his head as if he hadn't thought it. He hadn't even enjoyed the food that his maid, in her white cap, had laid on the table.

Mr. Klepman's house had almost a dozen ornate rooms. From across a spacious room, he heard the heavy step of his wife: a tall red-headed woman, swathed in silk, with diamonds dangling from her ears. She knew that her husband had her to thank for becoming rich, because it was only through her energy that the factory in Brick Street kept on its feet and hadn't gone under when the gentile partner, Tom Johnson, left them. Besides, it was due to her brains that they no longer lived in the small East End street and now belonged to the "highbrow" set.

Mr. Klepman's small daughter suddenly ran in through one of the doors, wearing a dainty pink dress with silk wings on the shoulders. Her shadow fell onto the pleasantly-decorated and elegant wood-paneled wall:

"Dad, I'm here," the child hugged her father happily, scrambling onto his belly, as if it was the stuffed back of her hobby horse. Mr. Klepman didn't kiss his child with his usual fatherly devotion; he just looked at her with indifference, because today he was feeling depressed:

"I've no time for you, dear," he answered the child, even though he wasn't hurrying to get to the factory to inspect the clothes and examine the new patterns.

A silent shimmer of silks floated toward Mr. Klepman, bringing behind it his wife. She threw her husband a pointed glance:

"You're still at home—apparently your business can run itself!"

The man with the long, flabby face and stiffly pressed trousers started pulling on his jacket and answered:

"Somehow, nothing is going right for me today."

"Come home in time for us to go to the Simons'." The wife waved off her husband with his painful kidneys.

. . .

In the midst of the city bustle, the car moved fast, passing rain-soaked horses and stressed-out people, all with their own jumble of thoughts spinning in their feverish heads day and night. A trembling in Mr. Klepman's nerves gradually shaped itself into an idea.

Small black houses with crooked roofs came into view on the opposite side of the road, and in Brick Street the fog had lifted. The car turned into the wide gate of the large house.

Electric lights burned in the factory. The pale girls who worked at small sewing machines on long tables looked up when the boss came in but kept on working silently. Mr. Klepman had no complaint with these girls as long as they worked quickly, without talking. He didn't like it when they talked at work. It came out of his wallet.

The manager looked Mr. Klepman straight in the eyes, with a semblance of submission that veiled a duplicitous shrewdness. He spoke quickly, tugging the ends of his pointed moustache, and accompanied his boss from one department to another. He showed him the cheap cloth from which they made expensive clothes:

"This is the cloth that I suggest we use."

To play up his importance and dedication to the business, the manager told Mr. Klepman with a sigh how difficult it was for him to maintain discipline. Despite the fact that only yesterday, in the presence of his boss, he had reprimanded the girls, they still went on giggling as soon as his back was turned, even for a moment.

Mr. Klepman felt an ache in his guts.

"Don't you know what to do with slackers like that?" said Klepman. "Let them work till the end of the week and then throw them out." Mr. Klepman was in a hurry to go, offered the manager a cigarette from his golden case, and bade goodbye with a tense, pompous expression in his eyes.

On the way home Mr. Klepman lay in his car, leaning with his head on the soft side panel, contentedly smoking a cigarette. His chicken soup with *kreplach* from BBB, Bertie's Best Beef restaurant in Whitechapel, had left him with a deliciously affable smile. The car glided along at a harmonious tempo, the rhythmic movement stimulating the blood flow to his stomach, digesting his food with considerable momentum and sending his brain a freshly cooked stream of energy.

This mood was similar to what he felt when he sat in a soft armchair with a glass of wine with his new "good friends," having eaten delicious turkey, baked potatoes, and peas (despite its not being Christmas) in his gorgeous house in Chelsea, which he had bought at a bargain price. This physical and mental confluence set up a train of thought, and it was good to mull over how well he had climbed the social ladder, how cleverly he ran his business, and how, after his partner Tom Johnson had left, he was once again sitting firmly in the saddle.

The desire to heighten this feeling of equanimity spurred him on to examine his situation in general, to convince himself that he was all right and everything was in order. However, he suddenly felt that something was preventing him from completely accepting that idea, and a disagreeable thought that had stayed with him since early morning and had kept slipping away now returned and nudged him, clawing at his heart. Again he felt an ache in his guts as he pictured in his mind's eye the girls in the factory laughing.

The chauffeur stopped outside Mr. Klepman's house. His tall red-headed wife stuck out her lipsticked lower lip with childish petulance. She gave her husband an impatient look, stretched out her plump hand, and looked at her gold watch.

"Have your tea, hurry up. We must get ready to go to the Simons' for supper; they have invited a marvelous Zionist speaker, Mr. Freydel," and she sang, "bim-bam-bom" to the melody of a Hebrew *hora* dance tune.

"It's all right, there's plenty of time," Mr. Klepman answered, giving his usual glance at the late evening paper. His attention was caught by the bold headline: "The Nazi Nuremberg Laws." Mr. Klepman sighed in deep sympathy with the Jews of Germany and read aloud: "restricted rights . . . persecution . . . boycott of Jewish shops . . ."

His wife gave a broad smile, and her face took on an oddly naive expression that was almost embarrassing:

"Isn't Mr. Freydel right when he says that all Jews, whether rich or poor, must unite for the nationalist ideal, and that we must all build up the national homeland together? Palestine is the only solution for the Jewish people." In broken English she parroted the hackneyed slogans she had heard with a flourish.

Mr. Klepman didn't reply to his wife's words; he was still absorbed in the paper. The frightful news of the persecution of the Jews in Germany had, against his will, brought a look of happiness to his face *because he was here in London*. And all at once a resolution emerged to the aggravating thought that had unsettled him the whole day. Mr. Klepman decided that tomorrow he would order the factory manager to put up a notice saying he wanted one hundred new workers. That would serve the girls right for laughing during his time.

ON THE MARCH
WITH THE HUNGRY

In the 1930s there were a number of weeks-long hunger marches by unemployed people from the north of England, Scotland, Welsh mining areas, and other rural communities. They arrived in London to petition Parliament and gather in rallies to publicize their plight and garner support. In 1931 the Conservative-majority national government had brought in a means test for unemployment benefits that was harsh, inequitable, and intrusive. It was hard to claim the benefit, and the initiative was extremely unpopular. The details in this story point to the largest of the hunger marches, the "Great National Hunger March against the Means Test," which arrived in London on 27 October 1932. The different groups of around 1,500 marchers were joined by 100,000 Londoners who assembled in rallies in Hyde Park and Trafalgar Square. There were clashes between marchers and the police, with considerable police violence.[1]

Lisky may of course be conflating more than one hunger march. In 1934 another large hunger march protested a new bill going through Parliament that would uphold the low rate of unemployment benefits and the means test. The Labour Party proposed amendments to the bill which would substantially raise the amount of unemployment pay, but the left was split on the action by the hunger marchers.[2] A 1934 article in Di tsayt condemned the "left of communist" march organizers, calling them agitators for a Marxist revolution. The writer of the article saw the hunger marches as dividing the Labour Party and Trade Union Congress, which wanted to fight the bill in Parliament, and the communists, who wanted to "pump up the mood and draw the worker into a militant place, preparing them for the social revolution."[3]

The story mentions Mrs. Barsht's visit to a soup kitchen. This would have been the Soup Kitchen for the Jewish Poor on Butler Street. (The street name was changed to Brune Street in 1937.) The numbers of people resorting to the soup kitchen for food during this time reflect how the 1930s Depression brought the heaviest demand for such services in twenty-five years; it went from serving twenty-seven families in 1920 to 866 families in 1931–32.[4]

All of a sudden the reddish-blue gas flames began to wane like the frail hearts of the hungry. Small and shrinking, they wavered to barely a flicker in the corner of the old black stove. The last remaining gas allowed the water in the tea kettle to hiss, but it could not boil. The three unemployed people waiting for a gulp of tea sensed the anticipated taste in their mouths disappearing.

Mr. Barsht swallowed the dry emptiness under his palate apathetically, showing no resentment in his dull, dejected eyes. His power to resist had been blunted by the long time he had been hanging about with nothing to do, unable to find any work as a carpenter, the occupation he had sweated over for many years. His idle hands, which lay useless, like the unattached crossbar of a carriage, now seemed to almost embrace the poverty that had held him in its clutches for several years.

He accepted each new disappointment with a kind of morbid joy, like a child who can't resist unjust beatings and so shouts *hit me, hit me*. Every stroke he received strengthened his new resolve, and clearly marked him on a downward trajectory:

"To hell with the gas!"

"Where can I get a penny?" Morry whispered to his mother. He wanted to throw a penny into the meter quickly, before the dying flames on the gas ring went out completely, because their matches had also just run out.

Mrs. Barsht looked at Morry and saw the teapot that was struggling in vain to boil. She considered asking a neighbor but thought: *I've already borrowed from her, and I've borrowed there as well.* She thought of the penny she had wasted the day before. An acquaintance had given her an address where she had been sure that she would find work:

"It was so far to walk, and when I was halfway there, I had to take the tram for a penny," she explained. "And in the end, they told me there was no work: 'Leave your address,' they said."

"I've heard that already!" Morry shouted. He didn't like his mother's cringing self-justification and was fired up by the injustice of it. Despite his hunger, his voice rang out like metal:

"I have to go to Trafalgar Square; the hunger marchers are coming today."

It was the second Sunday that Morry had marched in the London streets with the thousands of unemployed workers who had come from Scotland, Wales, and other coal-mining areas. For weeks the hunger marchers had marched to London to protest the government's failure to provide work for the millions of unemployed.

Morry became unemployed at the age of sixteen. He'd only worked for one year in total, from age fourteen to fifteen. Straight after leaving school he looked for a job. He read a notice on a large old gate of a small factory tucked away in a corner of a small black alley: "A strong boy of fourteen wanted." He knocked on the gate.

An Englishman with the cold, watery eyes of a seagull answered. Until recently this Englishman sat in a small office on the fifth floor of a skyscraper in the center of the city. He'd been doing financial business on the telephone for a long time, swindling people, until he managed to drive his friend into the clutches of the debtors and then to steal this factory away from him.

He asked Morry a few questions. Morry answered "yes" to all of them. The Englishman decided to give the boy a job for ten shillings a week.

"Come to work tomorrow," he said. Turning his head away, he crossed the extra sixpence off the form and added a zero, reducing the official pay to only ten shillings.

The factory manufactured small round boxes for pharmacies to use for anti-perspirant powder, Vaseline, and other health products. Apart from the fourteen-year-old boys, who were set to work at the heavy iron-pressing machines that produced metal lids, the Englishman employed only girls, who soldered with hot irons for long hours.

The first day they put Morry beside the machine of a worker who was one year older than him, to watch him, but after that Morry didn't see him again.

Morry worked and felt like an adult. He smoked cigarettes and came home with a sooty face. Mrs. Barsht was delighted with this flicker of new hope. But a year later the Englishman hung the same notice outside on the gate, placed a boy a year younger than Morry next to him at the heavy iron-pressing machine, and later that boy never saw Morry again. Morry became unemployed, returning home with his hope extinguished.

"Come to Trafalgar Square, Dad. You're also unemployed, and you, too, Mum." His voice echoed in the small kitchen.

In addition to her constant worry, Mrs. Barsht had a secret and shameful but stubborn plan. Dressed in a threadbare blue coat, with a small, misshapen hat on her head and a pot in her hand, she was ready to go to the soup kitchen. On the way she would drop by a small street where there was a large market, thinking that on Sundays there were always bargains at the stalls. Once there, Mrs. Barsht surveyed the leftover withered vegetables, the cheap pickled herring, and the out-of-date fruit that she used to buy for a rare penny. Today she couldn't buy anything, and this thought pierced her mind like a needle in the sole of her shoe. She would go without, just making do with the soup and bread roll they gave out at the soup kitchen. She couldn't go to Trafalgar Square—it was too far away—but she wanted to make sure Morry would march with them.

Workers carrying the red flag marched through Whitechapel. Morry yelled together with everyone: "We want work! We want bread!"

At three o'clock they dispersed at the enormous stone monument in Trafalgar Square, and mingled with the large crowd and the hundreds of police on horseback and on foot. The masses of dusty, gaunt, unemployed workers with bundles on their shoulders, who had marched for weeks to that day's demonstration, wearily wandered around the high stone monument in the square, where they were ready to shout about the deprivation and suffering of the enslaved and hungry.

Morry quickly moved around among the hunger marchers. His young, lively eyes shone with an impassioned desire to speak out:

"You see this," he said to one hunger marcher, pointing to his head. "It's a good job my hat is stuffed with a lot of padding." He stared at a tall policeman he could see at a distance: "What a dirty swine. He bashed me on the head. They've shown their true colors now."

Morry consciously kept control of himself, but his agitated bitterness increased, and he continued speaking:

"I know them, I've seen them every week, I know how vile they are. They pointed out the direction for our route toward Parliament, and when we gathered there, they charged us with their horses like wild beasts. People couldn't resist. The police rode their horses onto the pavement, what Tsarist Cossacks they are."

Morry and the hunger marchers were leaning against the stone surround of the water basin on the square. The water spurted from the fountain in a strong spray that made a lot of noise and prevented them catching the fervent words of a worker who was making an impassioned speech to the unemployed. The worker's words were an oft-repeated maxim yet felt new for the workers each day.

"The markets are overflowing, due to overproduction. The capitalists don't want to sell their merchandise too cheaply, so they're destroying whole ships and wagons full of produce!" he shouted.

"Hear, hear," the hungry replied.

With a furious gaze Morry repeatedly turned his head to the fountain:

"They've made the fountain this noisy on purpose!"

When Mrs. Barsht got home, she didn't find anyone in the house. It was already late. The street traders had all shut up shop. Road sweepers had swept up the rubbish and thrown it into a big old open cart that was dragged away with heavy steps by strong, broad-backed English horses. The street players were now performing cheap tricks, and young men in clean suits frolicked with dolled-up young women with shining eyes. The pubs were open. Penniless people hovered by the entrance doors, playing accordions, singing songs, and waiting, hoping someone would bring something out for them. Old women stood leaning against the walls with men's caps on their heads. They were very drunk and sung the well-known silly English folk song:

> Never mind the weather,
> Never mind the rain,
> Now that we're together,
> Whoops she goes again.

And they kept hopping and cheekily lifting their skirts.

• • •

The decision that Mr. Barsht had made tugged at him, stinging with a sort of dull, nagging pain, like an infected abscess that cried out to be squeezed to relieve the pressure.

The troubled thoughts he carried with him awakened all sorts of unpleasant feelings from his past experience. He kept remembering how he was left feeling embittered and wronged when he came back emptyhanded from the rich traders on a Friday night. He had taken his barrow laden with unfinished pieces of carpentry to sell to them; handcrafted pieces he had made when he still had the strength to cope with his circumstances.

Most of his deep and subconscious memories and impressions revolved around the lane where he had grown up. The merest association was enough for him to dream, or truly remember, and it brought his street to life in his mind as it was when, as a boy, he came here and moved next door to dockers who worked on ships on the Thames. He'd grown older together with the street, but many of the people of his past were now richer than him. Mr. Barsht often resented that so many shops had been established in the lane, and the shop owners had made a killing in rent. More than once it came into his mind how good it would be if he got back all those pounds he had paid out to the landlord for his small, poky rooms.

Mr. Barsht had already trudged over close to the big, smoky, black bridge where there was heavy traffic and people coming and going. He had already spent a few days wandering about under the bridge, but his hand had not yet wanted to obey him. Now his long back was bowed low, and his hollow cheekbones protruded sharply under the sunken, unshaven skin, like menacing signs that would induce foreboding in the onlooker. On the way to the bridge, however, he could not disentangle himself from the thoughts of his street.

Some local unemployed carpenters stopped him. As they talked, the smell of the tobacco constantly drifted across from the massive cigarette factory and wafted with a bittersweet smell into the noses of workers who had nothing to smoke and had gone there to get a sniff. It appealed to Mr. Barsht as well. Fragments of conversation surrounded him:

"They also stopped my dole," one said.

"Didn't you go to Trafalgar Square?" a second asked.

Mr. Barsht told them that his Morry was out there with the hunger marchers.

"They'll be passing a law soon that'll completely stop the dole," the bitter voice of the first one continued.

"For that amount of money, we'd be better off buying guns, powder, and gas masks."

"Have you read in the paper how many millions it costs to have a strong air force?"

"If only there was as much need for cabinetmakers as there is for armaments," someone said, laughing.

"Today there was an enormous demonstration," a newcomer added. "A miner spoke; he was railing against the means test."

"Were there any incidents with the police?"

"They arrested a few communists."

This gave Mr. Barsht a jolt, and he looked around uneasily. The newcomer continued: "I've just come from there. I came a bit of the way on the bus. The crowd will soon march through here."

The conversation then fell back onto the same well-worn subject.

"When they start throwing gas bombs, it'll be worse than it was in the Great War. When they dropped a bomb then, you could hide, even here under the bridge, but you can't hide from gas, and a good gas mask is expensive."

Mr. Barsht stood bedraggled and silently preoccupied. A sudden drum beat tore through his bitter apathy. From a distance the sound of workers' songs was heard. He pushed himself forward.

Destitute-looking people, both young and old, walked with drawn, pale faces and scrawny necks; some with open shirts, and others with scarves knotted at the neck. A strong police force on foot and horseback had accompanied the marchers on both sides from Trafalgar Square. The unemployed shouted:

"Down with the national government! Down with the means test!"

Mr. Barsht's long, stooped back straightened; he raised his head, looking for Morry. He thought he heard his voice. Suddenly, spinning in his mind's eye, he recalled the bruised mark from a rubber police truncheon that he had seen on Morry's neck and shoulders, and which the boy had tried to hide so that his father and mother wouldn't see it. The earlier interrupted conversation, with all its horror, suddenly came back vividly to him and fired him up with rage, and with an uncharacteristically brash voice he yelled out:

"We won't go into any new war; we'll take all the weapons into our hands, with all the gas and bombs they're preparing for us, and then poverty will be ended, and there won't be any more unemployed."

His gaze followed the hungry workers who were marching away. Their cry shook the cold walls of the buildings:

"We want work! We want bread!"

Arye Myer Kaizer

Kaizer chairing an Association of Jewish Journalists and Authors of Great Britain reception for the poet Avrom Sutzkever, May 1950. *Right to left*: Joseph Fraenkel, Moshe Oved, Sutzkever, Kaizer, and Jacob Maitlis. (*Loshn un lebn*, June 1950)

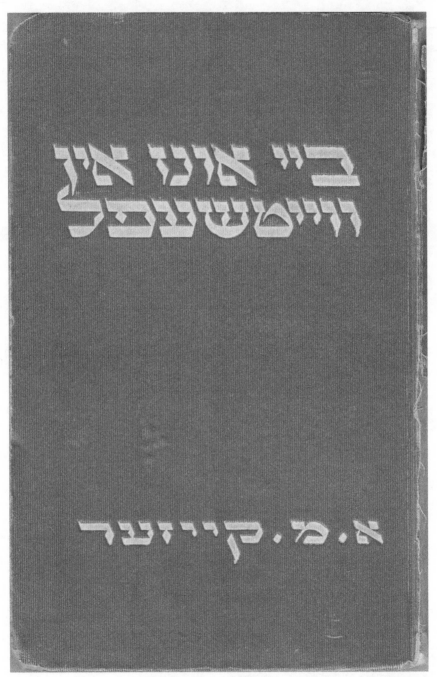

Front cover of *Bay undz in vaytshepl* (This Whitechapel of Ours), 1944. (Photograph by the author)

BIOGRAPHY

> Kaizer is not depressed with Whitechapel. He isn't in a temper, he isn't
> telling it off. The opposite, he understands Whitechapel. . . . Its garbled-
> ness doesn't make him angry, it simply amuses him, and he describes it
> lusciously and with good nature, and so his humor is healthy and useful,
> even for those he makes fun of.
>
> Morris Myer, *Di tsayt*, 1944[1]

Arye Myer (Arnold) Kaizer was born Leibush Arye Myer Michalenski in Yordanov (Jordanowo), Poland, on 8 February 1892, into a chaotic family. His father,
the rabbi Alter Noah HaKohen Michalenski, was a charismatic Talmud scholar
and kabbalist who left trails of adventure and misadventure behind him. One
such, involving arson and prison without trial, compelled him to leave Russia
for England in 1895 to prepare for a court case to clear his name. He arrived with
his wife, Tema Shinah, and their three-year-old son, Arye Myer, and settled at 27
Sidney Square in Whitechapel, in the East End of London. Alter Noah, with his
striking Hasidic dress and kabbalist custom of laying *two* pairs of *tefillin* when he
prayed instead of the usual one, became a recognized and eccentric figure. Hasidim would visit him seeking rabbinical advice. By his bar mitzvah, Arye had two
brothers and two sisters, and the family had moved to 37 Tredegar Square, Bow.
The family became naturalized British citizens, changing their surname from
Michalenski to Kaiser because of the spiritual significance of the Hebrew letters
in the new name.[2]

Arye Myer's first independent publication was an unusual and sensational
one. In 1909 his father, Alter Noah, sent two of his children—Haya Dina, aged
around fourteen, and twelve-year-old Isaac Moses—to Jerusalem with his elderly
mother. Alter Noah left the family in the care of Yaakov Herling, the owner of
the Warshawsky Hotel in Mea She'arim, the Hasidic area of Jerusalem, and he
paid Herling to look after them. In 1912 in Jaffa, Arye Myer, who was also then
living in Palestine and had been a regular contributor to the Jerusalem Yiddish-
language newspaper *Undzer bruder*, published a seventy-page pamphlet in Yiddish
under the name M. Cohen-Kaizer, with the title *Der bandit in yerushalayim oder
der makher fun varshever koylel* (The Brigand in Jerusalem or the Swindler from the
Warsaw Study House). The pamphlet was handed out on the streets of Jaffa, and

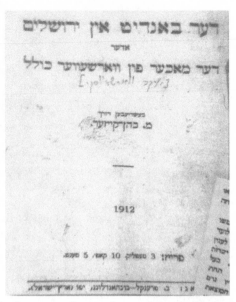

Alter Noah Michalenski Kaiser (1891); the cover of M. Cohen-Kaizer, *Der bandit in yerushalayim* (1912). (Courtesy of Rabbi Pini Dunner Collection, Beverly Hills, CA)

it accused Herling of keeping a house of disrepute, abusing and enslaving Kaizer's family, and raping his sister. Herling sued for libel, and Rav Abraham Isaac Kook, later to be the Ashkenazi chief rabbi of Israel, set up a tribunal of seven city elders. There followed a high-profile tribunal, with many interviews, which lasted weeks and was reported worldwide in the Hebrew and Yiddish press. The outcome was inconclusive, but Herling was not vindicated; there were accusations that the whole case was motivated by local disagreements within the ultra-Orthodox community.[3]

The young, politicized writer returned to London, where, at the start of World War I, he coedited *Der milkhome telegraf* (The War Telegraph) with the already established journalist and writer Avrom Margolin.[4] The newspaper lasted only a few issues before Kaizer (who now used a "z" rather than "s" in his surname) returned to Palestine with the Jewish Legion, 39th Battalion, of the Royal Fusiliers, fighting the Ottomans in the Jordan Valley.[5]

After the war Kaizer returned to London but did not remain in the East End. Instead he followed the waves of upwardly mobile Jews moving west to newer Jewish suburbs of North and North West London. He married Bertha Flider in his late twenties, and the couple moved to Fairholt Road, Stamford Hill, N16.

Just before World War II, they moved to North Crescent, in Finchley, N3, with their two teenaged children; after the war they settled on Armitage Road, Golders Green, NW11. All of these London districts were areas of Jewish settlement, with active Orthodox communities, large synagogues, kosher shops, and Jewish activity.

Kaizer was involved with Jewish community life in three spheres. First, he had employment as the secretary of the Federation of Jewish Relief Organizations (FJRO), working from London in support of Eastern European Jewish communities. Second, he was a contract journalist for *Di tsayt*, writing periodic travel reports from across Europe and weekly humorous sketches about London's East End Jewish community. Finally, Kaizer volunteered with Yiddish cultural organizations, organizing and chairing Yiddish-language events. Morris Myer, editor of *Di tsayt*, called him "a serious communal leader and a happy humorist."[6]

A SERIOUS COMMUNAL LEADER

In the mid-1920s Kaizer was the cofounder and secretary of the Federation of Jewish Relief Organizations, whose offices were based in Woburn House in Central London's West End. The organization worked to raise money through appeals and benefit events for supporting starving communities in Eastern Europe. They sent packages of Passover food to Russia and, after Hitler came to power in 1933, parcels of secondhand clothing to German Jewish refugees in Poland. Kaizer liaised with Eastern European communal leaders, government authorities, and American distribution bodies; on one occasion, in November 1939, his trip was facilitated by Foreign Secretary Viscount Halifax.[7]

Each time Kaizer returned from traveling on support and fact-finding trips, he produced reports in Yiddish. In 1930 his horrifying observations about life for Ukrainian Jewry were published in the pamphlet *Mir zenen hungerik* (We Are Hungry).[8] Between 1934 and 1940 his reports from trips to Eastern Europe appeared in *Di tsayt*, usually serialized over the course of a week. His trip to Lithuania in 1940 was published in English translation in the *Jewish Chronicle*.[9] Kaizer's Yiddish reports were reproduced in the European and North American Yiddish press: *La Journee Parisienne* (Paris); *Moment* (Warsaw); *Moment* (Kovno); *Canadian Eagle* (Montreal), and *Hebrew Journal* (Toronto).[10]

There was considerable public interest in Kaizer's trips, and *Di tsayt* and the *Jewish Chronicle* printed short informational notices telling readers when Kaizer embarked on trips and when he returned. On his return, they advertised where he was speaking about his observations. Between 1930 and 1944 Kaizer's name appeared more than fifty times in the *Jewish Chronicle* in relation to his relief work. Kaizer's high-profile journalism led to his name being included in Hitler's Black Book of "wanted" people to be arrested should the Nazis invade Britain.[11]

A HAPPY HUMORIST

For Yiddish speakers and readers of *Di tsayt*, Kaizer was possibly best known for his weekly sketches about different aspects of life in the community. These pieces were based on topical and local events happening in the streets, on buses, and in synagogues, and in domestic, community, or public arenas. Kaizer would find a funny or satirical angle and make fun of community foibles and indiscretions. Where others may have written angry social critiques, Kaizer made people laugh. He was published throughout the thirties and forties in *Di tsayt*. In 1944 he gathered a selection of his sketches from the 1930s and, with minimal updating of local references, published thirty-seven of them in the collection *Bay undz in vayt-shepl* (This Whitechapel of Ours).[12] The book versions are the ones translated here. Reviewing the book in 1944, Morris Myer wrote:

> Humor is distorted reality. It's that and not that. It's that way and not that way. And distortion can be funny, amusing. So where can you find more distortion than in Whitechapel? Here it really is like that, not how it should be, and the author with his naturally humoristic feel has seen all the distortions of Whitechapel.[13]

Kaizer knew the Orthodox and secular sections of the Jewish community inside out. His Hasidic background had given him knowledge of Torah and Talmud, liturgical text, and Orthodox and mystical practice; ongoing synagogue politics provided him with material to make fun of community affairs and religious activities.

Kaizer attended annual Zionist congresses, sending back daily reports that were published in *Di tsayt*. Although many of these were serious accounts, some were humorous sketches. One piece that mixed humor and fact began:

"Have you heard the one about the four delegates who went to the Zionist Congress in 1930? The first was a regular Zionist, the second, a revisionist, the third, a Poale Zion, and the fourth, a Mizrachi?" The joke sounds like the same sketch found in "Moses in London," but these lines in fact introduced a report describing the real disagreements being played out among the Zionist organizations.[14]

A YIDDISH ACTIVIST

Although Kaizer no longer lived in Whitechapel, he visited the East End regularly for events and meetings. Living away from the East End meant that he could not regularly attend Stencl's literary "Sabbath Afternoons," which would have been a long way to walk on the Sabbath. Kaizer was, however, intimately involved with Stencl's circle and the secular Yiddish literary community, and he was able to attend the monthly Friends of Yiddish Language events at the Ben Uri that took place on Sundays in West London.[15]

Kaizer had been the cofounder of the Association of Jewish Journalists and Authors in England in the twenties, and had remained active throughout the thirties and forties, organizing a variety of programs, mainly in Yiddish, such as the

Kaizer chairing a London YIVO reception for Sholem Asch, 1955. Asch, with the shock of white hair, is sitting next to Kaizer (behind the lectern). (Courtesy of the Mazower private collection)

popular "living newspaper" theatre event, where local Yiddish journalists, including Kaizer, gave talks on topical issues.[16] Through the Association of Jewish Journalists and Authors, Kaizer kept in contact with Yiddish writers in Eastern Europe, and these connections continued during and after the war.[17] Kaizer was also active in the London branch of the Yiddish Scientific Institute (YIVO), and served as its general secretary in the forties. In 1950 he promoted the contest *Mayn ershter yor in england* (My First Year in England), part of an international YIVO competition for immigrants to write Yiddish essays about their immigrant experiences.[18]

After *Di tsayt* folded in 1950, Kaizer's stories were published in *Loshn un lebn* and in two collections, *Vaytshapl lebt* and *Loshn un lebn almanak*. In 1953 Kaizer started preparing for a second book of stories and essays, but the publication never materialized.[19] He continued to be active in community events with the Association of Jewish Journalists and Authors, the YIVO London office, and various Zionist organizations, often chairing events and sometimes hosting them in his home on Armitage Road, Golders Green.[20]

FAMILY LIFE

Kaizer was a devoted family man with two children: a daughter, Nehama, and son, Arthur. The proud father even placed announcements in the *Jewish Chronicle* when Nehama won school and music scholarships at the age of eleven. Yet his family life also involved sorrow and tragedy. Nehama was married for just two years before she divorced in 1948, and she never remarried. Just a few months after Nehama's divorce, Kaizer's son, Arthur, tragically died at the age of nineteen.[21] Although Kaizer had four siblings, the extended family seemed to be fractured. Kaizer's younger brother Shlomo (Solomon) Kaiser lived across London in the Hasidic community in Stamford Hill. Shlomo wrote a memoir of their father, Alter Noah. A close friend of Shlomo, however, remembered him as a bachelor, with no extended family.[22]

Kaizer had a strong relationship with Israel. He and Bertha moved there in 1966, a year before he died at the age of seventy-five. All of Kaizer's death notices and listings in Yiddish and English lexicons put his birth year as 1896. Yet a range of official documents confirms his birth year as 1892.[23] Whatever the reason for the missing or mistaken years, Kaizer seemed to make use of every hour he was given, making a vital contribution to the Yiddish and Anglo-Jewish communities.

WHITECHAPEL: BY WAY OF AN INTRODUCTION

Apparently, when God created the world, he designed some places in pairs, two of each kind. For example, he bestowed upon Russia a small town called Belotzerkov or "white church," which the Jews nicknamed *shvartse tume*, or "black chapel." And in England he built a second Belotzerkov, which in English is called Whitechapel.*

You won't find any white church in our Whitechapel, and there is a hypothesis that it was the Jews themselves who named this patch of land beside the Thames "Whitechapel" after their beloved Belotzerkov. Most of the Jews who settled here came from Belotzerkov and brought their *shtetl* with them, with all of its mud and sewage, bag and baggage, and they didn't even change the name.

They hadn't actually intended to come to Whitechapel. They were heading for the *Goldene medine* of America. Human beings may travel, but it is God who holds the reins, and when their carriage pulled up in London, bang! A tire burst, and they got stuck, and so they stayed. And, as everyone knows, Jews are always scrambling toward the east, so they settled in East London, in Whitechapel. They unpacked their baggage, their bits and bobs, and began building a new life. They became tailors and market sellers, and some studied; and those who weren't suited to any trade became religious and community officers.

And Whitechapel grew. They established synagogues, study houses, religion classes for children, newspapers, theatres, and endless societies—one society after another with councils, arguments, and fights, according to the custom of the Jews

---

* Belotzerkov refers to Belaya Tserkov (today Bila Tserkva, Ukraine).

of all the Belotzerkovs. Whitechapel became a place of renown, and now it's quite something—Whitechapel!

Whitechapel, with its "Yiddish" synagogues housing Orthodox religious schools, where people study the *mishna* and recite psalms.** The doors of these synagogues are never shut, and people study and pray day and night. Whitechapel with its "English" synagogues, where there aren't enough people to make up a prayer quorum, so they hire men from the street and call them "*minyan* men." If you don't give them their fee, that's the end of the prayers, and the dead will be left without a *kaddish*.

Whitechapel, with its "red rabbi" who fights against the present system with all sorts of Torah verses, biblical commentaries, and other weapons, and the former ex-Bolshevik minister, a passionate socialist and devoutly pious: laying two pairs of *tefillin* and teaching a chapter of Karl Marx after prayers.

Whitechapel, with its burial societies, with both fat and thin corpses, and "burial members" who pay weekly dues so that after 120 years they will be buried well and the mourners will be provided with low chairs for the *shiva*.

Whitechapel, with its homely public bathhouse, where people clamber up to the top bench and yell "steam, steam." Buckets of water are poured over the burning-hot stones, and Motl the "beater" beats them for all he's worth. He gives them a powerful pummeling on the back and shoulders, just like back home in the *shtetl*. They bask in the luxury, melting with pleasure and groaning, "Oh, what a *mekhaye*."

Whitechapel, with its Christian missionaries who wear beards and eat only in kosher restaurants. On *Shabbes* afternoon, after his lunchtime *kugel*, the old missionary climbs onto a podium in the middle of Whitechapel and starts to give his "sermon to the Jews." Jewish passersby wander up, hang around, listen to him, spit on the ground, mumble "insolent rogue," and go off to pray *mincha*.

Whitechapel, with its weekday market that is closed on *Shabbes*—the "Lane" where people come from afar in their luxurious cars to buy pickled herring, stuffed carp, and rye bread. At a stall selling spectacles stands a man with a beard of biblical proportions who fits glasses while holding a prayer book in his hand. He puts a pair of glasses on a customer's nose, opens the prayer book, and tells them to read. It once happened that after trying on all the glasses the customer still couldn't read. The bearded stall-holder got furious and exclaimed:

** Here, the word "Yiddish" is describing the Yiddish-speaking immigrant synagogues.

"Mister, it's not spectacles you need, but a teacher."

Whitechapel, with its *Shabbes* market, which straggles along the broad Whitechapel pavement, and where Jewish beigel sellers swear that even though today is *Shabbes*, the beigels were baked today.

Whitechapel, with its kosher restaurants and hostels, where at one table a chap sweats over a large bowl of chicken soup with noodles, at another table a group is playing cards, and at a third table a teacher is teaching a girl to read Hebrew and recite blessings.

Whitechapel, with its "Jewish parliament"—the Board of Deputies, to which the Talmud Society delegates a colonel, the Mishna Society a half communist, and the Psalms Society a true socialist who gives sermons about this week's Torah reading.

Whitechapel, with its love of literature and its authors. No one in Whitechapel buys a Yiddish book in a shop, but rather the author stands at the entrance to every meeting and passionately publicizes one of his own pamphlets.

Whitechapel, with its foolish infatuations. When a guest comes, they make a fuss of him and lap up every word he says. But if he stays a moment more than he should, then—ugh! He's a nuisance, a loser, a pest.

Whitechapel, with her good friends—friends of Yiddish, friends of Hebrew, friends of Soviet Russia, friends of the Workers in the Land of Israel, and other types of friends, who would tear each other apart, were they not afraid of the cops.

Whitechapel, with its characteristic half-Englishy Yiddish. When Whitechapelers say "*zi geyt oys*," it doesn't mean, God forbid, that she's in the agony of death throes and "on the way out." On the contrary, it's a great joy for the parents because their daughter is "going out" with a boy and she's going to be a bride. Or when they say "*er hot ir ongeton ringen*," it doesn't mean, God forbid, that "he has put her in chains" but that a girl has been given an engagement ring by her fiancé, as is the custom in England.

So this is Whitechapel, the famous Whitechapel, which has outgrown its geographical borders and has spread across the whole of England. And I, Mr. A. M. Kaizer, myself a Whitechapeler from childhood, have created a portrait of our Whitechapel, may it live long. May the world look upon the face of my dearly beloved Whitechapel.

THE WHITECHAPEL
EXPRESS

Stamford Hill is located on a straight old Roman Road, and as East End Jews became upwardly mobile, some of them moved north, from Whitechapel, straight up the Kingsland Road to Dalston, and on up Stoke Newington Road to Stamford Hill. (See the map on page 103.) Stamford Hill was known as *di hoykhe fenster*, which literally means "high windows" and refers to high society or a wealthy suburb. Not all those living in Stamford Hill or Stoke Newington, however, were upwardly mobile. Some people shared homes or lodged with another family and still worked down in the East End. The early morning "workmen ticket" offered a return bus fare at a reduction in the usual fare, making the journey affordable.[1]

The 647 trolleybus (or Whitechapel Express) going south headed straight down from Stamford Hill, bearing slightly left at Shoreditch, to travel into the heart of the Jewish immigrant area of Whitechapel. This story about the 47 tram was first published in 1934, when trams were still running. In the late 1930s trolleybuses replaced trams, and the 647 trolleybus ran the same route. The 647 trolleybus seems to have become iconic, appearing in East End memoirs and songs such as *Der aldgeyt kar* (The Aldgate Car).[2]

The character Yerukhem, who pops up in this story to make comments, would have been familiar to Kaizer's readers from other stories he wrote. Kaizer calls Yerukhem "my *landsman*, who is known as the philosopher." In some stories, as here, he appears now and then. In other "Yerukhem stories," he is the sole narrator.[3]

Who doesn't know the Whitechapel Express? Who hasn't traveled on it? I don't think there's a single Jew in London who hasn't had the honor of bouncing along on the Whitechapel Express. If there is such a person, they should send me their photograph, and I will put it up in the museum of curiosities.

The Whitechapel Express, although it hasn't yet become bankrupt, has acquired an alternative name: "the Jerusalem Car." To tell you the truth, the sign on the trolleybus doesn't say Whitechapel Express or Jerusalem Car; it only has the number 647. Yet everyone knows that this is the Whitechapel Express, and if there is any individual who doesn't know, the bus conductor makes sure that they find out, because he shouts out "Whitechapel Express" at the top of his voice. No one smiles at this or complains because it is indeed the Whitechapel Express. The number 647 was only there by mistake.

The Whitechapel Express runs from Stamford Hill to the London docks, cutting through the innards of our densely populated *kibbutzim* of Stoke Newington, Dalston, Commercial Street, and Leman Street. It is packed with passengers. It seems to me that no trolleybus is as popular as this car. They say that it's the best deal because you pay cash—no credit! If only every shopkeeper did such good business. People push and shove onto the Whitechapel Express as if they're going to hear a Hasidic *rebbe*.

Who are the passengers? If you'd like to know, then take the trouble to step onto, or rather, shove your way onto, the Whitechapel Express in the late afternoon and start muttering the afternoon prayer. And if you quietly sing the melody from the liturgy *Ashrey yoshvey veysekho*, you'll see that the whole Express will sway and pray with you. Absolutely everyone, apart from the conductor, although sometimes he will, too, not because he's a Jew, but because he knows it by now.

The Whitechapel Express isn't just a Jewish bus but a whole Jewish *shtetl*. On a single journey you meet the rabbi, the *shochet*, the cantor, the synagogue warden, the religion teacher, and the upper crust of the area. And all the men are busy with something. Over there someone is engrossed in a book, mumbling the words under his breath as he reads interpretations of biblical passages. A second person also reads a religious book, mouthing out the words. If you look closely, you can see that he's reciting his daily psalms. A third person is totally absorbed in a Yiddish book, smiling into his beard as he reads a story by Sholem Aleichem. And almost everyone is reading a Yiddish newspaper. One reads the front page, another the serialized novel on the back page. It seems as if even the gentile conductor knows Yiddish because he peers into a Yiddish paper and asks its reader,

"What's the tip on the first race?" You see, the Whitechapel Express is not merely a bus; it is a cultural institution, a Whitechapel YIVO.

And what do the women do? They don't sit idle. One knits a sock, another shows everyone what a loyal wife she is by sewing the buttons on her husband's trousers. But even those doing nothing are doing something: They sit and bad-mouth their neighbors, or tell stories of their difficulties in coping with their in-laws, their children, and even their dear spouses.

All in all, the Whitechapel Express is lively and happy. My friend Yerukhem says that traveling on the Whitechapel Express is a thousand times more fun than traveling in a Rolls Royce. Despite the fact that he's never actually traveled in a Rolls Royce, he assumes that it would be a real torment to sit alone, in a stifling Rolls Royce, and not have anyone to chat to. One could go crazy from boredom. It should only happen to anti-Semites!

But it's different on the Whitechapel Express. You travel in a group, with dozens of Jews, and you feel like you're in your local bathhouse. This one tells a story, that one a joke. A strange child clambers onto your knee and takes off your glasses, while another child removes your hat, hits you on your neck, and says, "Uncle, give me a penny." If you refuse, he threatens to throw your hat out of the window. Or maybe you suddenly feel something dripping onto your neck and wonder where it's coming from. It's not raining, and the roof of the trolleybus, thank God, doesn't have a hole in it. But something salty is dripping down. Then you realize that the woman standing next to you, holding onto the bus strap, has a package of chopped herring in brine in the same hand. The paper bag has opened a tiny bit, and your bare neck is experiencing the taste of a drop of herring brine.

When all's said and done, it's a true pleasure to travel on the Whitechapel Express, especially on Thursday, when the whole of Jewish London goes down to the great market in the "Lane" to buy food for *Shabbes*. Traveling south are bags, baskets, suitcases, and especially women, a world of women.

As soon as the Whitechapel Express moves off from Stamford Hill, the clientele starts to appear. In Stamford Hill the well-to-do ladies stride onboard with fur coats and fine hats. In Stoke Newington, those boarding the trolleybus aren't ladies, but less well-off women: not dressed up in fur, though their woolen coats do have a fur collar. In Dalston, it's the poorer wives who trudge onboard, with plain coats without a scrap of fur on them, or with a worn-out collar from some sort of animal like a mangy cat. In Shoreditch no one gets on at all, because anyone going from there to the "Lane" or Whitechapel will go with the number 2—the legs. They can't spare the penny fare.

On the way home the Stamford Hill ladies, the Stoke Newington women, and the Dalston wives are all laden down with good things, especially fish, for *Shabbes*. If you want to guess where the women are going, this time don't look at their appearance, but cast an eye into the swollen bags they are carrying. The signs are as follows:

If a fine glossy, fat carp is sticking out of one bag—dressed in a silk coat and winking with one eye—it's going to Stamford Hill. If poking out of another bag is a half-dead, emaciated bream, that is going to Stoke Newington. And if popping out of a third bag is a small, sad, pale haddock with cloudy eyes, you can be sure it's on its way to Dalston. This tiny haddock, you should know, is not a singleton; it is merely the representative, the delegate of a whole "lot," of a bargain that was bitterly haggled over.

On this topic Yerukhem pronounces two brilliant thoughts. First, shortsighted people don't need to put on their glasses to see the tiny haddocks; they can be detected at a distance: They stink as much as his wife, Rashe-Gitl, if you know what I mean. Second, he maintains that you can't be certain that the haddock is going to Dalston. Today's world is topsy-turvy, and it could be that they're actually going to Stamford Hill. All haddock today are moving to Stamford Hill, and the apparent fat carp are not carp at all. They're just pretending to be carp, but really they're herring in disguise—it's a bluff. Oh, well, he may be right.

And so the Whitechapel Express, the *shtetl* within the city, goes there and back, and the whole way it's buzzing and swimming with Jewish life. There is, however, one part of the route where the Whitechapel Express becomes despondent. When it stops at the corner of Whitechapel and Aldgate, the bus empties, and it travels on alone, orphaned, passengerless, to the docks. The conductor becomes so dejected that he begins to yawn.

WHERE IT BUBBLES

In 1932 a small notice in the Jewish Chronicle advertised a new nonprofit project to establish a Jewish communal restaurant. The restaurant would sell meals at a minimum price to "remove the stigma of charity" associated with going to a soup kitchen.[1] The restaurant opened a year and a half later, on 3 May 1934, providing kosher meals for those in the Jewish community who were "on the verge of destitution." The kosher meal consisted of "bread, soup, meat or fish, vegetables, a sweet and tea for the small sum of 9d." The opening ceremony included lunch, followed by a toast from the editor of Di tsayt, Morris Myer.[2]

Around three weeks later, at a meeting of activists and benefactors, the chair, the Rev. H. Mayerowitsch, spoke of the responsibility of the Jewish community to raise money for the continuing upkeep and development of the Communal Restaurant, calling it "one of the greatest societal accomplishments of Jewish London." He spoke of the years of tireless work that had gone into the planning by a group of activists on the committee, and he also discussed "the issue of the haggadahs that were sent out and had only brought aggravation and great disappointment due to the poor response from the Jewish community." Two committees made up of the current activists were formed: a restaurant committee and a cultural committee. Kaizer was a part of the cultural committee.[3]

When I heard that in the heart of Whitechapel they had opened a remarkable institution, a sort of communal kitchen where the people of our community, like myself and other Jewish immigrants, could get a half-free lunch, I went to the head organizer for an interview. This is what happened.

Coming into the kitchen I found a hall full of people: workers, managers of workshops, owners of small and large factories, and the eminent local wealthy. Everyone was curious to know when they were going to start serving the lunches and whether it would really cost only ninepence a lunch. And why not cheaper?

One chap, the proprietor of a workshop with a pregnant-looking potbelly, squat and round as a bathtub, wanted to know what sort of soup they would be serving in the kitchen.

"I myself," he proudly informed me, "like an international soup. What I mean is a barley soup with short *lokshn*, *kliskes*, *farfl*, beans, small shallots, carrots, giblets, veal bones, and any other bones with meat on them. I want to know if they give that sort of international soup or just a simple broth made solely from chicken."

A second man, short and heavy like a butcher's block, wanted to know what sort of meat they would be serving:

"I have an inordinate love of turkey," he said with relish. "I don't mean the meat of the male, but meat from a female turkey. Roasted, and especially stuffed turkey, is my particular favorite. But if there's no choice, I will eat duck or a quarter of a goose, the hind part. I can't take beef, it's not to my taste."

A third person with chubby, pinchable cheeks was interested only in the compote.

"For me," he solemnly explained, "the essential part of the meal is the compote, the dessert. My favorite compote is pineapple. The tasty 'pine apples' that are served at weddings or the larger bar mitzvahs. If there are no pineapples, I also like the stewed plums, which should be served together on one plate with a large piece of rich fruit cake stuffed with raisins. But if you like, I would also gladly eat turnip *tzimmes* with a marrow bone, but see to it that there are enough marrow bones in the dish and I don't have to wait until another customer's marrow bone is freed up and comes to me secondhand."

A fourth guy, a Litvak, having listened to all the solemn declarations, pronounced with his regionally accented lisp:

"All these disses are only really delissous if you start with a bit of kosser herring with onion as an hors d'oeuvre."

And a fifth gloomy man with a gaunt face wanted to know if he could share his portion with his new son-in-law, a handsome gem of a young man to whom he had promised board and lodging for his first year of marriage.

"Where is the boss?" I asked the treasurer, who was standing with a wooden spoon, answering all these questions.

"Upstairs in the office. He's busy with today's post."

At full speed I legged it up to the admin office. But I could barely get into the room, because the whole office was covered with a mountain of envelopes and papers. No living soul was in the room. I just asked into the empty space:

"Is anyone here?"

A muffled voice answered, as if from the grave:

"Yeah, just coming."

It was hard to guess where the voice came from. It seemed to be coming from underneath the floor. But suddenly—Hear, O Israel! The great mountain moved. The envelopes scattered, the mountain exploded like a sneeze, and envelopes flew in all directions. It was nothing less than an earthquake. And, good God! From under the paper mountain, a head started to appear, and a moment later out crawled a complete person, and welcomed me warmly with a "*sholem aleykhem.*"

And who do you think appeared out of the tomb of papers? It was the head organizer himself.

"A good few checks have come in for your appeal," I said. "A good bit of post here, ha! You're drowning in checks."

"If only that were true," he answered with a sigh.

"Well, what's the mountain of envelopes?"

And he told me:

"When we sent out the letters for our appeal, we included a Passover *haggadah* in each one. Twenty-five thousand *haggadahs*. But oh, my, what a *megillah* we had with those *haggadahs*. People started searching for defects, mistakes, and omissions in them. The end result is that instead of checks, this whole mountain is returned *haggadahs*. The mountain is growing. The *haggadahs* are sending us crazy. We are simply, as you can see, drowning in *haggadahs*."

"What were the mistakes?"

"Have a read," and he handed me a bunch of letters. One person complained that there was a plague missing. In one of the ten plagues, the print was unclear and too faint to read. A second one sent back the *haggadah* because when his mother-in-law saw the pictures of the four sons, the wicked son's face looked like her own.

A third person, an Anglicized Jew wrote:

"It's a scandal, a disgrace, a shame! Every letter '*vov*' is either without a dot for the vowel '*o*' or without a dot for the vowel '*u*.' I have counted that there are three hundred thousand '*o*' dots missing and about the same number of '*u*' dots. I can only imagine what sort of management you have in the kitchen with so much punctuation missing. I am sure that you are a bunch of communists. The communists in Russia have these self-same *haggadahs*. I can see why you call yourself a 'communal center.' No, sir! I will not support the communist center in the East End."

"Now you understand," the organizer said with a small smile, "what we were looking for in the mountain of papers. We were searching for our missing vowels but found our vanishing dreams."

As I left the office, I stumbled into a second mountain of pots, pans, saucepans, plates, troughs, jugs, frying pans, bowls, pails, tubs, and I almost fell into a vat of boiling water.

"What are you cooking?" I asked the treasurer, who was mixing the bubbling water with a wooden spoon.

"For the time being," he explained, "I'm bubbling water to make steam. People love heat in the bathhouse, so when they see that there's steam in the kitchen, they'll start to believe that the kitchen really is a kitchen. Our dear customers, good health to them all, didn't believe in the whole kitchen plan at the beginning. They turned up their noses saying, 'Yeah, yeah, stuff and nonsense.' And even now when we have, thank God, our own building, that is to say, the building has us, they still don't believe that the kitchen will open. They say that they won't believe it until they can see that there's cooking going on, and something is bubbling. So, we've started to cook."

"Good luck with the cooking," I answered, and damp from the steam, I went off to write up my bubbling interview.

CHOOSING CANTORS

This story refers to two Jewish festivals.

Yom Kippur is the Day of Atonement, a fast day, and the holiest day on the Jewish calendar. The end of the fast is marked by the blowing of the shofar (ram's horn).

Simkhes toyre (Simchat Torah) is a joyful festival celebrating the Torah. It is marked by finishing the annual cycle of weekly Torah readings at the end of Deuteronomy and starting again from the beginning of Genesis. As part of the celebrations, the Torah scrolls are paraded around the synagogue seven times, and a prayer called Ato horeyso is read before each circuit. Each circuit is led by a different member of the congregation; this is one of the synagogue honors, which are sometimes auctioned off to the highest bidder.

Eyl mole rakhmim are the first words of the Prayer for the Dead.

The final joke in the story is a little obscure. The name Itche Mayer was used in jest as a disparaging name for a Polish Jewish religious zealot, named after the founder of the Ger Hasidim. Used here, it makes a satirical comment on the difference between religious style and custom. Immigrants from different areas of Eastern Europe (Poland or Lithuania) and different groupings (Hasidim or another religious sect) had their respective religious customs and styles of prayer. The East End was full of synagogues and small khevres (prayer rooms) that were established around these specific groups. There is also some self-parody here around Kaizer's own lineage and his own name.

It's lively in the Whitechapel *shtetl* because they're choosing a cantor.

Have you ever seen how a woman chooses a chicken for *Shabbes*? First, she pinches its flesh to see if there's enough meat on it. Then she blows the feathers to see if there's enough fat to make *shmaltz* for Passover. Well, this is more or less how they choose a cantor in Whitechapel. The congregation wants him to be both meaty and *shmaltzy*.

The cantors come from the four corners of the earth to audition. As you walk past a synagogue, you hear someone inside trilling, modulating, embellishing with ornaments, performing vocal tricks, and penetrating the highest echelons of heaven, while outside in front of the synagogue, you see a long queue of people jostling each other to hear the new cantor doing his trial set.

But if you think that this queue is the congregation, I beg your pardon, you've made a mistake. These are the newly arrived cantors, waiting to hear the word "next." Just like at the Labour Exchange. I asked the synagogue beadle:

"Why do the cantors stay outside? Why don't you let them go inside?"

"We'd gladly let them in," the beadle answered, "but the cantor who's 'doing his turn' at the moment won't let them." "The reason for that," the beadle explained, "is that every cantor has his own repertoire, and he's worried that another cantor will pinch it, and a cantor without a repertoire is, as you know, like a flock without a shepherd, like a cat without whiskers!"

"In our synagogue," the beadle continued, "all sorts of no-hopers have shown up, and we can't choose a cantor from among them. What's more, various trades and professions have ventured onto our synagogue podium. We've already had a doctor-cantor, a professor-cantor, a pharmacist-cantor, an engineer-cantor, and even a comedian-cantor. Oh, and was he a joker! The congregation really liked him. He put a kind of clowning into the prayers, with strange affectations and facial expressions. When he blessed the new moon, people were rolling about with laughter, and during the prayer confessing sins on Yom Kippur, everyone was doubled over giggling, such power he had."

"So why didn't you pick him?"

"Because a lot of the members specifically wanted the doctor-cantor because they maintained that a doctor in a synagogue is useful. It could happen that someone faints from hunger on Yom Kippur or that a woman chatting in the women's gallery is suddenly startled by the *shofar* blowing and goes into labor. Or on *Simkhes toyre*, when the scrolls are being carried round the synagogue, some of the members jostle each other, trying to elbow themselves into taking part in the *Ato horeyso* prayer, and people get bruised. It's a regular occurrence, and we have to bandage them up. So because of this, it's good if there's a doctor in the house."

"So why didn't you take the doctor?"

"Because we found out that he's not really a doctor. Listen, here's the story: It happened that during his trial service, because of all the pushing and shoving to get to hear him, a woman felt ill and a cry went up: 'A doctor! A doctor!' People ran over to the cantor and said to him, you're a doctor, do something, one of our congregants is dying! He answered that he is indeed a doctor, but not a medical one. So what do you think of such a doctor, eh?

"We also had a cantor from Hungary who boasted that he's a great Hebrew scholar and understands the resonances of translating from Hebrew into Yiddish. He certainly had a fine voice and wasn't bad at reciting the prayers. It was just because of a word, I swear to you, one word, that he failed to get the post. So here's the story: The assistant manager of our synagogue suddenly died, so we asked the Hungarian cantor, who was on trial that *Shabbes*, if he would sing the Prayer for the Dead. The cantor picked up the prayer book and began *Eyl mole rakhmim*. One could not have hoped for a better rendition. It would have moved the dead. It was a shame that the deceased assistant synagogue manager couldn't hear it. He always particularly liked a good Prayer for the Dead. He would have come back to life. And when our cantor came to the words 'who has gone to his eternal rest,' he began to show his true vocal brilliance. He sang 'who has gone,' first in a bass voice, and then 'who has gone' repeated in a tenor voice, a trill here and an ornament there, and, with a glance down at the prayer book, moved to a falsetto and sang with panache: 'who has gone to his *female*.'

"At this, there was such a commotion in the synagogue that the chandeliers began shaking. The relatives of the deceased wanted to tear the cantor apart like a piece of herring. Just to think, what a disgrace, what a desecration of the deceased, what a defamation (though maybe it's not such a defamation today, who knows?). All in all, it was a fine to-do.

"Our president went up to him, and angrily asked the cantor:

"'Hey, cantor, where did you get a "who has gone to his female" from?' The cantor pointed to the prayer book and answered him nonchalantly in German:

"'It is written right here in this Book of Common Prayer!'

"I snatched the prayer book out of his hand, or the 'book of common prayer' as he called it, and then everything was clear because it was written like this:

"'Who has gone to his (female: her) eternal rest.'

"And so the cantor showed us what a great scholar he was by singing the word 'female' right after 'gone to his,' and this was the cause of his horrible gaffe."

"So, as you've heard," the beadle ended his talk, "our synagogue is always lively and joyful, but we've not been able to choose a cantor. Oh, I've forgotten to say. Two new cantors are coming to us: one is Russian, indeed from *Sovietish* Russia. They say that he is a *bezbozhnik*. I don't know what that is, but I reckon that he's quite something. And the second cantor is coming all the way from China, where he is a general! His name is It-che may-uh. What an unusual name. Have you heard of him? They say that when he shoots out a high note in the Evening Prayer, he's a really big shot!"

RONI AKORE AND THE DRESSMAKER

The Torah, comprising the Five Books of Moses, is split into fifty-four named portions. Each Sabbath in the synagogue, one portion of the Torah is read from the Torah scrolls (some are double portions), so that over one year, the whole Torah is completed.

Maftir is the term used to describe the last few verses of each *Torah* portion.

The *haftoyre* is an additional reading from the prophets read after the Torah portion each week. They are usually different from one another, but occasionally one is read twice in a year.

Each week the Torah portion and *haftoyre* are read by the cantor, the rabbi, or a lay reader. If a thirteen-year-old boy has his bar mitzvah that week, it is customary for him to read that week's portion. Some bar mitzvah boys read the portion with the *maftir* and the *haftoyre*. Some boys read only the *maftir* and the *haftoyre*.

In Kaizer's story, the name of the Torah portion is *Ki seytse*. The *maftir* is the last few verses of *Ki seytse*. The name of the *haftoyre* is *Roni akore*. Another *Torah* portion, *Noyekh* (Noah), has the same *haftoyre*, *Roni akore*.

At the beginning of the story, Yerukhem is teaching the boys verses of Torah that look inappropriate. Many of Kaizer's readers would have known that the verse following those quoted concern circumcision, which is a contract with God, and particularly significant for a boy coming of age and studying for his bar mitzvah.

The term *rebbe* refers to the immigrant rabbis who studied for many years in Jewish seminaries. Reverend was the term used in Anglo-Jewish synagogues for ministers who had gone through a less rigorous training. The immigrants saw reverends as anglicized, less knowledgeable, and less orthodox.

The story mentions a speech. Yerukhem's anxiety points to this speech being at least partly in Yiddish. Books of bar mitzvah speeches in Yiddish, Hebrew, and English were published from the 1900s in London.[1]

Yerukhem, the teacher, tells a story . . .

Have I told you about my lovely bar mitzvah classes with my fine boys? May their days be lengthened and may they have good marriages. Oh, what scholars they are! What happy students, may God protect and save them. But do you think they want to learn? I tell you, not a jot! And do you think their fathers care? Nothing of the kind! My mother-in-law told me that the phrase in the women's bible, "As a father has mercy for his sons," really means that the father is no better than his sons.

If only the boys knew Yiddish, I would have already drilled a verse of the bible into their heads. If you know Yiddish, you've got a head start with Hebrew. In the old country it was a joy to teach the Torah reading to a boy. Who doesn't remember how their teacher sang their portion to them, translating the Hebrew to Yiddish with that beautiful bible tune?—they would sing the portion all about an *ishe*, a woman, just like this:

> *Ishe*—a woman,
> *ishe ki tazriya*—if a woman has conceived seed
> *veyoldo*—and borne
> *zokher*—a male-child
> *vetomo*—then she shall be unclean
> *shives yomim*—seven days—remember this, rascals, a whole seven days.

And the class absolutely had to remember. If not, they'd get a slap. Yet here, in blessed England, it's unfortunate, because every which way you turn, the boys only speak English.

I'll tell you a secret: I've already tried to teach my boys a verse of the Torah, and instead of translating into Yiddish, I translate into English with the same bible tune, like this: *ishe*—a *vooman*. But after singing *ishe*—a *vooman*, I didn't get any further, because you should have heard what happened next. The laughter and mockery at my English was over the top. And between you and me, why wouldn't they laugh? The word *vooman* doesn't sound nice. In fact, it's awful! It just doesn't compare with the translation into Yiddish, *ishe*—a woman. And since then I can't open a religious text with my class of scoundrels. As soon as I sit down to teach them anything, they all shout in unison, "*Rebbe*, give us *ishe*—a *vooman*."

Oh, well, I thought to myself, these boys won't become *rebbes* in any case, unless, possibly, they become reverends in the English synagogues. But even so, they still have to learn their bar mitzvah Torah reading . . . when I say Torah reading, what I really mean is just the last few verses of the Torah portion, just the *maftir*; that and their speech. And of course, as well as the *maftir*, they have to read the *haftoyre* verses from the prophets. So I started looking for a suitable *haftoyre*.

"What do you mean," you ask me, "you look for a *haftoyre*?" "I thought," you continue, "that every boy has his own bar mitzvah *Shabbes* when he turns thirteen, and he sings the *haftoyre* of that week." If you think so, I beg your pardon, but you are mistaken! Here in London, you have to start off with finding the shortest mini-*haftoyre* you can imagine for the bar mitzvah boy, so that he doesn't have to sweat over it and can quickly learn the Hebrew off by heart. And then that week will be chosen for his bar mitzvah. I've found that the shortest *haftoyre* is *Roni akore*, which is read in the middle of the summer, and it's attached to the Torah portion of *Ki seytse*. It's a tiny little *haftoyre*—only ten sentences long.

So all my bar mitzvah boys have sung the *maftir* of *Ki seytse* and the *haftoyre* *Roni akore* with great joy and merriment. It didn't even occur to me that it might be the case someday that two fathers who were members of the same synagogue would each want to have the *Roni akore haftoyre* for his son. But so it came to pass. There was an occasion when not two but *four* fathers of bar mitzvah boys all rushed in to the president of the synagogue, demanding the same *haftoyre* for the *Shabbes* of *Ki seytse*. They quarreled so much over *Roni akore* that they almost came to blows.

Of course, after that the president told everyone to go to the "*rebbe* of the *Roni akores*" and he'd show them how you can transform one *Roni akore* into four. They converged upon me full of rage, trying to be the first to make a deal with me. One of the group thumped on the table and yelled:

"I ordered a special *maftir* for my boy, not some cheap readymade one. I'll get you thrown into jail for these black-market dealings."

A second father added furiously:

"*K'seytse*, I'll give you such a *k'seytse* that you'll lose your appetite to be a *rebbe*."

A third asked, with a vicious smile:

"Is this your bar mitzvah factory where you manufacture readymade *maftirs* in stock sizes?"

And a fourth, an annoying little man with a high-pitched voice, shrieked:

"This can only happen to us Jews. It wouldn't happen among the *goyim.*"

So I thought that since they were really so impudent, I would get my own back by telling them exactly what sort of prodigies they have. This whole altercation was because of their precious darlings. So I responded:

"Listen to me gentlemen! Listen to this, sirs! *Your* boys, what they don't hear won't harm them, are not like *our* boys, our serious homespun youths—and if you keep provoking me, I'll tell you what your boys are: They are, sad to say, rascals, scamps, rogues, devils, ghouls, demons. Your boys would rather tame wild dogs than learn Torah. I wouldn't wish it on my worst enemy to tutor such a group. They make you lose the will to live. If I'd taught each one of them his own individual *maftir*, I'd have become a resident of Edmonton cemetery long ago. And I don't want that for the time being because I still have an agreement with this world—to live a bit longer. So *Roni akore* is the best *maftir* for them. It was made for them—it's a short, small, tiny reading, just two inches in length, which is not so difficult to devour. But even this olive-sized portion is not easy for them to digest. I've nearly drowned in sweat and foamed at the mouth 'til I got them to the place where they wouldn't stumble like blind horses in mud. You should see how well *Roni akore* works for them; it scampers like a foal. So, you belong to one synagogue, and each of you wants the *Roni akore* for yourself. Leave it to me! On my head be it. I'll find some sort of scheme to keep the wolf satisfied and the goat safe: All of you will be happy—both you and *Roni akore*. In the meantime, stay calm, don't get worked up. In the words of Rabbi Blockhead: 'Turmoil is not good for your bellybutton.' Off with you now and goodbye." And we parted as good friends.

Less than half an hour later, I received a telegram from one of the mothers of my bar mitzvah boys: a rather foolish boy with an unpleasant, grating voice. The mother was having a leisurely break at the seaside and sent me this telegram:

> Because my dressmaker can't *finndish* my dress in time for the bar mitzvah, I have decided to postpone the function. Arrange an extension with the synagogue until the beginning of winter.

What do you think of her *chutzpah*? For a year I had busted a gut for her brat.
By the time I had taught her nitwit of a son the *maftir* from *Ki seytse* and crammed in
the *Roni akore haftoyre*, my throat was raw. Now, without even having a holiday, I
was meant to start a new portion from the beginning. I sent her a telegram back
in her own choice English:

> Extension of *maftir* impossible. Had a hell of a job with *Roni akore*. Expe-
> rienced a year of hard labor until your boy took to it. Bar mitzvah must
> wait with *maftir* until the same time next year when *Roni akore* comes round
> again.

So how do you think she answered me? With this next telegram:

> Don't be crazy. Next year my dress will be out of fashion. To hell with *Roni*
> *akore*. Change station and tune in for another *maftir*.

What do you think of my luck? How would you like to do another six
months' slave labor and break stones with her boychick? She even thinks the *maftir*
is a wireless, a radio that you turn on, "tune in," and it'll sing to you.

For a day or two, I was at my wits' end until I realized that the *haftoyre Roni*
akore is read twice a year. It's also read in the autumn, attached to the portion of
Noyekh. I fired back this telegram: "Succeeded. Extension until *Noyekh*, but will
cost extra money." You may ask me why the extra money? Well, first, I have to
thoroughly coach her prodigy again in the reading of the *maftir* of the portion of
Noyekh, and second, I don't want her to think that you can just pick up a *maftir* on
the street. So then, what do you think she answered me?

"Money no object," she replied, "but it depends on what my dressmaker says
to *Noyekh*."

After further inquiries and investigations, the dressmaker ruled that it was
kosher, and I received a telegram that "*Noyekh* is okay, go ahead."

So I thought, if *Noyekh* is okay for my mistress by the sea, why would it not
fit the bill for my misters on dry land? I sent for my four *Roni akore* fathers who
belong to the same synagogue to tell them my plan: One bar mitzvah will take
place on the *Shabbes* of *Ki seytse*, and a second on the *Shabbes* of *Noyekh*. Then we
will have killed two *Roni akores* with one stone. As for the other two, they will
just have to wait another year until we read the same portions. My plan pleased

them, apart from the fact that they couldn't decide who should be the first two bar mitzvahs and who the last two. So I told them:

"Why bicker? Just go to your wives' dressmakers and ask them. They'll know what ruling to make."

My gentlemen laughed, exchanged sly glances, as if to say: "What sort of monkey-business is going on between our *rebbe* and the dressmakers?" I said to them:

"Don't laugh, gentlemen. If your wives' dresses aren't ready, not even ten *Roni akores* will help."

And you think was the end of it? The next day, three of my *Roni akore* dads let me know that they had to postpone their bar mitzvahs because the dressmakers were indeed not *finndished*. And a fourth announced that his wife's dress was now *finndished*, but, oh, my God, to such a terrible *finndish*: The dress was so badly cut that it pulled across the back. Nevertheless, he wants to *finndish* the bar mitzvah because it makes him sick. He's already fed up with the whole business.

And so, as you've heard, I have, thanks to the dressmakers, been saved from the hard drudgery of my bar mitzvahs. Say what you want. In a country where you can get an extension for a bar mitzvah because the dressmaker is not ready with the dress—in such a country you can make a living. You see, this London Jewish culture is such a treat. Oh, yes, a treat indeed!

WHEN YOU GO TO A YIDDISH THEATRE

In 1933, when this story was first published in *Di tsayt*, there were two Yiddish theatres in operation. The Pavilion Theatre on Whitechapel Road was a purpose-built theatre with a gallery and could seat more than two thousand. The Grand Palais on Commercial Road was a converted hall and seated around five hundred. The Pavilion closed in 1935, and the Grand Palais became a full-time Yiddish theatre. In 1936 the Jewish National Theatre was formed in Adler Hall on Adler Street, off Commercial Road, by Fanny Waxman and Meier Tzelniker. It was also a converted hall with a capacity of five hundred.

The newspapers *Di post* and *Di tsayt* published theatre reviews and reports each week, and often daily advertisements for the different shows performed by local companies and visiting actors and theatre troupes from America and Eastern Europe. The theatre repertoire changed weekly, and certain performances were promoted with "women-go-free" or "children-go-free" tickets.

By the time Kaizer's story was republished in 1944, there were still two Yiddish theatres although neither of them had a gallery. The Pavilion was closed, Adler Hall was now the home of the New Yiddish Theatre Company, and The Grand Palais had continued throughout the war under the direction of the actors Mark Markov and Etta Topel. The only break was when the Blitz made it impossible to perform in the theatre, and Markov and Topel performed on a makeshift stage in the underground in the West End.[1]

When you go to the Yiddish theatre and are shown your seat, just stay in it. Don't wander off in search of any other entertainment, or you could suffer my fate.

Even if the seat isn't that comfortable, stay in your place. After all, how long do you have to sit there? Two and a half hours! Sometimes maybe a whole three hours! But after that you're a free person, and at home you can sit wherever you want, even in your favorite easy chair with an eiderdown. But there are ways to deal with the myriad of troubles that happen in the theatre. A prudent chap will find a way to do this.

Let's say, for example, that you're sitting next to a woman who constantly cracks monkey nuts* and throws the shells into your lap. Your trousers get covered with shells. What should you do? Make a fuss in the middle of the play? Run off to another seat? No, you must simply take a brush with you and every few minutes brush the shells off your trousers until the woman has finished eating all the monkey nuts.

Or it could be in summertime, when the watermelons are in season, and you have a seat next to a woman holding a huge, red watermelon. In the middle of the play, the woman cuts up the watermelon and, "just for a minute," lays half of the watermelon in your lap, and the second half she puts, piece by piece, into her mouth. What should you actually do? Do you take the watermelon and throw it on the floor? No! A gentleman doesn't behave like that! Just be quiet, leave the watermelon in your lap, and look at the stage. You can be sure that the woman won't leave the watermelon with you, because she hasn't finished it. The night is grand, and the play is even grander. Ah, but what if the watermelon leaks, and you find yourself in an awkward situation? I've got a solution for that as well. Take a rubber sheet or a waterproof apron with you, and as soon as she sits down, spread it over your trousers.

If you're sitting upstairs in the gallery and you see a friend of yours downstairs in the stalls, someone from the old country, and you want him to know that you're also here in the theatre, don't get up and rush downstairs. It's better to shout down, catcall, whistle, or roar, but don't move from your seat. If your *landsman* doesn't hear you, then try to throw a banana at him. (I mean the skin—eat the banana first.) If it hits someone else and not him, don't give up. Try and try again. Eventually you'll get him.

So, I've shown you how you can sit in your seat quite comfortably, and peacefully enjoy the play without having to gad about from one place to another.

---

* Monkey nuts are peanuts in their shells.

If only I had been cleverer and done this last *Shabbes*, I wouldn't have experienced this embarrassing dressing down at a "child-goes-free" performance.

I had a yen to go to a theatre matinee. At the entrance there were hordes of children: fathers and mothers with children, grandfathers and grandmothers with grandchildren, uncles and aunts with nephews and nieces, little children and grown-up "thousand-week-old" children looking for marriage partners. Amid the noisy crowd of kids there was a little girl crying and trying to rush into the theatre—she wanted to be taken to her grandmother.

"Where," the usher asked her, "is your grandmother sitting?"

"She's on the stage!"

"How can your grandmother be on the stage?"

"She sings in the chorus, she's a chorus girl!"

I took the girl into the theatre on my ticket, led her to the stage door, to her grandmother, and took my seat. Next to me sat a woman in a fur coat, under which one could see a once-white apron. She had a large, full bag on her lap, and a small lad crawled at her feet playing with a ball. Every minute the ball rolled under our seats, and the lad crawled after it, getting under our feet and getting on our nerves so much that we had no idea what was happening on the stage. The woman couldn't bear it anymore. She grabbed the boy and threw him over her knee, lifted up his shirt, and spanked him so he would have something to remember.

The actors on the stage, hearing a slap, thought it was applause, and they politely bowed while the boy started crying loudly. Nothing could placate him, not even the silent pinches he got from his mother. People started shouting, "Quiet please!"

The woman took a chunk of *challah* with jam out of her bag, and the boy stuffed it into his mouth.

"So, get that down you! And be quiet!"

The boy was quiet, relishing the jam. But less than a minute later, he was crawling around me again, and I felt something sticky. Truly, I love jam and compote and other sweet things, but not on my trousers.

I got up to move, noticing that the front rows were empty. At first the boy with the jam crawled after me, but as I moved closer to the orchestra, I saw that I'd gotten rid of him, thank God. But after only a couple of minutes' peace, there they were again, my old neighbors, the woman with the boy.

"Hey, mister," she said to me. "He'll be a good boy, just give him back the *challah* and jam!"

I looked at the woman and grinned:

"What *challah* and jam?"

"Enough playing around. Give him back his *challah* and jam!" she answered.

I got angry and exclaimed:

"Why are you having a go at me? Who's taken any *challah* and jam?"

She flew into a rage and said:

"*Feh*, shame on you. A grown man playing such a trick on a little boy."

"Leave me alone!" I pleaded. "Let me see the play."

She grabbed the boy by the chin, pointed at me, and said:

"Tell me, darling, is this the man who took your *challah* and jam?"

The boy nodded. And that was good enough for the woman, who went as red as a beetroot and shouted:

"I can tell by your face what you are!"

A cry went up in the theatre:

"Quiet, shurrup, throw her out, the windbag."

The woman pointed her finger at me and cried:

"Throw *him* out, that glutton who has stuffed my boy's *challah* and jam down his throat."

"Throw them both out!" everyone shouted.

And that's actually what happened. Less than two minutes later, we were all outside: me, the woman, and of course the little brat. Even in the street the woman carried on cursing me. I shook her off with difficulty and ran home. As I came in the door, my wife asked:

"Couldn't you find a better place to keep your *challah* and jam than on your new coat, stuck right here on your behind?" And she peeled off the whole piece of that child's *challah* and jam, which had stuck to me while I was moving seats to look for a bit of peace in the theatre.

THE LUCK OF A TROLLEYBUS

A human being is like a trolleybus. A bus hurries and scurries, and a human does the same. A bus stops, and sometimes a human being stops, too. Someone may have a brother, and a trolleybus may have a brother-bus. And just as one person can be a scoundrel and the other a righteous fool, one can be stinking rich and the other dirt poor, so it can be between two trolleybuses.

Two trolleybuses stand at the top of Stamford Hill, blood relatives with identical faces from one womb. The only difference is that one is older than the other by six numbers. Written on one of their foreheads is 647, and on the other 653. But their destinies are totally different: One is lucky and happy, the second is so hapless, you wouldn't wish its fate on anyone.

Forty days before the 647 was born, it was decreed from above: "You will spend your life with poor people, and you'll stay poor all the days of your life." And that is how it has remained. At about seven in the morning, it is already besieged by paupers, workers who stream out en masse from their homes in the Stoke Newington "blocks," in their work clothes, caps on heads, black scarves around their necks, rough trousers held up with string, and metal-toed work boots. They set out for work with their lunches tied up in their red kerchiefs.

Later, when the clock strikes ten, the "tuppenny fares" begin, and the second category of passenger turns up. There are the women of the "impoverished rich" Stamford Hill families who have saved a few pennies and are going down to the Lane to grab bargains. The Stoke Newington grocers set out on their way to the East End to get a bit of stock on credit. And the simple Stoke Newington householders travel down to try and find work in Dalston, Bethnal Green, Spitalfields Market, Wentworth Street, Leman Street, all the affluent neighborhoods.

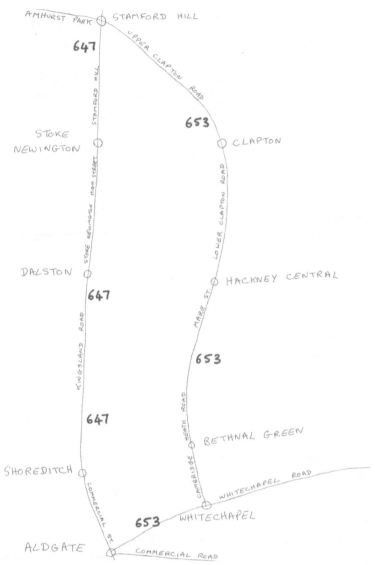

Routes of the 647 and 653 trolleybuses, late 1930s to late 1960s. (Drawing by Sarha Moore)

With all due respect to the 647, it is, as was decreed in heaven, a pauper, a beggar that has to make do with beggar fares. It does seem to take in a good amount of bus fares, but only in pauper-pence. The conductor runs around the bus more than once a day with ten shillings in his hand to change, but no one has that large a fortune. And when someone says that, thank God, he has change of ten shillings, and empties all the small change out of all his pockets, he still finds that it doesn't come to the full amount.

And it happened, that while a fully packed and cramped 647 was on its way to Stamford Hill, a man with a basket of beigels squeezed in at Commercial Street, or more accurately they squeezed him in, and his basket poked everyone in the ribs. The conductor shouted to the basket man, "Move along the bus." The basket man took another step. The more the conductor shouted, the farther the man with the basket moved on. But this was no easy task; it was truly like the parting of the Red Sea. When the bus arrived in Stamford Hill, the basket man moved forward from the back of the bus, and as the bus emptied, the conductor pointed out that he hadn't paid his fare.

"Fare?" asked the basket man, surprised. "Why do I have to pay a fare? Did I actually travel? I spent the whole time in the bus walking!"

This is the clientele of the 647.

Its brother, the 653 trolleybus, enjoys quite a different fate. Since the days of Creation, it was ordained to live among the wealthy, and to look affluent itself. It has a pedigree, it comes from "up west," from Tottenham Court Road, and on its way it travels through the old aristocratic neighborhoods of Euston Road, Camden Road, Seven Sisters Road, Amhurst Park, all distinguished streets. Just from these place names people know that this bus is not just any old trolleybus.

For that very reason it drives through these streets slowly and at a leisurely pace, the way of nobility. It drives particularly quietly and calmly in the morning in Amhurst Park, so as not to, God forbid, wake up the wealthy housewives, the ladies who don't emerge from their homes until 11 AM. It glides past Amhurst Park as if its wheels were well oiled. It doesn't begin to speed up until it gets over the border of Bethnal Green, and then, in the poor streets that lead to Whitechapel, it bowls along crazily as if it had committed goodness-knows-what kind of crime. At around six in the evening, it also runs quickly toward Amhurst Park, as it speeds along to bring the wealthy back home for dinner. In Amhurst Park people eat dinner at seven in the evening, not like the poor who eat at one in the afternoon.

The 653 has its own pedigree. It is really something. The seats are wider, softer, padded, and not worn out like on the 647. The rail and poles are coated with nickel. They are also made of nickel on the 647, but those are dull, while here they shine. Generally everything is much cleaner. The 653 is tidy, it sparkles. It seems to be a brother of the 647, but it is quite different. The 647, I am sorry to say, is a squalid, filthy, torn, and stained dung heap, while you can smell the opulence emanating from the 653.

On account of this, only respectable people associate with the 653. In the daytime you can meet an emissary from Galicia with a silk hat on his head and a leather briefcase under his arm, like a minister. He is going to the wealthy of Amhurst Park and Stamford Hill to raise money for a new *yeshiva* and at the same time to arrange a marriage for his teenaged daughter.

On the same bus as the *Galitzianer*, there is an Orthodox Lithuanian Jew with an old, greasy hard hat that he put on his head when he came to London thirty years ago. The hat has now fused with his head as if they are one. His face is like a black radish, which is not surprising, because if you eat radish with salt for thirty years on the trot, you will indeed have such a face and such a smell. He is on his way to see the Amhurst Park and Stamford Hill homeowners and offer them some real *Yiddishkayt*. He's taking with him a whole bag of religious items: pocket prayer books, *tefillin*, *mezuzahs*, *tsitses*, calendars, and books of psalms. In the meantime, he doesn't sit idly; he braids one of the *tsitses* fringes.

And there are men and women traveling with bags of wares: bed linen, women's underwear, tablecloths, hand towels, curtains, and other trifles that they are taking to the Amhurst Park and Stamford Hill ladies. The wealthy women are too lazy to go out and buy their household items. A traveling salesman or saleswoman does it for them. Furthermore, the customers don't have to pay the travelers in cash. They can pay in installments. Indeed, they'll still be paying when the Messiah comes!

You also meet older women dressed in their best, going from Whitechapel to Amhurst Park or Stamford Hill for the fresh air as if it were the seaside. Mothers come to their married children to convalesce. They travel with their crammed bundles and suitcases, just as if they really were going on holiday to the sea. Apparently the air in Amhurst Park agrees with them. One can recognize this in the flushed faces of those already on their way home with their baggage. My *landsman* Yerukhem says that the red flush is not always a sign of fresh air; it could well be that a mother-in-law has been slapped by her daughter-in-law.

As everyone knows, the idea of a rich trolleybus is pretty rich!

• • •

Two brother trolleybuses stand at the top of Stamford Hill that have one and the same aim in life—Whitechapel! And when they both arrive in Aldgate some time later, they greet each other with a *sholem aleykhem*. But their journeys to their goal are so different. One of them drags itself there with the poor, the destitute, and the urchins, and the second—with the rich, powerful, and respectable. So Yerukhem puts it: Everything must have its particular destiny, even a trolleybus.

SPRING IN
WHITECHAPEL

Spring is here! So says the Jewish calendar, and so say the poets. I went out to greet the spring. I wandered around Whitechapel for the whole day, with my head tilted back scouring the heavens for a patch of blue. I searched from Mile End Gate to Aldgate Pump for a hint of a sunbeam—but there was none.

A temperamental sky, cheerless and unsettled, covered with a grey blanket splattered with yellowish grey patches. Across its breadth hung a blue and white banner with a Yiddish caption: "Come to the Jewish National Fund bazaar in the Whitechapel Art Gallery." This banner has hung over this patch of sky for years, and it will hang and hang, just as the same grey sky will hang over our heads tomorrow and the day after.

I dropped my eyes to the ground and noticed how streams of murky water were running down the streets of Whitechapel, and I deduced from this that the ice had melted and that spring was really here. It reminded me of my *shtetl* before *Pesach*, when the snow melted and the gutters and puddles would flow rapidly, carrying chunks of dried up *cholent*, feathers, and leftover vegetables. Here too I noticed gutters clogged with fish heads, chicken innards, and other wonders. But my *landsman* Yerukhem the teacher, known as "the Philosopher," said I'd made a mistake, that these were not temporary flowing gutters, but permanent standing puddles that had become "naturalized" citizens of Whitechapel.

Spring! The festival of writers, of maidservants in love, and of cats who climb onto my roof every night and compete with the Yiddish theatre choir.

Spring! My soul becomes flooded with feelings of renewal. I want to bathe in the sun's rays, though Yerukhem advised me to wait until they build the *mikveh* for the rabbi of North Nothington.

Spring! I want to open the window of my back room to let in the spring air, except that the sash cords are broken, and the landlord, may his memory be blotted out, will not fix it.

Spring! I want to drown in light, but just out of spite, the electricity has failed.

Spring! I want to hear a new word, a fresh promise, bathed in green and washed with dew. But apart from the Friday night *Shabbes* supper in the Jewish Immigrant Shelter, I have nowhere to go.

In the manifesto of the London Jewish Mantle Makers' Union, I read that "the whole spring festival belongs to the proletariat!" I make my way to the union to see how the class-conscious workers meet *their* spring. The union is empty, dark, and dreary.

"Our members," I am told, "have become a tiny bit 'busy.' People are sweating until late in the evening, burning their eyes out by candlelight in order to grab whatever extra work they can. Please God, when the 'slack' returns, they'll come back to the union."

"And then?"

"Then they'll torment the secretary."

I bump into the organizer, who's wandering around with a dead flower in his lapel, and I ask him for a fresh word that will excite the Jewish masses. He wrinkles his forehead, thinks a while, and says:

"The work of the worker belongs to the workers themselves."

Scattered over the tables are damp, greasy dominoes, cigarette ends, and fish bones. As I stand there marveling at the spring atmosphere prevailing here, my eye alights on a sunbeam that has managed to sneak in: a long, narrow, bright stripe stretched out languidly across a double six. Good God! A sunbeam in the union and on a double six! But when I got closer, I saw that it was only a *loksh*, a poor, wretched, lonely, orphaned noodle that had slipped off a spoonful of milky *lokshen* that had been meant for the secretary's mouth. What bitter disappointment that a noodle had fooled me.

Looking for something new, I went off to the Yiddish theatre. I heard that there was a new play for spring that had the tang of earth and freshness. The spring plot of the play was this: It was night in a cemetery, and they were digging a new grave (in honor of spring!). They carried out a corpse of a young girl (to symbolize spring) and said the memorial prayer under a black wedding canopy. Suddenly in the dark night, a bright sun appeared. The stage was drenched with light (spring indeed!), and they said the mourner's *kaddish*.

I must confess that I sinned against the corpse in the theatre, and I beg her forgiveness because I didn't have the patience to wait until they'd buried her, and instead I ran out in the middle. However, I left her in the hands of good gravediggers.

From there I dropped in on the Beth Din Jewish Court, and my head started reeling with their spring problems, like *shechita* politics and the complexities of removing the hind parts of animals for kosher meat, and divorces. And I saw before me: congealed salt beef, a supervisor of kosher meat blind in one eye, a yellowing manuscript, a scribe who sniffed tobacco into his runny nose that dripped . . . Truly, the nuances of spring.

I went off to the shops to find a trace of spring but saw out-of-date cakes, stale matzah, and rotting plums. In one public house, however, I found something new. In the window, among the bottles of liquor, stood a glass vessel in the shape of a pig, and between the eyes of the pig was pinned a small printed card with the words "Kosher for Passover."

In the corner of Black Lion Yard, my eyes were drawn toward a Yiddish sign that was hanging across the width of the alley, which read: "Here you can get fresh milk straight from the cow." My spring fantasy blossomed: a green pasture with cattle freely roaming under the sun, and fresh, warm milk directly from the cow's udder.

"Where is the cow?" I asked the first person I saw walking toward me, a Jew with a bushy beard who was just coming out of the Black Lion Yard Hasidic prayer room with his *tallis* bag under his arm.

"You mean the creature?" he intoned in the sing-song voice of *gemara* study. "Go there to the spice shop."

The spice shop had all sorts of good smells that came from garlic sausage, sour gherkins, sauerkraut, kippers, herrings, petroleum, kindling smeared with tar, and other sorts of spring blooms. A red-headed man with a messy ginger beard in a ragged, quilted jacket with patched elbows was standing there, catching herring from a barrel and sorting them into milk and roe, fat and thin.

"A glass of milk from the cow?" I asked with a spring-like tone. With his right herring-briny hand, he took a glass that was green with mold, dunked it into a dirty pail, and poured it for me "straight from the cow."

Shattered from my hunt for spring, I went to a restaurant to cheer myself up, and on the table there were flowers. Flowers, flowers, flowers! The joy of my soul! Fresh roses bought a year ago at Woolworths, made of paper, a real treasure, and white and red lilies sewn out of rags. The "flowers" might even have had a fragrance had it not been for the cheesecake that was lying nearby.

I ate an ancient cutlet, washed it down with ginger beer and then went home to bed. There, under the warm featherbed, I felt for the first time that spring was here. However, the doctor who took my pulse told me that no, it was not spring, it was actually the flu.

MOSES IN LONDON

Some of these organizations and terminology are explained in the story. Here is a list for reference:

Agudas Yisroel—Ultra-Orthodox non-Zionist movement formed in Poland in 1912 with branches in London and across the world. Their desire to settle in Palestine came from a religious motivation.

Bund—The General Jewish Labour Bund in Lithuania, Poland, and Russia was a secular Jewish socialist organization founded in Vilnius in 1897. It was not a Zionist organization and promoted the idea of fighting for rights in the countries where Jews lived. Yet some of its members were also in the Poale Zion.

Central Rabbinical Congress (*Hisachdus harabonim*)—An ultra-Orthodox organization based in the United States.

"Discipline Clause"—Clause written on the back of the Zionist shekel, decreeing that the World Zionist Organization takes precedence over any other Zionist institution

Dorchester Hotel—A five-star hotel on Park Lane, one of the richest areas of London. It was often used by international Zionist leaders visiting London.

Mizrachi—Religious Zionist organization, founded in 1902 in Vilnius, which had branches across the world. The organization believed in combining Torah with *avoda* (labor; working the land).

National Fund or Keren Kayemet—Later called the Jewish National Fund; a fundraising organization to purchase land in Israel.

New Zionist Organization—Founded by Ze'ev Jabotinsky in 1935, when he left the Revisionist Zionists after an ideological clash. The group wanted independence from the World Zionist Organization.

Poale Zion—The Jewish Labor Movement was a Marxist Zionist organization of workers. The first British branch was established in 1903. Berl Locker was the general secretary of the World Union of Poale Zion. Malka Locker was a popular Yiddish poet who was married to Berl. Berl lived in London 1931–35, and they both lived in London 1938–48. The works of Moses Hess (1812–75) influenced Karl Marx and the early Zionist leaders of the Poale Zion. David Ben-Gurion was a Labor Zionist leader, head of the Jewish Agency, and later the first prime minister of the State of Israel.

Revisionist Zionists—Developed by Ze'ev Jabotinsky. They believed in the occupation of the whole Land of Israel, including Transjordan.

Shekel—The two-shilling membership fee of the World Zionist Organization. The hidden joke in the story is that the biblical Moses had instituted a half-shekel annual fee to count the population of the Children of Israel (Exodus 30:11–16).

Union of Orthodox Rabbis (*Agudas harabonim*)—Ultra-Orthodox movement established in 1902 in the United States.

United Israel Appeal (Keren Hayesod)—A fundraising charity for Jewish organizations in Palestine and later Israel.

Zionist Federation of Great Britain and Ireland—Founded in 1899 as a campaigning group for a homeland for the Jewish people.

Zionist Organization (World Zionist Organization)—Founded in 1897 at the First Zionist Congress. Its aim was to promote legal Jewish settlement in Palestine for farmers, traders, and artisans. The central office of the World Zionist Organization was at 77 Great Russell Street in Central London. Chaim Weizmann was the president of the Zionist Organization and, later, first president of the State of Israel. The poem *Hatikvah* (The Hope) was the anthem of the Zionist movement at the First Zionist Congress in 1897, and later became the national anthem of the State of Israel.

Some time in the distant future in one of our archives, this manuscript will be discovered.

After Moses led the Jews out of Egypt and sent them across into the Land of Israel, he realized that he hadn't provided himself with an immigration certificate and was, sadly, forced to remain outside the Holy Land. Moses discovered, however, that there was a Zionist organization in London with another leader, not named Moses but Chaim, and that they gave out certificates to the Land of Israel. Moses set out to visit them.

One fine day, a respectable man with a venerable grey beard, a dignified appearance, and a face glowing with light stood in the corridor of 77 Great Russell Street and asked for the general secretary. The girl at the reception desk asked him if he had an appointment. Moses replied that he did not have an appointment, but he had especially traveled here from far away on an important matter. The receptionist telephoned the general secretary's office, which called back to say that this Mr. Moses must explain what sort of business he had come about.

Moses told the receptionist that he was not a man of business and, indeed, was not coming on business, but he was a religious Jew and a leader of the Jewish people, and he needed an immigration certificate. The general secretary telephoned back to say that Mr. Moses needed to go to the immigration department. And so he did.

The immigration official looked him up and down and asked if he had about five hundred pounds, because then he would be able to go to the Land of Israel as a capitalist. Moses replied that, although he was a leader of the Jewish people, he had not been able to save five hundred pounds. Indeed, he was not like the leaders of today, and would not steal so much as a donkey from anyone.

"Do you have a trade?" the immigration official asked.

"The only trade I have," answered Moses, "is teaching Torah."

The immigration official got impatient: "We don't need teachers of religion in the Land of Israel, we need specialists. Can you plane a plank of wood? Can you break stones?"

Hearing the words "break stones" struck a chord with Moses, and he answered:

"I most certainly can break stones; once I hit a stone to get water from it."

"If that's the case," said the immigration official, "you can break stones in the Land of Israel to make roads. But it's not such a quick process. First, you will need to become a pioneer and do a few years' training. But just one moment, do you know Hebrew? And how old are you? Because if you're over thirty-five you can't get a pioneer certificate."

"Hebrew . . . ," Moses answered. "I do know a little Hebrew, but unfortunately, it's a while since I saw thirty-five."

"Well in that case," the immigration official quickly dismissed him, "you'll have to become a capitalist, or you won't get into the Land of Israel."

But Moses didn't want to become a capitalist. He didn't even know how to go about getting the right "stuff" to make himself into a capitalist. So he went to the left-wing Poale Zion, which doesn't approve of capitalism, thinking that they would help him get a certificate. In general Moses felt closer to the Poale Zion ideology, because he had been the leader of the Children of Israel and had given the Jews many social reforms: the law of leaving the land fallow every seventh year, and the law of nationalizing the land and freeing slaves every fifty years. Weren't these the essential principles of socialism?

The chairman of the London Poale Zion party simply asked him three questions. First, can he sing the *Bund* anthem, *Di Shvue*? Second, does he know Berl Locker? Third, has he read Malka Locker's poetry? When Moses answered no to all these questions, the chairman of the Poale Zion reprimanded him harshly:

"Bourgeois characters like you can't go to the Land of Israel. You darken the Poale Zion's class struggle. Capitalists like you should stay in exile."

Moses was very confused after this rebuke. One Zionist organization told him he had to become a capitalist to go to Israel, and the other one told him that he was *already* a capitalist and therefore could *not* go to Israel.

So Moses went off to find the Orthodox Mizrachi Zionists. The Mizrachi believe in the principles of Torah study combined with labor, so surely they would be delighted with him and would immediately give him a certificate for the Land of Israel. Moses looked for the Mizrachi organization in London for three days, but he could not find any Torah study or anyone laboring. Finally he got hold of the chairman of the Mizrachi, who didn't ask him three questions—just one.

"What do you think of my beard?"

Moses wanted to answer him with a phrase from the rabbinic commentaries: "Don't look at the beard but what's inside it." But realizing that you could not make an immigration certificate out of a beard, Moses went off angrily, disillusioned with the old Zionist organization.

So he went to look for a certificate at the New Zionist Organization, but they really tore a strip off him:

"Oh, are you *that* Moses," everyone yelled at him. "The infamous Moses who introduced that damned shekel fee and the Discipline Clause? Are you that very same Moses with the Marxist teachings that the left-wing have taken up? Go to Ben-Gurion. You are obviously a friend of his."

Bitter and offended, Moses went off to the ultra-Orthodox Agudas Yisroel. He imagined that the Aguda also had certificates for the Land of Israel. The Aguda was like his family, his intimate friends. They were the real guardians of his Torah. The leader of the London Aguda asked him a tricky Talmudic question.

"Which organization is more important: the Union of Orthodox Rabbis or the Central Rabbinical Congress?"

When Moses had no idea what to answer, the leader of the Aguda angrily exclaimed:

"Well, I can see that you're not Moses, because Moses would know that the Union of Orthodox Rabbis is more important than the Central Rabbinical Congress." And again, no certificate.

So Moses trudged off to the Central Rabbinical Congress. They consider themselves to be the real rabbis. The president asked him if he knew what *yoyvl* was.

"Of course," Moses replied excitedly, "the *yoyvl* is the fiftieth year, the jubilee year! It's my achievement, I set it up!"

"So," the president declared, "we would have to ask our secretary to call a meeting together, but we have a meeting only once in a *yoyvl*, and because he has recently called a meeting, you will have to wait until the next . . . *yoyvl*! In the meantime you can join us here and take a nap, grab forty winks."

So Moses dragged himself from one organization to the next, rebuffed at every turn, until he became ill from the great sorrow and heartache and ended up in the London Jewish Hospital. And Moses died.

As soon as it was known that Moses had died, the whole of London was upset, and every organization claimed him as their own.

"Our Moses," shouted the Zionist Federation, "who, for forty years in the desert, sang *Hatikvah* and devoted his life to the United Israel Appeal!"

"Our Moses," shouted the Poale Zion party, "who, even in Egypt, sang the *Bundist* anthem *Di Shvue* and fought for the Poale Zion's ideology of freedom."

"Our Moses," shouted the Mizrachi, "who gave us a special budget for the Zionist organizations to set up kosher kitchens in the Land of Israel."

"Our Moses," yelled the revisionists, "who introduced the biblical leadership structure for judges, captains, generals, and field marshals."

"Our Moses," intoned the Aguda, piously swaying, "who gave us our Torah, our bread."

And with the most beautiful eulogies and the warmest obituary notices that London is famous for, Moses was buried. "It was a magnificent funeral," wrote the

London Jewish newspapers. "Around one hundred cars followed the coffin." The National Fund decided to plant a "Moses Forest" in the Land of Israel, and the collection campaign for the Moses Forest started soon after the funeral, with a reception at the Dorchester Hotel. And soon after that, all other parties, organizations, and Polish federations were shaking their charity boxes for the causes close to Moses' heart: his Torah, his widow, his orphaned children, and his children's children. And the rattling of these charity boxes continues until this day.

TWO STREETS, TWO DESTINIES

This note can be read in conjunction with the map on page 16. From Gardiner's Corner in Aldgate, if you head east, you are walking along one of the two main arteries of the Jewish East End, Whitechapel Road. If, after a few yards, you turn diagonally right, it takes you along Commercial Road. This story describes the Yiddish culture of Whitechapel Road: kosher restaurants, such as Gradel's Restaurant at number 2–4 and the Jewish Communal Restaurant at number 214; the Whitechapel Library at 77–80, whose Jewish reading room had the largest collection of Yiddish books in the country, and the Whitechapel Art Gallery next door at 80–82, which exhibited Jewish artists such as Isaac Rosenberg in 1937 and Mark Gertler in 1949; the editorial offices of *Di tsayt* at number 325; the London hospital opposite Whitechapel Underground station, and the London Jewish Hospital farther along the road in Stepney Green, where it becomes Mile End Road; the Pavilion Theatre at number 191–93; the underground stations of Aldgate, Aldgate East, and, Whitechapel. The famous Petticoat Lane (the Lane) Market is tucked away behind Whitechapel Road; and the Makhzike Hadas synagogue was off Whitechapel Road on the corner of Brick Lane and Hanbury Street.

The busy Hessel Street Market was on a small street off Commercial Road, and directly opposite was the Grand Palais Theatre. The Temple of Art Yiddish Theatre farther along at 226 Commercial Road was an attempt to provide a higher quality theatre experience. It opened in 1912 but lasted only a few months, being unaffordable to East End workers due to the lack of a gallery with cheaper seats. Adler Hall, located nearer Aldgate, on Adler Street, just off Commercial Road, operated as an arts theatre during the 1940s.[1]

To my mind, nothing can be dearer or closer than two children of the same mother. Nevertheless, it sometimes happens that one is a redhead, the other has black hair; one is successful, and the other not. And so it is with two streets, Whitechapel Road and Commercial Road. They are like two brothers, two little boys who meet at Gardiner's corner, hold hands, and run along together. However, in fact, they are two different islands with two different destinies. Whitechapel Road is the lucky one, and Commercial Road the luckless one.

Whitechapel Road is the *nouveau riche* woman; the rich aunt dripping with diamonds, who burns electricity all day long.

"Let it burn!" she says. "What, can't I afford it?"

And Commercial Road is the poor relation who sits all day in her miserable little shop, straining her eyes for a customer.

Whitechapel Road lives very comfortably and lacks nothing. The pavements host the nicest cinemas, the best Jewish restaurants, the art gallery, the library with its Jewish reading room, the editorial offices of *Di tsayt*, the hospital, the underground station, and the famous "Petticoat Lane." And what does Commercial Road have apart from Hessel Street Market, which reminds one of Warsaw's shabby Smotshe Street? There is nothing else of note.

The merchants on Whitechapel Road removed the old windowpanes from their shops long ago and installed large, modern glass shop fronts. And they have moved out from the upper floors, where they lived for years, and made them into stockrooms or workshops. When it's time to shut up shop, the Whitechapel Road traders lower the shutters and go home, some in their cars and some with their season tickets to Kilburn, Hampstead, Golders Green, and even to the seaside. But when the shopkeepers from Commercial Road lock up their little shops with iron bolts, they clamber upstairs into their "hovels," and amid the commotion of a half-dozen precious offspring, they count up the day's takings.

On Whitechapel Road, so the story goes, there once were grocery and lemonade shops. "Right over here," and they point with their finger, "was a sweet shop with a small, dirty window that was speckled with flies. Today it is a first-class West End style boutique."

On Commercial Road you can still find little grocery shops where you can buy on a tab and wait until the wages come in at the end of the week to pay something on account or to settle in full. When the lovely summer weather comes round, these same grocery shops open a small window, put a little table outside with a soda fountain, and sell cold drinks, while small children buy a farthing-worth of sweets. The real business! And on the hot, muggy summer nights, the men of Commercial Road throw off their coats and waistcoats and sweaty collars and sit outside on benches on the street with the missus and take the air. It reminds you of your *shtetl* in the old country.

In the past Whitechapel Road also did this, but now the Whitechapel Road-ers take the air far away in Edgware. The Whitechapel Roaders see themselves as *city* people, civilized and modern, while the Commercial Roaders are small-town people, old-fashioned and backward.

And the Whitechapel Roaders say that the Commercial Roaders know this. They say that when Commercial Roaders need to come over to Whitechapel Road, they get up early in the morning, shave, and put on their *Shabbes* clothes because they know that in Whitechapel they can't appear in Commercial Road garb.

When they put on Yiddish plays in the Grand Palais or Adler Hall, the Com-mercial Roaders feel at home. They go to their theatre without a collar, with an open shirt—among their own people! And they take a few pounds of welshnuts, which they crack with their shoes just at the most dramatic moments. But when those same Commercial Roaders come to the Pavilion Theatre, they come dressed up in their best clothes, and they don't crack welshnuts but . . . monkey nuts, that national theatre food.* The Commercial Roader knows how to behave in Whi-techapel Road.

Therefore, when a Commercial Roader gets engaged to a Whitechapel Roader, it causes a big stir. People are jealous of the Commercial Roader:

"*Ay ay ay*, she's marrying a Whitechapel Roader. It must have cost a lot of money! Do you think they would have got him for free?"

Whitechapel Road may be lucky, but while Commercial Road has less luck, it has more *yiddishkayt*, certainly more religious observance. Commercial Road is packed with synagogues and small prayer rooms. When the Commercial Roaders pray or study Torah, there is a buzz in all seven heavens.

"We have made synagogues out of church buildings," say the Commercial Roaders with pride. "And we have totally driven out the missionaries. One final missionary left over from the ten plagues who gave sermons every week on the

---

* Welshnuts are walnuts in their shells. Monkey nuts are peanuts in their shells.

corner of Sidney Street was still wandering about here. We sent him packing, too. No missionaries around us! But they are still there lurking about in Whitechapel Road, with their sermons to the Jews." When the Whitechapel Roaders hear this, they retort:

"First, we have just one synagogue, the Makhzike Hadas, which outweighs all of your synagogues. And second, apart from driving out the missionaries, you have not created anything." The Commercial Roaders argue back:

"And we also have the Temple of Art Yiddish Theatre that was built, though not by us, on Commercial Road." The Whitechapel Roaders answer:

"And a real mess you made of the temple!"

And so they bicker and come to blows. Poor old Commercial Road! It has no luck. If I could, I would go to the eighteen righteous Jews in London. I would give them each a donation, so that they, the good Jews, could plead to God that Commercial Road should be developed and smartened up, and its luck should take a turn for the better, so that it would have the same prestige as Whitechapel Road.

Katie Brown

Katie Brown, c. 1920. (Courtesy of Geoffrey Shisler, private collection)

Brown's two book covers. Right: *Lakht oyb ir vilt* (Laugh If You Want To, 1947); left: *Alts in eynem!* (Everything Together! 1951). (Photograph by the author)

BIOGRAPHY

> With conscious perception and tragicomic situations, Katie's sketches, one after the other, tell of a type of life that is both known and not known. On one hand, it makes us want to turn away from it, and on the other, it gives us the feeling that it is ours, with all the poverty and sense of home that exists in this big world-city of London.
>
> Alegoryer, *Loshn un lebn*, 1947[1]

Katie Brown, the Yiddish "best seller" of Whitechapel, was born Gitl Bakon, into a traditional Orthodox family in Ulanov, Western Galicia (today, Ulanów, Poland), on 6 November 1889.[2] The youngest of five children, she received a religious and elementary school education until the age of twelve, when the family emigrated and settled in London. She worked in a tailor's workshop and joined the Workers' Circle, where she met Shlomo Brown, a cabinetmaker and a milkman who was the minutes secretary of the Workers' Circle Branch 1. When Katie was sixteen, they married, and Katie became the secretary of the Women's Section of

Branch 3. Katie described the Workers' Circle as such a close community organization that activists felt like family, and the annual conferences were an antidote to the struggle for daily living, providing a moment of ecstasy and excitement in a drab, painful world.[3]

By 1922 Brown had given up full-time tailoring to become a professional writer. She had five children under the age of fourteen. The Browns followed the Jewish custom of naming children after family members who had died. The oldest son, Yisroel (Izzy), was named after Katie's great-grandfather Yisroel Hillel Bakon. Hersh (Harry) was named after Katie's grandfather Hersh Leib Bakon. Sarah (Sadie) was named for Shlomo's mother, Sylvia (Sore), and their youngest son, Menashe (Moss), was named after Katie's father.

WRITING ABOUT WOMEN

Using the pseudonym *A poshete yidene* (An ordinary Jewish woman), Brown wrote the humorous advice column *In froyen kenigraykh* (In the Women's Kingdom) for the Yiddish weekly newspaper *Der familyen fraynd* (The Family Friend).[4] In her column, which was subtitled "Articles about women, the home, and family life," she wrote both the letters and the answers. She penned long, rambling letters from

Brown's husband, Shlomo, and daughter Sadie, c. 1930. (Courtesy of the Mazower private collection)

fictional readers with opinions and questions. Some of the letters are strident and uncompromising around relationship issues and gender roles, and some, written as men, display chauvinist or paternalist views. The letters often used cheeky and slapstick humor while revealing real problems that affected women. Brown's answers were more direct and sometimes conciliatory. Despite their tongue-in-cheek quality, the letters and responses raised a wide range of issues and displayed a spectrum of political and social positions about women, childrearing, the position of women in society, and marital relationships.[5] Brown's column was popular. When she took leave for a month to do some tailoring work and earn the living she could not make from writing alone, the editor told readers not to worry, because "our beloved *poshete yidene* would be returning soon."[6]

In 1926 *Der familyen fraynd* stopped publishing. Between 1930 and 1931, Brown edited the weekly page *Di froy un di familye* (The Woman and the Family) for *Di post*, which included long articles and short pieces on women in England and sexual politics. It was mostly written by Brown and included a regular poem, which she wrote under the name *Gitl bas menashe* (Gitl, daughter of Menashe).[7]

THE YIDDISH THEATRE AND CELEBRITY STATUS

During the thirties Katie and her husband, Shlomo, were both involved with the Yiddish theatre. Katie acted and wrote a number of full-length and one-act plays, some of which were produced in the professional Yiddish theatre and others performed by the Workers' Circle drama group. The play *Tserisene neshomes* (Torn Souls) was performed in the Pavilion Theatre in July 1920; her one-act play *Di antoyshung* (The Disappointment) was performed in the Workers' Circle in 1932; and the one-act *Bankrot* (Bankrupt) was published in her collection *Lakht oyb ir vilt* (Laugh If You Want To).[8] Brown also wrote original theatre songs and Yiddish versions of popular English songs. Sadly, none of the song lyrics survive.

Brown wrote occasional articles about the theatre. In a letter to *Di post* in 1934, she lamented the closing of the Pavilion Theatre, which had been a Yiddish theatre "synagogue," and she feared that the East End would be left with only poor quality popular Yiddish theatre from amateur actors.[9] Brown had an open home at 26 Chicksand Street, just off Brick Lane, in the heart of the Jewish East End. It became a magnet for writers, actors, and her many friends, who came to sing theatre songs and talk about the Yiddish theatre.[10]

The Woman and the Family page disappeared as a regular slot after 1931, but Brown's presence in *Di post* continued on a weekly basis with her published stories, sketches, and feuilletons. After *Di post* folded in 1935, she began editing the *Arbeter ring* journal of the Workers' Circle.

Brown's popularity gave her a local celebrity status. She was a familiar figure in Whitechapel. As she walked through the streets, people in the community pointed her out to their friends, telling them that she was *their* writer, who lived among them and wrote about them.[11] One reviewer described Brown's writing as:

> grabbing the comedy of daily life and happenings and transmitting them to the reader with a light touch. . . . She doesn't exaggerate. She doesn't make an effort to tickle you. She tells it simply, naturally, without a flowery word, just like a person would have told you, writing just what happens among poor people, annoying people, writers, actors, and community leaders.[12]

PUBLISHING THROUGH GRIEF AND TRAGEDY

During the forties, Brown was surrounded by death. Her brother Abraham died in 1940, her husband, Shlomo, in April 1941, her friend and comrade Baruch Weinberg, president of the Workers' Circle and editor of *Der familyen fraynd*, in October 1941, and her brother Harris in 1943. In an article written just after Weinberg's death, Brown cries: "One after another, one after another, they are going away from us and leaving wound after wound, pain after pain."[13] In 1943, with three sons in the British army, and the increasingly terrible news from Europe, Brown wrote a short, personal article titled "My Address Book." She describes her address book as a "souvenir" of comrades, friends, people from the old country, and members of the Workers' Circle. Each address brings her warm and homely memories of those people in prewar times, and she yearns for them. But they are gone:

> For each address only ruins now remain, broken, destroyed houses, families torn apart, every memory is of downfall and annihilation. The addresses are now no more than tombstones, cold, dead monuments of those who once existed and who will never return to the new world. And it gives me the strong impulse to destroy the address book and all its contents, which has already, in any case, outlived its life and is now worthless.[14]

Brown and her youngest son, Moss (Menashe), 1945. (Courtesy of the Mazower private collection)

The army addresses of her children stop her from doing so. However, her despair at the end of the article asserts: "Reality is strong and powerful and destroys all fantasies and dreams." Brown's grief at losing Shlomo pushed her into a depression from which she never completely surfaced. She took over his work at the Workers' Circle, but "she became very embittered, and her bitterness lost her many good friends."[15]

For the next few years, Brown wrote very little, although she still attended meetings with groups of writers, including the circle around Morris Myer and Avrom Nokhem Stencl's literary Sabbath Afternoons. Brown had not previously written for *Di tsayt*, where the regular column dedicated to humorous sketches was shared between Kaizer and *Der eygener* (Leon Creditor). However, after Morris Myer's death in 1944, Myer's son Harry, who was a close friend of Brown, took over the editorship of *Di tsayt*. Harry Myer did not have the depth of Yiddish culture of his father, Morris, and although many journalists stayed with *Di tsayt*, Myer needed to increase readership during what was going to be an inevitable slump. Myer offered Brown a regular contract, and she reworked around sixty of her stories that had appeared during the thirties in *Di post*; they now reappeared in their new form in *Di tsayt*. Brown's stories were sometimes considerably altered to update references and contexts from the thirties to the post-war forties. Brown and Kaizer shared the humor column from 1944 until 1950, when *Di tsayt* ceased publication.

In 1947, Harry Myer brought together a group drawn from Brown's community of writers to raise money to publish some of her stories from *Di tsayt* in book form.[16] The book, *Lakht oyb ir vilt*, came out six months later, with the advertisement announcing: "Laughing is healthy, and if you want to laugh and be healthy, buy this popular humorous book."[17] Although every reviewer found it necessary to remind the reader that Katie Brown had a female sensibility, was not writing "high literature," was not skilled in artistic techniques, and used simple words, the reviews were very favorable, and the book sold more copies than any other book published by a London Yiddish writer of the time.[18] Alegoryer (S. Palme), in his review in *Loshn un lebn*, described how Brown's characters disarmed both her readers and her critics:

> We have often read Katie's sketches that make us feel embarrassed because it seems as if we are seeing a known figure or type of person. And it also seems like you are seeing something that has a direct connection to yourself, and you therefore feel like you have accidentally stumbled upon a mirror and seen your own comic, distorted nose. And it annoys you, and you smile at the foolishness and laugh with everyone.[19]

Brown's second book, *Alts in eynem!* (Everything Together!), appeared in 1951, and in 1953 her novel, *Unter zelbn dakh* (Under the Same Roof), was serialized in *Di idishe shtime* (Jewish Voice).[20]

In the 1950s Brown struggled with her health, and when her oldest son, Yisroel, died in 1953, she was overcome with grief and had no strength to recover. Her penultimate story for *Loshn un lebn* was called "Es lakht zikh nisht mer" (There's Nothing More to Laugh About). The main character is a man full of joy and cheer who enlivened the lives of those who knew him and cheered up those who came to him depressed. Yet he became worn down by life's hardships and lost his joy in living. People's attempts to cheer him up were fruitless, and eventually

Brown, early 1950s. (Courtesy of Geoffrey Shisler, private collection)

he cried: "No, no, leave me alone. I can't have any more fun. I will not forget my troubles. They accompany me wherever I am and wherever I go."[21]

Little over a year later, after a week in the London Hospital, Whitechapel, Brown died.[22] She had not made a fuss about being ill, and many of her writer friends, including Avrom Nokhem Stencl, did not know of her death until after the funeral. In his obituary in *Loshn un lebn*, Stencl praised her:

> Everyone ran away from Whitechapel. She, the one-and-only Katie Brown, like a modest biblical woman, epitomized the verse "I am sitting amongst my people." . . . And she, the wise home-grown provider, concocted with a handful of grain, two potatoes, a sprig of parsley, and a sharp onion, a meal, tasty and steaming.[23]

A FOREWORD

This is Katie Brown's foreword to the book Lakht oyb ir vilt (Laugh If You Want To). It mentions the names of nine of her writer colleagues and friends who were all part of the committee that helped publish the book. Seven of the writers will appear in the final chapter of this book, where you can find biographies and more detail about their work.

- Harry Myer was the editor of Di tsayt from 1945, after the death of his father, Morris Myer. He edited and wrote articles and reviews for the paper.
- A. M. Fuchs was an established international Yiddish writer of essays and prose. He was the brother of Lisky.
- Moshe Oved was the president of the Friends of Yiddish Language. He was a poet, writer, and jeweler, and owned a jewelry shop in central London. He often financially supported other Yiddish writers and arts organizations.
- S. Palme (Bernard Savinski) was a poet who wrote prose under the name "Alegoryer"; he also authored a play for children.
- Joseph Hillel Lewy was a poet.
- A. N. (Avrom Nokhem) Stencl was known as the Bard of Whitechapel. He established and chaired the literary Sabbath Afternoons that became the Friends of Yiddish Language, and he edited the Loshn un lebn literary journal.
- Ben A. Sochachewsky was a poet, author, and journalist.
- Morris Katz was a journalist and playwright.
- Y. (Joseph) Tiger was a journalist who came to London in 1940.

Usually, when a professional writer publishes a work, they start with a foreword, where they introduce themselves: who they are, where they come from, how and why they came to write, how they became famous, and what the inspiration was for the work that will now benefit the world and their many readers (and this is not because the reader wants to know but because the writer wants to say it). And, as usual in such a case, imagination would take over, dragging fantasy to the highest heights, almost reaching the heavens. Later, in the postscript, the writer would come down to earth and become flesh and blood, like other earthly humans.

Unfortunately, I'm not a fantasist, and I'm not going to go about it that way. I don't need to introduce myself to you because you all know me. And if anyone out there doesn't know me personally, you know me from my sketches, from the characters I present to you and experience together with you, because I am also a part of your family and I feel your hardships and joys.

So, as you see, I haven't got anything to say in my foreword . . . but I also don't want to be totally silent, given such a promising opportunity. Also, my printer can't wait for my foreword any longer, because without being paid, he can't start printing the book.

I can see that he's right, and it has to be taken into consideration because, in spite of the fact that he's a printer, he's also a person, and a good one at that . . . So I've decided not to keep him waiting any longer. I invited all my writer friends over for a glass of tea to have a chat with them about my foreword, and leave any financial issues to my committee, which has raised the money to publish my book. All my friends came at the appointed time to mull over the important question of the book's foreword.

The first word came from my friend and editor, Harry Myer. His opinion and advice was not to write a foreword, for two reasons. First, it's not so important how we introduce ourselves. Second, if you have a foreword, then there has to be an afterword, which requires more paper, and paper is very expensive these days. You have to take that fact into account. In times like these, publishing a book costs a considerable sum, and you need to be seen to economize. He also considered a foreword completely unnecessary, because the author sometimes writes complete nonsense about themselves . . .

I saw that he was completely right. He's a clever and experienced person, and wants me to save money. He's a real friend.

But my friend A. M. Fuchs says that it *is* worthwhile to write a foreword, even if it costs more, because where does a writer have an opportunity to say whatever they want if not in the foreword of their own book? No one can advise an author on what to write in it because the foreword belongs to them, and with that sort of opportunity, one should write from the heart and let the reader or listener hear what they have to say. It's about time that what we say gets heard out there in public, rather than just talking about it among ourselves . . .

My friend Moshe Oved is of the same opinion, that I should write a foreword because every printed word in Yiddish is of great significance. One must take *that* into account and write even more, because in these dreadful times, when the Yiddish language is boycotted, assimilated, and substituted into foreign languages, we cannot engage with it lightly; the opposite: we must use it more. And if we don't, we're the enemies of the Yiddish language and not the friends . . . and with regard to the expenditure, don't worry, just leave it to him . . .

My friend S. Palme said that he is of Harry Myer's opinion that we have to economize on paper. And also, a second thing is that it will give someone else an opportunity, because he knows a writer who also wants to publish a work (and why not indeed). He has it all prepared, but the printer has said that there's a great shortage of paper, and he'll have to wait until other writers stop printing. He also admits that he's generally not into forewords because he knows from experience that the reader won't understand them. However, if it was an introduction, a preface, or a prologue, he would approve of it, because that's something completely different, especially if you can do it successfully in rhyme, and if it works well, then your readership will see that you don't only write prose but can write poetry too. And he assured me that even though he is a poet, he wouldn't be jealous of me.

Joseph Hillel Lewy, who is generally silent, said that he didn't have anything to say. He doesn't like meddling in yes-and-no debates. He doesn't like polemicists and doesn't want to be drawn into an uncomfortable situation. He doesn't want to make any enemies, because his motto is to live with everyone in peace. So he won't express any opinion and will leave that to my other friends.

The poet A. N. Stencl, who had deeply considered this important problem, agrees with having a foreword and even with an afterword on condition, speaking from his own experience, that it is written in a Yiddish that is understandable to the reader. And if I don't take his advice, I can't expect him to produce the traditional glass of tea in honor of me and my book *Lakht oyb ir vilt.*

Ben A. Sochachewsky then joined the discussion, and is of the opinion that a foreword is important not only in a book but even in a report, because it may be that the reader gets more enjoyment from the foreword than from the afterword. He said he was convinced that many regular readers read only the first chapter and leave the rest of the book or newspaper until they have more time and patience.

Morris Katz is thoroughly in agreement with Sochachewsky. He says that he has even written a foreword in his own plays in the form of a prologue, and he is sure that this has helped him with the great success he has had with his dramas.

Y. Tiger, who has the last word, is of the opinion that you have to have mercy on your readers because it's enough of an effort to read the book itself, and not to torment them with a foreword and afterword. It can have a bad effect on readers and make people stop buying Yiddish books, which would be terrible for writers who want to publish their works. And if writers don't want to be forced to beg readers to buy their book, they shouldn't write a foreword that readers don't want to read. And so, because there were different opinions among the writers who were gathered here, he proposed that we take it to a vote.

I didn't like that proposition, because I was sure that whichever vote would *not* be adopted would make the opposition view feel resentful, because everyone knows that their own opinion is right . . . and they do all have my welfare in mind. So I've decided not to write any foreword, and I hope that my numerous readers will derive pleasure in my postscript. And now, read on . . .

JEWISH READERS!

This story was published in *Di tsayt* in 1950 and was singled out in a review of the *Alts in eynem!* collection as "funnier than anything else in the book."[1] It was based on an earlier version published in *Di post* in 1934. In the 1934 version, the cheeky man badgering the man with the newspaper for his opinions on the news, asks:

"'What do you think will happen in the end with Hitler? How long do you think that evil man will be in power?' He pointed to Hitler's photograph in the paper. 'I'm telling you, it's an outrage that a Jewish paper publishes that *treyf* [unclean] head. What do you think?'"[2]

It makes a stark contrast to this later version, which mentions Korea, Belgium, and India—news without a Jewish angle.

Newspapers are read by civilized people across the world. For some, reading a newspaper is a daily routine, like any other regular, everyday activity.

Let's take, for example, the English. Every morning the trains, trams, and buses are packed with workers, each one holding their own paper, engrossed in reading it with interest. Whether they're reading sports, politics, current affairs, or theatre, readers sit quietly, undisturbed by anyone, so they can concentrate on the articles they are reading.

The Jewish reader, however, is different. For example, a Jew was walking slowly along the street, reading a paper he'd just bought, when a second Jew interrupted him and asked:

"Is there any news in today's paper?"

"There is," the first answered and kept walking.

"What is it then? Could you possibly describe . . . please tell me, I'm curious to know," the eager man kept asking as he followed him.

"I haven't got the time, I've got to go to work," the first one said, trying to get away.

"Oh, just let me have a quick look," said the other, and whipped the paper out of the first man's hands.

The man who had bought the paper was left standing aghast at the other's audacity and *chutzpah*, as the other bombarded him with questions:

"How do you think the war in Korea will end? Will it be soon or not? What do you think, mister, tell me, I'm curious to know. And what will happen with the atom bombs, will they be used or not? And what do you think of the saga with the Belgian King Leopold, may God have mercy on him, poor thing, what do you say?"

"Of course I feel sorry for him," replied the first man, rather overwhelmed, and he stretched out his hand to retrieve his paper. But the other wouldn't hear any of it. He turned the page quickly and kept asking:

"And what do you think about Mr. Nehru's attempt at peace? Now there's a person with a good heart, I wish him health and strength to avoid a war. And what do you think of the Jewish woman who gave birth to four Siamese twins? I wouldn't wish it on any Jewish mother . . . What? You don't believe it? I'm telling you, it's true because in my home *shtetl* the same thing happened, and when they grew up, they remained so loyal to each other that they didn't want to part, and so were forever together . . . Even our rabbi who was world-famous for performing miracles couldn't do anything in this case."

"Give me the paper, mister, and let me go. I haven't got time to hear what happened to you in your *shtetl*."

"No, I won't let you go, you've got to hear me out, just for a minute." And just to be certain of his listener, the second man slipped the newspaper under his arm and held the other man by the lapel.

"You see, at home in the old country," he continued, "this old regional police superintendent got married to a beautiful young girl. I tell you, she was gorgeous. All was going smoothly until the night of the wedding, when demons kidnapped the bride, and the old geezer was left standing like a fool in the marketplace . . ."

"I've already heard that story, my dear chap. Stop boring me, give me my paper, and let me go."

"Oh, all right, I can see that you haven't got time now, so I won't keep you any longer. I'll just have one more look and no more. It's just that I want to ask you something: Do you like the Yiddish theatre?"

"I don't know, I haven't seen it. Mister, will you leave me alone or not?"

"Oh, please be so good as to read that article for me," he implored, pointing to a theatre review. "I want to know if it's worth going to or not. I think
you must be an expert, so I want to know your opinion. I'd read it on my own
and not bother you because you need to get away, but I haven't got my glasses
with me, so I must trouble you, that's all, and then you can go off wherever
you need to."

"If you're so interested in knowing about everything written here, why
don't you buy a paper yourself?"

"What do you mean, I should buy one? My children buy two or three English
papers every day. I myself buy *The Star* so I can get a tip on the horses. Are you
suggesting I buy a Yiddish paper as well? Who do you think I am? Rothschild?
And secondly, I don't need to buy this paper, because I've snatched a look at yours
just now. I know everything from your paper, and it hasn't cost me a penny."

"In that case, my dear chap, you won't get another peek at mine," he answered
angrily, tore the paper out of the other's hands, and quickly ran away.

I witnessed a similar situation on a bus in Whitechapel. A woman was sitting there
reading a Yiddish paper, and a second woman, sitting next to her, glanced into it.
The first woman got annoyed at the cheek of someone else sticking her nose in her
newspaper and, in protest, quickly turned the page.

"Be so good as to let me finish that chapter of the serial," the second woman
asked. "I'm reading it with one of my neighbors. What I mean is, she buys it, and
I read it. But right now she's away on holiday and I'm in the middle of the serial
and I'm missing today's episode where the man comes in and catches his wife with
a lover . . . and I really want to know what's going to happen between them, you
know what I mean?"

The woman with the paper threw her a scornful look, folded up the paper,
and put it into her pocket.

"What are you frightened of? You think I'll bite off a bit of your paper? Ugh,
what a horrible person you are, you should be ashamed of yourself, for such a
trifle . . ."

"Missus, if you really want to know what happened between the woman and
her lover, be so good as to buy your own paper and don't look at someone else's,"
the first woman angrily retorted and moved away from her.

"Why would I buy a paper? Do you think everyone is as nasty as you? I'll just find someone who *will* lend me their paper, not like you . . . And you don't need to tell me what I have to do, it's none of your bloody business . . . It's really no wonder that there's so much anti-Semitism in the world," the woman finished angrily, and stood up to get off the bus.

Oy, Jewish readers!

KRISMES PREZENTS

Bazaars, a regular feature of the Jewish East End community calendar, were a way of raising money for different causes. In the thirties, when a version of this story first appeared, there were many bazaars advertised in the Yiddish press. The annual Workers' Circle bazaar supported the building of a convalescence home. The National Fund bazaar at the Whitechapel Gallery raised money for buying land in Palestine for Jewish settlement. A Jewish Community Council bazaar in 1937 raised funds to help the fight against fascism and anti-Semitism. They were significant events, running from one to four weeks, every evening except Friday, and Sunday during the day. They took months of planning and organizing, and the editors of the Yiddish press seemed to think that their readership would be interested in all sorts of details: appeals for help with planning, reports of committee meetings, and reports on the progress of stalls from businesses, synagogues, and societies. Bazaars of different political persuasions often ran at the same time, leading to competitive advertising in the Yiddish press.[1]

I don't know what it's like in other Jewish homes, but in ours I find it so stressful every year when the holy festival of *krismes* comes round. My children simply drive me crazy, constantly making plans for how to celebrate it.

First, they give me an ultimatum: that I have to buy each of them a *krismes prezent* if I don't want the festival to be ruined, because without *prezents*, *krismes* isn't *krismes*. And second, we have to celebrate by having a party with a green tree and red lights, just like decent, respectable Jewish families do.

While I don't like the idea of celebrating *krismes*—it was never done in my parents' home or anywhere in my family—I never say anything as long as they celebrate it at their friends' houses.

Today, however, my Rachel begged me to throw a *krismes* party for her at home. She said that every year she goes to her friends', but this year, she wants to invite her friends here. I complained and protested about our cramped flat, and our lack of money in these hard times, but it didn't help. Indeed, nothing helped, and I had to submit to the ultimatum.

From then on I didn't have a moment's peace. My head was constantly spinning, thinking about how to organize it all, the *prezents* and the party, because a promise is a promise.

A few days earlier I'd noticed a large poster on a wall in Whitechapel announcing the good tidings that, at this place on a certain day, there'd be a Hanukkah bazaar where people could find bargains, with the profits going to an important cause. On the evening of the Hanukkah charity bazaar, I took my mischievous Davy by the hand and went off to buy *krismes prezents*.

When we arrived, the square was already packed with customers who'd probably come for the same reason as me. The stalls were prettily decorated in all sorts of colored paper. Some had electric lights that shone like stars in the sky, and others had *krismes* decorations with slogans like:

"Don't walk past us, buy bargains at cheap prices."

"You need our goods and we need your money," and so on.

The stallholders were beautiful, well-dressed women, and charming girls who were drawing the attention of customers to their stalls. Davy, the little devil, nagged me to buy him everything in the bazaar. I managed to get away with only buying him a Purim rattle. I decided not to spend more than a few pounds, bearing in mind the *krismes* party that I had to throw for my pious children.

Unfortunately, we women have a weakness for buying everything we see, and there's no fighting such a desire. So I walked slowly from stall to stall and considered everything I saw, looked at each thing from every angle, considered it again, and put it back down, as one does.

In one corner I saw a stall with a sign "Only exquisite items sold here," which was very appealing. The stallholder, a pretty Jewish girl, also impressed me. I went over to look at the "exquisite items" in the hope that I'd find something there from our friend Moshe Oved's jewelry shop, because he's generous and often gives items to charitable causes. But no, the things on the stall were different. There was a pretty pair of ladies' shoes. I bought them for my daughter, who'd be going to a friend's wedding and had already bought an evening dress, which the shoes would match. The price was reasonable, so I paid and asked for them to be wrapped.

Davy had also seen a pair of trousers he really liked on the stall, and he begged me to buy them, promising to learn the Four Questions by heart for *Pesach* in return.* I was so happy that he remembered *Pesach* existed as well as *krismes*, that I bought the trousers for him. Then I remembered that my old man hadn't a decent shirt to wear, and especially now that we were going to be throwing an evening party for respectable company, I had to get him a *prezent*. At the same stall I bought him a white shirt with a collar and a red tie, just as he liked, thinking that he should look smart at least once a year. After this I decided not to spend any more money, and set off for home.

We were standing by the exit when I caught sight of a fur coat on another stall and had a sudden desire to get it. For many years I'd coveted such a coat and was jealous of any woman who owned something like that. I checked my purse and saw that I still had a few pounds left. I forgot about the party and decided to buy myself the coat. Decision made, I marched over to the stall, mulled over the bargain, tried it on, and liked how it looked in the mirror. With a happy smile, I thought to myself: Let my enemies eat their hearts out and think that I've won the Irish Sweepstake. They'd be so jealous of me. I bought it, they wrapped up the precious item, and Davy and I left.

On the way home I began to regret spending all my money, because now I'd have to work out how to borrow money to get the party together. If not, my daughter would move out, as she'd done a few times before, and I'd be without a breadwinner.

Getting home, out of breath from dragging the heavy packages, I arrived in the house puffing and thanked God that I hadn't run into anyone on the way. I instinctively felt that I should open up the packages on my own and have a look at my bargains. I set out the individually wrapped packages, looked at them, and thought I was going to pass out.

My Rachel's shoes were both for the left foot. Davy's trousers were full of holes, my husband's new shirt was stained, and my fur coat that I wanted to show off to my enemies was moth-eaten. Davy was afraid to come near me in case I took my anger out on him, and he cleared out of the house.

When my old man came home, my problems really began in earnest. He looked at the *krismes prezents* I'd spent so much on, was furious, and decided that

---

* The Four Questions are recited by the youngest family member at the Passover Seder.

there was no way we were going to have a *krismes* party, and not only that, but we were going to have a Hanukkah party instead. I was delighted and asked him when Hanukkah was. He said he didn't know. I said, How come you're a Jew and you know when *krismes* is but not when it's Hanukkah?

He replied that *krismes* came every year on the same day on the calendar, but Hanukkah doesn't, and he promised to ask the *shammes* of the synagogue.

So it was decided that this year we'd celebrate Hanukkah, and *krismes* would be left to the Christians.

But when he asked the *shammes* when Hanukkah was, the *shammes* looked at him as if he was crazy, laughed heartily, and said that "Hanukkah was two weeks ago."

So, as you can see, this year we're left without a *krismes* party and without a Hanukkah party. Oh, well, too bad, I thought. And when I thought it over, I realized I shouldn't take it to heart because the pounds spent on *prezents* had, in any case, gone to a good cause.

I NEED A FLAT

The children in Brown's fictional family both have anglicized Jewish names. The name Rachel, which would have been "Rokhl" in Yiddish, is written phonetically in Yiddish letters as Reytshl, to mirror the pronunciation of the English name. The name Davy is my translation of what Brown writes as "Deyvele" in the Yiddish text. The name David in Yiddish is Dovid, and with a diminutive, Dovidl, but in the stories Brown spells the English name Deyv (Dave) phonetically, with the Yiddish diminutive "le" at the end of the name.

This version of "I Need a Flat" from 1951 is based on a story from 1934. In the stories from the thirties, the Davy character is called "Yekele" (which would be Jake in English) as a diminutive of the name Yankev (Jacob). Yekele, meaning little fool, would have been recognizable to a Yiddish readership as the foolish hero of the children's book *Yekele nar* (Fool Yekele).[1] In addition, it is the name of the "ridiculous hero" of the comic Chelm stories.[2] For Brown to call her character Yekele is to set up the East End as Chelm, and to position Yekele as someone to be ridiculed. In contrast, the name Deyvele, or in my translation Davy, has no particular comic connotations.

If you have a flat to rent and want a quiet, decent tenant, then let it to me, and I promise you won't regret it. And if you particularly want a neighbor without children, I can assure you that mine are spirits, not children . . . I also want you to know that I don't quarrel with the neighbors, and I don't have a sewing machine, telephone, piano, refrigerator, lodger, or home help. I don't keep cats, dogs, or chickens. No one comes to see me, apart from a few friends who want to see what's going on at my place so that they can gossip about me.

At home it's blissfully quiet and peaceful. That's the sort of people we are. Yet with all these virtues, I've had no luck with any flat. I was thrown out of my last flat for such a trivial matter, it's not even worth talking about: This triviality was the radio.

No doubt you want to know how this happened, so I'll tell you. It all began when the long, cold, dark winter evenings drew in, and I became gloomy and dejected. Right after supper my children would disappear, and I'd be left sitting alone in the room, with just the four walls, lonely as a stone. I didn't know what to do with myself. I couldn't read because I was still waiting, after six months, for my free spectacles. There was no one to exchange one word with, so I just sat alone all night, contemplating my bitter fortune and weeping buckets of tears over all the dead members of my family, until I became sick with my nerves. I stopped sleeping and eating, and my health deteriorated.

I went to the doctor, and after I explained my symptoms, he diagnosed the cause and gave me a piece of advice. He told me to buy a radio. First, he explained, with a radio I wouldn't be alone in the house. Second, when I listened to music, I'd feel happier, and it'd be good for my nerves.

It wasn't so easy to do what he suggested, because my earnings today aren't what they once were. But what won't a person do for their health? I made the effort, took out my last few pounds, and bought a radio.

At first it was, indeed, a joy to have it in the house, and I blessed the doctor for his sound advice. When my two rascals went out in the evening, I sat down and listened to programs with interest. Even though I didn't really understand the news very well, I guessed what it was about. But I really enjoyed the music, especially the songs, and, most of all, I loved the operas. I would listen so intently that, more than once, I fell asleep to its sweet sounds.

But then I'd suddenly wake up when a singer sang *Eli, Eli* or *My Yiddishe Mame*. Oh, how this would make me cry my eyes out. It reminded me of my old mother and my childhood in the old country. But overall, I felt better, and my nerves became stronger, as if I had taken the best medicine.

However, calamity struck! My daughter Rachel caught the flu, and not being able to go out to work, was housebound. And this is when my troubles began. The radio became my mortal enemy, and I cursed the lives of those who had invented it. When my daughter was able to get up and move about, she immediately took the radio and began twisting the dials. I could have talked until I was blue in the face, but she took no notice of me and just did her own thing. If she heard a little bit of Yiddish music, it was like poison to her. I pleaded with her:

"For goodness sake, let me hear a bit of Yiddish. It fills me with joy."

"We don't need that," she replied. "I've been in England long enough, and it's time to forget Yiddish." And she kept twiddling the dials.

Her words hit me hard. I tried to make her understand that Yiddish is our mother tongue and that we don't need to be ashamed of it, especially now, when we've got our own land, Israel, where, God-willing, we will go. She answered that she didn't need any new country with a new language—she's fine here. She won't go there, and if I want to, I can go without her. And she ended up by telling me not to worry about her because she knows what's best for herself. Hearing these words, I was incensed, and I marched out of the house.

I wandered about in the street, thinking about the whole matter, and realized that it's only foolish mothers who can expect respect from their children. I decided not to say anything more and went back home. But this wasn't the end of it.

That evening after supper Rachel switched the radio to a station playing dance music, pushed the table and chairs away, grabbed my rascal Davy, and started to dance.

It was late. The neighbor downstairs complained that the noise was disturbing her, that she and her husband couldn't sleep, and that she couldn't bear it. They ignored her and kept on dancing. She knocked on the ceiling with a stick and yelled dreadful curses. Davy knocked back with a hammer, and they continued dancing. There was a terrible commotion. The neighbor came running upstairs in her pajamas, with her husband in his nightshirt, and they threatened to call the police. My daughter said she wasn't scared of a policeman because she pays rent, income tax, purchase tax, insurance, and can therefore do whatever she likes. The neighbors all came running up, shouting and yelling, spitefully adding their tuppenceworth, but to no avail.

The radio played, my children danced, and the couple downstairs were running up and down. I was apoplectic and begged God to bring on midnight quickly, when the radio would shut down and the war would end. But as the saying goes: God doesn't forsake us and doesn't spare us misery. Davy, the cleverclogs, found out that after midnight you could hear music from across the world, and he started retuning to Vienna, Berlin, Paris, and a minute later to Warsaw. I heard Polish being spoken, and despite the fact that I hadn't heard it for many years, I understood every word. Then he leapt straight over to Russia, where they were playing a jolly *Kamarinska* dance. Davy is pretty lively, and although it was already one o'clock, he crossed his skinny arms, threw out his feet from under him, and danced the energetic *Kamarinska*. The sweat ran down his forehead, his nose dripped, but it didn't bother him, he just kept going. I was afraid that the wife from the first floor would come back, and I finally managed to persuade him to switch off the radio, and we all went to sleep.

But it seems that my neighbor didn't sleep all night but instead spent it hatching plans for how to get rid of me, and first thing in the morning she went off to the landlord with signatures from all the neighbors on the street. The landlord immediately gave me notice and told me to move out. It was the last thing I needed, but he threw me, my two rascals, our baggage, and the radio out onto the street.

And so I decided to approach you to ask if you have a flat to let and want a quiet, decent, respectable tenant. Take me in, and I assure you that you won't have any regrets. On the contrary, you'll be absolutely delighted.

PESSIMISM AND OPTIMISM

"Pessimism and Optimism" was first published in *Di post* on 31 December 1934, and the changes in this later, revised form are particularly poignant. In the earlier version, the parents' political conversation runs:

FATHER—Another war is approaching, terrible times are on the way. Half the world will be slaughtered again.

MOTHER—Are you crazy? What are you doing having such sad thoughts? Hasn't Henderson just won a Nobel Prize for a peace initiative? Isn't that proof there won't be another war?

FATHER—So why are people making munitions day and night? They are making specials and working overtime.

In 1934 Hitler was in power, and many Jews were leaving Germany for Poland or other places in Europe. In London's East End, Mosley's Blackshirts were terrorizing Jews on the streets with anti-Semitic chanting and violence, and the government was beginning a rearmament program. At the same time, the Labour MP Arthur Henderson had just been awarded the Nobel Prize for "Peace through Disarmament." All these details are referred to in the 1934 version. In the story translated here, which appeared in *Di tsayt* in 1948, the family is still discussing politics, but this time it is about the role of the United Nations Organization (UNO) and the worry that the peace conferences and the Marshall Plan will fail.

What is pessimism and what is optimism?

When you find yourself in a bad mood, assailing your husband with accusations, complaining that he's worthless and the reason for all the misery you've had all the years of your married life and still have; living in a cramped flat without any decent clothes to wear like other women have, never going on holiday to get a bit of rest from your arduous work, and your life being a constant drag. This is pessimism.

And when your husband answers you coldly and calmly:

"Don't worry, darling, don't get worked up. It'll damage your beauty, God-forbid, and your delicate figure, and your health, which is dearer to me than my life. Don't imagine, my sweetheart, that we're the only ones who have it bad, who live in a small, uncomfortable flat and have no income. If it's any comfort, look at our *Litvak* neighbor over there. He doesn't have an income either." That is optimism.

Usually we women are more inclined to pessimism than our husbands, and that is probably because we are the weaker sex. We have to give birth and raise children, take responsibility for the house, do the housekeeping, sort out all the debtors who come demanding money, quarrel with the neighbors, and, from time to time, suffer our husbands' frivolity. All this takes its toll on us, and we're overcome with pessimism. All day we're angry and cross with the whole world and sometimes also with ourselves.

For quite a long time, I'd go around in precisely this mood. I didn't say good morning or have a friendly smile for anyone. People started avoiding me. The children stopped talking to me altogether. But I stuck to my guns and gave in to my feelings.

Until one day when my old man got exasperated with me for being constantly angry and upset. He pointed out that my actions had chased away all our friends, who often used to come round for a game of solo, and now he had no one to play with. Furthermore, I'd let myself go and am not the woman I used to be. Bitterness had aged me and wrinkled my face, making me look years older than I am. And finally, he warned me, if I carry on like this, he'd leave the house, and I wouldn't know where he'd gone. And he walked out of the room, shutting the door.

These last words about my appearance really shocked me, and, on top of that, I really didn't want to be abandoned. I know what it means to be an abandoned wife because my mother suffered that fate. I seriously contemplated this issue, and when I looked at myself in the mirror, I saw the changes in my face and my angry eyes and was dismayed. I decided to change my character immediately.

I became friendly to everyone at home. The children exchanged glances and couldn't believe that such a change had happened to me so suddenly. I responded lovingly to every word my husband spoke to me, and if he complained about something, I comforted him and assured him that all would soon be well.

In short, I became a 100-percent optimist. The children championed my bright view of the future. But my husband couldn't really live in peace for too long because he enjoyed bickering with me. He maintained that once in a while it's simply essential to fight a bit, to get annoyed for a while, and after that, when you make up, life is invigorated.

The other day, for example, we were discussing the news during supper, when my hubby said:

"There's no peace in the world. People are constantly arguing. They organize conferences to meet today, but they met yesterday, and they'll meet tomorrow, and I bet that nothing will come from all those meetings. The UNO isn't any good, or the congresses or the Marshall Plan. Every country is making munitions, and who knows how this will end."

Afraid of making him angry, I replied with my usual good-natured smile:

"Don't be daft. How can a person with such sharp intelligence believe such nonsense? After all, we hear that all nations want peace."

He answered:

"So why are they working at making so much ammunition and calling people back to military service?"

I said that all this was to maintain the peace. The armaments are being produced only for defense purposes and not, God forbid, to attack another country. He said:

"So why have they invented the atom bomb?"

I said that our trustworthy providers felt sorry for the thousands of citizens, their families, and small children, who ran into the shelters during the war. So they've devised a solution, namely the atom bomb, so that if, God forbid, there was another war, these poor people might not have to run away again.

My daughter, who was on my side, replied that the boy she's going out with—who's very clever, reads lots of books and newspapers, and goes every Sunday to Hyde Park to hear the speeches—assured her that there would never be another war. So, what better proof do you need? Also Davy, who's got a broad view of life and politics, wanted to bet all of his pocket money that there wouldn't be another war. It's just my old man who stubbornly sticks to his position.

After supper my daughter looked out the window and said:

"Mum, I promised Benny I'd go to a dance with him today. But the sky's black, and it looks like rain. What should I do?"

I answered:

"Get dressed up, darling, and go. It won't rain, the dark clouds will pass. Go on, don't be frightened, and have a good time."

Reassured by my optimism, my daughter put on her dance frock and flimsy silk shoes and was about to go, but hesitated at the door because it had started spitting with rain.

"Go on, darling. Your mother has pronounced that it will be alright," my old man joked at my expense. In spite of being a bit worried, I didn't want to give in to him in this case and told her to go. Davy was delighted by my heroism, and my daughter followed my advice and went to the dance.

Later a violent storm broke out, with thunder and lightning. I was shame-faced in front of my husband, who'd made fun of me, and as a protest I went to bed. But I couldn't sleep. I lay there anxiously as every roll of thunder tore at my heart. I shook with fear and began to reproach myself: What sort of mother was I to have ordered her to go to the dance? If, God forbid, she caught a cold, it'd be my fault, and I'd never forgive myself. It plagued my conscience, but with all my will-power, I managed to suppress my feelings. I lay there terrified until late at night, when, on hearing her return, my heart stopped racing, and I finally fell asleep.

But I had achieved my goal. Optimism prevailed.

BREADWINNERS

"Mum!" yelled my Rachel this morning from her bedroom.

"Yes, darling, what do you want?"

"Make me some sandwiches because I'm going out today . . ."

"What sort of 'going out' do you mean?"

"Don't ask any questions, Mum, just do what I'm asking you. It's a nice day, and I'm going out."

"Who with?"

"Charlie."

"Oh, with Charlie now? Yesterday it was with Benny, the day before David, today Charlie, and who will it be tomorrow?"

"Oh, Mum, don't be sarcastic. Charlie's a lovely boy, and he loves me . . . so he says."

"So what else is new. And where are you 'going out' to? Am I allowed to know?"

"Hikin'."

"And where is that, which neighborhood?"

"Nowhere, Mum, you go off into the forest, through fields, along straight and twisty paths, walking until you get tired, then resting and then going farther."

"What's the point in that? I can't see the fun in dragging yourself around the countryside. Rachel, just come here a moment. I want to ask you something."

Rachel ran in, laughing loudly, and when I saw her I nearly fainted . . . she was wearing a pair of trousers, with an open-necked man's shirt, a pair of large, heavy boots, a rucksack on her shoulders, and a cigarette in her mouth.

"My daughter," I cried out in anguish, "are you out of your mind? What's the matter with you? Have you no respect for your father and mother, for God, or for anyone? Oh, my God. If your father could see you now, he'd die of shock."

"Shut up, Mum, don't talk nonsense," my daughter answered angrily. "You're so old-fashioned, but me, I'm modern. I'm much more comfortable in trousers, like you are in a dress."

"Rachel," I said bitterly, "you should take off the trousers. I'm telling you, I won't put up with this, it's not fitting for a Jewish girl, and even more for you whose grandfather was a rabbi. Are you listening or not?"

"How many times have I told you not to call me Rachel, but Ray? You get it, Mum, Ray, not Rachel. You've been in London for so many years already, and you can't talk like a normal person . . . It's disgraceful, I'm embarrassed in front of my friends when they come over here."

There was a knock at the door:

"That's Charlie, Mum, you've got to be nice to him, okay? Speak to him in English because he doesn't understand Yiddish—and don't call me Rachel," she ordered.

A young man came in dressed just like my Rachel.

"Charlie, this is my mother," Rachel introduced him.

I wanted to get back at her, so I pretended not to hear.

"Mum, this is my Charlie," Rachel said angrily and threw me a hostile glance. I felt quite scared of her and gave a strained smile.

"You look exactly the same," I forced myself to laugh despite my anxiety. "It's hard to tell which of you is the man and which the woman. These strange modern fashions!"

"That's all right, Mum, we won't make that mistake," said Charlie with assurance.

"What sort of *Mum* am I to you? What cheek! The first time I see him, he already . . ."*

"You see, Mum," Charlie explained, "I'm going out with your daughter, and I'm sure it'll be okay."

"So you're going out with my daughter. And you tell me it'll be okay, and on account of that you call me *Mum* already, huh? Everything's so simple today, no marriage, no contract, no best man, no wedding ring, just like that, anything goes. You don't care what other people think. So that means that you all do whatever you want, and you call it modern. And you want me to join in and dance with pride, huh? Rachel, I won't stand for this carrying-on. Are you listening or not? I'm

---

* In Cockney English, the word "Mum" is used as the polite form of address, "Ma'am." As articulated in London, the two words sound almost identical.

telling you to stay at home today, and as far as I'm concerned, he can 'go out' on his own. I haven't brought up a girl to dress in men's trousers and go off wandering around in forests and fields with a strange boy. I didn't behave like that at all!"

"Mum," Rachel warned, "remember that if you meddle in my business, I'll leave home like I've done before. And you'll have to pay for the radio, the sewing machine, the furniture, and the insurance agent all by yourself again. Remember, you'll be sorry, and you'll come round to me and beg and cry for me to come home. Be careful, Mum, before it's too late. Because this time I won't feel sorry for you."

I almost fainted with shock when I heard this, because I know Rachel and know that she means what she says, and if I have to rely on her father's earnings, we'll die of hunger three times a day. So, with great reluctance, I answered:

"All right, my daughter, I won't say anything more. Yes, I'm sorry, I was upset and was talking nonsense, and I promise you that I won't do it anymore. So, why are you standing there? You wanted to go. You've got sandwiches, a couple of oranges, a bottle of milk. Take it and go! Go, have a good time. I will tidy up your bedroom, polish your shoes, do the laundry, and when you come back full of the country air, everything will be in good order. How long will you be away, my child?" I concluded, full of anguish, biting my lips.

"A few days," Rachel said curtly.

"Oh, a few days—and nights?" I repeated, being careful not to show my anger. "Will you have enough sandwiches for the two of you, or should I make a few more?"

"Enough, enough. Don't bother, Mum. It's getting late, we've got to go."

"Go and take care, God forbid anything bad should happen to you. Take a coat and an umbrella in case a storm breaks in the middle of the night and you'll be lying under the open sky, and might, God forbid, catch a cold. And make sure you don't climb any high mountains."

"It's all right, Mum."

"And I'll pray to God that I live long enough to see you married properly, and get joy from you, my child."

"Don't worry, Mum."

"So goodbye, goodbye children, go well and come back well . . . Yes, Rachel, just one minute, I want to ask you something."

I took her to one side and whispered:

"Tell me, my child, is he at least Jewish?"

Instead of answering, she hooted with laughter and, together with Charlie, left the house.

DAVY BECOMES A PRIZE FIGHTER

Kid Berg and Harry Mizler were both Jewish boxers brought up in the East End of London. When this story was first published, these boxers were particularly successful and well known.

Jackie "Kid" Berg was born Judah Bergman. He became the World Junior Welterweight Champion in 1930 and the British Lightweight Champion in 1934–36. Harry Mizler was born Hyman Barnett. He won a string of British titles as an amateur, including the bantamweight title in 1930 and the featherweight in 1932, and competed for Great Britain in the 1932 Summer Olympic games. On turning professional, he won the British lightweight title in 1934.[1]

Of particular importance was that Berg and Mizler displayed their Jewishness in the boxing ring with pride. Kid Berg had a Star of David on his shorts, and Mizler had a Union Jack on one leg of his shorts and the Star of David on the other. In 1933 Berg married a gentile actress, Bunty Pain. Harry Mizler, on the other hand, married his Jewish wife, Betty, in "the big wedding of the East End" in Philpot Street Synagogue.[2] The story from 1934 and that published in Brown's collection in 1951 are identical, other than the Davy character's name being Yekele in the earlier version.

"Mum," said my Davy the other day.

"Yes, son?"

"I want to ask you a question, but you mustn't laugh at me."

"Of course, go on, ask away."

"What's an 'income'?"

"It's something we don't have, son."

"What do you mean?"

"Right now there's nothing for the rent, nothing to cook, no clothes, no shoes, and no money to go to the pictures. That's what having no income means, and without that, my son, life is as bitter as death. But why are you suddenly asking a question like that?"

"You see, Mum, I saw how my pal Sammy's mother got all dressed up and went out, and then Mrs. Cohen said to Mrs. Levy that she's going out looking for an income. And then Mrs. Levy smiled in a funny way."

"Aha, now I see," I said.

After a few moments Davy spoke again:

"Mum."

"Yes."

"I want to go out, too."

"Where to?" I asked.

"Looking for an income for you. You've got no money, so I'm going to learn a trade, and earn money, and I'll give it all to you, and you'll give me spending money."

"Oh, you kids are all so kind when you're young—how wonderful it'd be if you never grew up . . . because later, when you're big, you'll think differently."

"Mum, you leave it to me, it'll be okay," my precious boy replied eagerly, and off he went out of the house.

I laughed heartily at my breadwinner. However, the following week this is what happened:

My daughter was going out with a very nice boy. He used to come round to our house and was almost like one of our own children. I don't need to tell you what it means, in times like these, to get a nice boy for a girl without a dowry, because you already know it yourself. I'm telling you that everyone in Whitechapel was jealous of me because of this match. And everything was going just as we would have hoped.

In short, it had reached the stage where he was about to give her an engagement ring. And since his parents hadn't been to our house yet, we decided to invite them one *Shabbes* for tea.

I can't tell you how much I and my daughter worked on the house during the week because, as you can imagine, scrubbing away poverty is no mean feat. We tidied up, cleaned the rooms, polished the spoons and forks, moved the table to the middle of the room, and really transformed the place, just like spring cleaning before *Pesach*. We bought a few pretty things at Woolworths and hung some colorful decorations on the walls. I'd bought some fruit and baked a fine *strudel* for the guests. Everything was ready.

On *Shabbes* afternoon I borrowed some chairs from the neighbors, and a couple of glasses and a few dishes, and set the table to look beautiful. I sent Davy out of the house, asking him, for heaven's sake, not to come home too early, and we got ready to entertain the guests.

They came, as expected, at the right time, and we ate and drank. While chatting, I found out that they were very important people: He was the warden of a synagogue, and she was president of the *Agune* Society. My daughter couldn't take her eyes off her bridegroom-to-be the whole time. What can I say? I nearly burst with pride. It's no small thing to marry into a family of this pedigree.

As I got up to offer more tea, we heard a loud knock on the door. My stomach lurched, as if I'd known that some sort of mishap was about to happen.

A moment later the door burst open. and Sammy's mother rushed in shouting, swearing, and calling me all the names under the sun, in front of the strangers, saying that my Davy had given her Sammy a black eye and twisted his left hand.

If a pit could have opened up, I'd have sunk into it with embarrassment.

"Thank you for telling me, missus!" I said, holding in my anger (while thinking "to hell with you"). "What on earth are you doing making such a scene? Is it my fault? Go away," I spluttered. "Please leave me in peace."

But my pleas didn't help. Seeing strangers, she took the opportunity of an audience and started up again:

"I'll have you charged, that's what I'll do. People who have kids like yours—ruffians like yours, shouldn't live among respectable people—living with savages would suit them better. Just you wait, I haven't finished with you yet. I'll show you what I can do," she continued, wagging her finger at me. "Everyone knows what you and your family are like."

I couldn't control myself anymore. I went up to her, opened the door, and threw her out of the house. I won't tell you what she shrieked from the other side of the door.

The prospective in-laws exchanged glances for a moment, then got up, said a cursory goodbye, and left, taking their precious son home with them.

My daughter went into her bedroom, sobbing bitterly. I was left alone to contemplate the table covered with sandwiches and cakes that were lying there, untouched.

Just then Davy came into the house with a triumphant laugh. I grabbed hold of him, taking my rage out on him.

"You scoundrel!" I shrieked. "Why did you hit that boy, what have you got against him? You've ruined your sister's future."

"It's alright, Mum, don't get worked up," he said, smiling. "It was only a friendly fight. You see, Mum, I'm going to become a professional prize fighter, and bring you in an income. Oh, Mum, you should've seen Sammy's black eye." Despite my anger, he laughed happily.

"You're going to pay for this, you brat. You want to be a prize fighter, do you? Lucky me! Your grandmother would turn in her grave. I'll box your ears if you don't get that idea out of your head. That's not a profession for a Jewish boy."

"Why not?" Davy argued. "Isn't Kid Berg a Jewish boy? Isn't Mizler a Jew? They were famous and earned loads of money, and their mothers were proud of them . . . Please, Mum, don't be old-fashioned. Every morning before a fight, I'll pray like I was taught for my bar mitzvah, and I'll wear a Star of David in the ring to show that I'm a religious Jew. Don't you get it, Mum? Don't you see how much you'll be respected because of me?"

"Oh, so in the morning you'll pray, in the fight you'll wear a Star of David to show that you're a Jew, and no doubt you'll get married to a gentile girl. Yes, yes, I understand the business. I don't want that sort of income. Thanks, but no thanks." Davy turned and ran out of the room.

The next day a letter arrived from my daughter's ex-fiancé. He wrote that he can't come round anymore because his mother said that he's still got time before getting married, and when it comes to that point, he'd let her know. Meanwhile there's nothing more to say on the matter. After my daughter had read the letter, she laid her head in her arms, and tears streamed from her eyes.

My heart ached. I wasn't destined to have any luck, I thought to myself, and cursed the hour of my birth.

Davy however, continued to practice: punching other boys and getting broken bones himself. But, he said, it doesn't matter; he wants to become a prize fighter and provide me with an income!

MY PRINCE,
THE SOCIALIST

In this story Davy is a young socialist. Yet in an earlier version of this story from 1933, called "Yekele Makes a Speech," Yekele is a young communist. When Yekele is asked what the Young Pioneers group he has just joined is, he tells his mother that it is a "group of young people committed to making everyone into communists, and when everyone becomes communists, then the whole world will be a free country." The free country that inspires Yekele is Russia, and on the street corner he shouts from his soapbox:

"We must have a free country, like Russia. We don't care what Lloyd George said, what Baldwin said. We must all be united in the front, never mind the back. We must fight with sticks, with shovels, and even with pokers if necessary until we sort out the enemy like we sorted out the Russian tsar."[1]

Although Brown did not identify as a communist, the Workers' Circle Branch 3, where she was the secretary of the Women's Section, was known as a communist-leaning branch. Jewish communism in the UK in the thirties was identified with antifascism, and the Workers' Circle was particularly active in fighting the British Union of Fascists. In contrast, in this later version, published in *Di tsayt* in 1950, it was an entirely different environment, and communism was replaced with a socialist pacifism.

I'm telling you, the youth of today are unbearable. You have to put up with all sorts of problems. And on top of that, they drag you into the most terrible trouble, which you then have to endure for the rest of your life. I'm talking about my son, Davy, who you already know a bit about from my previous stories.

The boy's a firebrand with the gift of the gab, a nose that sniffs around where it shouldn't, a brain working day and night planning new tricks, and a tongue that is out more often than it's in. And despite the fact that I'm his mother, I have to tell you the truth, I don't know where I got such a scoundrel from, or whom he takes after. His father and I are two quiet, calm people. We don't argue when he's in earshot, and the neighbors have a really good impression of our family life.

Any trouble I had with him when he was little was easy to cope with. For example, he smashed a couple of the neighbor's windowpanes. That was merely foolishness, it could happen. When he fought a boy and knocked out his two front teeth, I could forgive him that, too, because they were both bashing each other about. It's better that Davy got him than the other one got Davy. I could even forgive how, when his *rebbe* was teaching him his bar mitzvah portion, he was counting the hairs in the *rebbe*'s sparse beard. But what he did to me on the eve of *Pesach* goes beyond the limit, and is simply too much to bear.

A few days before *Pesach*, Davy came home from school very jolly and told me that he had joined a group called "the Young Pioneers." I didn't like the sound of that at all. I felt that it wasn't entirely kosher, and that Davy had stuck his nose into something fishy. But I responded to him calmly:

"Davy, my son, tell me, who are these 'Pioneers,' and what are their aims?"

He told me clearly and plainly, that it was a group of boys committed to making propaganda for peace across the world, and when everyone listened to them and became a socialist and did away with capital, then the whole world would be a free country, and everything would be all right. No one would have to work, everyone would have what they wanted, and his dad would not have to be a tailor's presser.

"Tell me, son," I asked him respectfully, because I was afraid that he'd become angry, "is this anything to do with politics, or, God forbid, with war?"

"Oh, no, Mum," said Davy, laughing at my ignorance. "No politics and no war."

I felt slightly relieved. But from that day on, he began disappearing from the house for hours on end. One morning I noticed that my red pajamas were missing. I suspected that Davy had taken them out of the house, and I urged him to tell me what he'd done with them. But he categorically denied it and swore that he didn't know what I was talking about.

A day later, the *rebbe* came over to give Davy his lesson, but as usual, he wasn't there. The two of us ran around looking for him, but he wasn't anywhere. Maybe something had happened to him. We couldn't understand where he was going every evening and what he was doing.

Until the first Seder night came round. I'd been working until I was exhausted, preparing the Seder, boiling and roasting, just as God had commanded. I was busy the whole day and hadn't noticed that it was hours since my son had been home, and I'd forgotten to tell him that this evening we were celebrating the Seder, and he had to ask the Four Questions. Night started to draw in. I started preparing the table, putting out the glasses, the wine, the finely cooked fish that filled the room with its enticing smell, and a bowl of tasty dumplings. The house was bright and warm. My husband came home from synagogue. We wanted to perform the Seder, but my jewel-of-a-boy was not there.

After half an hour we became impatient. My husband went out onto the streets looking for our prince. And I was left sitting miserably at home, wondering where on earth my only son had vanished to. In a while my husband came running in, half-dead with fright and agitation. Wringing his hands, he said:

"Come with me and see if you feel proud of your jewel."

My heart sank with dread, and I followed him outside. When we got to the corner of our street and I saw what was happening, I almost fainted.

Davy was standing on an orange box. Next to him was a large stick with my red pajamas hanging from it, looking like a flag. Around him stood a whole bunch of rascals like him, and Davy was giving an impassioned speech, waving his skinny, grubby arms about, shaking his head, and shouting at the top of his voice:

"We must have a free country. We must stop the atom bomb, the hydrogen bomb, and all other bombs. We must not be afraid of the law." He pointed to a policeman who was standing and listening to his speech and laughing.

"We must all be united, and our slogan must be 'no more wars,'" he yelled, wiping his dripping nose.

"Hear, hear," his friends the "Pioneers" shouted.

I was utterly shocked to hear this speech, and immediately ran over to him, beseeching him:

"Davy, think of your mother and father, stop talking like this. You'll bring us into the firing line. They'll send us out of the country. What will we do? We're so poor. Come home instead, we've got to celebrate the Seder. It's all prepared, and we have to start, it's getting late. You are the prince tonight and must sit at the table by your father. What are you doing to us, you wretched boy?"

But Davy didn't want to listen.

"We socialists," he said, "don't go in for that sort of foolishness." He cleared his throat, pulled up his trousers that were falling down, and was about to start speaking all over again.

By now a large crowd had gathered around Davy, and I saw that this wasn't going to work just with gentle persuasion. I nodded at my husband, and he got my drift.

With a sudden grab I tore my pajamas off the stick, so that at least they would be without a flag. Then we both seized Davy by the arms and dragged him away from there. There was a ruckus among his friends and loud laughter from the crowd. We just about managed to drag him into the house and forcefully sat him down at the table.

He was clearly very hungry, and when he saw and smelled the fine food on the table, and especially the bottles of wine, he immediately forgot his socialism with the Pioneers, and with a mischievous smile, his eyes began to sparkle with happiness.

I dragged him into the kitchen, gave him a bowl of hot water, and told him to wash himself so that he'd look respectable at the Seder. He did what I said, and as he was doing that, I took the opportunity to tell him clearly that this whole episode he was engaged in was not fit for a Jewish boy. What have socialists and Pioneers got to do with us? Let the English get worked up about all that. A Jewish boy has to think about Israel, our own country, which was so difficult to establish, and we have to fight to keep it. And all young men and women should become involved in the youth *aliya*, go there, and help build up the country for our people, for the orphans who have survived from the six million Jews who perished in the camps.

Davy stared with large, intelligent eyes and admitted that I was right.

Soon after, we sat at the Seder table. Davy made the blessing over the wine with his father and asked the Four Questions. He even read the second half of the *haggadah* for the first time, because in other years he had only eaten and gone to sleep. But this year he said everything that he was meant to say and ended up with "Next Year in Jerusalem."

TOO JEWISH

An acquaintance of mine, a quiet and respectable woman, poured her heart out to me. Her father, she said, had been a kind, Orthodox Jew in the old country. Everyone in their town envied her for having a father like him, and envied her mother for having such a husband. She was truly blessed with him. He was as wise as King Solomon, as radiant as the sun in the sky, and as honest as they come. Businessmen would come to him for advice, and his kindness had no equal. He would give his last bite of food to a hungry pauper. He came from a line of scholars that went back generations. In short, he was pious and generous to everyone.

It was now a few years since he died, and she desperately wanted someone to be named after him. But, as if she was trying too hard, nothing happened, no baby boy was born in the family. But when one has patience and faith, one is rewarded. Her eldest daughter, who was very well off and lived in an affluent London neighborhood, finally got pregnant after ten years of marriage.

Imagine the mother's joy when she heard. She knew from the depths of her heart that God had answered her prayers, and she'd now have the opportunity to name a child, if it was a boy, after her father. She said that recently her father had appeared to her in a dream several times, begging her not to forget him, and she had promised that she would not.

Months passed by, one after another, during which she visited her daughter a number of times, but she didn't want to say anything about her request before, with God's help, the child was born.

Meanwhile they made lots of preparations: buying everything for the new and important guest, the baby who was coming after years of hope and despair. This child was the only thing they lacked.

A while ago, my acquaintance continued, she received a telegram from her son-in-law saying that her daughter had been blessed with the birth of a son.

Her joy was twofold: first, that the birth had gone smoothly, and second, that this child was the boy she'd prayed for, who would take her father's name.

That very day she began running around, happily telling the family the good news, and she put a notice in the classified section of the London *Tsayt* so that all her good friends would know her joy.

That night she was too excited to sleep. She thought about the present she'd chosen for the child, because he wasn't just any child or any grandchild; he was truly a part of her father, with his name. Her father had been called Yisroel, and she decided to only call him Yisrolik until he grew up, went to *heder*, had his bar mitzvah, and when he was called up to read the Torah, he would then be called Yisroel, but until then he would be little Yisrolik. What a wonderful name, a proper Jewish name that fills one with pleasure.

Early next morning, she got up, dressed smartly, bought an expensive bouquet of flowers, and went to see her daughter. Her daughter greeted her very warmly, kissing her just like a daughter should, and assured her mother that from today she would see how much she valued and respected her.

The mother was delighted with her daughter's words and knew in her heart that her daughter would fulfill her desire. Just to be totally sure, she asked if they had chosen a name for the baby.

"No, not yet," the daughter replied. "But we're going to give it some thought, and we'll no doubt choose a lovely name for him."

"In the Jewish community, we don't just pick a name out of thin air, darling," the mother said tenderly. "We call children the name of a grandfather or an uncle, and as we're talking about this now, let me ask you, darling, to name the child after my father. Believe me, he deserves this; he loved you dearly and carried you in his arms when you were a child." And she told her about her father's ancestry.

"Okay, Mum," the daughter said pleasantly. "I'll discuss it with my husband, and I'm sure he won't have any objection. What was the name of my grandfather—Yisroel, wasn't it?"

"Yes, yes, that's what he was called, and that's what you should name the child, may he live long."

As they said goodbye, the daughter apologized to her mother that she wouldn't be able to invite her to the circumcision, because in the maternity home she was in, they wouldn't allow anyone apart from her husband to be present. But she assured her that she could come with the whole family to the party they were having a week later. The mother was a little put out by this:

"What?" she said. "What do you mean I can't be at the circumcision of my first grandchild?" But then she realized that this was London and not their little town back in the old country, and here you have to do what you're told.

On her way out a nurse led her into another room and showed her the child. She all but wept with excitement, and when she looked closely at the little soul, she saw that he looked exactly like her father, and she was overjoyed, above all because he would have her father's name. As it turned out, all her plans came to nothing.

The day after the circumcision, she received a letter from her son-in-law in which he apologized, explaining that it pained him to say that he couldn't, with the best will in the world, fulfill her desire, and despite his having "tried his best," it wasn't possible to name the child after her father. He'd come to the conclusion that the name Yisroel simply wasn't suitable . . . It sounded too Jewish. Particularly in the neighborhood where he lived, it wasn't the done thing to give a child a Jewish name. It wouldn't fit in with the neighbors, or in the school he'd attend, and even he would find it hard, because then people would know that they were Jewish, and these days you had to be careful with this kind of thing.

If her father had been called Gershon, Henech, or Aaron, you could translate the names into George, Henry, or Irving, but Yisroel is more difficult because it can't be modified. So they've given the child the name Mackenzie, a real English name of which you can be sure he won't be ashamed. However, if she really wants to name a child after her father, she only needs to wait until her East End daughter gets married and has a child. There it doesn't matter what a child is called. In the East End there are lots of Yisroliks, so there can be another one, but for this baby, it's not suitable.

My acquaintance was furious with her son-in-law, the snob, and cried bitter tears for her luckless father.

WHEN A WOMAN
BECOMES A PERSON

Although no one wants to interfere in the relationship between husband and wife and create a row that sets them at each other's throats, I'd like to persuade you that sometimes it's absolutely necessary and, in many cases, brings unexpectedly good results. Now let me convince you.

Yesterday my old man came in from outside, upset and burning with rage.

"How's it possible?" he fumed. "How could you do this to me? My own wife laughing at me, making fun of me, calling me a loser, unhappy, clumsy, and all sorts of other things. It's completely out of order! My own wife!"

"Imagine," he said to me, barely containing his anger. "I was walking about in Whitechapel when I was stopped by my *landsman* Yashe, who told me, and actually showed me in black and white, what you wrote about me in the papers. And Yashe gave me a right earful: How come I don't say anything? How come I don't protest about it in the strongest terms? And not only protest but boycott you. According to him, I should boycott you like they boycotted that evil Hitler. Yashe says that he's known me longer than you've known me. He remembers me from the old country, and he's certain that I'm not what you call me."

"It is true," my husband admitted, "I'm not earning a wage, and you've had to suffer as a result, and I've not been able to give you what you deserve as my wife . . ."

"So," I butted in, "if that's really true, why are you fuming?"

"I'm allowed to fume," he yelled in outrage and stamped his foot, "when my own wife writes such things about her husband. Have I got the right to be furious or not?"

"Yes, yes," I confessed. "You've got the right, I admit it."

"Maybe I don't earn anything, but even so, you're not short of anything. I make sure we've got everything we need in the house, but still you grumble and write about me in the papers."

To give him an example of my thinking, I told him a story. A woman went to the rabbi, complaining about her husband being fit for nothing, that he was utterly useless.

"Do you have children?" the rabbi asked.

"Yes, Rabbi, I have four clever boys," answered the wife.

"So why on earth did you tell me that your husband was fit for nothing?" the rabbi probed.

"Oh, Rabbi," sighed the woman. "If I'd relied on him for that, I wouldn't have even had one of them . . ."

This set my husband fuming all over again. I continued:

"Listen, nothing good will come of your raging. It won't help anything. As long as you don't get work and bring in some money, I won't stop writing about you."

"How about," he suggested, "we make a plan, and you, my dear wife, get a job? Modern women aren't like those of the past," he explained, and told me that he knows many women who manage workshops, are dressmakers, masseuses, manicurists, and other things that make a good living. "These women are a blessing from God, both to their husbands and really to themselves as well . . .

"Their family lives very well, they have their own car, become more fashionable, and make lots of friends, thanks to the wife. But most important, it's better for a woman not to be dependent on a man. She should be a person, not just a woman. The days when women were tied to cooking, baking, and having children are over. Nowadays you can find an answer to everything. So why shouldn't a wife do useful work and support her husband?"

Indeed, after hearing his argument, I realized that my husband isn't such a fool as I thought. I discovered that he's a man just like all others, with the same desires, the same thoughts and aspirations, and possibly he's also actually right that today's woman shouldn't be reliant on her husband, looking for him to provide everything she needs. So we decided to change jobs. He'd stay at home and do all my work, and I'd go out and learn a trade so that he wouldn't want for anything, because he'd have my income. He'd live contentedly and make a good life for himself.

After a great deal of thought, I concluded that this was a practical plan, and I advise every woman to do the same as me. If you want your husband to value you, care for you, and truly love you with all his heart, then you must become the breadwinner. Give him the opportunity to walk around with his hands in his pockets, be a charitable person, a community provider, go to cultural events, be the president of a society, or the warden of his synagogue. This will bring him respect and fulfillment from your pay packet. And you'll also benefit from his status. He'll become a good, honest, and faithful husband, such as he's never been before. He'll give you lovely presents and lots of joy. Nothing will be too difficult for him or too expensive for him to buy you . . . And if you really want to be completely generous, let him do what he likes with his money, spending it on whatever his heart desires. Pretend not to notice that it was your hard-earned pounds. Believe everything he tells you, and even if you're convinced that he's lying, ignore it and don't say anything. Because when it comes to it, you're still the wife and he's the husband. And if, from time to time, it really gets to you and you can't bear it any longer, your patience explodes, and you have to discuss matters with him, then do it quietly and modestly, so that no one can hear. Everyone will have the impression that you have a happy life together, and for this alone, he'll love you all the more, because men hate to be blamed in public. They always want to look like gentlemen, so that they can please others—and they need clever, modest women to help them. So this is my advice to women who want to lead a quiet, honorable, and good family life.

I thank my husband's *landsman* Yashe for meddling in our relationship, because his provocation gave my husband new ideas. Ideas can turn into reality and, who knows, it may be women's salvation.

A NEW PLAY IN
WHITECHAPEL

The London Yiddish theatre changed its repertoire weekly, so there was a constant search for new material. The theatres produced Yiddish classics and popular works by writers such as Abraham Goldfaden, Jacob Gordin, and Joseph Lateiner, and plays translated from other languages into Yiddish; many plays came from the Yiddish stages of Eastern Europe and America. However, there were also a number of home-grown playwrights, such as Brown, who produced occasional local plays.

The story "A New Play in Whitechapel" was published in *Di tsayt* in 1944 and has two theatre references readers would have recognized. The actors Brown mentions but does not name are Etta Topel and Mark Markov. The two took over the direction of the Grand Palais in 1939 and stayed in London for ten years, becoming popular and renowned.[1] An earlier version of the story, called "Der yid mit der piese" (The Jew with the Play), was published in *Di post* in 1931. The stories are almost identical, but in the earlier story, the two actors are named Julius Nathanson and Ludwig Satz, both visiting actors in the 1931–32 season. The play mentioned in both versions is *Alts far kinder* (All for the Children) by the American playwright Rokhl Semkof, and it was performed at the Pavilion Theatre during that season with Satz in the cast. Although *Alts far kinder* was not performed in 1944, this reference remains in the later story.[2]

A final inside joke is the reference to the aspiring playwright being sent to Brown by the Journalists' Union. Both A. M. Kaizer and the internationally known arts critic Leo Koenig were chairs of the Association of Jewish

Journalists and Authors from the twenties to the late forties. The reference may have been aimed at either of them, both of whom Brown knew well.

I was invited to submit an article to a journal. I accepted the invitation with delight and, having decided to write a short story, got straight down to work.

I sat down at my desk enthusiastically one evening, pen in hand, and searched for a theme that would be both interesting and intelligible. Today, with God's help, there are lots of subjects: all kinds of problems with daily life, family tragedies, and even tragicomedies that happen during wartime. But you have to be careful not to trample over the reader's strained nerves.

Naturally, it's a difficult task, and you have to concentrate intensely to think of a topic. I sat there racking my brains until finally I found what I was looking for—a wonderful idea for a short story. With a contented smile I dipped my pen into the ink and began this important work. Barely had I started writing the first words when there was a knock at the door.

Irritated, I decided not to answer it. A few minutes later, the knock came again, and despite my annoyance, I was curious to know who it was, so I curtly answered, "Come in."

Slowly and hesitantly, an elderly man entered. He was thin and pale, with a grey, spiky beard and spectacles on his long, bony nose, over which peered two bloodshot and weary eyes. He held a stick in his hand and a portfolio under his arm and asked me respectfully:

"Are you Katie Brown?"

"Yes," I told the uninvited guest. "What do you want?"

"I've been sent to you," he answered, slowly sitting down on the edge of a chair.

"Who by?" I asked, keen to know.

"The Journalists' Union," he answered with a happy smile, certain that this was a good recommendation.

"What about?"

"I've written a play about Whitechapel for the Yiddish theatre and wanted to read it to the central committee. The secretary sent me to you, saying that you're involved with the Yiddish theatre and you're a real expert on Yiddish drama. So that's why I'm here. I really want to read it to you so that you can give me your opinion."

And with these words, he took out his play, took off his glasses, and wanted to get down to work. I understood straightaway that someone had played a trick on me and sent me a person I could not extricate myself from easily, so I resolved to get rid of him right away and replied:

"I'm sorry, mister, you must forgive me, but I haven't got any time."

But the man wouldn't hear of it.

"I won't keep you long," he begged. "The play is very short: only four acts and ten scenes, a prologue, and an epilogue."

Hearing this, my heart sank, and I felt faint. With an effort I asked:

"Have you written anything else other than this play, I mean, like something for a paper or a journal?"

"No, not yet," he said naively. "But I'm considering taking up the profession."

"What made you think of becoming a writer?"

"To tell you the truth, it's hard for people like me today. The workshop where I worked shut down, and I won't get taken on by a large factory because they say I'm too old and can't work hard enough. I can't live off the ten shillings a week old-age pension. I've thought and thought about what new work I could do, and I came up with this plan. Since they always need new plays for the Yiddish theatre, I'll turn to that trade, and so I've created my first work." He pointed with pride at his manuscript.

"And you haven't read it to anyone yet?"

"Yes, I've read it to my wife and my children and my good friends. Everyone said that it's a good play."

"And anybody else?"

"My colleague, a playwright."

"And what did he say?"

"He said that it doesn't work, that it needs more excitement and comedy, because the audience, he says, wants to have a laugh. He says the writer has to include lots of comic scenes, and if he doesn't, the play won't be successful, and he'd have wasted his time. But I don't agree with his opinion. You see, he's just a nobody who doesn't want me to have the glory and the joy. So please let me read it to you, and you'll see that it's not just a play, but a work of art."

"In that case, I've got some good advice for you. I know where your work will get lots of glory and money," I replied. He stared curiously as I continued:

"You know that here in London there's a good theatre company that per-forms a new play every week. The lead actor is a slim, handsome, and very talented young man. The leading lady is a very good actress: a great artiste, a beautiful woman with large black eyes. And besides that, they are very liberal people and pay well for every new play. Take my advice and go and read your work to them."

When I mentioned their names, he seemed a little embarrassed and answered:

"Yes, I've heard of them."

"Have you seen them performing?"

"No, not yet."

"Why not? Someone like you, who wants to become an important and famous playwright, must see such artists perform. It'll help you considerably."

"I'm so busy writing that I don't go out of the house for days on end. Just one evening I unexpectedly *did* go out and wanted to go to the theatre. The nice lady at the box office told me that they had *All for the Children* playing that day, so I went home because plays for children are not for me. You understand that?"

"Do what I say. Read your play to the two artists. They're bound to buy it from you and pay you well."

He looked rather shamefaced and replied:

"I've already read it to them."

"So what did they say?"

"He said that the play was very good, but impossible to perform. Possibly, he said, it could be fixed by discarding two acts and six scenes, and with the remainder he'd manage to do something. But he said that he didn't have any time now because he's terribly busy with a string of new plays he's just received from America."

"And what did she say?"

"She just said that I shouldn't throw anything away because every word is a pearl. The only problem is that she'd need a new costume in each act, and she wouldn't be able to buy them at the moment on her clothing coupons, so they'll have to set the show aside for later."

"As I see it, dear mister, your first play hasn't had much luck. Now follow my advice. Go home and write a second one, but don't rush it; let it take two or three years. The longer you take, the better it'll be . . . and when you're ready, then come and read it to me, and I'll give you my best advice."

He no longer had anything to say, but I noticed that my words hadn't discouraged him. He put his new livelihood back in its package, stood up, smoothed his beard, glanced into the mirror, blew his nose, put on his glasses, bid me a cordial farewell, and was off to look for a new victim.

But I didn't start my short story that night. I couldn't for the life of me remember what the theme was, all because of the elderly Jew and his play about Whitechapel.

THE LITERARY LANDSCAPE OF LONDON'S YIDDISHTOWN AND THE FIGHT FOR THE SURVIVAL OF YIDDISH, 1930–50

London Friends of Yiddish Language reception for the Canadian Yiddish poet Chava Rosenfarb, Saturday, 5 March 1949, in the Bernhard Baron Settlement at 33 Berner Street, E1. Front left is the novelist Esther Kreitman; obscured behind her is Chava Rosenfarb. Next to Kreitman is the writer and jeweler Moshe Oved and, moving right, the journalist Joseph Fraenkel. Behind Fraenkel, in the hat, in front of the window, is possibly Katie Brown. Third from right is the poet S. Palme; moving left is the cultural activist Judah Beach; and out of focus, sitting at the table, is the poet Joseph Hillel Lewy. (Courtesy of the Mazower private collection)

A selection of Yiddish books published in London, by London Yiddish writers. *From right to left*: A. N. Stencl, *Vidervuks* (London: Loshn un lebn, 1952); S. Palme, *Ringen un keyten* (London: 1947); Lisky, *Melokhe bezuye* (London: Narodiczky and Sons, 1947); Lisky, *Gezangen tsu medines yisroel* (London: 1968); *Yoyvl-almanak—loshn un lebn* (London: Narodiczky, 1956); Moshe Oved, *Vizyonen un eydlshteyner* (London: Narod Press, 1950); A. N. Stencl, *Vaytshepl shtetl debritn* (London: Loshn un lebn, 1961); Itzik Manger, *Volkns ibern dakh* (London: Narodiczky, 1942); Lisky, *Produktivizatsye* (London: Narodiczky, 1937); Brown, *Alts in eynem!* (London: Printed by N. Zilberg, 1951); Brown, *Lakht oyb ir vilt* (London: N. Zilberg, 1947); Kaizer, *Bay undz in vaytshepl* (London: Narodiczky, 1944); Morris Myer, *Idish teatr in London 1902–1942* (London: Narodiczky, 1943), Moshe Oved, *In kheyder arayn* (London, Narodiczky, 1945).

In the crowded, busy East End of the thirties, amid the world depression, and the anxiety of daily struggles, a group of Yiddish writers and publishers found ways to continue to develop a local Yiddish print culture. They were passionate about the Yiddish language and keeping an engagement with it before it disappeared into an English-speaking Jewish world. This is an episodic snapshot, gleaned mostly from reports in the London Yiddish press. It places Katie Brown, Arnold Kaizer, and Summer Lisky in the context of a small but buzzing Yiddish literary community of the thirties and forties; a community producing their perspectives on the world, on Jewry, and on the Jewish East End.

In addition to publishing their work, Yiddish writers took part in literary debates and activities. They chaired societies, gave lectures, performed as living

newspapers, and gave public readings from their works. The activities were organized by the few Yiddish-language organizations and also Jewish societies and
institutions that had Yiddish-speaking members. In the East End, there was the
Workers' Circle, which promoted Yiddish culture and had a full program of
activities directed at working people; and the poet Avrom Nokhem Stencl's literary "Sabbath Afternoons" in Whitechapel drew a large crowd for recitations
and song. Based in the West End, the Ben Uri Art and Literature Society held
debates, cultural events, and exhibitions. The Association of Jewish Journalists
and Authors, with Kaizer as its honorary secretary, met mostly in North West or
Central London, and held events with local and visiting writers.

The writers attending these public events, whether poets, fiction writers,
humorists, essayists, or journalists, were a diverse and changing group of both
established, published writers and what the critic N. M. Seedo called "Saturday
writers" and "part-time poets," who would "fill the room with a kind of marketplace hullabaloo."[1] These public events were directed at a wide audience of Yiddish speakers in an attempt to stem the decline of the Yiddish language in London
and counter the attempts at eradicating Yiddish for future generations. The Jews'
Free School (JFS), for example, where the majority of Jewish pupils were immigrants or children of immigrants, banned the speaking of Yiddish and encouraged
pupils to refuse to speak Yiddish at home with their parents. This school policy
worked so well that school inspectors in 1939 praised the quality of the pupils'
English speech.[2] The *Jewish Chronicle*, on the other hand, which had been opposed
to Yiddish from the 1880s, began to develop a benevolent interest in Yiddish culture, listing events, reviewing books, and even profiling Yiddish writers.[3]

Alongside the public literary events, writers and journalists gathered in private,
more intimate groups to discuss Yiddish writing and publishing, encourage and
support each other's work, and consider how to increase public engagement
and sell more books. The groups congregated around particular individuals, and
London's Yiddishtown was not short of inspiring and magnetic personalities who
gave a wealth of energy to Yiddish writing and were household names in the
community. The art critic and journalist Leo Koenig met with artists, writers,
and intellectuals of the North West London suburbs. The editor of *Di tsayt*, Morris Myer, met regularly on a Friday with a group of journalists in Whitechapel.
The prolific writer Sholem Asch met with individual writers and attended literary groups on his frequent visits to the metropolis.[4] Stencl had an "inner circle"
that met nightly in Carlos' Café on Fulbourne Street. The printer Narodiczky,

published hundreds of Yiddish books and pamphlets from his press and home at 48 Mile End Road. He hosted a salon with Yiddish and Hebrew writers, who also sometimes lived there.[5]

Writers were busy, and the same names appear over and over again in newspaper listings and post-event reports. But it was almost impossible to make a living from writing for the Yiddish press in Britain, and few were full-time professional writers. It was expensive to publish in book form, particularly when the audience for Yiddish writing was diminishing. It was not easy to organize a Yiddish-language literary culture in London that was of interest to regular Yiddish-speaking workers. The Yiddish speakers who moved out of the area joined communities where English was the dominant spoken language. Yiddish activities across London were becoming more and more of a niche culture.

The East End community described by the Yiddish writers was also being documented in the English language. There were a growing number of novelists writing in English about the lives of Jewish immigrants and the children of immigrants in British Jewish communities. The writers had been brought up in those Jewish areas and had heard Yiddish in their families or neighborhoods, yet they lived their lives and wrote in English. Simon Blumenfeld published *Jew Boy* in 1935, and Willy Goldman's *East End My Cradle* was published in 1940. In Jewish Manchester, Louis Golding's *Magnolia Street* was a 1932 best-seller, and he was an influential figure. The most revered Anglo-Jewish writer was still Israel Zangwill, who had died in 1920, but whose novel *Children of the Ghetto*, published in 1892, was seen as a touchstone against which to compare other Jewish novels in English. The critic Leo Koenig, in reviewing Louis Golding's work in *Di tsayt*, referred to Zangwill more than he wrote about Golding.[6]

There was limited contact between Yiddish and English writers. One place where the writers mixed was in the political sphere. Blumenfeld was a member of the Workers' Circle and took part in establishing the antifascist "1942 Committee." Both organizations included many Yiddish writers.[7] The writers knew each other's work: English Jewish novels were reviewed and sometimes translated for the Yiddish press, and occasionally vice-versa, with the *Jewish Chronicle* reviewing Yiddish books.[8] Yet the contact was limited, because writers like Goldman were trying to break away from what they saw as the confinement of their close Jewish immigrant community background. And the English writers generally did not speak Yiddish.

One bridge between the two worlds was the translator Joseph Leftwich, who was an integral part of both circles. He edited *Yisroel*, a collection of around one hundred stories, some by Jewish writers in English and others translations of stories from Yiddish and other European languages into English. Around two dozen of the writers were British Jewish writers, although fewer than a handful were Yiddish writers.[9] Even Leftwich, however, saw the two groups as quite separate. The focus of the Yiddish writers was on preserving Yiddish and documenting the Jewish East End, whereas the English writers were unconcerned with Yiddish.

THE WORKERS' CIRCLE (*ARBETER RING*)

The most active institution with a focus on the Yiddish language was the Workers' Circle or *Arbeter ring*, which put on a vibrant array of events and performances in Yiddish and about Yiddish.[10] The London Workers' Circle was established in around 1909 as a mutual aid organization. Workers paid a weekly fee, and the circle provided sickness benefits, a social club, and cultural programming. It was different from other mutual-aid groups and "Friendly Societies" in that it was run by workers for workers, promoted a secular Jewish culture, and had a progressive outlook. Workers held a range of positions on the left: They were socialists, Bundists, communists, and Labor Zionists. The circle offered a collective way to politically engage with social activism, supporting Jewish causes and defending Jewish rights in antifascist campaigns. Lisky describes the central organizing role of the Workers' Circle in the 1936 "Battle of Cable Street" in his novella *Melokhe bezuye* (A Humiliating Profession).[11]

The Workers' Circle's central venue was Circle House on Great Alie Street in the East End, and seventeen branches across Britain served their local areas. Each branch had its own identity, put on its own activities, and directed its political activism to its membership's allegiances.[12] Circle House was a hubbub of activity day and night, hosting branch and committee meetings, lectures and classes, drama and singing groups, and members organizing cultural events and political campaigns.[13]

Of paramount importance was the circle's relationship to Yiddish, and it actively promoted Yiddish events and activities. It had a Yiddish library and a Sunday school that taught Yiddish to children. The London Workers' Circle maintained good contact with Yiddish-speaking communities on the Continent, and over the years a huge number of internationally famous writers, progressive

Circle House, Great Alie Street, E1, 1937–38. (Courtesy of Tower Hamlets Public Library)

thinkers, and intellectuals spoke at Circle House.[14] Local members included most, if not all, of the Yiddish writers described here: Brown, as already mentioned, was the secretary of the Women's Section of Branch 3; Morris Myer was the first chairman of Branch 1; Lisky was on the Workers' Circle committee for the support of the Vilnius Yiddish Scientific Institute (YIVO); Koenig wrote for the

Arbeter ring journal, as did the popular poet Itzik Manger, who lived in London for nearly a decade during the war. Brown, Kaizer, Myer, Stencl, the poet Moshe Oved, and Joseph Leftwich all spoke there.[15] By 1935 its membership was greater than 2,700. There were so many events—including lectures, discussions, performances, dances, debates, classes, and concerts—that one critic suggested there was a surfeit of activities and leaders.[16]

The Sunday-night classical concert series featured internationally renowned singers and musicians and proved particularly popular in attracting the younger members "by the hundred," who queued up before the programs began to make sure they would be admitted.[17] The protagonist of Simon Blumenfeld's novel *Jew Boy* explains how the concert series was set up by Workers' Circle enthusiasts, but the older members worried that the youth preferred dances and would not be interested in classical music. They were proved wrong.[18]

However, this hive of activity was not the whole story. In an article in 1934, the cofounder and secretary of the East End Workers' Circle, Mick Mindel, bemoaned the workers' lack of interest in coming to cultural events and, in particular, Yiddish cultural events. He saw the mass of Jewish workers as not interested enough in Yiddish books, Yiddish theatre, and other branches of artistic and cultural life because they were "stunned from crises: revolution, war, fascism, Nazism, and other misfortunes." They had no attention for more intellectual or educational events, and in any case, Yiddish was less understandable for the younger generation.[19] This is backed up by a rather abashed, somewhat tongue-in-cheek article by Katie Brown, who told the unfortunate tale of what happened when she gave a lecture in Yiddish at Circle House. She had felt thrilled to have been asked by the Workers' Circle to talk to a politically engaged audience where she would get a spirited response, and she spent considerable energy writing her speech. The Workers' Circle promoted the lecture with notices in the Yiddish press and posters on the walls. However, despite Brown being a well-known and beloved writer and activist, and despite there being a room full of people playing dominoes and chatting next to the lecture hall, she drew merely a handful of audience members, including a couple of children. Her disappointment was only marginally relieved when the chairman told her not to take it personally. It happens all the time![20]

Clearly, members were going to concerts and other social activities, but events with a focus on the Yiddish language were less of a draw. Despite the leadership's best attempts at educating their membership, the Workers' Circle did not always provide the type of events for which workers would leave their dominoes and chats.

THE WEST END CIRCLES: BEN URI AND LEO KOENIG

This was no isolated complaint. In 1933 a "literary and musical evening" was held for the Ben Uri Art and Literature Society's annual general meeting, at which Kaizer was one of the speakers. The meeting took place in the gallery of the Jewish Communal Centre on Woburn Square in the West End, and founding member Judah Beach reported that

> [for] eighteen years the Ben Uri has tried to elevate the situation of the masses. It wanted to enrich their taste for the beautiful artworks of Jewish artists and for Yiddish literature. But, unfortunately, the masses have stood at a distance and have had very little interest in the society.[21]

The Ben Uri was founded in 1915 at a meeting in Gradel's Restaurant in Whitechapel. It was established in the heart of the Jewish East End, with the aim of "fostering and developing Jewish decorative art" and supporting Jewish artists to create and exhibit work.[22] High on its agenda was a commitment to Yiddish culture: literature, theatre, and music. It hosted a wide range of talks by writers, literary critics, and intellectuals. There was considerable discussion among Ben Uri's membership over the society's balance between art and Yiddish literature, with complaints that its emphasis was on collecting artworks more than on developing a Yiddish library.[23] By 1933 the Ben Uri had moved to Woburn House in the West End. The move west made the art exhibitions and literary activities less accessible to Yiddish-speaking, working-class Eastenders. Some asserted that the move was due to the indifference of Whitechapel Jewry rather than the lure of a higher-brow West End culture. In any event, the move effectively placed the Ben Uri more firmly in the middle-class, North West London community.[24]

Closely associated with the Ben Uri from its founding, and of great importance to Yiddish writers of the time, was the journalist, writer, and critic Leo Koenig. Koenig's interests lay in Yiddish culture across the Yiddish-speaking world, and his writing covered art, politics, and philosophy. He provided critical reviews of artists' and writers' work. Koenig gathered a circle of Yiddish-speaking intellectuals around him—mainly artists and writers, including Lisky and Kaizer. Many but not all in his circle were upwardly mobile and middle class, living in the northwest suburbs of Golders Green, Hendon, Willesden, Brondesbury, and other areas.[25] Kaizer was precisely on just such an upwardly mobile trajectory, moving from the East End to North West London, as was Lisky, who had moved out of the East End to Stoke Newington after the war.[26] These writers may have written and conversed in Yiddish, but they were generally a part of the Anglo-Jewish English-speaking milieu as well. They often met at Koenig's house on Hurstwood Road, Temple Fortune, North West London, for tea and discussions on the nature of art.[27]

Leo Koenig was born in 1889 in Salen, in the province of Minsk; he studied at the Bezalel School of Arts and Crafts in Jerusalem and moved to London in 1914. He became an essayist and critic, writing about art, Yiddish literature, and Jewish issues, and was widely published across the Yiddish-speaking world. He was instrumental in establishing a Yiddish branch of the international PEN club. In London, he was a founding member of the Ben Uri, for which he edited the Yiddish art journal *Renesans*.[28] He wrote a daily column for *Di tsayt* and occasional pieces for the *Arbeter ring*, coedited the journal *Eyrope*, and later wrote for *Loshn un lebn*. Among his many publications was a novella, *Shive*, published in 1934, about an East End family mourning for their father. In 1948 he published *Dos bukh fun lesterungen* (The Book of Blasphemies).[29]

Koenig had a detailed and broad knowledge of European literature and culture, and his Yiddish essays, published widely in America and Poland, were often controversial, initiating discussion in the Yiddish press. Seedo suggested that Koenig was aloof, and that he ignored local writers and only "condescendingly obliged the editors of the Jewish dailies by writing for them."[30]

Koenig's daily column for *Di tsayt* was a solid fixture on page 2 of the paper for decades. He wrote about world literature, art, and culture. In 1934 Koenig's novella *Shive* came out in English; it was translated by Joseph Leftwich under the title *A Week After Life*. The *Jewish Chronicle* and *Di tsayt* reviewed the book within a few days of each other. The *Jewish Chronicle*'s review was short and damning: highlighting its inaccessibility for a gentile audience and suggesting that Leftwich could have found a better outlet for his excellent translation talent.[31] In contrast, Morris Myer gave it a glowing review in *Di tsayt*: "The writer has looked the truth in the eyes and has related this truth to us and the world. In a world of falseness of concept and art, drawing out the truth is one of the greatest achievements."[32] The

Yiddish press, in this instance, was clearly going to protect its own. Myer would not have wanted to lose a main contributor to his newspaper.

Koenig's *Dos bukh fun lesterungen* (The Book of Blasphemies) also had a critical reception. Stencl called it Koenig's "latest philosophical theses, ambitious treatises with all sorts of clumsy and stylistic pretentions." Stencl remembered going into a bookshop with Koenig. The bookseller was honored that Koenig had come in personally to deliver the book, and searched for the best place to display it. Stencl recalls how he smiled as Koenig's heavy tome was placed in a position of honor, next to Whitechapel's "best seller"—Katie Brown's *Lakht oyb ir vilt* (Laugh If You Want To).[33]

JOURNALISTS' CIRCLES: *DI TSAYT* AND MORRIS MYER

Di tsayt had been established by Morris Myer in 1913, and he remained its editor until his death in 1944. The press offices were based at 325 Whitechapel Road. Myer filled his daily paper with national and international news; reports of international congresses and local meetings; features and articles on politics and culture; serialized stories, short stories, feuilletons, poetry, and sketches; theatre reviews; and local notices, listings, and news from synagogues and organizations. He placed serious politics next to sensationalist news and back-page, gripping, easy-read serials that ended with cliffhangers. There were set spots in the paper reserved for regular items. One prime slot, set halfway down page 2 twice a week, had a satirical sketch or humorous story that was rotated among several writers, the three main ones being "our three Whitechapel humorists: *Der eygener*, Katie Brown, and Kaizer."[34] *Der eygener*, or *An eygenem*, as noted earlier, was the pseudonym of Leyb Sholem (Leon) Creditor.

> **Leyb Sholem (Leon) Creditor** was born in 1875 in Lithuania; he immigrated to London in around 1905. He was possibly the first professional Yiddish journalist in Britain, working for *Der idisher ekspres*, *Der idisher dzurnal*, and later *Di tsayt*, and periodicals, including *Loshn un lebn*. He was one of the editors of *Teatr shpigl* (Theatre Mirror). He wrote essays and a play, and under the pseudonym *Der eygener*, he wrote humorous sketches. He financed Stencl's first book of poems in London. From 1951 he coedited *Di idishe shtime*.[35]

Over Morris Myer's three decades at the helm, he gave work to probably the whole circle of local Yiddish writers, as well as those from further afield in Europe and America.

> Morris Myer was born in 1879 in Romania and came to London in 1902. He was active in labor organizations and published *Di sveting sistem, vi vert men fun ir poter* (The Sweating System, How Does One Get Rid of It). He translated British and European plays for London's Yiddish theatre, including Shakespeare's *Merchant of Venice* for the Pavilion Theatre in 1912. He founded *Di tsayt* (The Times) in 1913, and he edited it for thirty years. He also edited its evening edition, *Di ovent nayes* (The Evening News), from 1914 to 1940. He was one of the main contributors to Zalmen Reyzen's lexicon of Yiddish literature, and he produced the book *Yidish teater in london* (Yiddish Theatre in London, c. 1943). He was the vice president of the Federation of English Zionists and a member of the Board of Deputies of British Jews.[36]

Myer was a pivotal figure in Anglo Jewry. He was active and highly respected across the Jewish community, in both the established Anglo-Jewish institutions and the immigrant East End. He epitomizes the integration of people with immigrant backgrounds into leadership positions in the Anglo-Jewish establishment.

Myer was active in probably all the London Yiddish cultural institutions, yet his reach extended beyond London, as *Di tsayt* traveled to other communities in Britain. Stencl called him an excellent journalist and an even better speaker.[37] In a passionate memorial piece, Brown describes how Myer was at the center of a small circle of journalists who met regularly in a "prominent teashop in Whitechapel" and who were "Hasidim around their *rebbe*." She commented on his dynamic presence, his approachability, and his centrality to the writer community. The writer Esther Kreitman also remembered Myer's "august presence" at the weekly Friday meeting of journalists and literati.[38] Lisky recalled how Myer's breadth of reading allowed discussions with him on dialectics, relativity, Kant, and Spinoza, and Myer was frequently asked to give lectures on Jewish history, politics, and culture.[39]

Myer was particularly interested in the Yiddish theatre, writing theatre reviews under the pseudonym *Kritikus.* He could be outspoken and pompous; his criticism could be sharp, and cultural meetings were not always smooth affairs. For example, when the Vilna Theatre Troupe visited London to perform at the West End Fortune Theatre in 1934, they attended a reception with local Yiddish writers at Circle House. Discussion, however, descended into argument. Myer gave an analysis of the expressionism of the new Vilna troupe as a significant development compared with the impressionism of the old troupe. This was met with irritation by the Vilna Theatre Troupe's leader, Mordechai Mazo, who objected to Myer's definitions and went on to chastise him for being too harsh on weak performers in his theatre reviews, saying that he "lacked forgiveness." There was some commotion as the chair tried to smooth things over, and Myer argued back that artistic truth was more important than any other consideration.[40] Critics did not hold their punches.

In around 1943 Myer gathered many of his theatre articles in his book *Yidish teater in london* (Yiddish Theatre in London); it was published with the patronage of a nineteen-member committee that included Kaizer and Lisky. This was not an unusual way to publish, and the introduction to the book by the committee gives an idea of the esteem in which Myer was held. The committee represented twelve organizations: cultural groups (including the Friends of Yiddish Theatre, the Workers' Circle, the Ben Uri, and the Association of Jewish Journalists and Authors), trade unions, aid organizations, and Zionist groups.

THE GLASS OF TEA AND SHOLEM ASCH

The main type of event organized by the Yiddish writers' community for local and visiting writers were receptions. There were receptions when a local author published a book or a popular writer celebrated a decade birthday, but most often when a writer from abroad was passing through London. These receptions may have been in time for afternoon tea, but even those in the evening were called *A gleyzl tey lekoved* . . . (A glass of tea in honor of . . .). Despite the informality of the "tea" concept, these were formal affairs with a set order of how things were run. The chair of the event would introduce the writer. A number of writers would give prepared talks on different aspects of the writer's latest book, and an actor would recite parts of the work. The writer would be invited to respond, there would be some time for questions, and, finally, there would be a vote of thanks, followed by the tea. The tea was as important as the formal part of the evening. Lisky describes how the "poets, journalists, critics, essayists, and humorists drank tea and discussed liquor" in an atmosphere of gossip and jostling for position.[41] Sometimes the event would end there, but with a particularly popular guest there might be some musical entertainment and a write-up in the Yiddish press.

One of the most extravagant occasions was the "grandiose reception" in 1933 in honor of a visit by the celebrated Sholem Asch. The reception drew a large local crowd and special guests from as far afield as Paris, Warsaw, and Palestine. After the twelve speeches about Asch's life and work (all reported in detail in the full-page report in *Di tsayt*), Asch gave a powerful response, talking about the role of Jewish writers and arguing that, although critics had compared him to Tolstoy and Balzac, he saw his work as coming from the love of the ordinary Jew and the people of Israel. This brought a standing ovation.[42]

> **Sholem Asch** was the most famous, prolific, and popular living Yiddish writer at the time, and a familiar face in London. Born in Kutne (Kutno), Poland, he lived in various places in Europe and was naturalized in America in 1920. Asch published scores of works: novels, including *Motke ganev* (Motke the Thief, 1916); plays, including *Got fun nekome* (God of Vengeance, 1907); and essays. He was a controversial figure, unafraid to address taboo subjects, such as Christianity in *The Nazarene* (1939). He was made honorary president of the Yiddish PEN Club in 1932.[43]

Sholem Asch had a special connection to London. He had first visited in 1906, when the actor Jacob Adler, Sholem Aleichem, and Asch had all stayed in the Three Nuns Hotel on Aldgate High Street in Whitechapel. He also had a longstanding contract with Morris Myer to write for *Di tsayt* from its early years. Whenever he moved between Europe and America, he stopped for a few days in London to visit Myer and others.[44] Later, his daughter Ruth Shaffer lived there with her family. Asch may have on occasion slipped into London without the Yiddish press knowing, but announcements of his arrival regularly appeared in the papers: He was coming to visit his daughter and staying a few days; he was giving a lecture; he was weak from working so hard and coming to convalesce so no one must disturb him; he was talking at an exhibition at the Ben Uri gallery; or he was writing a new book and should be left in peace. His lectures on Palestine, on Polish Hasidism, and on the Yiddish book crisis were all reported afterward in the paper. Indeed, Asch was in press notices just as often when he was not in London:

for publication of a new work, for publication of a new English translation, for a controversy over a medal awarded to him by the International PEN club, and so on.[45] Asch was a favorite of newspaper editors, and both *Di post* and *Di tsayt* serialized his works.[46] In addition, many of his works were published in England with English translators. London was like home turf, and he could always be sure of a good turnout for a reception during his visit.

Asch's 1933 reception was therefore a big event, and after the "cup of tea" interval, there was another special guest. The writer Malka Locker read "prayers" from her latest poetry collection *Du* (You) and sung in Yiddish to an enthusiastic audience response.[47]

> Malka Locker was born in Kitev, Eastern Galicia (today, Kuty, Ukraine), in 1887; she lived in London for ten years between 1938 and 1948. She was a poet and composer who read and sang at local and international events. In 1938 she wrote the choral works *Luekh trts"v* (1935–36 Calendar) and *Luekh trts"kh* (1937–38 Calendar), which were staged in Vienna and London. Among her publications is the poetry book *Shtet* (Cities), about London, which was published in 1942 by Narodiczky Press. Her husband, Berl Locker, was the general secretary of the World Union of Poale Zion (Labor Zionists) and a member of the Zionist Executive in London.[48]

Sholem Asch had no formal circle of writers around him, but he was highly respected, and writers found opportunities and occasions to engage in discussions with him. He was well acquainted with London writers and a close friend of the writer, jeweler, and sculptor Moshe Oved. Asch used to visit him in his jewelry shop, Cameo Corner, and they would walk in the park to discuss political and cultural issues, art, writing, and the old country.[49]

Oved was a familiar face in events across London. He was a cofounder of the Ben Uri and contributed financially to many Yiddish organizations and individuals. Brown mentions him in a sketch as donating jewelry to charity.[50]

> Moshe Oved (Edward Good) was born in Skempe (Skępe), Poland, in 1885, and came to England in 1903. He was a poet, writer, and cultural activist. A jeweler by trade, he was involved in running the Ben Uri for

many years. He ran a small shop in the West End called Cameo Corner, which attracted many Jewish and English customers, including Queen Mary. He was the president of the Friends of Yiddish Language. His poems and prose were published in the art journal *Renesans*, *Di tsayt*, Stencl's *Heftlekh*, and *Loshn un lebn*. His memoirs, *Vizyonen un eydlshteyner*, appeared in English as *Visions and Jewels*.[51]

Oved, like Myer, acted as a sort of bridge between east and west. He was involved in most of the Yiddish-language circles and deeply concerned about the rift between Anglo-Jewry and Yiddish culture. He blamed the West End Jewish intellectuals for not supporting Yiddish culture and singled out the upwardly mobile arts activists, such as those at the Ben Uri, for not having the spiritual strength to explain the significance of the arts to East End working people.[52]

Although receptions that were expected to fill a large hall took place at Circle House, the Whitechapel Gallery, the popular Stern's Hotel in Aldgate, or the Pavilion or Grand Palais theatres, smaller receptions took place in restaurants or even in the homes of community activists, and had a similar format. These smaller meetings did not compromise the quality of the speakers, and they allowed the writers to have more intimate conversations with guests. During a visit by Asch in 1932, he gave a talk about the situation for Yiddish literature to a group of local writers at the home of Ben Uri founding member and treasurer Yankev Seres, on Bethune Road, Stamford Hill.[53] This gathering had been organized by the Ben Uri, and the chair of the evening, Moshe Oved, mentioned how a couple of months earlier they had had the honor to hear the Hebrew poet Chaim Nachman Bialik in the same room, where he talked about the situation of Hebrew literature.[54]

THE EAST END CIRCLE: "SABBATH AFTERNOONS" AND AVROM NOKHEM STENCL

There are competing anecdotes attached to how the poet Avrom Nokhem Stencl arrived in London. Yiddishist Dovid Katz, who lived in London, lodging with Lisky during the 1970s, remembers that Stencl and members of his "inner circle" would relate the story of how Stencl escaped Berlin in 1936, crossing the border in a coffin. Katz also heard from Lisky, who was in Stencl's "outer circle," that the coffin story was a small incident at the beginning of his journey.[55] The more likely version is that the Quaker Christabel Fowler facilitated his escape by inviting him to London to write an article on English art.[56] Whether or not there is any basis to the coffin story, or whether it is a myth, it is worth repeating, because Stencl became an important figure for the creation of Yiddish mythology as he wrote his beloved Whitechapel into his poetry published in London.

Avrom Nokhem Stencl was born in 1893 into a Hasidic family in Tsheladzsh (Czeladz), Poland. He fled to Holland in 1919 to escape conscription, and from there to Berlin, where he became a Yiddish poet of some acclaim, publishing poetry and essays. He arrived in London in 1936 and became a cultural activist for the Yiddish language. He published dozens of poetry books and pamphlets, including *Londoner sonetn* (London Sonnets, 1937); *London lirik* (London Lyric, 1940); *Yidish* (1941); and *September motivn, harbst un nile lider* (September Motifs, Autumn, and Neilah Poems, 1942); and he edited the literary journals *Heftlekh* and *Loshn un lebn*.[57] His work appeared in Leftwich's *Golden Peacock*, and his Berlin poems were published in translation in 2007. From 1938 he ran the *Shabbes nokhmitog* (Sabbath Afternoon) weekly literary group, later called "the Friends of Yiddish Language." He lived in Whitechapel for some forty years.[58]

As soon as he arrived, Stencl began producing his own poetry in pamphlets published by the Narodiczky Press. He also wrote for *Di tsayt*, although this part of his career did not have an auspicious beginning. Yiddishist and tailor Majer Bogdanski recalled a story, told to him by Stencl, that the first time he gave Morris Myer a manuscript of a poem for publication in *Di tsayt*, Myer took it away and "improved" it beyond all recognition. When Stencl saw the result, he refused to allow its publication and demanded the manuscript back, but Myer would not return it. Stencl opened the window of his flat and yelled "Police!" and Myer capitulated.[59] This incident did not seem to affect their ongoing relationship, and Myer published many of Stencl's poems over the next decade.[60]

The most inspired and long-lasting of the regular literary events was the weekly "Sabbath Afternoons," which began in 1938. These gatherings were based on a similar Yiddish literary circle in Berlin, where in 1936 the group had been inaugurated in secret, posing as an engagement party, with Stencl as the groom and his friend, the actress Dora Diamant, as the bride.[61] In 1938 in London, no such care was needed and, encouraged by Diamant, Stencl ran the London Sabbath Afternoon meeting in the Jewish reading room of the Jewish Shelter at 63 Mansell Street in Whitechapel.[62] It brought together writers and intellectuals who read their own work and that of others to an engaged and critical audience. One of the regular readers was Esther Kreitman.

> **Esther Kreitman** was born in 1891 in Bilgoray (Biłgoraj), Poland. She left Poland at the start of World War I, coming via Berlin and Antwerp to London, where she lived for nearly forty years. She translated essays by George Bernard Shaw on women and socialism into Yiddish. She published two novels—*Der sheydim tants* (Dance of the Demons) in 1936, and *Brilyantn* (Diamonds) in 1951—and a collection of short stories titled *Yikhes* (Lineage), 1949, some of which were set during the Blitz. Her fiction appeared in the Yiddish press and in *Loshn un lebn*, and most of her work has been translated into English. She was the sister of Israel Joshua Singer and Isaac Bashevis Singer. She was also related by marriage to Lisky whose niece Lola married Kreitman's son Maurice Carr.[63]

In addition to giving writers the opportunity to read their own work, each Sabbath Afternoon had a specific focus. It might have been the anniversary of a Yiddish writer, a Jewish festival, a new work published by a local writer, or a visit by a guest from abroad. The contributions of readings, oratory, and song would be connected to that theme. Lisky and Brown were regular attendees. Lisky described the Sabbath Afternoons in his novella, *Melokhe bezuye*. Brown wrote about Stencl in the introduction to *Lakht oyb ir vilt*, and later, Brown, Kaizer, and Lisky were all regularly published in Stencl's journals.[64]

THE YIDDISH CULTURE ASSOCIATION (YKUF)

In 1938 a small group of writers established a London branch of the international communist-leaning YKUF, naming it the *Yidisher kultur-gezelshaft, YKUF, London*. Myer was the chair, Lisky the secretary, and Oved the treasurer.[65] The organizing committee, including Seedo, Stencl, and Leftwich, arranged a number of lectures and events.

N. M. Seedo, the pseudonym of Sonia Husid, was born in Sekuran, Bessarabia (today, Sokyriany, Ukraine), in 1906 and educated in Vienna. She belonged to the illegal communist party in Romania. She arrived in London in 1930 and became active in Yiddish literary culture. She wrote on psychology and literature in works that included *Di dialektik fun gefil un gedank* (The Dialectics of Thought and Feeling, 1941). She wrote essays and reviews of the works of Yiddish writers in *Loshn un lebn* and was a regular participant in Stencl's Sabbath Afternoons. In 1964 she published a memoir in English, *In the Beginning Was Fear*. She was married to Lisky. Her brother was the poet and story-writer Mordecai Husid.[66]

YKUF's inaugural debate took place at Circle House in February 1938. Moshe Oved's opening speech was downbeat, bemoaning the loss of Yiddish culture. He expressed his frustration that, after London's vibrant and noisy Yiddish existence before World War I, there was now "a sort of silence." The only scurry of activity happened when there was a guest from abroad. He claimed that the Yiddish cultural community had become apathetic, and that the self-criticism that had once pushed creativity forward was no longer there. Morris Myer countered that this was a worldwide problem: Cultural revival happens only when people feel excited and hopeful. But now everyone's culture was suffering, and Yiddish cultural revival was impossible in such an unsettled world. The translator Joseph Leftwich added a more optimistic perspective: "People create things here without a fanfare. We don't have to cry and shout about Yiddish disappearing."[67]

Under Seedo's initiative, YKUF organized a lecture course at King's College, University of London, on the development of the Yiddish language and literature, hoping to later establish a chair in Yiddish at the university. The first three lectures were given by the distinguished and pioneering linguist Solomon Birnbaum, and the following three lectures on Yiddish literature were given by Leftwich. The lectures attracted more than two hundred people.[68]

The translator and community activist **Joseph Leftwich** was born in 1892 in Holland and came to England as a child. He held a number of organizational positions with the Poale Zion (Labor Zionists), the Jewish Telegraphic Agency, and the Federation of Jewish Relief Organizations. He was one of what came to be called the "Whitechapel Boys" group of writers, and he served as the representative of the Yiddish PEN to the international PEN. Leftwich translated large amounts of Yiddish literature and essays, including the poetry anthology *The Golden Peacock* (1939), in which he included a number of London writers. He continued to publish into the 1970s.[69]

An important issue that had come up at the YKUF inaugural meeting was the subject of Yiddish publishing. Lisky was critical of the small number of Yiddish books being published, and he stressed how important they were to Yiddish speakers. One response by YKUF, London was to produce the periodical *Yidish london*, edited by the committee of contributors. The first edition included poetry and essays by the entire editorial board and four or five other local writers, including a poem by Brown. Stencl's essay pondered on the challenge to date:

It has not been easy to plough the arid cultural-earth in London. The field of Yiddish culture is hard and stony. Hard, as is every place that has not felt the warm kiss of human work for a long time. Optimism and purpose are therefore needed for building and fighting, and the iron patience of a robust peasant awaiting the fruit of the soil hidden under its wild grasses and swamps that draw in and kill creative activity. Not one attempt disappears, not one effort is in vain.[70]

THE YIDDISH LITERARY CIRCLES AND THE YIDDISH THEATRE

A major player in the continuity of Yiddish as a vibrant language was the Yiddish theatre. The Yiddish theatre was an institution that was based on spoken Yiddish, and it attracted large audiences throughout the 1930s. It was attended by writers who wrote reviews, articles, and critiques of plays. Morris Myer wrote hundreds of theatre reviews in *Di tsayt*. The theatre was loved, criticized, and made fun of, as in Kaizer's humorous sketch about audience behavior in "When You Go to a Yiddish Theatre," which is translated in this volume.

There was a two-way relationship between the literary circles and the Yiddish theatre. Actors, directors, and playwrights were often part of the literary circles, and they orated at writers' receptions and events. The Yiddish writer and theatre producer Abish Meisels translated *The Merchant of Venice* and *Othello* into Yiddish, wrote his own plays for the London Yiddish stage, and authored a novel, *Der volentir* (The Volunteer), which was serialized in *Di tsayt in 1942*. The actor and playwright Joseph Markovitsh wrote many popular plays and songs, some on the theme of London, and also *melo-deklamatsyes*, which were dramatic poems in rhyming couplets accompanied by orchestra.[71] The actress Dora Diamant and the actor Mark Markov often read from writers' works at literary events such as Stencl's Sabbath Afternoons. Stencl praised Diamant's wonderful recitations from the great Yiddish writer I. L. Peretz, and Markov had the leading male role at the Grand Palais Theatre, performing together with the actress Etta Topel.[72] Their shows were advertised daily with photographs in *Di tsayt*. Markov and Topel both humorously appear incognito in Brown's story "A New Play in Whitechapel," which is translated in this volume.

In the other direction, the theatre offered considerable support to writers who wrote plays among their more established writing. Brown wrote at least one full-length play, a few one-act plays, and many theatre songs, which were performed both on the professional Yiddish stage and by the Workers' Circle theatre group. The theatre journalist Samuel Harendorf produced the big hit *The King of Lampedusa* in 1943 at the New Yiddish Theatre on Adler Street. The writer Max Ellenzweig had one play produced at the Grand Palais in the mid-1940s, and the poet S. Palme wrote a play for children in 1923 and another play performed at the Grand Palais in 1942.[73]

THE STRUGGLE FOR THE SURVIVAL OF YIDDISH IN A WAR-STRUCK CITY

On the eve of World War II, Katie and Shlomo Brown and two of their five children were living in Chicksand Street, just off Brick Lane, in Whitechapel. Brown was editing the *Arbeter ring* journal of the Workers' Circle. Arnold and Bertha Kaizer, with two teenagers, had just moved farther west to North Crescent, in Finchley; and Arnold Kaizer was working for the Federation of Jewish Relief Organizations.

Morris Myer, postcard, L. and J. Suss's Prize Pictures, 25 Whitechapel Road, c. 1920. (Courtesy of the Mazower private collection)

Sholem Asch speaking at the London YIVO reception in his honor (1955). (Courtesy of the Mazower private collection)

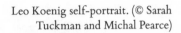

Leo Koenig self-portrait. (© Sarah
Tuckman and Michal Pearce)

Moshe Oved in his
jewelry shop Cameo Cor-
ner, Museum Street, close
to the British Museum
c. 1950. (Courtesy of
Goldie Morgentaler,
private collection)

Portrait of "Hinde Esther Kreitman," by Hazel Karr, granddaughter of Esther Kreitman, 2018. (Courtesy of the artist)

Leyb Sholem (Leon) Creditor (*Der eygener*), c. 1950s.

Dora Diamant and Avrom Nokhem Stencl. The inscription in German on the back of the photo reads: "Mit einen guten Freund, A. N. Stencil, an einen Badeort. Sommer, 1950" (With a good friend, A. N. Stencl, at a seaside resort, summer 1950). (Courtesy of the Lask Collection)

Malka Locker (left) and N. M. Seedo (right), 1940s. (Courtesy of the Mazower private collection)

A. M. Fuchs c. 1930s (Courtesy of
Hazel Karr, private collection)

S. Palme, pen name of Bernard
Savinsky, who also wrote under
the name Alegoryer c. late 1940s.
(Courtesy of the Mazower private
collection)

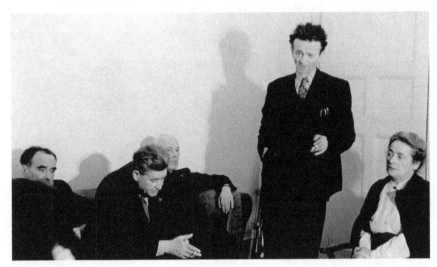

Itzik Manger at a London literary meeting, 1940s. (Courtesy of Goldie Morgentaler, private collection)

Joseph Leftwich as a delegate at the 1966 P.E.N. Congress in America. From *Loshn un lebn* (May–July 1966).

Summer Lisky and Sonia Husid (Seedo), with a newborn, were living in the East End and working on the publication *Yidish london*. They were all busy writing, and deeply involved in both Jewish community work and attending Yiddish-language events.

Despite imminent war, the Sabbath afternoon meetings gathered momentum. In fact, attendance numbers were bolstered by writers, journalists, actors, and intellectuals arriving in London who had escaped Europe at the last moment. In reports in *Di tsayt*, there seemed to be new journalists welcomed to London at almost every "glass of tea."

In September 1939 a YKUF-sponsored reception honored Moshe Oved just before a trip he was making to America. It took place at Stern's Hotel on Mansell Street, with a crowd of writers, artists, and Oved's friends.[74] The meeting followed the usual formalities. It was opened by Leftwich, who emphasized how Oved was one of the few Yiddish writers to publish works in both Yiddish and English. Lisky spoke about the theme of nature in Oved's prose. The next speaker was Lisky's brother, the established Yiddish fiction writer A. M. Fuchs, who had himself recently arrived in London from Vienna.

> Abraham Moshe Fuchs was born in 1890 in Yezerna, Eastern Galicia (now Ozerna, Ukraine). He was a member of the writers' group "Yung Galitsye" (Young Galicia) before he left for the United States in 1912, where he wrote for *Forverts* (the Yiddish *Daily Forward*). He returned to Europe in 1914 and lived in Vienna until 1938. He was a prolific writer of articles and books of stories of Jewish Galicia, including *Oyfn bergl* (On the Hill, 1924). Fuchs escaped Austria and, via France, arrived in England in 1939, where he was interned on the Isle of Man for three months. He lived in London for ten years, writing for *Di tsayt*, coediting the journal *Eyrope*, and occasionally contributing to *Loshn un lebn*. He was the brother of Lisky and his daughter married Kreitman's son. In 1950 he settled in Israel.[75]

Fuchs welcomed journalist colleagues who had also recently escaped Nazi violence and arrived in London via Prague and Vienna. This escape route was familiar; the poet Joseph Hillel Lewy had arrived that way just a few months earlier. Lewy was already well known in the Yiddish world, and he had quickly become an integral part of the London writers' community, writing and publishing in London.

Joseph Hillel Lewy (Levi) was born in Kroke (Krakow), Poland, in 1891. He lived in Germany until early 1939, when he managed to reach London, where he lived for the rest of his life. He published three books of poetry in London: *Kroke/poeme* (Krakow, poems, 1941), *Ven di velt brent* (When the World Is Aflame, 1943), and *Mayn tate der soyfer un andere poemes* (My Father the Scribe and Other Poems, 1949). He wrote occasionally for *Di tsayt* and *Loshn un lebn* and had works translated by Leftwich for his anthology *Golden Peacock*.[76]

At Oved's reception, there were nine speakers, including Esther Kreitman and the librarian of the Whitechapel Library Reading Room, Mara Doniach. In Oved's response to the speakers, he explained how the purpose of his trip was to forge new links with American Yiddish writers and strengthen existing contacts between American and English Yiddish literary circles. The evening ended with a reading of Oved's poetry by Abish Meisels, who had arrived from Vienna a year earlier.[77]

THE START OF THE WAR

Despite the vibrancy of some of its earlier events, the YKUF group did not manage to keep going through the war, and the attempt to set up a Yiddish chair at King's College collapsed due to lack of funding. But Stencl's Sabbath Afternoons kept on throughout the war, now taking place at the Reading Room in Adler House on Adler Street. After Oved returned to London, he gave a lecture on the art of writing at a Sabbath Afternoon gathering. As Oved was known outside of Yiddish circles, his lecture was attended by a local councilor and Anglo-Jewish artists from the Ben Uri Society. They were not Yiddish speakers, so Oved spoke in English. This was extremely unusual for a Sabbath Afternoon meeting, where Yiddish typically was the only language used. Indeed, in his daily dealings Stencl refused to engage with anyone in anything other than Yiddish. This rare occasion shows the respect offered to Oved by the Yiddish writers in appreciation of his organizational and financial support. No doubt after the talk, when "close friends and colleagues spent time with him in a warm atmosphere over a cup of tea," they reverted to Yiddish.[78]

In July 1940, a Sabbath Afternoon was dedicated to the local poet S. Palme on the publication of his new book *Tsvishn fir vent* (Within Four Walls). By this time, the numbers attending the Sabbath Afternoons had risen to more than a hundred each week, and significantly more for special events. Lisky, Oved, and Stencl introduced Palme's work, and the Yiddish actor and orator Mark Markov recited two of his poems.

> **S. Palme**, the pen name of Bernard Savinski, was born in 1888 in Mezritsh (Międzyrzec), Poland. He arrived in London in 1910, where he remained, apart from four years in Soviet Russia after the 1917 revolution. He published verse and prose in just about all the London Yiddish press: *Der idisher dzurnal*, *Di post*, *Der familyen fraynd*, *Di tsayt*, *Loshn un lebn*, and other publications. He sometimes wrote under the pseudonym Alegoryer. His books included a play for children, a novella, and a number of books of poetry, including *Farviste erd* (Scorched Earth, 1943) and *Ringen un keytn* (Links and Chains, 1947).[79]

At the end of Palme's Sabbath Afternoon, Brown's friend and neighbor from Chicksand Street, the London editor and journalist Ben A. Sochachewsky, made a speech suggesting that the difference between literary celebrations organized by Jews and those organized by non-Jews was that the Jewish one was free. This comment may have been an inside joke or dig at some English literary event that had been expensive to attend. More likely it was a cheeky aside to the religious attendees, as Sochachewsky went on to add that on the Sabbath everything Jewish is free: It's free to go and hear the Torah reading on a Sabbath morning and free to hear a secular Yiddish poet's work on a Sabbath afternoon. It is doubtful whether either of these were indeed free, because people paid memberships both to their synagogues and to the Sabbath Afternoon circle. No doubt Sochachewsky's joke was taken to mean that the numbers attending the Sabbath Afternoon compared favorably with those of many local synagogues.[80]

> **Ben A. Sochachewsky**, born in 1889 in Lodz, Poland, came to London in around 1914. He was a prominent figure on the London literary scene: a poet, satirist, editor, and Hasidic storyteller. He was a journalist and edited the humorous weekly *S'hitl* in 1932. He was on the editorial staff of *Di tsayt* until it folded in 1950, after which he founded and edited *Di idishe shtime*. Between 1948 and 1957 he published five long novels that were serialized in those two papers.[81]

Sochachewsky ended his talk by acknowledging the role of Israel Narodiczky and his press, which had published Palme's book (and indeed had published Lisky's book and would go on to publish Kaizer's a few years later), and who made Yiddish publishing possible in July 1940, even as they were surrounded by the chaos of war.

YIDDISH AND THE BLITZ

On 6 September 1940, *Di tsayt* announced that the next day's Sabbath Afternoon would be the first of three lectures by A. M. Fuchs. The first lecture would focus on Yiddish poetry in London: Oved, Locker, and Stencl. The second lecture would be about political journalism in London, examining the work of Leftwich, Myer, and Koenig.[82] The third would be announced later in *Di tsayt*.

At 4 PM on Saturday, 7 September, however, no one attended the lecture. The cancellation notice was provided by the roar of German bombers as the Blitz began pummeling South East London and, as the day moved on, reaching the East End. The Blitz over London ran for fifty-seven consecutive days and nights, bringing all East End activity to a virtual standstill.[83]

But that same month, before Fuchs's talk could be rescheduled, Stencl produced the first issue of a new monthly Yiddish literary journal containing his own and around ten other London writers' contributions in poetry, prose, and essays relating to Yiddish literature. He did not have enough money to pay for printing the journal, so Narodiczky loaned him the funds to produce the first edition.[84] Stencl recalled that this was during the first days of the Blitz, when even *Di tsayt* had ceased publication for a few days.[85] It was a time when no one considered founding a new literary journal in Whitechapel. But the bombing of the East End was a spur, because the Yiddish word needed to survive these dangerous streets. It was an hour before nightfall, on the eve of Rosh Hashanah, the Jewish New Year, and Stencl barely had time to grab the five hundred copies and run into the nearest shelter before the bombing began. Thousands of people were sheltering there. In one corner there were Orthodox Jews praying the New Year liturgy, and "danger hung over everyone's head . . . At that moment, how close people were to God, and my heart felt close to every Jew there. Yes, it turned fantastical, if not fanatical. In that dreadful night, if I had had one thousand copies, I would have sold them all." Stencl made enough to repay the loan, and more.[86]

The new journal did not have a name. Each edition had its own title, but they were informally called *Stencls heftlekh* (Stencl's Pamphlets); some were

Copies of Stencl's *Heftlekh* and *Loshn un lebn*. (Photographs by the author)

sixteen pages and some were forty. Stencl became a familiar figure, standing at the door of every literary or Yiddish-language event, selling his *Heftlekh* and, later, *Loshn un lebn*. The Narodiczky Press printed them all, and after Narodiczky's death in 1942, his sons, who continued the business as the Narod Press, kept publishing the journal regardless of whether the cost of the printing was paid each time.[87]

The Blitz continued to devastate the East End. During one bombing raid, Circle House was damaged, destroying the large hall where so many Workers' Circle events had been held. Hundreds of members of the Circle were fighting in the war, and activities were reduced, although the *Arbeter ring* journal was still being published.[88] During another bombing raid, Esther Kreitman was seen running, terrified, through the streets of Whitechapel, clutching the manuscript of her first novel, *Brilyantn* (Diamonds).[89] In yet another bombing raid, Stencl's small room off Commercial Road and his whole street were completely destroyed. With it went all his books and papers, leaving him to live in a rest home for air-raid victims, where he began writing poems about that very air raid. His friend and colleague Joseph Leftwich remembered how Stencl refused to be bowed; he was undeterred in his mission to ensure that the Yiddish language was not bombed out of existence:

Some will say that the man is mad to go on, heedless of everything that is happening around him and to himself, writing and printing and selling—he is his own bookseller—his poems and essays. The truth is, the man is "possessed." No matter what is happening to him, there is nothing more important than to express himself . . . in his beloved Yiddish. . . . He is a fanatic. But it needs a fanatic to stick to his guns in spite of everything that happens.[90]

As the bombing over London became less intense, with night raids becoming more common than daytime attacks, Fuchs's lecture was finally rescheduled for a Sabbath Afternoon in early November. The report in *Di tsayt* ran:

"When the canons speak, the muse is silent," says a Latin proverb. The Yiddish muse, however, will not be silenced, even when Hitler's bombs are smashing and canons are thundering. The spiritual Yiddish word will surely survive all destruction of the Nazi destroyers.

In the reading room of the East End of London, better to say, in the shelter of the cellar of the reading room, there was recently an important literary event, while outside in the neighborhood bombing raged from Hitler's airplanes. This is a strange part of Jewish spiritual life.[91]

Before Fuchs began his talk on the three Yiddish poets—Locker, Oved, and Stencl—he welcomed a special guest: a fourth poet, who had just escaped to London as a refugee from Europe and who was already busy in local literary circles. The poet was the highly praised and popular writer Itzik Manger, and Fuchs began his lecture with praise for Manger's "beautiful word-magic" inspired by folk poetry.[92]

Itzik Manger was born in Czernowitz, Bukovina (today, Chernivtsi, Ukraine), in 1901. He started publishing poetry in his twenties, while living in Bucharest and Warsaw. He reached London in 1940 with the help of the Romanian PEN club, which had managed to secure a Romanian passport for him just in the nick of time. While in London he published a number of works, including the poetry collections *Volkns ibern dakh* (Clouds Over the Roof, 1942), and *Der shnayder gezeln note manger zingt* (The

Tailor-Apprentice Notte Manger Sings, 1948), and the play *Hotsmakh-shpil* (Hotsmach Play, 1947). He was one of the editors of the journal *Eyrope*, and he occasionally wrote for *Di tsayt* and the *Arbeter ring*.[93]

Manger lived in London for more than a decade and became an important figure on the London literary scene. His London publications were made possible by the patronage of Benzion Margulies, the founder of the Ohel Club, a meeting point for Polish Jewish writers and artists in London.[94] Although Manger's poetry was loved, he could be a difficult character when drunk. In one sketch Lisky portrays a London literary event where a beloved poet is treated with courtesy and respect even when he rudely demands alcohol at a meeting, and his request is carried out with great sensitivity. However, when the poet later becomes aggressive, he is thrown out of the meeting. Whether or not this sketch was based on a real event, it would have been a familiar episode.[95]

Fuchs's lecture analyzed the work of the three London poets, showing with expressive language how, for each of them, their inspiration came from biblical and religious themes. He praised Locker as having "lively sparks of fire of historical women prophets in her soul," where "her books speak of the prophecies of national Jewish tragedy and existence." Oved's quiet simplicity "borrowed from the hot breath of deep mysticism, the godly-perception of life and nature, and a connection to a high ethical Jewish spirit." Fuchs called Stencl "the Hasid of Yiddish poetry," whose "every phrase is a colorful picture, every word is significant," and whose "artistic eye is always astonished by God's world."[96]

The connection to spirituality and an ancient past would have emerged as a theme even if the lecture had been given two months earlier, as first scheduled. However, it must have seemed particularly poignant during the Blitz, when prayer was higher than usual on peoples' agenda. This literary meeting to discuss poetry, in the middle of bombing raids, to a smaller crowd than the usual hundred attendees, acknowledged the richness of their Yiddish legacy and the importance of warmth and support.

YIDDISH PUBLISHING AND CULTURAL INITIATIVES DURING THE WAR

In the first years of the war, the Narodiczky Press published nearly two dozen Yiddish pamphlets, including Stencl's *Heftlekh*, and English information booklets translated into Yiddish. It also published nine Yiddish books by London authors, including Seedo, Palme, Lewy, Sochachewsky, Lisky, and Stencl. The most expansive publication was Seedo's *Di dialektik fun gefil un gedank* (The Dialectics of Thought and Feeling). In her later memoir, Seedo describes how Lisky took over the technical sides of its publication, printing, and corrections, while she was juggling feeding a tiny baby. When it came out in 1941, Lisky "pulled a few strings" with his comrades in the Association of Jewish Journalists and Authors to throw a lavish reception in her honor, which Oved financed. Seedo, depressed by the news from Europe, felt she could not go through with it and wanted to cancel, but Lisky demanded that she attend. For many in the community, balancing huge despair with maintaining a Yiddish literary public life was a supremely difficult choice.[97]

Single-mindedness and hard-headed obstinacy, however, were the preserve of many of the Yiddish writers. These may have been positive traits in the fight to keep Yiddish on the agenda, but, war or no war, they also led to anger, arguments, and disagreements, both within groups and between groups. The London literary scene was split between the West End middle class and the East End working class, and although there was significant crossover—as with Lisky, Kaizer, and Oved—there was a certain amount of squabbling and hurt feelings. Lisky paints a picture of hierarchies of writers and individuals anxious about their work, feeling underappreciated and snubbing each other. Seedo writes of the competitive environment where writers tried to conceal their vanity and vulnerability. Kreitman spoke harshly of how writers respected her writings but not her as a writer.[98] Leo Koenig noted in his diary of 14 November 1942: "Went to Stencl's Literary Afternoon in the Shelter—a poor show reeking of working people."[99] The class snobbism and condescension between the West End and East End circles may have created a rift between writers, yet they often reconciled, and Koenig's writing frequently appeared in Stencl's *Heftlekh* after the war. Stencl had also not been on speaking terms for years with Asch after Asch had declared that Hebrew would be the force that would assimilate Jews and that Yiddish had no future. Yiddish scholar Leonard Prager recalled Stencl spluttering when reminiscing about this incident, and how Stencl nearly threw an inkwell at Asch. They finally made peace only a month or so before Asch's death.[100] Possibly the most notorious incident of disagreement was a feud between Stencl and Itzik Manger. At one point, recalled the artist Joseph Herman, "with the wrath of a prophet, he [Stencl] threatened him [Manger]: 'I will see that you never again walk through the streets of White-chapel.'" This dispute had no resolution and led to litigation. Dovid Katz recalls that Lisky remembered the name of Stencl's lawyer, but no further details.[101]

After Russia entered the war, a group of East European immigrants, including many communist members, set up the Jewish Cultural Club to raise the profile of the plight of Russian Jews. The group held events and produced the first issue of a Yiddish journal called *Eyrope* in 1943. Its editorial team included Koenig, the scholar Chimen Abramsky, and recent immigrants Manger and Fuchs. But the journal lasted only one issue, dissolving due to disagreements among the editors.[102] Stencl's *Heftlekh*, on the other hand, were already nearing their fortieth issue, possibly because Stencl was the sole editor and made all the editorial decisions. At the Jewish Culture Club offices, a meeting was called between the club's committee and Stencl, who represented the Sabbath Afternoons, to find ways they could work together. A report in one of the *Heftlekh* described how the two sides presented their opinions and decided that there was no antagonism between the organizations, which were working toward the same goal of increasing Yiddish-language culture in London. They therefore agreed to start attending each other's events, and indeed, the Culture Club editors were all later published in Stencl's journals.[103] In early 1943 the Sabbath Afternoons had a name change, becoming *Di fraynt fun yidish loshn* (the Friends of the Yiddish Language), with Moshe Oved as president and Stencl as "spiritual guide."[104]

In September 1943 a project of the Association of Jewish Journalists and Authors that had been developing for years came to fruition with the opening of the Folk House in a large building on Adler Street that had previously housed the Jewish National Theatre and had been slightly damaged in the Blitz. The move was designed to provide a place for Yiddish activities that was not connected to just one of the established organizations and groupings, thereby bringing in a broader audience. The activists setting it up included Kaizer, Lisky, Seedo, and Myer. The two-story building housed a large lecture hall and concert space, offices for different community organizations, smaller rooms for cultural activities, a drama studio, a music room, a library and exhibition space, and a home for the New Yiddish Theatre Company. The center opened with a community event that featured contributions from writers and poets and a lecture by Morris Myer on the theme "Good News for the New Year." In February 1944 Sholem Asch's play *Motke ganev* was performed there by Markov's Yiddish theatre troupe.[105]

Although its goal was to unite and unify the disparate London cultural institutions, activities, and resources, and provide a cultural home for all Jewish adults and youth, the Folk House, by the time it opened, had an even more urgent sense of duty. Its statement of purpose, published in Yiddish and English, clearly cries: "We, here in England, are the only free Jewish community in Europe; we alone have escaped the ordeal. Sacred is the duty we owe the millions of our brethren." The continuity of Jewish and Yiddish-language culture had become a spiritual necessity.[106]

This lament was repeated by the Jewish Culture Club, which in April 1944 opened their own center outside the East End, on 70 Cazenove Road in Stoke Newington, serving the Jewish and Yiddish-speaking Russian activists of North London. A moving article in one of Stencl's *Heftlekh* of April 1944 described how it was essential that people not give up on Yiddish culture. Hitler may have destroyed the generations of Yiddish writers that would have followed in the tradition of the great Yiddish writers, but now London Jews had to take their place in the future of Yiddish culture.[107]

Toward the end of 1944, Morris Myer, who had been so involved with Yiddish cultural institutions, and in particular, the Folk House, died. For days, writer after writer, including Brown, Kreitman, and Lisky, penned articles and obituaries.[108] Myer had been instrumental in publishing and supporting all the London Yiddish writers and had acted as a bridge between the East End immigrant community, the North West London communities, and the Anglo-Jewish establishment. His son Harry Myer took over the editorship of *Di tsayt*, and although he was a good journalist, he was the next generation and did not have the same background in Yiddish culture.[109] Writers like Kaizer and others were loyal to the paper, and Brown, a close friend of Harry Myer, reworked scores of her stories for publication. However, with a declining readership, *Di tsayt* lasted only another five years.

During the war years a total of fifty-six Yiddish books were published in London. Although a significant number, this did not stop Joseph Hillel Lewy from complaining that had things been better organized, twice that number could have been published. Israel Narodiczky was the main publisher of Yiddish books, publishing under the name Narodiczky Press or Narodiczky and Sons. After his death in 1942, Narodiczky's sons took over the business as the Narod Press. Narodiczky and his sons were generous with their terms, allowing authors to pay back loan money slowly, as the books sold. But it was not easy for authors to sell their own books, and most writers, including Brown, managed to publish only with the patronage of family and friends.[110]

In September 1945, in an article marking the fifth anniversary of the *Heftlekh*, Stencl admitted that the journal had not really brought out new talent, but that it had encouraged established writers to produce new material when they had been dormant.[111] After 1946 the *Heftlekh* became the literary journal *Loshn un lebn* (Language and Life), which came out sometimes fortnightly, sometimes monthly. There were stories, poems, and articles by fifteen or twenty mainly local writers in each issue, with regular contributions from all the writers mentioned in these chapters.

YIDDISH CULTURE AFTER THE WAR

Much of the East End was rubble. Many of the older community activists had died; Jews had moved out of the East End, dispersing into other areas of London, and the community that remained was in decline. It was a community in shock, trying to deal with the impact of the Holocaust, the loss of family, and the loss of Yiddish culture. In 1946 the writer H. Leyvik was on his way from New York to examine the situation for survivors in Displaced Persons (DP) camps in Europe. He stopped in London, with time to walk through the debris of the East End to a Friends of Yiddish meeting. He described "*Yiddishkayt* crying out from the ruins." On coming into the meeting, he was moved by the warmth of the dozens of people, many of them writers he had met on an earlier visit to London before the war, and others whom he had read. But the warmth sat atop hopelessness, and he wrote in his diary: "The naked lonely destiny of our literature here felt greater than loneliness. Every writer felt like an orphan. I felt it in Fuchs. I felt it in Koenig." Leyvik, on his way to witness the devastation the Holocaust had wrought, was only too aware of the break in continuity for every Jew who had once come from Eastern Europe. Yet Leyvik was staggered by Stencl's commitment: "It may thunder or lightening or throw bombs over London, he won't give up the time that they gather together. Under the effect of his stubbornness, a hundred people join him in the atmosphere of Yiddish language, Yiddish literature, and Yiddish song."[112] Leyvik's visit coincided with the publication of the first edition of *Loshn un lebn*. Stencl described how he handed a copy to Leyvik, who "held the first copy of the journal in his hands and his face shone."[113] Despite Stencl's perception of his reaction, Leyvik remarked with gloom that in all of these one hundred faces there was not one young person, and he left feeling unable to be optimistic about Yiddish in London.[114]

Yet through the late forties, Yiddish did not disappear. Receptions continued for local writers and international visitors, including Lisky's brother-in-law, the writer Mordecai Husid, who was the guest of honor at a Friends of Yiddish Language gathering in 1947.[115] The Friends of Yiddish Language also added a new monthly literary event on Sunday afternoons at the Ben Uri Gallery, thus including those who did not travel to the East End for the regular meetings on the Sabbath.[116] Members of London YIVO began working more intensely on the publication of a book about Jewish life in England in the previous forty years.[117] The Whitechapel Library had a Jewish reading room with the largest collection of Yiddish books in the country. Brown's first book, *Lakht oyb ir vilt*, was published in 1947, and *Loshn un lebn* continued and expanded, sometimes running to sixty pages, sometimes ninety.

There may even have been more events than usual, as actors and writers living in America stopped on their way to visiting communities in mainland Europe to offer their support. In 1947 there were a string of receptions hosted by different groups for the popular and influential Yiddish stage and film actor, director, and writer Maurice Schwartz, who was passing through London on his way to giving a series of concerts for the Jewish refugees in the DP camps in Germany. He attracted a large crowd at the reception organized by the Association of Jewish Journalists and Authors at the West London Esplanade Hotel, Warrington Crescent West. The first to welcome him was the chair, Kaizer, followed by a host of contributions from Oved and Palme, the actor Meier Tzelniker, Harendorf, Kreitman, the journalist Joseph Fraenkel, Lewy, Sochachewsky, Harry Myer, and Lisky.[118]

When one looks through the pages of *Loshn un lebn* from 1948, the amount of cultural activity is striking, with an event almost every night of the week. *Loshn un lebn* was full of poems, stories, and essays on literary subjects: generally critiques of international Yiddish writers' work and Yiddish in the new State of Israel. There were also local debates, reports of literary meetings, and community-centered discussions. Cultural news provided short paragraphs of happenings by key community activists and local Yiddish writers and visitors to London. Finally, there were listings and ads for the Friends of Yiddish Language weekly meetings, the Friends of Yiddish monthly event at the Ben Uri Gallery, Workers' Circle lectures, and plays at the Yiddish theatre. Despite Leyvik's hopelessness, the cultural news from the *Loshn un lebn* of February 1948 recorded seventeen items. Around half of the news items are local. The other half is a mixture of events featuring Yiddish writers from abroad visiting London or popular writers publishing books in London. These included the poet Chava Rosenfarb, who published her poetry book and later visited in March 1949, and Avrom Tsikert, whose poems appeared in London Yiddish journals.

Friends of Yiddish Language reception for Chava Rosenfarb on Saturday, 5 March 1949, at the Bernhard Baron Settlement at 33 Berner Street, E1. Standing at the back are, from right, Judah Beach, Chava Rosenfarb, and A. M. Fuchs. Two spots to Fuchs's right, sitting in front of the window, is Mark Markov, and next to him, with the moustache, is the journalist Ben A. Sochachewsky. In front of Rosenfarb are Esther Kreitman and Moshe Oved. (Courtesy of Goldie Morgentaler, private collection)

The list of cultural events from *Loshn un lebn*, February 1948

- Chava Rosenfarb has produced a new book in London, with the financial support of Moshe Oved.
- A second, expanded edition has come out of a Joseph Hillel Lewy poetry book, published by Narodiczky.
- A book of poetry by Avrom Tsikert is in the process of being prepared.[119]
- A new story of London Jewish life written by Ben A. Sochachewsky is about to start being serialized in *Di tsayt*.
- The London painter Alfred Wolmark is celebrating his seventieth birthday with an exhibition at the Ben Uri Gallery.
- The London Tate Gallery has a large exhibition of Marc Chagall.
- The famous artist Mane-Katz is currently in London, and there will be a "Glass of Tea" in his honor at the Friends of Yiddish Language.
- Lena Pilchowsky, the wife of the well-known painter, has passed away in London.
- There will be a memorial at the Friends of Yiddish Language for the great actor Solomon Mikhoels.
- The famous actress Ida Kaminska will be performing at the Alexandra Theatre.
- Moshe Oved gave a lecture to the students at Oxford.
- The famous activist from Brussels, Herschel Himelfarb, is now in London for some time and will give a series of lectures.
- The well-known journalist Hillel Seidman will stop in London on his way to the DP camps in Germany.
- Dr. Shimen Ravidovitsh, the Hebraic scholar at Leeds University, is going on a lecture tour to America.
- Our Mendele celebration, with the participation of the actor Yidl Goldberg and singer Hannah Metzger, was a great success.
- Shlomo Auerbach gave a talk about Sholem Asch at the Workers' Circle.
- The secretary of the tailor's union, the Yiddish journalist L. Fayn, has been awarded a medal by the king.[120]

On the next page of the same edition of *Loshn un lebn*, the events section listed lectures and classes every Thursday evening and Sunday afternoon at the Workers' Circle, a tea party for the London *Fraye arbeter shtime* (Free Voice of Labor) group, a lecture on Sholem Asch at the Ben Uri Gallery, a banquet celebrating five years since the official start of the *Fraynt fun yidish loshn* (Friends of Yiddish Language), and a concert of folk songs at the Whitehall Theatre, Trafalgar Square, organized by the Jewish Workers' Relief Committee. And there were still new plays opening at the Yiddish theatre!

There is no doubt that *Loshn un lebn* was striving to promote as full a picture of Yiddish-related activity as possible, and it is true that many of the same group of writers and cultural activists were attending all the events. But it is against this background that, in the summer of 1948, Lisky wrote an article trying to make sense of what had been left from the war. It is a provocative piece, again rehearsing the familiar complaint about the disintegration of a London Yiddish culture, due to assimilation and the anglicized Jewish youth who were the products of the English schooling system and knew no Yiddish. He laid out London's pedigree of Jewish writers, including Yosef Haim Brenner and Morris Winchevsky, who, for the time they lived in London, made the city their home and fully engaged with the place and the community in their poetry and prose. But Lisky argued against a nostalgic harkening back to the past. These writers did not stay in England, and one of London's problems was that it was serving as an inn on the way to somewhere else.[121]

Itzik Manger penned similar despair, but also cautious optimism. He mulled over how many well-known Yiddish writers and cultural activists had lived at some point in Whitechapel, and mused:

> Whitechapel has a lot of failings. It is often rightly criticized. It is a hard ground for Jewish community work. Much is sown, but little grows. . . . But when someone will write the history of the Whitechapels, they will have a lot to say. They will not only reprove. The historian will also find words of compassion and praise. They will not only mention the dreaminess and passivity, but also the many attempts that were made, the benevolent obstinacy, the terrific strength and streams of energy, that were invested in the work.[122]

And to end with Stencl's stubborn optimism:

> If our blood is being sucked out of us, with as much as is left, we shall go
> on, firm in the faith that the coming generations will not shame the past,
> and that the Yiddish literature that is being created in and about our epoch
> will be the expression of our conflict and pain, and will contain the hope
> and the joy of being able to bear everything and to bring it to life.[123]

Maybe the names are not lasting. Maybe you had never before heard of Kaizer, Lisky, or Brown, Lewy, Sochachewsky, or Palme, Seedo, Creditor, or Locker, Oved, Myer, or Koenig, Leftwich, or Fuchs. Maybe you had not heard of Kreitman or Stencl. Maybe the only names in this chapter that are familiar are those of Manger and Asch. But all these names, together with more than treble the number who wrote for newspapers and journals, left a considerable amount of writing: literature that can be enjoyed today on its own merits, and within its historical context. Reading London Yiddishtown, we find vibrant activity within a diminishing, saddened, but always passionate community. This is the story of our London Yiddish past, of a heroic fight, and one worthy to be remembered.

APPENDIX

References for the Yiddish Stories

YEHUDA ITAMAR LISKY (I. A. LISKY)

All Lisky's stories translated here are taken from his collection *Produktivizatsye* (London: Narodiczky, 1937). Some early versions of the stories appeared in *Di tsayt*. Later publications are from *Vaytshepl lebt* (London: Narod Press, 1951) and *Yoyvel almanakh* (London: Narod Press, 1956).

Story title	Earlier version in *Di tsayt*, 1930s	Story collection, *Produktivizatsye*, 1937	Republication
Produktivizatsye		72–84	*Vaytshepl lebt*, 1951, 25–33
Fashistishe rekrutn	"A shuster in london," 8 October 1931	87–95	"Der naketer kop," *Yoyvel almanakh*, 1956, 19–25
Idialistishe spekulatsye		98–101	
A gine a tog	"Di gele late," 25– 27 December 1934	104–14	
Natsionale gefiln—un klasn interesn	"Der oyfgekume- ner gvir," 24– 26 November 1931	117–24	*Vaytshepl lebt*, 1951, 33–40
In marsh mit di hungerike		127–36	

ARYE MYER KAIZER (A. M. KAIZER)

Nine out of Kaizer's ten stories translated here are taken from his collection *Bay undz in vaytshepl* (London: Narodiczky, 1944). Apart from the introductory story, which was written specifically for that collection, those I was able to trace appeared first in *Di tsayt*. Later publications are from *Vaytshepl lebt: Loshn un lebn almanak* (London: Narod Press, 1951) and *Loshn un lebn*.

Story title	Earlier version in *Di tsayt*, 1930s	Appearance in *Bay undz in vaytshepl*, 1944	Republication
Vaytshepl: Anshtot a hakdome		3–6	
Der "vaytshepler-ekspres"	21 October 1934	17–20	*Vaytshepl lebt*, 1951, 9–12
Dort vu s'bulbet zikh	c. 1934 (see pre-story note)	25–28	
M'klaybt khazonim	13 March 1932	33–35	*Loshn un lebn*, September–October 1967, 9–11
"Roni Akore" un di "dresmekerin"	Unfound. Any time from 1932		*Vaytshepl lebt*, 1951, 12–16
Az ir geyt in idishn teater	23 March 1933	29–32	
Dos mazl fun an omnibus	"Der mazl fun a tremvay," 24 June 1935	21–24	
Friling in vaytshepl	24 April 1932	9–12	
Moyshe rabeynu in london	10 April 1936	75–79	
Tsvey gasn—tsvey mazoles	26 January 1932	13–16	

KATIE BROWN

All of Brown's stories translated here are taken from her collections, *Lakht oyb ir vilt* (London: N. Zilberg, 1947) and *Alts in eynem!* (London: N. Zilberg, 1951). Apart from the introductory story, which was written specifically for *Lakht oyb ir vilt*, they are all updated versions of stories that appeared in some form in *Di post* in the 1930s and were published in their new forms in *Di tsayt* in the 1940s and 1950s. The one later publication was in *Vaytshepl lebt: Loshn un lebn almanak* (London: Narod Press, 1951).

Story title	Earlier version in *Di post*, 1930s	Edited version in *Di tsayt*, 1940s and 1950s	*Lakht oyb ir vilt* (1947) and *Alts in eynem!* (1951)	Republication in *Vaytshepl lebt*, 1951
A vort oyf tsu frier			*Lakht*, 3–6	
Idishe lezer	4 July 1934	30 August 1950	*Alts*, 111–14	
Krismes prezents	"Dos vaybele hot rekht," 18 March 1934	14 December 1949	*Alts*, 9–12	
Ikh darf a dire	"Alts tsulib dem radyo," 26 February 1934		*Alts*, 64–67	
Pesimizm un optimizm	Post–31 December 1934	2 November 1948	*Alts*, 165–68	
Parnose gebers	"Der mames nakhes," 10 July 1935	23 May 1945	*Lakht*, 99–102	118–21
Deyvele vert a prayz fayter	"Yeykele vert a prayz fayter," 28 November 1934		*Alts*, 20–23	
Mayn prints der sotsialist	"Mayn Yeykele halt a spitsh," 3 December 1933	6 April 1950	*Alts*, 153–56	

(continued)

Story title	Earlier version in *Di post*, 1930s	Edited version in *Di tsayt*, 1940s and 1950s	*Lakht oyb ir vilt* (1947) and *Alts in eynem!* (1951)	Republication in *Vaytshepl lebt*, 1951
Tsufil idish	"Faln tsu faln iz nit glaykh," 11 October 1931	19 June 1946	*Lakht*, 51–54	
Ven a froy vert a mentsh	10 September 1933	15 May 1944	*Alts*, 108–10	
A naye piese in vaytshepl	"Der id mit der piese," 27 December 1931	15 May 1944	*Lakht*, 83–86	

GLOSSARY

Agune—woman who is denied a divorce by her husband and so is trapped in a marriage.

Aliya—going to live in Israel. The youth *aliya* rescued children during the war and survivors after the war and took them to live in Israel.

Ato horeyso—prayer said on *Simkhes toyre* when parading the Torah scrolls.

Bar mitzvah—boy's coming-of-age ceremony at thirteen years of age.

Bezbozhnik—(Russian) godless.

Challah—braided loaf of bread eaten on the Sabbath.

Cholent—Sabbath stew of meat, potatoes, and beans.

Chutzpah—impudence, gall.

Eyl mole rakhmim—opening words of the Prayer for the Dead.

Farfl—noodles.

Feh—ugh.

Galitzianer—a Galician Jew. Someone who came from Galicia, a region alternately claimed by Poland and the Austro-Hungarian Empire. Today, it is part in Poland and part in Ukraine.

Gemara—The Talmud. The oral Torah and commentaries regularly studied by Orthodox men.

Goldene medine—lit., golden country. Often meant to refer to America. Not always positive.

Goyim (sing. goy)—gentiles.

Haftoyre—a reading from the Prophets read on Sabbath after the Torah reading.

Haggadah—prayer book for the first two nights of Passover.

Hatikvah—(The Hope) poem written in 1878 by Naftali Herz Imber. It was the anthem of the Zionist movement and, later, of the State of Israel.

Heder—religious school for young children.

Kabbalist—a follower of the *Kabbalah* and related works of mystical and esoteric writings originating in the twelfth and thirteenth centuries.

Kaddish—prayer praising God. Recited by mourners for eleven months after a parent dies and for thirty days after the death of a spouse, sibling, or child.

Kibbutz/kibbutzim—collective agricultural village(s) in Palestine and, later, Israel.

Kliskes—egg drops.

Kreplach—meat dumpling.

Kugel—noodle or potato pudding.

Landsman—person coming from the same town in Eastern Europe.

Litvak—a Jew from Lithuania (historically included Latvia and Belarus).

Loksh/lokshn—noodle(s).

Maftir—last few lines of the Torah portion.

Megillah—a scroll with a biblical book read on certain festivals. In the story "Where it Bubbles" it is used in its slang meaning—to make a long, complicated situation out of something.

Mekhaye—delight.

Mezuzah—parchment with Torah verses inside a case attached to doorposts by many Jews.

Mikveh—ritual bathhouse.

Mincha—evening prayer.

Minyan—a quorum of ten men for prayers.

Mishna—the Oral Law, said to have been given by God to Moses.

Mizrachi—religious Zionist organization. See the background note on page 111.

Neilah—final prayer on Yom Kippur.

Pesach—festival of Passover.

Rebbe—Hasidic rabbi.

Seder—first two nights of Passover.

Shabbes—the Sabbath.

Shammes—beadle, sexton.

Shechita—ritual slaughter of animals for kosher meat.

Shiva—seven-day mourning period.

Shmaltz/shmaltzy—grease/greasy.

Shochet—ritual slaughterer for kosher meat.

Shofar—ram's horn blown in synagogue during the High Holy Days.

Sholem aleykhem—warm greeting, hello.

Shtetl—small town in Eastern Europe.

Simkhes toyre—Simchat Torah. Festival celebrating the end and beginning of the Torah cycle.

Strudel—cake with an apple or other fruit filling.

Tallis—prayer shawl.

Tefillin—phylacteries: small boxes containing verses from the Torah worn by Jewish men during their morning prayer.

Torah—the Five Books of Moses.

Treyf—unclean, not kosher.

Tsitses—tassels on prayer shawl or vest; ritual fringes.

Tzimmes—stewed fruit or vegetable dish.

Yeshiva—religious seminary for boys and men.

Yiddishkayt/Yiddishkeyt—Jewishness, aspects of Judaism. Yiddishkayt is the pronunciation in London.

YIVO—Acronym for the *Yidisher visnshaftlekher institut* (Yiddish Scientific Institute); based in Vilnius before the war, with branches in additional cities, including London.

Yom Kippur—Day of Atonement. Fast day ten days after the New Year.

NOTES

A NOTE ON THE YIDDISH

1 Khone Shmeruk, "Dray londoner Yiddisher gasnlider fun far der ershte velt-milkhome," in *Studies in the Cultural Life of the Jews in England*, ed. Dov Noy and Issachar Ben-Ami (Jerusalem: Magnes Press, Hebrew University, 1975), 116.

INTRODUCTION

1 I use the term "Yiddishtown" to mean the part of the East End that had a large Jewish population, similar to the way in which what was later called "Banglatown" denoted an area of the East End with a large Bangladeshi population.

2 For an in-depth analysis of the Yiddish East End in these years, see Vivi Lachs, *Whitechapel Noise: Jewish Immigrant Life in Yiddish Song and Verse, London 1884–1914* (Detroit: Wayne State University Press, 2018).

3 Katie Brown, "I Need a Flat," in *Alts in eynem!* (London: N. Zilberg, 1951), 64–67. For an overview of this second generation and their relationship with Yiddish, see the introduction to David Dee, *The "Estranged" Generation? Social and Generational Change in Interwar British Jewry* (London: Palgrave Macmillan, 2017), 1–6, 21–80.

4 Henry Felix Srebrnik, *London Jews and British Communism* (London: Vallentine Mitchell, 1995), 28–29.

5 For an analysis of Zionism in Britain at this time, see Stephan Wendehorst, *British Jewry, Zionism, and the Jewish State, 1936–1956* (Oxford: Oxford University Press, 2011), 292–307; David Cesarani, "One Hundred Years of Zionism in England," *European Judaism: A Journal for the New Europe* 25, no. 1 (1992): 1, 43–45.

6 Daniel Tilles, *British Fascist Antisemitism and Jewish Responses, 1932–40* (London: Bloomsbury Academic, 2014), 101–14, 123–34.

7 V. D. Lipman, *A History of the Jews in Britain Since 1858* (Leicester: Leicester University Press, 1990), 203–23.

8 See David Cesarani, "The Transformation of Communal Authority in Anglo-Jewry, 1914–1940," in *The Making of Modern Anglo-Jewry*, ed. David Cesarani (Oxford: Basil Blackwell, 1990), 115–40; Lipman, *A History of the Jews in Britain*, 203–23.

9 Wendehorst, *British Jewry*, 292–307.

10 Bill Williams, "'East and West' in Manchester Jewry, 1880–1914," in *The Making of Modern Anglo-Jewry*, ed. Cesarani, 20–31.

11 http://blogs.bbk.ac.uk/events/tag/history-of-art/. Accessed 2 May 2020. For Oved, see "Kultur yediyes fun do," *Loshn un lebn* (February 1948), 63.

12 See Leonard Prager, *Yiddish Culture in Britain: A Guide* (Frankfurt am Main: Peter Lang, 1990), 38–42.

13 Stencl, "A. M. Kaizer," *Loshn un lebn* (September–October 1967), 70.

14 Esther Kreitman, *Blitz and Other Stories*, trans. Dorothea van Tendeloo (London: David Paul, 2004).

15 Katie Brown, *Lakht oyb ir vilt* (London: N. Zilberg, 1947); *Alts in eynem!* (London: N. Zilberg, 1951); *Unter zelbn dakh*, serialized in the weekly *Di idishe shtime* (6 November 1953–25 June 1954).

16 Biographical information from Prager, "Brown, Katie," in *Yiddish Culture*, 177–78.

17 Katie Brown, *Life Is a Dance—You Should Only Know the Steps*, trans. Sydney Bacon, with Rose Kashtan; illus. Gail Geltner (Toronto: Bacon Publishing, 1987). Sydney was Brown's nephew: the youngest son of her oldest brother, Hersh (Harris).

18 "Arye-Meyer Kayzer," *Yiddish leksikon*, http://yleksikon.blogspot.com/2019/03/arye-meyer-kayzer.html. Accessed 23 January 2021.

19 A. M. Kaizer, *Mir zenen hungerik* (London: Federation of Jewish Relief Organizations, 1930); reports in *Di tsayt* on trips to Austria, 15–19 February 1934; Belgium, 13–14 January 1935; Germany, 7 September and 9 November 1936; Poland, March–May 1940; "In the Hell of Nazi Poland," *Jewish Chronicle*, 1 March 1940, 14.

20 The Association of Jewish Journalists and Authors is called different names in different sources: Its official name was the Association of Jewish Journalists and Authors in England (Kaizer's letterhead of 1 May 1931). In the mid-1940s the *Jewish Chronicle* generally referred to it as "the Association of Jewish Journalists and Authors of Great Britain." Throughout the 1930s and 1940s, other sources refer to "the Association of Jewish Writers and Journalists," "the Association of Jewish Writers," and other permutations. In 1933 a notice in *Di tsayt* referenced an inaugural meeting for the "Farband fun yidishe shriftshteler, dzurnalistn un kultur tuer in england gegrindet in london" (*Tsayt*, 2 June 1933). These were almost certainly the same organization, or branches of the same organization, as can be seen in a letter in the *Jewish Chronicle*, "Help for Germany," 26 March 1948, 15. For consistency, I have used the "the Association of Jewish Journalists and Authors," sometimes adding "in England" or "of Great Britain" for clarification.

21 A. M. Kaizer, *Bay undz in vaytshepl* (London: Narodiczky, 1944).

22 Biographical information from Prager, "Liski, Yehuda Itamar," in *Yiddish Culture*, 418; "Y. A. Lisky," *Yiddish Leksikon*, http://yleksikon.blogspot.com/2017/04/y-liski-i-lisky.html. Accessed 30 August 2020. Various sources disagree on the year of Lisky's birth. It is in fact 12 July 1899. Dovid Katz, "I. A. Lisky, 1899–1990," in Katz, ed., *Oksforder Yidish*, vol. 2 (Oxford: Taylor and Francis, 1991), 277.

23 I. A. Lisky, *Produktivizatsye* (London: Narodiczky, 1937); *For, du kleyner kozak!* (London: Haseyfer, 1942); *Melokhe bezuye* (Narodiczky and Sons, 1947).

24 I. A. Lisky, *The Cockerel in the Basket*, trans. Hannah Berman (London: J. S. Bergson, 1955); Lisky, "Geese," trans. Hannah Berman, *Jewish Literary Gazette*, 15 March 1951, 2.

25 Lisky intended to publish "Ideological Speculation" in English translation and had started working on it with Isaac Panner, a journalist, communist activist, and biographer of Sholem Asch then living in London. Lisky made two changes to the text. The tea became wine, and Lyons Corner House, a café popular with Jewish youth, was changed to the up-market Trocadero in the West End. In a handwritten message below the typed English text, Lisky explained that these two changes were to underline the issue of money, because they "were more in keeping with a wealthy man's actions." This translation was never published. "Ideological Speculation," unpublished ms. (Francis Fuchs, personal collection).

26 In "Moses in London" Kaizer names the largest and most-established organizations. The real state of affairs was more complex and diverse. In 1929 there were 144 Zionist organizations affiliated with the Zionist Federation. By 1939 there were 250. The main groups had subgroups and offshoots, youth sections, and branches in different locations. Lipman, *A History of the Jews in Britain*, 179; Dee, *The "Estranged" Generation?* 244–51.

27 Todd M. Endelman, *The Jews of Britain, 1656 to 2000* (Berkeley: University of California Press, 2002), 234–35.

28 Image of Mosley in his Rolls Royce Bentley at *The Times*, "Mosley aces quiz over press watchdog funding," https://www.thetimes.co.uk/article/mosley-faces-quiz-over-press-watchdog-funding-fw6fmxn7f. Accessed 26 November 2020.

29 Listings for events, *Jewish Chronicle*, 9 June 1939, 48; 22 October 1948, 6.

YEHUDA ITAMAR LISKY

1 Y. H. Levi (Lewy), "Iber i a liskis tetikeyt un zayn shafn," *Tsayt*, 3 February 1943, 2.

2 These early memories were the inspiration for stories set in Jewish Poland. Introduction to I. A. Lisky, *The Cockerel in the Basket*, trans. Hannah Berman (London: J. S. Bergson, 1955), 9.

3 Dovid Katz, "I. A. Lisky, 1899–1990," in Katz, ed., *Oksforder Yidish*, vol. 2 (Oxford: Taylor and Francis, 1991), 277; Bella Fox telephone conversation with author, 13 July 2020.

4 Naygreshl was a published Yiddish poet and Yiddish activist in Vienna who wrote articles and poems for the local Yiddish press and edited the journal *Yidish*. Yiddish Leksikon, "Mendl Naygreshl," http://yleksikon.blogspot.com/2018/01/mendl-naygreshl-neugroschel.html. Accessed 11 November 2020.

5 Katz, "I. A. Lisky, 1899–1990," 277.

6 Simo Muir, "Chusid, Mordechai," in *Kansallisbiografia-verkkojulkaisu*, Studia Biographica 4 (Helsinki: Suomalaisen Kirjallisuuden Seura, 1997).

7 Di Bloggerin, "Yehuda Itamar Lisky: Yiddish Poet, Story-Writer, Newspaper Editor," http://dibloggerin.blogspot.com/2014/12/yehuda-itamar-lisky-yiddish-poet-story.html. Accessed 24 June 2020. Shia is short for the Yiddish name Yehoshiye (Joshua).

8 I. A. Lisky, "Zalmen reyzn a simbol fun zaftiker shvarts erd," *Tsayt*, 9 November 1930, 2; Levi (Lewy), "Iber i a liskis tetikeyt," 2. The reviewer Undzer Makshiv used the metaphor of Lisky bringing a suitcase with him but not showing anyone the contents straightaway. Undzer Makshiv, "Y A Lisky—tsum ovent fun idisher dikhtung vos iz arazhirt lekoved im," *Idishe shtime*, 14 March 1952.

9 Dovid Katz, "Y. A. Liski (I. A. Lisky)," *Forverts*, 24 May 1991, 19.

10 N. M. Seedo, *In the Beginning Was Fear* (London: Narod Press, 1964), 293–94.

11 From postmarks on letters in the private collection of Francis Fuchs.

12 Introductory note to his translation of a chapter from A. M. Fuchs, "The House on the Hill," *Jewish Literary Gazette*, 11 May 1951, 2; Levi (Lewy), "Iber i a liskis tetikeyt," 2.

13 Postcard from Mordecai Husid to Sonia and Lisky, 27 March 1935. Private collection of Francis Fuchs.

14 Mordecai Husid, *Formen in bren* (Vilnius: Kletskin Printing House, 1937); I. A. Lisky, *Produktivizatsye* (London: Narodiczky, 1937).

15 "A shuster in london" (A Cobbler in London), *Tsayt*, 8 October 1931, provided a half of the story "Fascist Recruits." "Oyfgekumener gvir" (Social Climber), *Tsayt*, 24–26 November 1931, was an older version of "Nationalist Feelings and Class Interests." "Di gele late" (The Yellow Star), *Tsayt*, 25–27 December 1934, is the same story as "A Guinea a Day." Lisky was still called the "young talented Lisky" in 1943, suggesting that he would still develop and grow. Levi (Lewy), "Iber i a liskis tetikeyt," 2.

16 Morris Myer, "Dertseylungen fun i a liski," *Tsayt*, 30 December 1936, 2.

17 Ibid.

18 Seedo, *In the Beginning*, 299–300. The Association of Jewish Journalists and Authors is often called by other names. Seedo calls the association "the Jewish Writers and Journalists Organisation."

19 YKUF (IKUF) was the communist-linked Yidisher kultur-farband (the World Jewish Cultural Union), established in 1937 in Paris. The London branch was named the Yidisher kultur-gezelshaft, as displayed on the front cover of their journal *Yidish London* (London: YKUF, 1938). See also Henry Felix Srebrnik, *London Jews and British Communism* (London: Vallentine Mitchell, 1995), 14.

20 "Society for Yiddish Culture: University of London Course," *Jewish Chronicle*, 14 October 1938, 4.

21 Seedo, *In the Beginning*, 320.

22 The 1942 Committee had a broad remit to incorporate all political positions and demonstrate British Jewish support for the Soviet Union. "Committee: Aid-for-Russia Fund," *Jewish Chronicle*, 4 September 1942, 16; Henry Felix Srebrnik, *London Jews and British Communism* (London: Vallentine Mitchell, 1995), 89.

23 Francis Fuchs telephone conversation with the author, 19 June 2020, and email, 30 June 2020.

24 Anecdotes suggest that they argued publicly about ideologies. They would sit in the park outside their home in Stoke Newington, and Seedo would call Lisky "Fascist," to which Lisky would retort "Comunistke." Di Bloggerin, "Yehuda Itamar Lisky."

25 Lisky, *For, du kleyner kozak!* (London: Haseyfer, 1942); *Melokhe bezuye* (London: Narodiczky and Sons, 1947).

26 "Excursion into 'Yiddish-Land,'" *Jewish Chronicle*, 7 October 1949, 5.

27 Seedo, *In the Beginning*, 298.

28 Lisky, "Geese," trans. Hannah Berman, *Jewish Literary Gazette*, 15 March 1951, 2; Lisky, *The Cockerel in the Basket*, trans. Hannah Berman (London: J. S. Bergson, 1955).

29 A manuscript survives with Panner's muddled translation, which mistakenly switched the two main characters, and Lisky's corrections and changes. Unpublished ms. (Francis Fuchs personal collection).

30 Conversation with Bob Chait, 8 April 2019.

31 "Y. A. Liski (I. A. Lisky)," *Yiddish Leksikon*, http://yleksikon.blogspot.com/2017/04/y-liski-i-lisky.html. Accessed 12 July 2020

32 "Yehuda Lisky," *Jewish Chronicle*, 11 May 1990, 14.

LISKY: "PRODUCTIVIZATION"

1 Daniel Tilles, *British Fascist Antisemitism and Jewish Responses, 1932–40* (London: Bloomsbury, 2014), 101–14, 123–34; Henry Felix Srebrnik, *London Jews and British Communism* (London: Vallentine Mitchell, 1995), 14–15, 24.

2 David Rosenberg, *The Battle for the East End: Jewish Responses to Fascism in the 1930s* (Nottingham: Five Leaves Publications, 2011), 67–77, 143–44; Tilles, *British Fascist Antisemitism and Jewish Responses*, 109–13.

3 Todd M. Endelman, "Fighting Antisemitism with Numbers in Early Twentieth-Century Britain," in *Patterns of Prejudice* 53, no. 1 (2019): 9–22.

4 See, for example, Gennady Esteraikh, "Changing Ideologies of Artisanal 'Productivisation': ORT in Late Imperial Russia," in *East European Jewish Affairs* 39, no. 1 (2009): 3–18.

LISKY: "FASCIST RECRUITS"

1 Juliet Gardiner, *The Thirties: An Intimate History* (London: Harper Press, 2010), 268–69.

2 For an overview of the fascist approach to the East End, and changes in the policy of anti-Semitism, see Daniel Tilles, *British Fascist Antisemitism and Jewish Responses, 1932–40* (London: Bloomsbury, 2014), 31–86; Thomas P. Linehan, *East London for Mosley: The British Union of Fascists in East London and South West Essex 1933–40* (London: Grank Cass, 1996), 64–76.

LISKY: "IDEOLOGICAL SPECULATION"

1 David Cesarani, "One Hundred Years of Zionism in England," *European Judaism: A Journal for the New Europe* 25, no. 1 (1992): 42–44; David Cesarani, "The East London of Simon Blumenfeld's Jew Boy," *London Journal* 13, no.1 (1987): 49–50.

2 "Tsu farkoyfn land in erets yisroyel—a shaliekh in London," *Tsayt*, 5 June 1934, 6.

LISKY: "A GUINEA A DAY"

1 "Jew Süss (1934)," *BFI Screenonline*, http://www.screenonline.org.uk/film/id/570808/index.html. Accessed 14 July 2020. "Jew Süss (1934)," BFI National Archive, Youtube, https://www.youtube.com/watch?v=dMTHwuQnIKA, 55.41–58.45. Accessed 14 July 2020.

2 "Jew Süss (1934)," *BFI Screenonline*.

3 "Jew Süss at the Tivoli," *Jewish Chronicle*, 12 October 1934, 43; "The Tivoli: 'Jew Süss,'" *The Times*, 5 October 1934, 5; "Pre War East End Memories from Aldgate Pump to All Stops East, by Dr Cyril Sherer, now in his 80's and living in Israel," *Jewisheastend*, https://www.jewisheastend.com/cyril.html. Accessed 14 July 2020.

LISKY: "ON THE MARCH WITH THE HUNGRY"

1 Juliet Gardiner, *The Thirties: An Intimate History* (London: Harper Press, 2010), 47–51, 159.

2 Ibid., 161.

3 "Di arbetsloze hunger marshers," *Tsayt*, 25 February 1934, 2.

4 "Soup Kitchen Annual Meeting: Increasing Demand on Institution's Resources," *Jewish Chronicle*, 4 November 1932, 15. The soup kitchen handed out soup, bread, and sardines on specific days. Had Mrs. Barsht gone on the day of the march of 27 October 1932, which was a Thursday, she would have received soup, pilchards, and an extra portion of bread to last over the weekend; advertisement, "Soup Kitchen for the Jewish Poor," *Jewish Chronicle*, 2 December 1932, 31. See also a 16mm amateur film, "Soup Kitchen" (1934), BFI Player, https://player.bfi.org.uk/free/film/watch -soup-kitchen-1934-online. Accessed 30 June 2020.

ARYE MYER KAIZER

1 Morris Myer, "Bay undz in vaytshepl," *Tsayt*, 27 June 1944, 2.

2 Kaizer's birth date is disputed. See 229n23. "Kaizer, alter noach," in *The Palgrave Dictionary of Anglo-Jewish History*, ed. William D. Rubinstein, Michael A. Jolles, and Hilary L. Rubinstein (London: Palgrave Macmillan, 2011), 500; Harry Rabinowicz, *A World Apart: The Story of the Chasidim in Britain* (London: Vallentine Mitchell, 1997), 53–56; "A Talk with a Chosid," *Jewish Chronicle*, 25 January 1895, 9. Kabbalists use the art of *gematria*, taking the numerical equivalents of Hebrew letters to make spiritual connections between words and their associations. It is also worth noting that in the naturalization papers of 1904, the name Michalenski is misspelled by the English official as Michalankis.

3 Ouzi Elyada, *Hebrew Popular Journalism: Birth and Development in Ottoman Palestine* (Abingdon: Routledge, 2019), 217–34. Tom Segev, "Good Old Days in Eretz Israel," *Haaretz Online*, https://www.haaretz.com/1.5124560, 3 February 2012. Accessed 12 May 2020. Rabbi Pini Duner, "Rav Kook and the Warshawski Hotel Affair," https://rabbidunner .com/the-warshawski-hotel-affair, 11 January 2019. Accessed 12 May 2020. Yad Izhak Ben-Tzvi, "Teuda mishpat diba: Yaakov yosef herling neged alter noach Kaiser," https://

www.ybz.org.il/_Uploads/dbsArticles/katedraonefortytwoprotocolofdibakook.pdf. Accessed 29 November 2020.

4   Leonard Prager, "Kayzer, Arye-Myer," in *Yiddish Culture in Britain: A Guide* (Frankfurt am Main: Peter Lang, 1990), 358. Margolin had been the editor of *Der bloffer*, a London satirical periodical. Vivi Lachs, *Whitechapel Noise: Jewish Immigrant Life in Yiddish Song and Verse, London 1884–1914* (Detroit: Wayne State University Press, 2018), 201–12.

5   "J/2280, Pte Kaizer, Leibush Myer," Royal Fusiliers, Regiment of Corps, Roll B Sheet, No. J. 272. www.ancestry.com.

6   Myer, "Bay undz in vaytshepl."

7   "Passover Relief for Russian Jews," *Jewish Chronicle*, 5 February 1932, 16; "Federation of Jewish Relief Organisations: Second Hand Clothing Parcels," *Jewish Chronicle*, 7 July 1933, 34; "Federation of Jewish Relief Organisations: Committee Formed in Paris and Cape Town," *Jewish Chronicle*, 15 December 1933, 26; "A m kayzers bazukh in idishe institutsyes in poyln," *Tsayt* 10 July 1934, 2.

8   A. M. Kaizer, *Mir zenen hungerik* (London: Federation of Jewish Relief Organizations, 1930).

9   Reports in *Di tsayt* on trips to Austria, 15–19 February 1934; Belgium, 13–14 January 1935; Germany, 7 September and 9 November 1936; Poland, March–May 1940; "In the Hell of Nazi Poland," *Jewish Chronicle*, 1 March 1940.

10 Letter on Kaizer's headed notepaper to the editor of the *Forverts*, 1 September 1936, YIVO Archives Territorial Collection, England.

11 Forces War Records, "Arnold Meer Kaizer," *onderfahndungsliste G. B.*, Hitler's Black Book, www.forces-war-records.co.uk/hitlers-black-book/person/15/arnold-meer-kaizer. Accessed 25 March 2020.

12 A. M. Kaizer, *Bay undz in vaytshepl* (London: Narodiczky, 1944). Stories first published: "Two Streets, Two Destinies," *Tsayt*, 26 January 1932, 2; "Choosing Cantors," *Tsayt*, 13 March 1932, 2; "Spring in Whitechapel," *Tsayt*, 24 April 1932, 2; "When You Go to a Yiddish Theatre," *Tsayt*, 23 March 1933, 2; "The Whitechapel Express," *Tsayt*, 21 October 1934, 2; "The Luck of a Trolleybus," *Tsayt*, 24 June 1935, 2; "Moses in London" *Tsayt*, 10 April 1936, 2.

13 Myer, "Bay undz in vaytshepl."

14 Kaizer's reports on Zionist Congresses for *Di tsayt* were published over consecutive days:1–22 July 1931; 16–29 August 1932; 22 August–3 September 1935; 8 January–17 March 1947; 15 December 1947–1 January 1948.

15 These ran on the first Sunday of the month and were advertised each month. *Loshn un lebn*, 1948–53.

16 The journalists included Kaizer himself, Oved, Fuchs, Creditor, Lisky, and Sochachewsky. *Jewish Chronicle*, 9 March 1945, 11.

17 Kaizer maintained his Eastern European concern. At a reception for the visiting author Melech Ravitch in 1950, Kaizer expressed worry that the Association of Yiddish Writers of Poland had dissolved, and that the group was forming a writers' club within the Polish Writers' Association. He saw this as communist pressure and worried about the status of the Yiddish language. *Jewish Chronicle*, 7 July 1950, 6.

18 YIVO letter to members about upcoming events, signed by Kaizer, E. W. Poldolsky, and A. R. Rollin, 8 March 1951, YIVO Archives Territorial Collection, England.

19 Community notice in *Loshn un lebn*, May 1953, 40.

20 These were often recorded in notices in the *Jewish Chronicle* and *Loshn un lebn*. For example, "A YIVO reception in his home," *Jewish Chronicle*, 20 March 1953, 31; "Taking part in a living newspaper," *Loshn un lebn*, March–April 1957, 57.

21 Sympathy announcement in *Loshn un lebn*, March 1949, 65.

22 A friend of Shlomo Kaiser who sat beside him every day in synagogue witnessed him "always scribbling," and was the signatory of his probate. He was not aware that Shlomo had any family and had never heard of Arye Myer Kaizer. However, he did know about their famous father, Alter Noah Kaiser. When Shlomo died, the friend in the community arranged for his burial in Israel. Conversation with E. K., 13 February 2019. After A. M. Kaizer died, a neighbor used to visit his wife, Bertha, and daughter, Nehama, who were living together in Golders Green. She was the only regular visitor and knew of no other family members. Telephone conversation with Naomi Klein, 27 January 2019.

23 Kaizer's parents' naturalization papers of 1904 record the ages of the children. Arye Myer was twelve. In addition, the record of the court proceedings in Jaffa in 1912 gives Kaizer's siblings' ages during the episode surrounding the publication of *Der bandit in yerushalayim*. This corresponds to the ages on the naturalization papers. This is also confirmed by the 1939 England and Wales register: www.ancestry.com. Accessed 27 April 2020.

KAIZER: "THE WHITECHAPEL EXPRESS"

1 Workmen's tickets had begun on the trains but were later extended to include trams and trolleybuses in London. For early instances of train use, see Simon T. Abernethy, "Opening Up the Suburbs: Workmen's Trains in London, 1860–1914," *Urban History* 42, no. 1 (2015): 70–88. See also Mike Hazell, "Bus Stop" (chapter 2, part 1), *BBC: WW2 People's War*, https://www.bbc.co.uk/history/ww2peopleswar/stories/89/a3084789.shtml. Accessed 23 August 2020.

2 Eddie Summers, "The 'Jewish' Trolleybuses of the East End—Gone but Not Forgotten," *Jewish News*, https://jewishnews.timesofisrael.com/the-jewish-trolleybuses-of

-the-east-end-gone-but-not-forgotten/. Accessed 2 February 2019. Author collected three versions of the popular song "Der aldgeyt kar" (The Aldgate Car): printed lyrics by a resident (name unknown) at Vi and John Rubens House, handed to Yiddishist Chaim Neslen in 2008; recordings from author interviews with Irving Hiller, 29 November 2010; Lou Segal, 10 March 2011.

3 In many stories Kaizer makes this plain; for example, in "Un mayn landsman yerukhem der melamed vemen m'ruft 'der filozof." Kaizer, "Shver tsu zayn a rov," *Tsayt*, 30 November 1936, 2.

KAIZER: "WHERE IT BUBBLES"

1 "A Jewish Communal Restaurant," *Jewish Chronicle*, 24 December 1932, 29.

2 "Jewish Communal Restaurant: Substantial Meals at Nominal Cost," *Jewish Chronicle*, 11 May 1934, 26. See also "The Jewish Communal Restaurant," *Jewisheastend*, https://www.jewisheastend.com/soupkitchen.html. Accessed 6 July 2020.

3 "Di naye folks-kikh noytiks zikh in ayer hilf," *Tsayt*, 1 June 1934, 6.

RONI AKORE AND THE DRESSMAKER

1 Leonard Prager, *Yiddish Culture in Britain: A Guide* (Frankfurt am Main: Peter Lang, 1990, *137–39*).

KAIZER: "WHEN YOU GO TO A YIDDISH THEATRE"

1 Leonard Prager, "Barmitzve speeches," *Yiddish Culture in Britain: A Guide* (Frankfurt am Main: Peter Lang, 1990), 53–54, David Mazower, *Yiddish Theatre in London* (London: Museum of the Jewish East End, 1987), 20–23, 67.

KAIZER: TWO STREETS, TWO DESTINIES

1 The Jewish East End of these two roads are introduced in two Springboard videos by Aumie Shapiro. The Whitechapel Road video is "La Boheme to Gardiners: The Sights and Sounds of the Jewish East End," written, directed, and narrated by Aumie Shapiro (Springboard Education Trust, 1989), https://www.youtube.com/watch?v=oA1DTYGs2tc. Accessed 29 January 2021. The Commercial Road video is "Going Down the Jewish East End with Aumie Shapiro," written and directed by Aumie and Michael Shapiro (Springboard Education Trust, n.d.), https://www.youtube.com/watch?v=F9pdGKpLm90. Accessed 29 January 2021.

KATIE BROWN

1 Alegoryer (S. Palme), "Lakht oyb ir vilt," *Loshn un lebn*, September 1947, 51.

2 The term "best seller" was used in Stencl, "Keyti Braun," *Loshn un lebn*, May 1955, 4.

3 Katie Brown, *Life Is a Dance—You Should Only Know the Steps*, trans. Sydney Bacon, with Rose Kashtan; illus. Gail Geltner (Toronto: Bacon Publishing, 1987), 12; Brown, "Mayne ayndruke fun konvenshen fun arbeter ring," *Post*, 4 April 1933; "Oyf a komitet zitsung fun brentsh eyns," *Arbeter ring*, September 1942.

4 "In froyen kenigraykh," *Der familyen fraynd*, from 5 January 1923 to 30 April 1926.

5 Brown's column was almost a parody of the American immigrant advice column *A bintel brif* (A Bundle of Letters), which appeared in the Yiddish daily *Forverts* newspaper. Isaac Metzker, *A Bintel Brief: Sixty Years of Letters from the Lower East Side to the Jewish Daily Forward* (New York: Schocken, 1971).

6 "In froyen kenigraykh," *Der familyen fraynd*, 16 March 1923, 3.

7 "Di froy un di familye," mainly weekly, 38 issues, 1 January–10 September 1930, 3.

8 *Jewish Chronicle*, 15 June 1951, 6; *Tsayt*, 1 January 1932, 3; Brown, "Bankrot," in *Lakht oyb ir vilt* (London: N. Zilberg, 1947), 165–84.

9 Gitl bas-menashe, "Vegn yidishn teater," *Post* (1934).

10 Rokhl Mirski, "Oyfn frishn kever fun keyti bron," *Loshn un lebn*, May 1955, 13.

11 Ibid.

12 L. Sh. Creditor, "Lakht—oyb ir vilt," *Tsayt*, 22 October 1947, 2.

13 Brown, "Borukh Vaynberg—vi ikh hob im gekent," *Arbeter ring*, October 1941.

14 Brown, "Mayn adresn bikhl," *Arbeter ring*, April 1943, 6.

15 Mirski, "Oyfn frishn kever," 14; Brown, "A brif fun keyti bron," *Tsayt*, 3 February 1941, 2.

16 "Keyti brons humariskes," *Tsayt*, 2 April 1947, 3.

17 There were ads for *Lakht oyb ir vilt* in *Di tsayt*, 31 January 1949, and throughout February 1949.

18 Stencl, "Keyti Bron," *Loshn un lebn*, May 1955, 3.

19 Alegoryer, "Lakht oyb ir vilt," 50.

20 Brown, *Unter zelbn dakh*, serialized weekly in *Di idishe shtime*, 6 November 1953–25 June 1954.

21 Brown, "Es lakht zikh nisht mer," *Loshn un lebn*, July–August 1954, 18.

22 Mirski, "Oyfn frishn kever," 14.

23 Stencl, "Keyti Bron," *Loshn un lebn*, May 1955, 3.

BROWN: "JEWISH READERS!"

1 Hersh Shistler, "Alts in eynem," *Loshn un lebn*, February 1952, 31.

2 "Vi azoy yidn leyzn a tsaytung," *Post*, 4 July 1934, 2.

BROWN: *"KRISMES PREZENTS"*

1 "Vaytshepl iz haynt andersh," *Post*, 10 March 1933; "Der bazar efnt zikh in a vokh arum," *Tsayt*, 11 March 1932, 3; bazaar ad, *Tsayt*, 6 December 1937.

BROWN: "I NEED A FLAT"

1 Shloyme Bastomski, *Yekele nar: A maysele far kleynere kinder* (Vilna: Di naye yidishe folksshul, 1920), 3. The introduction reads: "There once was a little boy. His name was Yekele. Just like all Yekeles are fools, our Yekele was also considered a fool, and they called him 'Yekele fool.'" See also Nicholas Alexander Block, "In the Eyes of Others: The Dialectics of German-Jewish and Yiddish Modernisms," PhD thesis, University of Michigan (2013), 48n.17, https://deepblue.lib.umich.edu/bitstream/handle/2027.42/100095/nblock_1.pdf?sequence=1. Accessed 25 July 2020.

2 Solon Beinfeld and Harry Bochner, *Comprehensive Yiddish-English Dictionary* (Bloomington: Indiana University Press, 2013), 343.

BROWN: "DAVY BECOMES A PRIZE FIGHTER"

1 *The Palgrave Dictionary of Anglo-Jewish History*, ed. William Rubinstein, Michael Jolles, and Hilary Rubinstein (London: Palgrave Macmillan, 2011), 78, 679–80.

2 "Harry Mizzler [*sic*], a Boxing Story," Jewisheastend, https://www.jewisheastend.com/redmans.html. Accessed 9 July 2020.

BROWN: "MY PRINCE, THE SOCIALIST"

1 Brown, "Mayn yekele halt a spitsh," *Post*, 3 December 1933.

BROWN: "A NEW PLAY IN WHITECHAPEL"

1 David Mazower, *Yiddish Theatre in London* (London: Museum of the Jewish East End, 1987), 23.

2 Leonard Prager, *Yiddish Culture in Britain: A Guide* (Frankfurt am Main: Peter Lang, 1990), 112, 572.

THE LITERARY LANDSCAPE OF LONDON'S YIDDISHTOWN AND THE FIGHT FOR THE SURVIVAL OF YIDDISH, 1930–50

1 N. M. Seedo, *In the Beginning Was Fear* (London: Narod Press, 1964), 304.

2 Gerry Black, *J.F.S.: The History of the Jews' Free School, London since 1732* (London: Tymsder Publishing, 1998), 126–28.

3 David Cesarani, *The Jewish Chronicle and Anglo-Jewry, 1841–1991* (Cambridge: Cambridge University Press, 1994), 78, 100, 203.

4 Maurice Carr, "The Singer Family–the Other Exile–London" (unpublished manuscript, archive of Hazel Carr, chapter 38). Available in French translation as *La Famille Singer: l'Autre Exil, Londres* (Lormont: Le Bord de L'eau, DL2016); information about Asch from David Mazower, email correspondence, 15 April 2020.

5 Marion Aptroot, "Israel Narodiczky and His Whitechapel Press," in *Jewish Books in Whitechapel: A Bibliography of Narodiczky's Press*, compiled by Moshe Sanders, ed. Marion Aptroot (London: Duckworth, 1991), viii; Dovid Katz, email correspondence, 7 April 2020. Chimen Abramsky suggested three circles, Koenig's, Stencl's, and Asch's (interview with Chimen Abramsky by Yiddishist scholars Misha Krutikov and Gennady Estraikh, 8 July 1997, audiotape, Whine private collection).

6 Leo Koenig, "Luiy golding: Der populerer idish-englisher novelist," *Tsayt*, July–August 1940, 2. Writing about the East End includes journalist's vignettes, such as A. B. Levy's *East End Story*, which was first published in the *Jewish Chronicle* in 1948; the works of novelists such as Alexander Baron, Wolf Mankowitz, Arnold Wesker, Roland Camberton, Ralph Finn, Emanuel Litvinoff, and Bernard Kops; and dozens of often self-published memoirs.

7 See "To Aid Russia: 1942 Committee Set Up," *Jewish Chronicle*, 3 July 1942, 11.

8 A very short piece about the novel *Jew Boy* has a photograph of Blumenfeld and his family in their garden ("A bukh vegn istend," *Post*, 14 July 1935, 7). See also "Excursion into 'Yiddish-Land,'" *Jewish Chronicle*, 7 October 1949, 5; Joseph Leftwich, "Books and Bookmen: The Real East End," *Jewish Chronicle*, 10 February 1933, 18.

9 *Yisroel: The First Jewish Omnibus*, ed. Joseph Leftwich (London: John Heritage, 1933); an ad for *Yisroel* listed the authors in *Jewish Chronicle*, 21 January 1933, 23.

10 In America at this time, the *Arbeter ring* was translated as "Workmen's Circle." In Britain it was always the Workers' Circle.

11 Lisky, *Melokhe bezuye* (Narodiczky and Sons, 1947), 55–65.

12 Rudolf Rocker, *The London Years* (Nottingham: Five Leaves Press, 2005), 126–27; Baruch Weinberg, "25 yor arbeter ring," *Post*, 9 December 1934, 2; Henry Felix

Srebrnik, *London Jews and British Communism* (London: Vallentine Mitchell, 1995), 24; David Mazower, "Love Labours Lost," *Jewish Socialist* 40 (1999): 19–21.

13 Despite being a secular organization, Circle House is mentioned in the obituary for Shlomo Brown as a venue where synagogue committee meetings took place. L Belkin, "Baym frishn kevr shloyme braun," *Arbeter ring*, April 1941, 6.

14 David Mazower, "Love Labours Lost," 21; Seedo, *In the Beginning*, 312.

15 "Der arbeter ring," *Post*, 4 December 1930, 4; Itzik Manger, "Farvos shaygt vaytshepl?" *Arbeter ring*, January 1942, 4; Leo Koenig, "Di yidishe literatur in di milkhome yorn," September 1942, 6; "Yiddish kultur ovnt in London," *Tsayt*, 8 March 1938.

16 Creditor, "Undzer kulturele institutsyes," *Post*, 27 January 1933.

17 The Radical History of Hackney (blog), "The Workers' Circle—Fighting Anti-semitism in Hackney," lecture by Jack Pearce 1966, https://hackneyhistory.wordpress.com/2018/04/08/the-workers-circle-fighting-anti-semitism-in-hackney, 2.26–5.40. Accessed 2 August 2020. See also "The Workers' Circle London," tape 03–3, January 1966, on Youtube, https://www.youtube.com/watch?v=c8wOWOrXgyw&t=433s. Accessed 26 November 2020. Jack Pearce (Jacob Pines) was the chairman of the Workers' Circle in the 1950s. He was a member of the Communist Party and secretary of the Jewish Peoples' Council against Fascism and Anti-Semitism. See David Mazower, "A. L. Cohen's 'The Memorable Sunday,'" in *Remembering Cable Street: Fascism and Anti-Fascism in British Society*, ed. Tony Kushner and Nadia Valman (London: Vallentine Mitchell, 2000), 202, nn. 4, 7.

18 Simon Blumenfeld, *Jew Boy* (London: London Books, 2011), 73–74. (First published in 1935 by Jonathan Cape.)

19 Morris Mindel, "Di kulturele tetikayt oyfn yidishn gas," *Arbeter ring*, August 1934, 4. Mindel's speech listed literary activities in London at the Mantle Makers' Union, the Ben Uri, and among the anarchists, Bundists, and Poale Zion (Labor Zionists), which he saw as "spontaneous and chaotic." Morris Mindel's son, Mick Mindel, was a tailors' trade union activist. See Anne Kershen, *Uniting the Tailors* (Abingdon: Routledge, 2013), 179–82. Morris Mindel's activism is reported in an interview with Mick Mindel by Andrew Whitehead (London: British Library Sound Archive, 1988, CD10 + CD 11/1: Mick Mindel). For the relationship between Morris and Mick, see Jonathan Freedland, *Jacob's Gift* (London: Penguin, 2005), 91–108.

20 Katie Brown, "Nokhn krizis," *Arbeter ring*, 6 October 1935, 6.

21 "Der idisher kunst farayn ben uri," *Tsayt*, 25 February 1934, 2. For Beach, see Lily Ford (Birkbeck, University of London), "Hopscotch in the Archives: Reflections from the Ben Uri Researcher in Residence," http://blogs.bbk.ac.uk/events/2015/06/19/hopscotch-in-the-archives-reflections-from-the-ben-uri-researcher-in-residence. Accessed 26 November 2020.

22 "The Art of the Russian and Polish Jews: Lecture by Mr Pilichowski," *Jewish Chronicle*, 4 February 1916, 14.

23 David Mazower, "Ben Uri and Yiddish Culture," in *Ben Uri: 100 Years in London—Art, Identity, Migration* (London: Ben Uri, 2015), 38–51.

24 Rachel Dickson, "A Real Temple of Jewish Art? A Century of Ben Uri in London, 1915–2015," in *Visualising a Sacred City*, ed. Ben Quash, Aaron Rosen, and Chloe Reddaway (London: I. B. Tauris, 2017), 280.

25 David Mazower, email correspondence, 15 April 2020.

26 Despite the upward mobility, Lisky was "barely solvent." Francis Fuchs, email correspondence, 30 June 2020.

27 Ester Whine, email correspondence, 3 June 2020; Lisky gives a fictionalized account of a reception in Koenig's house: *Melokhe bezuye*, 70–93.

28 For Koenig's editorial input into *Renesans*, see Alex Grafen and William Pimlott, "Jewish Art and Yiddish Art History: Leo Koenig's *Renesans*," *Shofar: An Interdisciplinary Journal of Jewish Studies* 40, no.1, due March 2022.

29 "Leo Kenig," *Yiddish Leksikon*, http://yleksikon.blogspot.com/2019/04/leo-kenig .html. Accessed 6 July 2020.

30 Seedo, *In the Beginning*, 299.

31 "Notes on Books and Authors," *Jewish Chronicle*, 6 July 1934, 23.

32 Morris Myer, "Leo Koenigs bukh in english," *Tsayt*, 21 June 1934, 2. The book was later serialized in Yiddish in *Loshn un lebn*, starting in July 1950 (pp. 10–19).

33 Stencl, "Keyti Braun," *Loshn un lebn*, May 1955, 3.

34 Stencl, "A. M. Kaizer," *Loshn un lebn*, September–October 1967, 70.

35 Leonard Prager, "Kreditor, Leib-Sholem," in *Yiddish Culture in Britain: A Guide* (Frankfurt am Main: Peter Lang, 1990), 383.

36 Prager, "Mayer, moris," in *Yiddish Culture*, 443; "Morris Myer," *Jewish Telegraphic Agency*, 22 October 1944, 4.

37 Stencl, "Moris mayer o"h," *27 yor soviet-rusland* (heftl), November 1944, 38.

38 Brown, "Undzer moris mayer o"h," *Tsayt*, 8 November 1944, 2. Brown does not name the teashop. In a memoir of his mother, Esther Kreitman, Maurice Carr remembered that he could not visit his mother on a Friday because she was a regular attender at Morris Myer's Friday circle. Maurice Carr, "The Singer Family–the Other Exile–London."

39 Lisky, "Der konserkventer mentsh," *Tsayt*, 23 November 1944, 2.

40 "Di arbeter ring un di 'vilner,'" *Tsayt*, 27 April 1934, 6.

41 Lisky, *Melukhe bezuye*, 12.

42 "Di grandieze oyfname far sholem asch," *Post*, 17 November 1933.

43 Prager, "Ash, sholem," in *Yiddish Culture*, 129–30.

44 Mazower, email correspondence, 13 June 2020.

45 "Sholem ash kumt oyf a bazukh nokh london," *Post*, 25 January 1932, 1; "Sholem ash in London," *Post*, 13 June 1933, 1; "Der poylisher khsidizm: Sholem ashes fortrog baym ben uri," *Tsayt*, 15 July 1933, 2; "Sholem ash iber der matsev fun idishn shriftshteler un der krizis fun idishn bukh," *Tsayt*, 4 March 1932, 4; "Sholem ash in english," *Tsayt*, 19 December 1930, 2; Leo Koenig, "Shrayber un politik," *Tsayt*, 13 January 1933, 2.

46 For example, *Farn mabl*, *Tsayt* (1930); *Moskve*, *Tsayt* (1930–31); *Di tsines kvart*, *Tsayt* (1931); *Gots gefangene*, *Post* (1932).

47 "Di grandieze oyfname far sholem asch."

48 Prager, "Loker, malke," in *Yiddish Culture*, 420; "Malke Loker," *Yiddish Leksikon*, http://yleksikon.blogspot.com/2017/02/malke-loker-malka-locker.html. Accessed 13 August 2020.

49 Moshe Oved, *Vizyonen un eydlshteyner* (London: Narod Press, 1950); Moshe Oved, *Visions and Jewels* (London: Faber and Faber, 1952), 83–87.

50 Brown, *"Krismes prezents,"* in *Alts in eynem!* (London: Zilberg, 1951), 10.

51 Prager, "Oyved, Moyshe," in *Yiddish Culture*, 502. For examples of Oved's poetry in *Renensans*, see "Ikh un der tog," *Renesans* 2, no. 1 (1920); "Der geburt funem morgn," *Renesans* 2, no. 3 (1920). For Oved's connection to the Ben Uri, see Mazower, "Ben Uri and Yiddish Culture," in *Ben Uri: 100 Years in London*, 43.

52 "Der idisher kunst farayn ben uri," *Tsayt*, 25 February 1934, 2. For Beach, see Lily Ford, "Reflections from the Ben Uri Researcher in Residence," http://blogs.bbk .ac.uk/events/2015/06/19/hopscotch-in-the-archives-reflections-from-the-ben-uri -researcher-in-residence/. Accessed 2 April 2020.

53 Yankev Seres was active in the YIVO London branch and served as treasurer of the Ben Uri, where he was active for more than forty years. He argued for the move of the gallery from Whitechapel to the West End. Prager, "Seres, Yankev," in *Yiddish Culture*, 573.

54 "Sholem ash iber dem matsev fun idishn shriftshteler un der krizis fun idishn bukh," *Tsayt*, 4 March 1932, 4. It is worth noting that, for many writers with Orthodox backgrounds, there was not necessarily any conflict between Yiddish and Hebrew.

55 Email correspondence with Dovid Katz, 11 April 2020.

56 Heather Valencia, "Czeladz, Berlin and Whitechapel: The World of Avrom Nokhem Stencl," *European Judaism: A Journal for the New Europe* 30, no. 1 (1997): 7.

57 A selection of Stencl's Whitechapel poems, previously published in pamphlet form, appear in Stencl, *Vaytshepl shtetl dbritn* (London: Loshn un lebn press/Narod Press, 1961).

58 Dovid Katz, "Stencl of Whitechapel," *The Mendele Review: Yiddish Literature and Language* 7, 30 March 2003, http://yiddish.haifa.ac.il/tmr/tmr07/tmr07003.htm.

Accessed 26 November 2020; A. N. Stencl, *All My Young Years: Yiddish Poetry from Weimar Germany*, trans. Haike Beruriah Wiegand and Stephen Watts (Nottingham: Five Leaves, 2007). Wiegand and Watts are currently working on a translation of a collection of Stencl's London poems with Francis Boutle Publishers (forthcoming).

59 Majer Bogdanski, "Londoner yidishe shrayber," *Oksforder Yidish*, vol. 3 (Oxford: Oksforder Yiddish Press, 1995), 799.

60 For example, *Tsayt*, 25 March, 16 April, 25 November 1938; 26 July, 9, 23, and 30 August 1940.

61 Kathi Diamant, *Kafka's Last Love* (London: Secker & Warburg, 2003), 191.

62 Ibid., 240–41. The Jewish Shelter had moved to 63 Mansell Street in 1931. It was a modern new conversion that offered space for Yiddish cultural events. Ben A. Sochachewsky, "Undzere londoner institutsyes shelter: 4. Der idisher shelter," *Post*, 13 February 1931.

63 Esther Kreitman's *Der sheydim tants* was translated by her son Maurice Carr, with the title *Deborah* (London: W. and G. Foyle Ltd., 1964). It has been republished several times. *Diamonds*, trans. Heather Valencia (London: David Paul, 2010). Lola was the daughter of Lisky's brother A. M. Fuchs. It was a close-knit community, and Maurice Carr writes how his mother was annoyed with him because Lisky gave Kreitman the news of Lola's pregnancy before Maurice had the chance to tell her himself. Maurice Carr, "The Singer Family–the Other Exile–London."

64 Lisky, *Melokhe bezuye*, 42–53; Brown, *Lakht*, 5.

65 See this volume, "Yehuda Itamar Lisky," 225n19.

66 "N. M. Seedo," *Yiddish Lexicon*, https://yleksikon.blogspot.com/2018/04/n-m-sido -seedo.html. Accessed 22 May 2020.

67 "Idisher kultur ovent in London: Vegn der oyflebung fun shprakh un literature," *Tsayt*, 8 March 1938, 3.

68 "Educational Opportunities: Yiddish Language and Literature," *Jewish Chronicle*, 7 October 1938, 32.

69 *The Golden Peacock: An Anthology of Yiddish Poetry*, translated, compiled, and edited by Joseph Leftwich (London: Robert Anscombe & Co., Ltd, reissue 1944). See also Alexander Grafen, "The Whitechapel Renaissance and Its Legacies: Rosenberg to Rodker," PhD thesis (University College London, 2020), 30–43, 51–61.

70 Stencl, "Notitsn," in *Yidish london* (London: YKUF, 1938), 60.

71 Prager, "Mayzels, Abish," in *Yiddish Culture*, 446–47; *Der voluntir* was serialized on the back page of *Di tsayt* throughout 1942; David Mazower, "Stories in Song: The Melo-deklamtsyes of Joseph Markovitsh," in *Yiddish Theatre: New Approaches*, ed. Joel Berkowitz (Oxford: Littman Library of Jewish Civilization, 2003), 119–37;

Vivi Lachs, *Whitechapel Noise: Jewish Immigrant Life in Yiddish Song and Verse, London 1884–1914* (Detroit: Wayne State University Press, 2018) 161–62, 194–200.

72 "Shoyshpilerin dore diamant fort tsu gast in di kemps," *Loshn un lebn*, August 1948, 64.

73 Leonard Prager and S. J. Harendorf, *Der kenig fun lampeduse/The King of Lampedusa*, ed. and trans. Heather Valencia (London: Jewish Music Institute/International Forum for Yiddish Culture, 2003); Prager, "Palme, S.," in *Yiddish Culture*, 505.

74 Sam Stern's Hotel and Kosher Restaurant at 3 and 5 Mansell Street, Aldgate, opened in 1928 and was a popular venue for Jewish weddings and other functions. It was bombed during the war but continued operating until it was sold in 1952. David Dee, *The "Estranged" Generation? Social and Generational Change in Interwar British Jewry* (London: Palgrave Macmillan, 2017), 36–37.

75 Prager, "Fuks, Albert," in *Yiddish Culture*, 256–57; "Avrom-Moyshe Fuks," *Yiddish Leksikon*, http://yleksikon.blogspot.com/2018/10/avrom-moyshe-fuks.html. Accessed 13 August 2020. See also 237n63.

76 Prager, "Levi, Yoysef-Hilel," in *Yiddish Culture*, 406.

77 "Dikhter un mentsh: Gaystraykher ovent lekoved moyshe oyved far zayn opforn keyn amerike," *Tsayt*, 1 September 1939, 7; David Schneider, email correspondence with author, 12 July 2020.

78 "Oveds fortrog," *Tsayt*, 19 April 1940, 2.

79 Prager, *Yiddish Culture*, 505.

80 "A gleyzl te lekoved dem dikhter s palme," *Tsayt*, 19 July 1940, 2.

81 Prager, "Sokhatshevski, Ben-A," in *Yiddish Culture*, 611–12; *The Palgrave Dictionary of Anglo-Jewish History*, ed. William Rubinstein, Michael Jolles, and Hilary Rubinstein (London: Palgrave Macmillan, 2011), 929.

82 "Literarishe fortrog fun dem shriftshteler a m fuks," *Tsayt*, 6 September 1940, 2.

83 A full rundown of the first day of the Blitz and its effect on London's East End can be found at the *Guardian* Datablog, "London Blitz 1940: The First Day's Bomb Attacks Listed in Full," https://www.theguardian.com/news/datablog/2010/sep/06/london-blitz-bomb-map-september-7-1940. Accessed 11 April 2020.

84 Bogdanski, "Londoner yidishe shrayber," 799–800.

85 *Di tsayt* did not appear 9–12 September 1940, and only one issue covered 13–16 September. Prager, "Di tsayt," in *Yiddish Culture*, 651.

86 Stencl, "Lekoved dem fuftsikstn heftl," *Fuftsik yidish-heftlekh*, 15 March 1944, 1–2.

87 Aptroot, "Israel Narodiczky," ix.

88 David Mazower, "Love Labours Lost," 21.

89 Stencl related this story to Bob Chait. Stencl had encountered her on the street. Bob Chait telephone conversation with author, 9 August 2020.

90 Joseph Leftwich, "Poet and Fanatic: Stenzel Goes On," *Jewish Chronicle*, 5 March 1943, 16.

91 "Idishe dikhter in london: A literarishe fartrog beeys der bombardirung," *Tsayt*, 15 November 1940, 3.

92 Ibid.

93 Prager, "Manger, Itzik," in *Yiddish Culture*, 435.

94 Benzion and his brother Alexander were great patrons of the arts. In 1942 they established the Ohel Club. *Palgrave Dictionary of Anglo-Jewish History*, 644–45.

95 Lisky, *Melokhe bezuye*, 51–52.

96 "Idishe dikhter in london," 3.

97 Seedo, *In the Beginning*, 324–25. Seedo uses the term "Jewish Writers and Authors Association." This was her unofficial title and would have been the Association of Jewish Journalists and Authors.

98 Lisky, *Melokhe bezuye*, 12–15; Seedo, *In the Beginning*, 307; Maurice Carr, "The Singer Family."

99 Unpublished manuscript diaries of Leo Koenig; from a phone conversation with Ester Whine, 14 April 2020.

100 Leonard Prager, "Avrom Nokhem Stencl," *The Mendele Review: Yiddish Literature and Language* 21 and 23, February 1995, n17. Part 1: http://www.columbia.edu/~jap2220/Arkhiv/vol04%20(1994-5)/vol04336.txt Part 2: https://www.ibiblio.org/pub/academic/languages/yiddish/mendele/vol4.337. Both accessed 1 February 2021.

101 Josef Herman, "Avrom-Nokhem Shtentsl (1897–1983)," *Di goldene keyt*, 112 (1984), 140. Dovid Katz recalls Lisky telling him that the lawyer who knew all the details was a Dr. Okin. Katz, "Stencl of Whitechapel," n.22.

102 Prager, "Eyrope," in *Yiddish Culture*, 225; Mazower, email correspondence, 20 April 2020.

103 "Fraynt fun yidish-loshn un der yiddisher kultur-klub," *London vaytshepl: Finf yor milkhome*, heftl no. 56 (September 1944): 31–32.

104 The statutes of the *Fraynt fun yidish loshn* were published in *Loshn un lebn* (February 1948): 62–63; "Literary Sabbath Afternoons," *Jewish Chronicle*, 2 April 1943, 18.

105 "Dos folkshoyz in vaytshepl," *Tsayt*, 16 September 1943; Srebrnik, *London Jews and British Communism*, 27; notice of upcoming performance, *Tsayt*, 28 January 1944.

106 "The Jewish Cultural Centre," *Cultural Topics*, 1944, 2 (English section).

107 Abraham Boymeder, "Tsu der efenung fun undzer nayem yidishn kultur hoyz," *A peysekh un perets heftl*, April 1944, 34–35.

108 Kreitman, "Moris mayer o"h," *Tsayt*, 22 October 1944, 2; Brown, "Undzer moris myer," *Tsayt*, 8 November 1944, 2; Lisky, "Konserkventer mentsh," *Tsayt*, 23 November 1944, 2.

109 Stencl, "Di oysgegangene tsayt," *Loshn un lebn*, December 1950, 1.

110 Y. H. Levi (Lewy), "Iber londoner shrayber un zeyerer bikher," *5-yor yidish-heftlekh*, September 1945, 22–23.

111 Stencl, "Di noytikeyt fun a yidish literarishn journal," *5-yor heftlekh* (1945), 1, 3–4.

112 H. Leyvik, *Mit der sheyres hapleyte* (New York: Tsentrale yidishe kultur orginizatsye, 1947), 42–44.

113 Stencl, "Dos tsente yor fun yidish-heftlekh: Un 4 yor fun der dzurnal 'loshn un lebn,'" *Loshn un lebn*, April 1950, 4.

114 Leyvik, *Mit der sheyres hapleyte*, 42–44.

115 "Dertseylungn fun m khusid," *Loshn un lebn*, September 1947, 48–49.

116 Friends of Yiddish Language at the Ben Uri were advertised each month. *Loshn un lebn*, 1948–53.

117 "Zeks khadoshim YIVO arbet;" *Loshn un lebn*, January 1947.

118 "Moris shvartses kaboles ponim," *Tsayt*, 3 July 1947.

119 "Avrom-Pinkhes Tsikert," *Yiddish Leksikon*, http://yleksikon.blogspot.com/2019/01/avrom-pinkhes-tsikert.html. Accessed 15 June 2020.

120 Jacob Lewis Fayn O.B.E. See "Fayn, Yankev-Leybush," in Prager, *Yiddish Culture*, 231.

121 Lisky, "Efsher darf take London brenen," *Loshn un lebn* (August 1948): 36–39.

122 "Farvos shvaygt vaytshelpl?" *Arbeter ring*, 1942, 4.

123 Joseph Leftwich, "Poet and Fanatic: Stenzel Goes On," *Jewish Chronicle*, 5 March 1943, 16.